I, NANO

J.F. Lawrence

JFL Press

ISBN: 978-1-7356301-2-0

Cover design by: J.F. Lawrence
Printed in the United States of America

For my kiddos, who inspired and encouraged me to write this book and listened to early version. You mean the world to me.

CHAPTER ONE

Resistance

Out on the rattling balcony, I close the shipping container door, slow enough to quiet the creaking of metal on metal, careful not to wake my folks. The squeaks and groans of our well-oiled hinges fade into the metal symphony of the blocks. In the darkness before dawn, I feel my way to the rusty ladder and place my boots gingerly on each rung before I step down, sure to distribute my weight between hands and feet.

On the second-floor landing, I open my patched backpack and retrieve the two squares of tofu I saved from breakfast. I slide the wrapped bits into Laticia's lockbox, imagining her irresistible toothy grin when she finds them.

Mazz, we can't keep doing this, says Lii, my AI implant. He sends the emotional equivalent of a head shake through our bond. *We don't have spare calories to give away, even for Laticia.*

I'll survive. I can't stand by and watch her olive cheeks slim down further. Besides, rule three: we take care of our own. We blockers need to stick together.

The first signs of light paint the skies a hint of cyan as I descend to street level. This is the freest I'll feel all day, streets empty of vendors and scavengers, too early for government enforcers or Resistance fighters. I toss my skateboard to the street and push off, enjoying the way the wind flows over my shaved scalp.

On wheels, I glide around potholes, hop over cracks, and jog over sections too torn up to ride. I arrive at the bus stop early and practice jumping off a set of stairs. Adrenaline kicks in as I fly through the air and flip my board just right. On my second try, I land a five-forty rodeo flip, a trick I wouldn't consider a few weeks ago.

We're improving faster and faster, Lii says. *This is wicked fun.*

I practice the rodeo three times without error but torque my ankle on the fourth try. I walk it off but take it easy after that. Twelve minutes later, a graffitied bus rolls up. I plop into the last empty seat as the transport lurches forward behind a slow produce truck. Nuts and bolts rattle every time the tires hit a pothole or jounce on a crevice in the road.

Outside the cracked window, the container blocks slide by in a mosaic of faded colors and rust. What I would give for Lii to overlay reality with the digital veneer of perfection again, to return to the shared delusion, the heavenly facade that keeps us happy, no matter how complacent it makes us.

Would that I could, Lii says, his common refrain for consistently glitching.

We pass into the wastelands between the decay of the container blocks and the shining towers of downtown. While everyone else sees a beautiful park honoring those we lost in the AI War, all I see is the radioactive remains of buildings and piled rubble.

Gleaming skyscrapers loom before us to remind everyone of their place in society as much as the marks on our necks. The pinnacles with their triangle tattoos serve the supremes with their diamond marks. Uppers with their circles serve the Pinnacles. Blockers with our double lines serve the uppers. Blockers work so we don't starve.

I pull out my datapad and scroll through a new graphic novel. In this one, Hazel Gray searches for an antidote to the curse that turned her into a half-cougar, half-human hybrid. She's stuck in limbo, neither accepted by animals nor humans. I can empathize.

When we approach the wall ringing downtown, the enforcers "randomly" select our bus for inspection. An enforcer dressed in a green uniform and a bullet-proof jacket climbs the stairs. Good. It's Smithson, one of the better ones. He looks around, eyes surveying faces with enhanced speed. His hand rests casually on his combat rifle.

Smithson nods to me and says, "Hey Mazz. Let's check your bag and get along with this." While the tension builds between blockers and uppers due to the escalating Resistance attacks, the enforcers typically don't mess with regular commuters. Uppers don't like it when their blocker servants are late.

I offer my worn-out backpack and turn my skateboard over so he can see I'm not concealing anything. My pack holds nothing except for my water bottle and measly lunch. Like every other time, he finds nothing of concern.

I smile when he slips a cocoa cube into my bag, grateful for the millions of medical nanites inside, more life-sustaining micro-bots than I get in a week's worth of government-supplied algae tofu. If not for our dependence on the trickle of life-sustaining bots, we would have overthrown the establishment decades ago. Without them, radiation would have killed us long ago, and who would do the bidding of the uppers? The act of giving me these little cubes on occasion directly flaunts the norm. Smithson is definitely one of the good guys. I don't dare eat the cube yet in case someone is watching. For show, he moseys to the back of the bus, humming a catchy tune.

"Stand up," Smithson says, his voice full of agitation. My head swivels in unison with the other passengers. His rifle tip presses against the back of an upper's head. That's strange. Enforcers never bother uppers. Then again, I've never seen an upper on one of our buses before. I should have noticed him when I boarded.

Upon closer examination, the man painted over the blemishes and wrinkles on his face and masked his double-lined neck tattoo with an imperfect circle. Uppers don't have either.

Does he have prosthetics to fill out his sunken cheeks?

Yes, Lii says, nervousness raising his pitch an octave. No wonder Smithson escalated so fast.

Two more armored enforcers board the bus, scanning the bus with rifles swinging past us. I point my nose and eyes forward, sticking to Rule Seventeen–don't draw attention. My chest thumps extra hard when the barrels swing past me. I'll never get used to that feeling.

Smithson yells, "I told you to stand up!" An uncomfortable quiet settles over the bus, so silent one might hear the repair nanites working on the brakes. I hold my breath, fearing that even the subtle in and out of my chest could siphon an enforcer's wrath in my direction.

I involuntarily blink at the thud of metal on flesh, pretty sure the crunch sounded of broken bones, something made easier by years of malnourishment. It wouldn't be hard for Smithson to crumple the man.

Don't look, Lii warns me, though he needn't have said anything. There is no sense in following him into the detention center, possibly with broken bones of my own, possibly dead. Rule six: don't mess with enforcers.

After a short scuffle, Smithson shoves the faux upper along the aisle. Blood drips from the imposter's busted nose, but he holds his head high. He might be smiling or grimacing. It's impossible to tell with the prosthetics and makeup. Something about him smells of Resistance.

The other two enforcers follow Smithson off the bus and I join the other passengers in a communal sigh of relief. The bus pulls into traffic and I almost look out the window to see what's happening, but no good can come of showing concern.

There are tons of rumors about blockers who elevate to upper status, but it can't be as easy as dressing like one. The diamond-caste supremes rigged the system to keep everyone where we are, spurred into endless work by the promise of eternal life offered by the trickle of government-supplied nanites. The government doesn't do it out of the kindness of their hearts. She who controls the nanites rules the world.

We are as close to jumping tiers as it comes, Lii says. *There are only a few seats in upper schools offered to blockers each year. And as bright as we are, we barely lasted nine months among them.*

I slip the cocoa cube into my mouth and force myself to return to my graphic novel. The dose of medical nanites from the cube fills me with tendrils of warmth. These bitty tendrils provide the hope of eternal life and promise the higher-ups that they don't have to pay for healthcare. I could–

Boom! The windows rattle and the bus bucks under us. Flames and smoke engulf the detention center. A pulse of pressure smacks my ears, muffling all but the lowest notes.

Holy frak! That guy was Resistance, a suicide bomber. If they'd searched him earlier, would he have detonated with us onboard? They usually keep blocker casualties to a minimum, but you never know.

Put it out of your mind, Lii says.

Easier said than done. Smithson was among them. Nevertheless, I follow the blocker way and face forward, pretending that I don't care. Nothing to see here. Move along.

Focus on the warmth of the cocoa cube, Lii suggests.

I only need to survive four more days of high school. Then I'll be done with riding buses back and forth across the wasteland. Life will return to normal.

CHAPTER TWO

Safe Room

I don't care a nanite's ass about the history of China. It has no practical application in real life. But does that stop Ms. Dillinger from droning on? Nope. Not at all.

Anyone can learn the facts, Lii says in his frustrated parent voice. *But understanding how things work is power.*

The relevance of today's bombing far outranks centuries-old politics, but does she talk about that? No. The Resistance fighters attack at least once a week now, yet we never hear about it at school. Instead, Ms. Dillinger blabbers on. And, she always sticks to the propaganda, not the facts.

"The Orbem Imperium rose from the ashes of the nuclear war caused by the Republic of China. Without..."

I nearly died this morning. I mean–

Crack! Countless shards of window explode into my third-period history room, flinging me from my seat to the cement floor like nothing more than recycled tinfoil. My skull ricochets off something hard, bouncing my gray matter around inside. Shrieks fill the air. I think my voice joined the collective.

Is this another Resistance bombing? Pain stabs the left side of my face, arm, and leg.

We're cut up, Lii says. I stare, dumbfounded by the layer of glass shards embedded in my left arm. So much silver glitter. *We trained for an attack all year. Don't panic now. Stay low and get to the safe room.* I flail to my belly and army-crawl to the corner, toward safety. Pain shoots up my body every time I use my left leg, so I let it lie dead on the floor, pushing harder with my right.

I nearly pass by Renata, who still sits in her seat, hands flung over her head. She wails so loud my right ear resonates at a high pitch for the second time today. She may have a few crystalline splinters, but not a fraction of mine. I never accredited her with an overabundance of smarts.

She's panicking, Lii says. *Do something.*

Argh. I reach up and yank her to the floor. "Move!" I yell. Instead, she curls into the fetal position and continues her shriekfest. My annoyance spikes to a new level as I hook my fingers through her belt loop and haul her behind me. As a healthy upper, she weighs more than me. But, I apprentice with my parentals on their welding jobs most weekends and during school breaks, so I'm stronger than I look. Tugging her along magnifies the pain in my left thigh and forearm.

Lii says, *I'm trying to staunch the blood flow. The nanites from the cocoa cube might be enough to patch us up if you stop moving.*

Stop moving? And stay out in the open? Fat chance.

Stop moving, Lii says icy cold, serious enough to freeze me in place. Everything goes dark as I shrink into nothingness. I can't break rule number one: please don't die. Something pops within me.

The next thing I know I'm lying belly down in the red-lit safe room, fingers still hooked into Renata's belt loop. Screams and whimpers fill the air as thick as blood. I must have blacked out. The back right part of my head thumps like a drum, probably a concussion. Someone steps on my cut-up thigh, nearly making me pass out again. I howl and struggle to my feet with my cut-up leg trailing behind as if a badger were clinging to it, claws fully embedded.

I try to heft Renata but the agony in my thigh spikes to new levels, nearly making me pass out again. My head reels as her shrieks elevate above our classmates and change from those of panic to ones of pain. I wedge an open space above her curled form, but my classmates push back in the small safe room, which doubles as a materials closet. I sway like a toy boat on crashing waves. Pain stabs at my arm and leg wherever they rub against me, sending slivers deeper into my skin.

Lii, can you do something about the pain? No response. Lii? Please don't glitch now. The metallic taste of blood dripping down the back of my throat nearly makes me gag. Noted: bloody nose.

The door clicks open and the red light turns to green. "All clear," says Mr. Hussain, the school's bodyguard slash janitor, with two lines on his neck. "False alarm." It doesn't feel like a false alarm to me. My wounds are very much real. He says, "No bombs and no signs of Resistance."

We file back into the classroom where broken glass sparkles on the floor like millions of diamonds. The path I swept clean of glass dust in my army crawl is streaked with red. Blood. If I weren't in so much pain, I might appreciate the beauty of it all. Not an ounce of glass remains in the window frame next to my seat.

"Mazz!" Ms. Dillinger yells as she grabs my good arm with an iron grip. "You took it too far this time."

"I didn't do it." Those words tumble out of my mouth all too often. I hate this posh school and all the uppers in it. "Look at me," I say, seeing the full extent of my wounds for the first time. Blood seeps from dozens of cuts on my arm below my short sleeve. A several-inch shard impaled my thigh. It hurts all the more now that I see it. My pants are soaked with blood and crimson dribbles over my shoe onto the floor. Patches of glittering rubies match my footprints. That's too much blood.

Without thinking, I yank the large fragment out of my thigh with a hiss. Now the blood spills faster, flowing with the metronome of my heart. I nearly fall over in pain as I press my palm to the open gash. My vision blurs for a moment as I teeter. If not for Ms. Dillinger's hand clamped on my arm, I would surely slump to the floor, no more than a gelatinous sack of flesh. When my head clears, over half the class stares at me with evil eyes though none of them suffered more than a nick.

Focusing on Ms. Dillinger, I ask, "Would I do this to myself?" The fury in her eyes tells me all I need to know. She made up her mind. To her, the two lines on my neck practically make me Resistance. So I shut my trap: rule twelve. Beyond my edicts of survival, the pins and needles that sting from my nostril to my jaw dissuade me from yapping my mouth further.

I look around to see which one of my classmates did it. Or maybe they conspire together. Whoever it is, keeps resorting to more drastic measures, escalating eye for eye with The Resistance.

She hands me over to Mr. Hussain who gingerly leads me to the hallway. As a blocker, he treats me with far more consideration than all of the uppers put together. The sympathy in his eyes tells me that he knows I'm guilty of growing up in the blocks. Every step hurts more and pumps more blood from the gash in my thigh.

Lii glitches in and digital murals cover the walls in dazzling colors. Student art lines the corridor. The smell shifts from that of a stale armpit to one of vanilla and lavender. The cracks in the floor disappear. The hallway radiates beauty, serenity, and timelessness. A few paces later, Lii's simulated velum malfunctions and I return to reality.

Mr. Hussain gives me a shoulder to lean on as we walk to the bathroom, where he hands me a first-aid kit. An ambulance will surely be here to take care of the uppers in a minute or less. I look awful in the mirror, with sparkly red glass splinters glittering on the left side of my face and blood shining from nose to chin. I'm amazed at how many tiny holes riddle my shirt and pants.

Dizzy as I am, I fall to the toilet and focus on the large gash in my thigh, smearing it with nanite cream and bandaging it tight. When the twirling blur stops threatening to make me blow chunks, I start picking out the larger shards and rub the cuts with nanite cream.

After I don't know how long, I stand again and hobble to the mirror to see my face, I look like a half-pizza, half-human hybrid. It takes several minutes to extract dozens of bitty fragments. In time, Lii and the nanites will stop the bleeding, mend the cuts, and take down the redness. But it's gonna hurt for a few days. With so many slivers embedded in my skin, it will probably take all night to pick them out. One of the shards narrowly missed my jugular. I don't know whether to consider myself lucky or not.

When I exit the bathroom, Mr. Hussain says, "You're a tough kid. None of them would be standing if they took that blow." I don't feel tough. I hurt everywhere but nod, regretting the motion instantly when my vision blurs again.

We stop at my locker, where I pull off my bloodied shirt and tie it around the large slash in my leg for extra support and cloth to soak up the blood. Then I pull on my gray hoodie, careful not to tug at the remaining glass splinters.

As we turn the corner to Principal Jean's office, she says, "Mazz." I've seen this room too many times of late. I nearly laugh upon seeing her. Does she know her blouse looks like a clown's wig? Could that possibly be what she's going for? Or is she relying on her avatar to fix that atrocity? Instead, I thin my lips and nod wordlessly. Again, rule twelve: shut your trap.

Damn, my leg hurts!

Principal Jean's face bunches up in a half snarl. "Another inexplicable incident. This has your telltale enigma shattered all over it. What do you have to say for yourself?"

"I was just sitting there." Telling her that my classmates set me up will only rile her up. We have covered this crap so many times we might as well be sewage treatment techs. She surely watched the classroom's surveillance cameras while waiting for me and saw that I didn't do anything, as always. But that won't stop her from sticking the blocker with the blame, especially since I sat closest to the shattered window.

"You burned your last chance three chances ago. You're suspended for the rest of the year."

I almost laugh. There are only three more days until summer.

"You'll be lucky if your classmates don't sue."

I want to say, "Empty threat. Blockers don't have anything an upper would want."

I'm done with this place. Why do I need to go to school anyway? With two more years of apprenticing, I'll be able to join the Welders' Guild. What more do I need?

You were here for very good reasons, Lii says in his patient mentor voice. *A world of difference separates the ability to access information and knowing how and when to use it. Plus, with prestigious schooling, you could have chosen the highest-paying welding jobs.*

Now you show up. How is my body doing? Nothing. Lii? He withdrew again.

"You are a clever young man. As smart as they come. If only you put that mind to..." Can she see the essence of who-gives-a-damn spilling out of my ears? With a wave of her hand and a closed-eyed shake of her head, I am dismissed. I hike up my blood-soaked pants and limp out of her office.

Mr. Hussain and I stop by my locker again. With my pack over my shoulder and my skateboard in hand, I hobble through the school's front doors for the last time. I gingerly step on my skateboard and let gravity pull me down to the bus stop, the breeze stinging my wounds.

Fourteen minutes later, I board the bus back to the blocks but the stop-and-go traffic is mostly stop. The enforcers are searching every blocker vehicle in response to this morning's Resistance attack. It's a typical reaction. Gunk up the blockers' lives to make us dislike The Resistance. But it only fuels our anger for the uppers and especially the enforcers.

Enforcers. Damn. I can't imagine that Smithson survived this morning's blast.

I take the extra time to free more splinters from my arm and leg. I wish Lii would respond but the worst of the gashes don't hurt as sharply, which means he and the nanite cream are doing their jobs.

An hour later, we reach the gates and it's our turn to be

inspected. Blackened rubble occupies the space where a large cement building used to be. Expecting a full search, I already opened my pack, set my skateboard wheel-side-up, and placed my hands on the seatback in front of me. This isn't going to be like one of Smithson's routine inspections.

Four enforcers that I don't recognize board the bus, pointing their guns in every direction. I try not to flinch each time the barrels swing past me. With my fresh scars and the copious amounts of dried blood caked to my pants, I stick out like a flamingo among pigeons. Blocker by blocker, they search our belongings.

An enforcer, one I haven't seen before, dumps out my bag, dropping my datapad to the floor with a clatter. Ahh, man. Please don't be broken. My tofu splats on my skateboard, fortunately still in its wrapper. He opens my water bottle and dumps it out, soaking my datapad.

The enforcer orders me to "stand and turn to the window," then frisks me while another enforcer points his gun at the back of my head. The first enforcer pats me down, each touch rubbing my clothes into my cuts and glass splinters. "How did you hurt yourself?" he asks, a bit of sadistic pleasure leaking into his voice. Hurt myself? More like how did someone hurt me? Always blame the blocker.

"An accident at school," I say. Best to stick to the truth, but not elaborate.

"A blocker at school downtown?" he says, disbelief plain. He unties my bloodied shirt from my leg, which threatens to make me blackout again. I have to bite my cheek to keep from shouting in pain. Evidently, one patdown isn't enough proof of my innocence, so he gives me a twice over, rougher this time. Silence. He's probably checking my records, hopefully seeing that I wasn't lying. Inwardly, I say, please don't detain me. Then it's over and they move on to their next victim.

When they're done and the door closes, I slump, exhausted and broken. I tie my shirt around my leg again and pick up my datapad. Frak! It has a new scratch down the center. A series of rainbows reflect from the screen, a sign of water damage. Rule thirty-six is in full force today: suck it up on bad days.

CHAPTER THREE

Scavengers

Rather than limp home from the bus stop, I risk reopening my cuts by skating across the cracked blocker streets. No tricks today. Slow and steady as Dad always says. Even still, my left leg protests like a Resistance riot. Speaking of Resistance, I cross the street to stay clear of a new red "R" inside a circle. Their sign. Rule thirty-nine: stay away from The Resistance.

A crusty-skinned man, a sign of radiation sickness, with missing front teeth and sunken eyes extends his arm at throat level, attempting to clothesline me. I recognize him as one of the local chapter of scavengers who has tried to "help" me several times. Like most starved blockers, he's pretty slow, so I duck and swerve.

My dodge sends me careening toward a tofu vendor's cart. Thirty-six! I won't be able to miss the cart. I leap off my board, feeling a ticklish twinge in my gut, run over the top of the cart, and land on my board again as it spits out the other side. My leg unleashes a new torrent of suffering.

How in all that is nanite did I manage that? It shouldn't have worked.

"Hey!" the mustached fu peddler yells after me. "You..." My heart pounds too hard to care what curse he bellows after me.

I pick up speed and skate around the corner only to find five more scavengers standing in my path. Crap! It's Gunther and his crew. I'm overdue for a walloping and I'm riding too fast to stop. Paying too much attention to them, and not enough to the pothole in the road, my board stops underfoot while I keep going, momentarily airborne like the world's worst gymnast. Landing fuels the flames of my shredded left side. As my knees hit the ground, they add to my bouquet of pain.

"Get up," Gunther says, low and gravelly. From what I hear, the more crazy and dangerous you are, the more spoils you get from the daily collection. With mismatched brown and blue eyes, dozens of piercings, and face and neck tattoos, Gunther doesn't need an avatar to look the part. I have a feeling that my skateboard, backpack, and datapad will be in their loot today, not that they will go for much at the market.

I push myself up, rough pavement digging into my palms. With a single hand, Gunther pulls me up by my hoodie, easily lifting my skinny body off the ground. Face to smelly face, he taps my right temple with his revolver.

"You look like an upper dressed in blocker clothes." Really? With bandages, fresh scabs, and blood-caked clothes? "Your skin is smooth like them." He runs the back of his tattooed hand across my good cheek. What a fitting end to a thirty-sixer of a year. A blocker to the uppers and an upper to the blockers.

"Velta," he says, eyes darting to his side. "Lighten this upper's load, will you?"

"Got it, boss," Velta says, her voice vacant as if she's only slightly connected to reality. A skinny wafer of a woman with blisters all over her lips yanks my pack gruffly but it sticks to my shoulders, popping my spine. She yanks again with a grunt, but instead of my pack coming loose, the front of my hoodie tears from Gunther's grip. I drop to my knees with my backpack still in place.

I can't help but yelp in pain. How much more can I take? Gunther's boots smell of all the horrible places he stomped today. His boot potpourri wafts with hints of blood, grease, and the cringe-worthy afterglow of excrement. I know what's coming. Never disobey a scavenger, even by accident: rule thirty. They make an example out of you every time.

One laceless boot pulls back. My hands shoot up to protect my head. This is gonna suck. In anticipation of my teeth flying from my mouth or my nose shattering, I fasten my eyes shut.

"Ahhh!" Gunther yells. When I open my eyes, Gunther growls from on his back, holding a bootless and sockless foot with toes twisted in every unnatural direction. What an idiot? No wonder he didn't land a kick. I'm amazed that he could even stand with that mutilated foot.

Recognizing my chance to escape, I hook my skateboard, toss it in front of me, and dash to catch up. I push through the pain and kick as fast as my junker of a leg will tolerate. I'm too fast for any of them to catch up, which was the reason I took up skating in the first place. After rounding four corners in six blocks, I slow down. The wound in my thigh ripped open and bleeds freely again. I tighten my make-shift tourniquet and keep hobbling home.

About ten minutes later, I grunt up the rickety ladder to my shipping container, one lopsided step at a time. On the second-floor landing, I knock on Laticia's door, but she isn't home. Probably at the textile factory. I consider giving her another pair of tofu squares, but I really do need them now with all my cuts. Two more flights up, I carefully unlock and open the puke green door, heedful to keep the hinges from squeaking. What a thirty-sixer of a day.

CHAPTER FOUR

Home

At dinner time, I bite into a square of fu and nearly spit it out. What flavor is that supposed to be? I almost curse out loud, but Mom and Dad are still sleeping.

Mac and cheese, Lii says, having unglitched momentarily.

That is not, I repeat, not, mac 'n cheese. Maybe cheesy puffs and fermented applesauce. Why can't you do anything right?

After my fourth bite of tofunky, I hear Mom and Dad bumping and thumping from behind the curtain that covers the back end of our container. I'm not afraid of punishment, but I really don't want to go through another round of, "I didn't do it."

Dad pulls the bedroom curtain aside and sits down next to me. "What happened?" He has a look of concern when he sees the scars on my face. He steals a half square of my dinner and takes a seat. His large, angular frame makes the whimpering chair and chipped orange table look like a toy set.

What should I lead with? Scavengers? Enforcers? Resistance? Damn this was a thirty-sixer. I decide to go with "A window at school exploded and I got the blame."

"And you didn't do anything?" asks Mom. She looks over my scars with deep concern, cupping the uninjured side of my face.

"No. I tried to explain that I was hit harder than anyone else but they wouldn't listen. Look at my clothes?" I tried to sew up the new cuts but didn't have a chance to wash them without making a bunch of noise.

She nudges my hair to the side and kisses my forehead. I hate it when she does that. I'm glad Laticia isn't here to see it. "It looks like it hurt."

"Still does," I say. "Lii took care of the worst of it but ran out of nanites. I'll have scars for a while."

"Your 'incidents' are getting worse," she says, examining my poorly-mended pants. She runs her hand over the pant leg where the glass bled me good. "They've never hurt you before. Did anyone else get hurt?"

"Not much. The sabotage grows worse every day." I shouldn't have said that. They get weird whenever I mention my theories of retribution for daring to attend an upper school. "Or it was getting worse. They suspended me until the end of school." I barely hold in a smile. School and limbo are over.

Dad hands me a full square of his fu and nods for me to down it. I really don't want to, but he'll keep eyeing me until I do.

"And is Lii still glitching?" Mom asks. She knows the answer, but I shake my head anyway. That's the thing I don't get. How are they messing with him? It shouldn't be possible to influence someone else's AI. But they managed it somehow.

Dad squeezes my good shoulder with his powerful hands and says, "Well, if you're done with school for the year, you're on full-time apprentice duty starting tomorrow. Rest up and recover tonight." They steal concerned looks between each other but don't seem interested in delving further into the inexplicable. I decide to keep my mouth shut about the rest of today's crapitude. Rule thirty-four: what they don't know won't hurt them.

Neeeh! Neeeh! Neeeh! Lii blares the absolute worst alarm into my head.

Damn it, Lii. I don't have school today. Let me sleep.

About that. Principal Jean reversed your suspension.

Argh. Why does she keep withdrawing my reprieve from that damn school?

No clue. Pep up. It's our birthday, Lii says.

Yeah. Today has to be better. I look over the edge of my bunk but my parentals aren't home. Lately, their job keeps running long. I jump off my bed, prepared to bounce off their mattress, and land my skateboard but only manage to collapse. My leg still lacks the strength for that sort of abuse.

I serve myself some breakfast tofu, which is the remaining cube from last night's dinner. The longer the stuff's been open, the worse Lii sims it. "Bleh! Lii, what is that supposed to be? Snail slime with pumpkin-spiced grapes?"

Eggs and toast, he says.

"Please. Pretty please, stop simming tofu. The plain stuff tastes way better."

Would if I could.

I'm not sure how long I've been sitting at the table forcing squares down my gullet before I notice a message on the kitchen whiteboard. It's Mom's loopy handwriting.

> *Mazz,*
> *Happy Birthday! It amazes me that you are seventeen years old. I'm so proud to be your mom. We will be home and awake after school to celebrate.*
> *Love, -Mom*
> *P.S. We have something special planned.*

"Something special," I say, feeling the words tumble around my mouth. That means it's more than the usual cake and a new shirt. What does she have up her sleeve? Maybe new wheels for my board? A pair of Soul Stompers would be cool even if they're used. They're supposed to broadcast an avatar of their own, so it won't matter how much Lii messes up.

With a grunt, I go about preparing for another school day, a day I thought I'd have off. With my best shirt stitched up like Frankenstein's monster, I dress in my next best.

Why did Principal Jean change her mind?

Rule forty-one: don't try to understand uppers.

I go to pull out a tofu package and find a bottle of chocolate milk with a frayed red bow on it. The note says, "Drink up." Nano! I haven't had milk in ages, especially not the sweet stuff. I sigh in relief when Lii doesn't sim it to taste like raw chicken and pickles. It's thicker than I remember but just as good.

After sipping the glorious stuff for a few minutes, I smile. The writing wasn't Mom or Dad, so it was probably Laticia. How could she afford this? I can imagine her bright smile and the twinkle in her dark brown eyes.

After emptying the bottle, wishing that I'd saved some for lunch, I realize there is a rolled-up note in a baggy at the bottom of the bottle. Pretty slick move, Laticia.

On one side, it reads "Sir Mazzen Erwin Becker." Nobody ever uses my full name, except Mom when she's angry. Laticia knows I hate my middle name and loves prodding me with it, confirming my suspicions. The note might as well be address to Supreme Mazz. I shake my head and read the other side.

> *Mazz,*
> *In light of the accident yesterday, today is your testing day. The bottle juiced you with extra nanites. You may see, hear, and encounter strange things.*
> *It will be okay. I'll be there in case anything goes terribly wrong.*
> *Regards,*
> *- Bender*

"As if." I roll my eyes so far that if I had x-ray vision, I'd see my spine. This is another attempt to push her theory that the sabotage is actually Lii accidentally setting off nanites outside my body. It's a ridiculous idea, of course. If AIs could activate nanites like that, one could kill people with a thought. Besides, it doesn't explain why the accidents started as soon as I began attending Desmond High. I push the idea out of my head and ride my board to the bus stop, my leg hurting far less than I expected.

CHAPTER FIVE

Bender

During first-period phys ed, Coach Short announces that "Today, we'll play basketball." The class splits down the middle between lovers and haters. While I used to enjoy team sports, I now reside on the hater side of the class. Why can't we run or skate? I'm great at dodging and running from scavengers, but those skills don't translate to team sports, at least not here.

Weee, basketball, Lii says with false glee. *I can't wait to see what happens today.*

I'm picked last, even behind Perri Greene, who compulsively picks at her teeth when she thinks nobody is watching. For twenty-two minutes, I manage to remain as far from the ball as I can without getting yelled at by Coach Short. Rule seventeen: fade into the background. He bellows, "Mazz, take Sebastion's spot!" I must have stepped too far away from the action.

"Yes, sir," I say. What would Coach do if I ran the other way?

Two more days here, Lii says. *Don't blow this one last chance.*

"Keltin," Mr. Short hollers. "Pass the ball to Mazz." Keltin hesitates, giving Coach a questioning look. Nobody covers me. Begrudgingly, he tosses the orange ball and I catch it. I'm pretty sure he isn't my saboteur, but I can't rule him out. Nobody comes to cover me, so I dribble the ball while the other team parts before me as if a sentient flesh-eating bacteria oozes from my pores.

"Shoot, Mazz." Mr. Short casts his hands up like I don't know how. Looking back and forth between Short and Keltin, I freeze. I close my eyes and throw the ball in the direction of the hoop.

The metal net clanks and Keltin says, "No way." I open my eyes to find everyone gawking at me.

"Great job," Coach Short says with a cheesy fist pump. "You swooshed it." Why won't they stop staring at me?

Boom! Basketball shrapnel flies in every direction, sending everyone running.

And there it is, Lii says as if this were the funniest thing to happen in years.

"Mazz," Coach Short growls. "Bench. Now!" It's always the blocker's fault. At least he didn't send me to Principal Jean.

After phys ed, my classmates resort to stupid stunts to get me in trouble. Apparently, I stole Doug's shoelaces. Rhenate threw her lunch into the air and claimed I blew it up. Jett said I locked him in the bathroom. I guess the hoaxes are so transparent that the teachers don't banish me to Ms. Jean's office. That or the faculty decided to go easy on me because it's my birthday. I suspect the prior.

Either way, I find myself on the bus after a full day of class. After I cross over the wasteland, delayed again by the enforcers, I blankly look out the window, wondering about Laticia's prank. Was it a clue about Mom's special plans for tonight? It doesn't make sense.

My senses go berserk when a semi-truck hauling one giant metal beam careens through the intersection at us. I can practically taste the fear among my fellow passengers. The truck's front bumper rattles in my ear. The oil stains on the over-strained motor pique my nostrils. I brace for impact and wait for the sound of squealing tires to transition into crunching metal.

My chest constricts so tight I can't breathe. The world around me ignites in a purple-blue overlay on top of reality. A loud *crack* sounds from inside me. Did I have a heart attack? Or an aneurysm? Then, it's over.

I'm no longer inside the bus, but sitting on the street corner, faced with the strangest bus accident I've ever seen. The bus and semi rest in the intersection melded together middle-to-middle as if they were built that way: an x-shaped pair of conjoined twins. There are no signs of bent metal, broken headlights, or shattered glass.

Lii, what's going on? He withdrew. I pat myself down to see if I sustained any injuries. Other than my cuts from yesterday, a new headache, and a bloody nose, I look like the picture of health.

What the? My butt remains planted on the bus seat, but with bolts anchored to the cement rather than the bus. Lii? Silence. Is this a sim? Or a dream? Nothing. Passengers flee from the bus, uninjured as far as I can tell.

I swipe up my backpack and skate down the street. Rule twenty-six: don't wait for trouble to find you. I draw my hoodie over my face. My legs shake with the effort of holding me up. After rounding the street corner, I kick my board into my hand and lean against the decaying facade of a permanently-shuttered machine shop. My chest heaves harder than after any workout.

For some reason, I start laughing uncontrollably, half suffocating. What the heck just happened? That was insane. I check myself again for injuries. Nope. My nose still bleeds down the front of my hoodie but I prefer that over a nasty case of road rash. I erupt into another fit of laughter. What is wrong with me?

I need distance. I drop my board and lazily kick forward, taking a circuitous route home, pleased with how my leg holds up. Not wanting to run into Gunther after yesterday's encounter, I ride in random directions. After a few blocks the clouds adopt a sickly green tinge and rain picks up fast. Good. That'll keep the scavengers indoors. They can't afford more radiation. The raindrops grow heavier and the wind picks up. I duck under the purple awning of an abandoned locksmith as the large droplets transition into pelting hail.

"Odd weather today, eh Mazz?" a man says in a London accent only a foot away from me. I jolt and spin my head so fast I'm surprised it doesn't snap, spinal cord and all. He isn't a scavenger with his upper's circle tattoo, so my heart decides not to burst in panic. His cheekbones are high, eyes sharp, giving him the look of a Persian Supreme. If he were a blocker, he might look like an older version of me but far more handsome.

His blue sandals, Hawaiian shirt, and every-colored swim shorts make him look ridiculous. Is that a lei made of real flowers? My neck hairs raise as my body tries to decide between fight or flight. How does he know my name? And as importantly, was he there a second ago?

"Yeah," I respond. Rule thirty-five: the fewer the words, the better. I'm less likely to stick my foot in my mouth. An invisible gremlin squeezes my brain tighter by the second.

"You'll remember the note I left this morning," he says. His eyes dart this way and that. Sketchy.

"Uh?" I say dumbly.

"I put the note in the bottle," he says. "And, happy birthday, by the way."

Splick. Who is this guy? Was he in my container while I was sleeping? WTF! Creepy McCreeperson. And how does he know it's my birthday? Stalker much?

We may want to leave now, Lii suggests, more than a bit of tension pushing through our bond.

Again, my body freezes between fight and flight. I'll go when it stops hailing. He would have attacked right away with the element of surprise if he meant harm. Plus, I'm too tired to run anyway.

"As the note said, I'm Bender." He holds out his hand to shake. I look out at the worsening weather and pretend that I don't see his outstretched palm. Awkward silence. "Also mentioned in the note, the milk was juiced with nanites, so your innate abilities ramped up today."

He pauses, possibly expecting me to say something, but I

keep my mouth-hole shut. "Do you know how you swooshed, then blew up the basketball this morning?"

"Uh." My jaw hangs open.

Danger, Lii says. *We should run for it.* I stand still, looking back and forth between Bender and the hail, which pummels the ground even harder now with larger ice balls.

Apparently comfortable with a one-sided conversation, he says, "Or how that truck melded with your bus?"

Lii's right. I should split. Still feeling exhausted, I double down on silence.

"I was watching to make sure nothing dangerous happened today." His eyes never stop scanning the block.

"Ha," I laugh. I'd hate to see what this guy thinks is dangerous if a bus accident doesn't count.

"You acquitted yourself very well today." Definitely a stalker. I really need to get out of here. "You have a knack for nano influence, you know? You're naturally as strong as they come."

"Nano influence?" I mentally kick myself for joining him in the Land of Crazy. Rule thirty-eight: don't engage weirdos.

"I think of it as bending the world's nanites to my will. Doctor Fontein calls it nano influence." Hmm. Bending, bender. Obviously not his real name.

"Doctor who?" I ask before I realize what spurts out of my yapper.

We really should stop opening our mouth, Lii says. Waves of annoyance waft off of him. *This guy is the supreme of Nutsville.*

"Doctor Fontein," Bender says calmly, though his eyes bounce around like balls on a ping pong table. "She studies nano influence, the link between one's AI and the nanoscopic bots outside our bodies. Similar to how AIs use nanites to keep everyone healthy from radiation and normal illnesses. Rare individuals like us can control the nanites that repair things like the bus's tires, regulate the weather, and mine for resources."

"Ha," I laugh. "Laticia, come on out. You got me." I look around for her.

Completely in character, he says, "Specifically, you and I

control the nanites that transport material and other nanites. We're nano kinetics. Other types of nanos control weather nanites, magnetic nanites, water purification nanites, or mining nanites."

"Man, you're good." I almost pat him down to look for cameras but stop short.

"Mazz." A stern flash in his eye makes me back up. He doesn't seem full of anger, but he has a focus that says he could kill me instantly if he wanted. Crazy and dangerous. Great combo. "You can also phase as you did with that semi-truck and teleport as you did to the street corner. Both, impressive feats for someone untrained like yourself."

Did he say teleport? I ask Lii.

I do believe he did.

Bender nods when I nervously glance at him. "Strange accidents happen more and more frequently the longer you attend Desmond High. You've lived without an overlay for a while. It's part of our influence."

Lii says, *Don't start believing this guy just because he knows a few things about us.*

"That's why I'm here. You don't know how to control your innate skills yet. You need to reign in your abilities properly or these misfires will keep springing up when you least want them. More people could get hurt."

He stops talking. Am I actually listening to him?

"Usually, nanos manifest their influence when they're young, but being a blocker, you never had enough nanites for it to manifest. So, you're a late bloomer if you will."

This is too elaborate to be a prank.

"I spiked your bottle with nanites so I could observe your latent abilities. A test that you passed with more potential than anyone. With practice, you could hone your skills."

I ask, "And where would I practice?"

Stop opening our mouth.

"When you get home today, you'll find an invitation to Camp Astrid, a summer-long camp for young nanos like yourself."

With a shake of my head, I recognize the con. Mom and Dad are rich for blockers, having specialized work skills. He wants to dig into what they saved for school. "No thanks. I don't want whatever you're selling."

"Really?" Bender asks. "You don't have any interest in learning how to use your nano influence? And you aren't concerned that you might hurt someone?"

I shake my head, looking out at the storm, which switched from hail back to heavy rain, splashing cold water all over my shoes and drenching the frayed cuffs of my pants. Yet, water bounces away from Bender as if an invisible barrier shields his sandalled feet. His shins are as dry as–as something dry.

"You should know that Camp Astrid is free for families that can't afford it."

"What?" I ask, thrown off guard. It's too good to be true. Nothing is ever free: rule twenty-two.

"Camp Astrid won't cost your family a single credit. Your parents will be thrilled by the opportunity."

"Really?"

Who is crazier? Lii asks. *Him for preaching this particular brand of insanity? Or you for listening?* I can't argue that the AI-nanite-theory doesn't make some sense, being Laticia's leading hypothesis, but…

"Your influence won't go away, so the sooner you master it, the sooner you'll be safe."

"Safe?" I ask. Is he threatening me?

"Nano-influence isn't supposed to happen," Bender says, scraping grains of golden sand out from under his thumbnail. "If you keep drawing attention to yourself, the wrong sorts might take notice. You can't tell anyone except your family. Norms can't know. Do you understand?"

Nice scare tactic. Then again, it does have a grain of truth to it, like the grains of beach sand he scraped from under his nail. I ask, "What do you get out of this?"

"You risk your life and the safety of the entire nano community every time you have a public misfire."

That's exactly what a con man would say.

"All you have to do is respond to Dr. Fontein's invitation. Let us know you're coming." The weather mellows bit by bit and my legs almost feel normal. I'll be able to run for it in another minute or two.

"Seeing is believing," he says. He sticks his leg into the rain. The heavy droplets bounce off something invisible only inches from his skin. A pink and white drink with a pineapple wedge on the rim puffs into his hand. He takes a sip. "Mmmm. Tastes great, but I let it warm too long. Tea is more appropriate for this weather. One moment." He vanishes with a faint ffwup.

Holy splick! I swipe my hands through the air where he stood a second ago. How? Lii, am I going crazy?

If so, then we both are.

Then you glitched some strange sim, right?

Nope, Lii says, a sense of awe bubbling through our bond. *One hundred percent physical reality.*

I don't believe his royal glitchiness and stomp the ground on the hunt for a trick door, then look up into the awning in search of a hiding place. Nope. That was a slick illusion. One part of me wonders how he did it, but the stronger part is glad that he left.

Another puff announces his re-emergence into time and space. He cradles a large travel mug in his hands, steam wisping from it. He also changed into a black and gray camo shirt and black tech pants. Fully-laced, calf-high combat boots replaced his sandals. His hard edges soften as he sips the steaming drink. "Mmm. That's better."

Then he's back to the intense man, on the lookout for what, I don't know. Scavengers? Resistance? Enforcers? The tea vanishes to be replaced by a bullet-proof vest like the enforcers wear. As he swings it on, he says, "I'll come knocking another day. I don't want to disturb your birthday more than I already have." He snaps a holster with a black pistol to his belt. I step back. Technically, people aren't supposed to own guns, though the scavengers and Resistance flaunt that rule.

"Uh, okay," I nod. I'm not sure what I'm more afraid of, this guy showing up at my container door or being alone with a gun-toating magician.

Bender smiles again. "See you soon. I must be off to other... matters." An enforcer-style semi-automatic rifle materializes in his hands, its strap already slung around his torso. I step back again, nearly tripping into a puddle.

Is this physical reality, Lii? Not some digital effect?

Yupadoobers, Lii says, awe wafting from his core. *Insane, but real.*

Bender walks into the rain, an invisible umbrella overhead. A tactical helmet fastens itself into place. His boots tread on top of the water-filled potholes, not through them. Not possible.

"Don't worry about Principal Jean or your teachers," he says with a wink. "There's a reason they never stick to their threats to kick you out."

He checks one of his magazines for bullets and says, "I almost forgot. You'll want to eat extra cake when you get home. Nano-influence drains us of both nanites and sugars. You overused your influence. That's why your nose bled." Bender snaps into a swirl of nothingness, leaving a wave in the puddle upon which he was standing.

This can't be.

By the time I arrive home, I'm drenched from head to toe and weary legs. If he told the truth–a big if–an invitation awaits me at home. A real summer camp. If this is legit, I won't have to work with my parentals on their endless welding jobs.

The upside of the rain is that it keeps the scavengers away. If only it would rain every day. As I open our container door, my lips curl despite my exhaustion and a nagging burr that needles my mind. White lab coats, ultra-clean surgical rooms, and empty prison cells.

CHAPTER SIX

Birthday

"Surprise!" Mom, Dad, and Laticia yell as soon as I swing the door open. Glitter flies everywhere to the sound of string-poppers. Confetti sticks to my wet skin and drenched clothes, leaving no part glitter-free.

"Happy birthday!" they shout, grins across their faces. I nearly drool when I spy a dark brown cake set on the kitchen table with four lit candles. The icing looks amazing, even with the specks of glitter that land on it. Better yet, a box covered in bits of every kind of wrapping paper rests in a seat with a white envelope on top.

Mom ushers me to "come sit" at our too-small table and pulls out the chair for me as if I'm royalty.

"Make a wish and blow out your candles," Dad says in his husky voice, clapping me firmly on the shoulder. I close my eyes, breathe in, and silently wish, "Make Bender's camp the real deal." As I open my eyes, the cake explodes with chunks hitting my face, wet hair, and soaked hoodie. The candles flew off to who-knows-where.

An open-mouthed look of horror mars Mom's face. "My cake."

Laticia mouths the word, "Classic." Her wide smile says, "I hang out with you because I never know what's going to happen." Damn, she's beautiful. Dark skin, deep brown eyes, and frizzy hair. While strange things often happen around me, this is by far the weirdest incident I've seen outside school before today. Laticia and Bender's explanation of nano influence does fit, especially since this happened at home, and not at school like they usually do.

I expect them all to ask what happened, but Dad smiles and says, "Well, let's have some cake." He swipes a piece off his shirt and shoves it into his mouth. "Del-ish-ish! The best exploding cake I've ever had." Rule fourteen: roll with it.

While the others scoop cake bits from their clothes, I reach for the envelope that had several names crossed out before receiving the "Mazz" label. I wipe a layer of frosting from it into my mouth. Fan-tab-u-lous. I retrieve the letter and read it aloud.

"Dear Mazzen and Parents. On behalf of Camp Astrid, a place for talented children to grow, we are pleased to invite Mazzen to join us this summer. Camp Astrid will cover all costs including supplies and food. Our activities last from June fifth to August eighteenth."

"Please find the attached pamphlet explaining everything you need to know about camp. We eagerly anticipate your reply. Sincerely, Doctor Fontein, Head Counselor."

Mom tries to brush glitter out of my wet hair and says, "That's what we couldn't wait to tell you. I received this message yesterday. We printed it out at Guild headquarters last night so you could open it up."

Could Bender really be legit? The invite doesn't say anything about nano-influence or Bender's warning of danger. What will they think when they hear why they really invited me?

That can be a conversation for another day, Lii says. *Cake and presents are for today.*

I smile broadly.

"We thought you'd love it," Mom says through a beaming smile. "Here's the pamphlet." She sends Lii a digital file, which he tries to display but fails, always the glitcher.

Having finished several upper-sized bites, Dad says. "We got you something." He reaches over the cake remains and grabs the crazy every-color present, which looks like someone ran over an upper's birthday party with a lawnmower and spat this box out.

"It's not new, mind you," Mom says. My gifts rarely are, but any present is better than no present. "We cleaned it up and mended the holes, so it should do the trick."

"Well," Laticia exclaims with wide eyes and an expectant expression. "Open it already." Without needing to be told twice, I dig into the wrapping paper and the box beneath. I pull out a floppy green canvas duffle like they use in the military.

"It's a bag!" Mom says, obviously incapable of handling the suspense. "So you can pack your stuff for camp." In an instant, a bundle of cloth and a zipper transforms from a simple bag into a summer-long escape ticket.

"Are you sure you're okay with me skipping out on my apprenticeship?" I ask.

Dad winks and says, "You can't pass this up. Do you know anyone who went to a summer camp? Now, look inside."

I open the bag and find a K-bar knife sheathed in black leather, the kind they use in the special forces. I flick it over in my hands and pull it from its sheath. While used, the blade feels sturdy and weighs almost nothing. The edge could slice the electrons from an atom. I can't believe how many rations this must have cost Mom and Dad.

Dad smiles, as proud as I've ever seen him, and says, "It's for whittling at camp. You're of an age that you can be trusted with such things."

"Thanks, Dad," I say, rolling the knife in my hand. Setting it down, I reach into the bag again, this time pulling out an olive-green, long-sleeved shirt that might have once belonged to an upper. It's big for me, but perfect for camp. "Thanks, Mom."

Will they allow me to keep these once Bender pays us a visit? Will they understand? I'm tempted to share the note I got from Bender, but go with rule forty: Why do today what can be put off until tomorrow?

◆ ◆ ◆

I feel like mashed tofu when Lii blares the most annoying morning alarm in my head. Was yesterday a dream?

Neeeeeh! Lii buzzes. *Wro-ong.*

I extend my foot and feel the canvas duffel at the foot of my bed, which I packed with gear for camp despite the fact that I won't leave for two weeks. Half the night, I sorted and re-sorted my stuff into "go" and "stay" piles, never packing the bag even half-full.

Opening my bleary eyes, I catch sight of the printed invitation to Camp Astrid resting on our kitchen table, right where I'd left it. I peruse the digital brochure, which Lii eventually figured out how to display. The pictures show giant trees, sandstone rock outcrops, old wooden cabins, rock climbing, swimming, campfires, and the works. The photos show campers that look as young as six and as old as eighteen, though all uppers.

I bound down from my bunk, bounce off my parent's bed, twist a three-sixty, and land in the kitchen, where I serve up a mangled slice of leftover cake. Pure bliss. The more I think about it, the more I'm convinced that Bender is legit. I can't be the only human plagued by strange accidents, so someone must be able to explain the bus accident and the exploding cake. Why not him?

I float through my normal daily routine of getting to school without a hitch, not worrying about a thing. Heeding Bender's warning, I leave my skateboard at home in case someone saw me flee the accident. At school, I ignore the judgmental looks. They can think what they want. They're norms. I'm nano.

I don't care when Coach Short sends me to the principal's office after Keltin's pant legs spontaneously shred at the cuffs. Principal Jean simply sends me back to the gym with only two words: "Get out." As minutes pass into hours, and hours roll into a complete school day, my mood continues to improve.

Then, as I step onto the bus, my danger senses spin to a perfect ten. All the passengers face forward, stiff and upright, their gazes not budging to watch me enter. A conspicuous man dressed in a tight-fitting black shirt and black techwear pants sits rigidly at the back of the bus. His sharp blue eyes dart from passenger to passenger. His hair screams of military perfection. Is he a government agent as Bender hinted at? I avert my eyes, take a seat near the front and pretend to be immersed in a sim like everyone else. Rule seventeen: blend in.

I disembark one bus stop before the accident and walk away quickly, eyes on the lookout for scavengers and men in black. While I shouldn't, I can't resist rounding past the intersection of the crash. The bus and eighteen-wheel truck are gone but the intersection is full of excited blockers. Twitchy enforcers weave among them. Scavengers too. One blocker looks up to the sky wearing a cardboard sign that reads, "X marks the spot. The aliens are coming."

Two watchful men dressed in tactical wear stand out like enforcers, though nobody seems to notice them. I'm pretty sure that the bulges at their hips are concealed pistols.

Let's not find out, Lii says. It was a bad idea to come here.

I pretend to not notice the agents and walk in the opposite direction from home. A few blocks away, I loop around toward my block, backtracking once or twice just in case.

When I get home, I take two slices of cake to Laticia's container. After crushing the cake, we play Kongo Killer, one of the better games that still exist on a datapad. The temptation to tell her threatens to unravel me like a poorly-nit sweater. Why not? She knows everything about me. Shouldn't I tell her? No, it's better this way. She'd needlessly worry.

Keep telling yourself that, Lii says.

And what if it all turns out to be a scam? Would she keep hanging out with such a sucker?

You do realize how quiet you've become, don't you?

I know, but what should I do about it?

CHAPTER SEVEN

Accidents Happen

I hate the blocks in the summer. Without air conditioning, my clothes stick to me with endless sweat and the stacked containers smell putrid. They were meant to be temporary, and that was a century ago. At least we have a cool breeze tonight.

"Are you ready?" Dad asks after breakfast or dinner or whatever you call the evening meal. He whirls his hand and points out the door. Dad loves to be punctual, and for him, that really means early.

"Ready," I say. With a grunt, I heft my backpack, which now serves as a tool bag. We head five blocks north, then climb seven flights to a collapsed section of shipping containers. I nervously follow Dad as he winds across a beam twenty feet in the air. He picks a path through the chaos of fallen metal to find good contacts to weld. After a lengthy discussion of why he uses a TIG versus a MIG weld, he begins showering the contact between two metal lengths. The white and gold sparks spray like reunification day fireworks, but better.

Sitting in the flickering light of the welder, I peruse Camp Astrid's digital pamphlet, trying to avoid the fact that we're sitting on a six-inch beam twentyish feet above the next solid surface. I distract myself by picturing the camp forests, the old wood cabins, the fire pits, and the stomach-gurgling s'mores.

Wait a sec. How can they have a pamphlet for a secret camp depicting people who aren't supposed to exist?

Simple, Lii says. *Those are avatars and digital renderings. The whole thing is a lie.*

Fu–

Clang! Something snaps overhead. A set of large beams fall toward us, creating an avalanche of metal debris. The world slows and my chest clenches. I'm gonna die. I don't want to–

With the loudest noise I've ever heard, one that rattles my bones, the rubble stops only feet overhead, a jumble of wreckage. Metal hangs precariously above us, beams sticking out at odd angles, rusted sheets bend this way and that, impossibly balanced on something I can't see.

Dad deftly hops to a crouched position on the narrow beam and frantically looks me over, patting my body down like a medic. "Are you hurt?" he asks, wide-eyed. I don't know how to answer. I don't feel any pain, but I'm paralyzed with my arms locked overhead. "Move!" he yells.

"I can't," I yell back, my voice cracking. Frak! The metal heap should have hit us. Why can't I move?

With the skill and confidence of someone who has worked for decades on jobs like this, Dad hops over to another beam, then back behind me. I feel like one of those elderly anti-AI zealots who carry heavy loads wherever they go, a display of the burden that humans should carry. My eyes droop.

Dad grabs the straps of my backpack and tugs me away from the suspended metal. As soon as I slide out from under it, the debris plummets in a deafening cacophony and collects more iron on its way down. I can't believe that I'm not dead.

"Are you okay?" Dad asks frantically patting me down in another round of father-medic.

"No," I hear myself say as black holes puncture my vision and darkness engulfs me in an impenetrable ink. I feel sickeningly weak. What's happening? Dying is against the rules.

◆ ◆ ◆

"Son," Dad says, nudging my shoulder. I open my eyes, head cleaving in pain. Splinters and sandpaper compose the makeup of my being. Even the dim light in our container stings my eyes and the gentle groans of the blocks ring in my ears. "Oh, thank the nanites. There you are."

"What happened?" I croak, raising my hand to my forehead. I taste blood in my mouth, the sign of yet another bloody nose. Lii, fix me up. Lii, are you there?

"You saved us," Dad says, pulling me to a sitting position on the floor and hugging me in an embrace that might as well be a trash compactor. The accident must have strained all of my six hundred and forty muscles and tested the limits of every joint.

"No, Dad. I was stuck and you saved me."

Dad cups my head so he can look in my eyes and says, "You stopped the collapse mid-fall. No injuries other than your nose." There is stone-cold love in his eyes mixed with something else. Pride? Fear? Is he scared for me, or of me?

"You threw your hands up and the wreckage froze," he says and lifts me to sit in one of our undersized chairs. "Once I pulled you out from under the floating scrap, the metal fell again and you passed out. It was…"

"Nano-influence," I say before realizing that I'd spilled a can of hex nuts. I've been so close to telling him for weeks that it slipped out all on its own.

Dad nods and says, "I know. And Camp Astrid is–"

Dad jumps at a firm knock on our container door, then spins in a hunched position and rushes to the front, bent at the waist and legs as if to pounce like a wolf. He soundlessly withdraws his "anti-theft" metal pipe from beside the door and pulls a handgun from his waist. Since when has Dad had a gun? With a smooth, swift motion, he shifts his eye past the peephole, rather than pausing to look through as I would have. Without dropping the pipe, he unlocks the door and ushers someone in.

When he steps aside, Bender nods, a grave expression cutting lines across his forehead. This time, he's dressed in black blocker clothes, ratty shoes to match. Half-smiling and half-worried, he says, "Good evening, sonny."

"Bender," I try to say but a dry fit of coughs seizes my body like a medieval torture device. With the intention of standing, I only manage to slump out of my seat.

"Come sit," Dad says as he lifts me into the chair. "Thanks for coming so quickly."

A normal-sized chair coalesces beside our small table and he plops into it, shoulders slumped but fingers twitchy, tired but ultra-aware. Dad looks uneasy at the spontaneously materializing furniture but swallows the impossibility like a champ, then takes his seat between Bender and me.

"SitRep?" Dad says, all business, like an army officer. The militaristic edge is natural on his tongue, but strange to hear.

Bender scratches his beard and says, "I surveilled the site of the accident. As far as I could tell, the event went unnoticed. No witnesses. A camp of homeless was nearby, but they were simmed out, completely unaware."

"Bravo Zulu," Dad says. If I'm not mistaken, that translates to "good job" in army-speak. He nods and says, "That confirms my observations."

Bender hands me a candy bar and a bottle of chocolate milk and says, "Eat up." The milk sports a bland label of "Nano-Milk" and a red cross. The bar reads "Nano-Bar" with the same red cross.

"Drink, son," Dad says, both commanding and gentle. "They contain nanites and nutrients. Army medics use them for wounds." No further encouragement needed. I'm not that addled. I don't bother to listen as they discuss who-knows-what in hushed tones. The inner caramel mixes with the chocolate crust and crunch waffle to yield the perfect balance of flavor and texture. I can't taste the nanites, but when they hit my stomach, a feathery warmth spills through me, filling me with a deficit I didn't know could exist.

Bender snaps his fingers several times in my face and says, "We cannot allow you to draw the wrong sort of attention. There are those that would use your nano-skills for...let's say less than moral purposes."

Mom arrived sometime while I was focused on the buzz from the milk and bar. My folks share a glance that communicates something important, likely sending rapid-fire digital messages back and forth. I used to be able to do that.

Bender explains that "Mazz has more natural ability than anyone we've found in a decade. Camp Astrid is his only option for a normal life. We can't delay." Dad looks worried, but not Mom. They digested the news of my nano-influence far smoother than I thought.

Bender fixes me with an intimidating gaze and says, "In the name of prudence, you will stay hidden indoors until you come to camp. Another incident risks all of your lives. Are we all agreed?"

"Affirmative," Dad says, sounding the military man again.

"Agreed," says Mom. None of them bother to look at me for confirmation and like that, I am completely homebound for a week.

Bender dispatches the remains of the sweets with a flick of his finger and says, "Too many nanites will instigate another accident. No more attention. Got it?"

I nearly object to the loss of the sweets and again at the accusation, but rule twelve: shut your trap. Under the combined glares from all three adults, I say, "Fine."

"Mazz," Laticia pounds on my container door with her usual thump, thump, pause, tap at three in the morning. Since I stopped apprenticing, Mom took her on but lets her come home early so she can rest before reporting for her factory job. She receives half a brick of tofu a night for her efforts, easing her hunger and the starvation of her father. I toss down my datapad, soar out of my bunk, twist, land on my skateboard, thud-thud-thud my way across the uneven floor, and slide to a stop at the door.

"Come in, m'lady," I say, pulling the door open and bowing deeply. She dressed in her black shirt that is ripped in all the right places. Somehow, she makes blocker clothes look good. Her short black hair is mussed up and frizzy in her signature look, which I know is for my benefit, since everyone else sees her avatar. I try not to give her a once-over, but my eyes slip to the deep V in her shirt for a fraction of a second.

"Still grounded?" she asks as soon as she's inside, air-quoting "grounded." Being stupid, I didn't plan out my lie about stealing candies in advance. I couldn't provide details like which candies I stole or where the crime supposedly happened.

You're the worst liar on this side of the wastelands, Lii says.

"When are you gonna tell me why you're really stuck at home?" she asks. Her smirk splits one part happy and four parts pissed. Or maybe nine parts pissed. Few of my memories lack her before I started at Desmond High. We share everything. No secrets. "I'll quit coming by if you don't tell me. I can tell you're itching to spill the tofu."

I give her what I hope looks like an "I'm sorry" expression and purse my lips. "I can't."

Her face brightens as if her irritation spontaneously washed away, but I know better. "Wanna play poker?"

"Yes," I say, glad for the change of topic. She fetches a deck of cracked and bent cards from her back pocket and we sit at the table, her in the full-sized chair Bender conjured. We must be the first people to play a physical card game in the last century, so the deck only cost a half square of tofu.

About ten rounds of poker later, she sprays her cards at my face. I flinch and miraculously, the cards bounce away as if deflected by an invisible barrier. We both stare in surprise until she laughs triumphantly, jumps to her feet, hands held high over her head. "I knew it. Superpowers!" She bounces and spins a few more times. Pointing at me with both hands, she says, "And I know that camp has something to do with it, so you might as well tell me."

"Fine," I say, both nervous and relieved. "But you have to keep it secret."

"You know I will," she says in mock offense. "And who would I tell? Nobody asks about you anymore."

I should probably be offended, but I'm not. "Now, don't freak out but I can control nanites outside my body." Yes. Finally! The pressure valve releases. "It's called nano-influence, and it isn't supposed to happen, ever."

"Yeah, and…" she says as if I was an idiot, shaking her head.

"And if the wrong people found out, then…"

"They would either kill you or dissect you," she says as if it's no big deal. "Tell me something I don't know."

"How could you know?"

"Well, I didn't know-know but it was the only viable explanation. I told you my theory months ago, but you wouldn't listen. And don't think for a second that I didn't investigate the welding accident."

Seeing my face blanch she says, "Don't worry. Nobody else put two and two together."

"Why didn't you say anything?" I ask.

"I was waiting for you to tell me," she says. Her squinted eyes tell me that I failed an important test. "It took you long enough. Didn't I deserve better than your lies?"

"Yeah," I say. "You did, but I swore I wouldn't tell anyone."

I spend the next hour filling her in on everything, from the bus accident to a detailed description of the falling metal at the job site. She asks all sorts of questions about the black-clad agent types and Bender, about whom I know very little. Within an hour, we joke about my influence without the tension that she arrived with.

As she prepares to leave and slides the cards into her back pocket, she says, "Thanks." Then she leans in and kisses my cheek, her lips soft and warm, sending tendrils of pleasure down my spine. We share a gaze, her eyes glistening and beautiful. She turns on her toes and skips out the door. "See ya."

I'm left a puddle of confusion.

CHAPTER EIGHT

Camp Astrid

After eight days stuck in my container with only occasional visits from Latisha, I have a serious case of boreditis, and can't wait to go. The trip will take most of the day, transferring between three buses and two trains through cities and the wildlands. I check the time on my datapad: six-thirty. Laticia and my parentals should be back from the night shift by now.

I want to see them before I go. Especially Laticia. We haven't talked about the kiss or our shared look, and I don't know what leaving all summer will do to our relationship.

"Okay," I say, "Time to go." I easily lift the olive duffle over my shoulder, aware that its minimal contents aren't well suited for a summer-long camp in the woods. I open the door to find Bender on the other side with an uneasy grimace and keyed-up eyes. Baggy dark-gray blocker clothes mostly cover a set of beige army fatigues. He smells of desert and gunpowder. A layer of sand and dust covers his tan combat boots.

Without asking, he pushes his way in and bites into a nano-bar, quickly closing the door behind him. "What's going on?"

"We decided to transport you to camp in a less conventional manner."

"You mean?" I snap my fingers. It doesn't escape me that he

said, "you," not "all the campers." Did I attract too many eyes? Or do they think I'll misfire again? Either way, they're singling me out before I even arrive. Not a great start.

"Are you ready to go?"

"Yeah." I pat the duffle. I wish I could seeing Laticia and my rents before I go but if wishes were rainbows, the world would be a kaleidoscope of color. "What should I do? To, you know..."

"Don't worry. I'll do all the work but try not to puke." A dizzying vertigo grips me, collapsing my innards as if squeezed by King Kong. Something pulls me into a pin-sized hole and blows me out the other side.

Keeling over, my morning tofu makes an unwelcome return. When my stomach stops conspiring against me, I take a look around. We stand inside the ruins of a roofless cement-walled room. A layer of dirt and rubble covers the floor, from which bushes and an impossibly tall tree sprout.

Douglas fir, Lii says, surprisingly on point rather than glitching. Green moss grows in patches from its thick, coarse trunk. Branches splay out overhead, rimmed with bushy green bunches of needles. Farther above, through the gaps in the tree, the sky shines a turquoise blue, so different from the toxic cadet-blue of home.

Lii says, *The air is almost pure here, but the radiation is higher than the badlands back home. Don't worry though. There are so many nanites here that we can heal from almost anything short of a rod to the head.*

The sweet and earthy smell of the forest contrasts so completely from the blocks that I hardly believe this is the same planet. Something taps my shoulder and I jump, but nothing is there except for a splotch of water. More drops hit the forest floor around me.

Outside the ruins in which we materialized, the forest reaches to the sky with millions of pointy green needles. The trees with dark rust-colored trunks ascend even higher into the heavens.

Redwoods, Lii says.

They must be a hundred feet tall.

Some are over two hundred feet, he says as if reading from a textbook.

Dew clings to ferns, bushes, and an unending layer of brown needles and branches that cover the forest floor. We stand on a gently sloping hillside where the loose combination of twigs, needles, loose dirt conspire to slide out from under me. Trees and half-buried foundations stretch out in all directions as far as I can see.

A chitter to the side sends my heart racing and winds my muscles tight. *A chipmunk,* Lii laughs. Bender's half-smile reddens my cheeks. He pulls off the blocker clothes, revealing a full complement of beige military uniform and gear, including a flak jacket and numerous pockets holding ammo and who knows what else. He removes the body armor that has the name tag "M. Weather" on it and it disappears. I bet he has all sorts of aliases.

Offline, Lii says. *I can't reach the outside world. It's terrifying.*

"Offline?" I ask.

"Yeah," Bender says. "You can't access the global network out here unless you're a nano hacker. Dr. Fontein chose this spot so you can focus on your skills and not a bunch of digital distractions."

I tilt my head and ask, "And the radiation?"

Bender looks out over our surroundings, his nose twitching, and says, "The nuclear contamination means most people won't come around, giving us peace and quiet."

"You'll also notice the excess nanites, which make it easier to learn your nano-skills." Bender juts his chin in a direction indistinguishable from any other and says, "Let's go see camp, shall we?" Without waiting for me to agree, he strides off along a thin, barely noticeable path through the ruins and trees. I don't get how he knows where he's going. Every direction looks the same.

Lii says, *I can't get GPS and my internal compass keeps spinning.* Not too surprising for Lii but I suspect these failures play into our proximity to Camp Astrid.

As we walk, Bender removes item after item from his person and inspects them, each disappearing in turn. The trail winds this way and that, yet without much attention, he picks offshoots that make no sense. It's strange to have so few people in so much open space.

"Why didn't we teleport into camp?" I ask.

"Groups of...unsavory people would love nothing more than to find a camp full of nano kids. We added defenses to keep them away but they also block us. I could have pushed us through but that would make your pukathon back there seem like a ladybug's burp."

My legs aren't used to the uneven ground and intermittent branches, so different from the potholes and tire ruts of home. While lightweight, my duffle keeps snagging on sticks and bushes.

After a minute, we turn right onto a road, half cement and half divot and bump. Ferns and grasses sweep against my pant legs, streaks of dew soaking my shins. Bender wordlessly walks ahead of me, his synthetic clothes wicking water away, and heavy boots apparently choosing their own way when the road splits left or right.

In several places, buildings toppled over the road, which we would either walk around or over. Twice, we traverse over the collapsed sections of overpasses that block our way.

About ten minutes later, a wall of interwoven wood, metal, stone, and cement rises fifteen feet into the air. A pair of mismatched towers flank a tall open metal gate, giving off the vibe of a werewolf's prison. Out of place, a purple and black tarp hangs between the towers saying, "WELCOME to CAMP ASTRID."

"This is Southgate," Bender says as we walk beneath the towers. "Four gates mark the north, east, south, and west entrances to camp."

Inside, trees ring a courtyard with the remains of a truly massive tree trunk at its center. Wood cabins built on the remains of older buildings peak out from between the redwoods.

Dirt and sawdust paths wind off in five directions.

A tall woman with thick black hair pulled back in a bun, dressed in sporty shorts and a purple Camp Astrid tee-shirt approaches. The square mark of the pinnacle caste is barely visible against her dark skin. I've never been this close to someone of such status before.

She and Bender tap fists. She smiles and says, "Bender, how good to see you?" Her resonant voice and South African accent ring with power. Her vibrant amber eyes practically shine. If I believed in auras, this woman would glow brighter than the sun.

"Dr. Fontein," Bender says with an edgy smile. The two of them couldn't look more different, Bender militaristic and edgy and Dr. Fontein casual and calm. Yet under the surface, both emanate a dangerous intangible power, picked up by a nagging otherly sense.

Turning to me with an inner vibe that makes me want to shy away while outwardly presenting a demeanor gentle enough to reassure me, Dr. Fontein says, "This must be young Mazz."

"Yes, ma'am," I say, feeling my palms sweat under her scrutiny. An indescribable part of me squirms. If I didn't know any better, I would think that she senses my every thought.

"Welcome," Fontein says offering a fist to bump. "Your cabin is Steadfast Corner, near Northgate." She points toward a rusted metal sign that says "Cabins" with an arrow pointing up a dirt path. "You should be able to find your way. Bender and I have things to discuss." I wonder what those "things" might be, but decide to keep my trap shut: rule twelve.

I follow the hand-painted signs down a well-trodden path. Alone, I notice the unsettling bird calls and the creaks of trees, which juxtapose the familiar clangs and bangs of home. At a fork in the path, another sign directs me left to the "gents" side of camp. Where are the other campers?

Confidently, Lii says, *They should get here later today.*

"And how would you know?"

They have a local camp network cut off from the rest of the world. This place feels amazing.

I cross a wooden bridge over a hazy stream. Dozens of signs with names like "Peacocks" and "Argonauts" point in offshoots from the main trail. The old cabins of rough-hewn planks on top of aged cement foundations perfectly nestle into the forest as if grown alongside the trees. The scattered drips of water give it an creepy ax-murderer vibe.

Following the signs that say "Steadfast Corner," I eventually find my cabin, the last one in the bunch. Between the trees, a pair of towers loom like Southgate. Steadfast resembles the other cabins but noticeably leans to the right and has a canvas tarp rather than wood. Pounding echoes from within adding to the murdery vibe.

I poke my head inside, letting my eyes adjust to the dark interior. Wood bunks line the walls, six to the left and another six to the right, each bigger than my bed at home.

"Mazz," says a guy with straight black hair, slender eyes, and a slim but full build. Circle marks of an upper on his neck. He's dressed in a dark-brown, tight-fit shirt, forest-green hiking pants, and thick-soled boots. Upper clothes. He hammers a half-rusted nail into the corner of a bunk. "Dr. F said you'd be arriving early. I'm Miles, your cabin leader."

I'm here for five minutes and they already talked about me. So much for rule seventeen and not standing out. He holds out a fist to bump, either missing that I'm a skinny blocker or pretending not to notice.

"I'm Miles. Let me finish this board. Go pick a bunk." He's way too friendly to be trusted. "The early familiar gets the nanites, right?" I get the gist, but what's a familiar?

At the back of the cabin, I toss my duffle onto the top bunk left of the frail rear door. Someone neatly laid out sage-green shirts with "Steadfast" embossed on the shoulders in each cot. The synthetic material stretches like the one Mom gave me on my birthday. I quickly pull it over my shirt, hoping that I won't stand out as much this way.

"Most of the campers will arrive later today," Miles says after pounding in a few more nails. "Steadfast is for fifteen years and older. We have a bunch of different kinds of nanos in here: rock, electric, vibration, chemists. You name it. And now, with you we have kinetics, phasing, and teleportation."

Noted, I say inwardly. Lots of types of abilities.

"I'm an adapter."

"A what?"

"I can use skills that others around me use naturally."

I nod.

"You deserve a proper tour but I have lots to finish up. Why don't you walk the inner perimeter of camp? Get the lay of the land."

"Cool," I say, hoping I don't look as out of place as I feel. I don't want to traipse around the forest alone, ax murderers and all, but refuse to sound like a coward. Outside, I walk to the amalgamated towers. The materials interweave in ways that defy understanding. Boards grew through stone. Metal fronds braid through cement. Rock flows through metal sheets. I touch a bulge of protruding stone to make sure it's real. I marvel at the contacts of metal on metal, which show no signs of welding junctions. I can't help but check if this is a dream

Not a dream, Lii confirms.

Unlike the towers, the massive doors consist of solid metal, though made from many pieces, all rusted except the hinges. Again, no hints of welding. I peak through an eye-level slot in the large barrier. Outside, broken foundations line a road, trees growing indiscriminately among them. It reminds me of the wasteland back home, but with a real forest growing through them rather than a digital overlay.

A trail runs on the inside of the tall walls in both directions. Choosing a direction at random, I head left. It will take a while for me to get used to the unevenness of the forest floor, especially near the walls. Shortly, I find the hazy stream I crossed earlier and jump across, getting mud all over my shoes.

A bit later I come upon Westgate, which matches the other two in so much as random combinations of materials can match each other. A quaint stone and wood cottage labeled Braunwyn nestles under the tower. The craftsmanship stands in a separate class from the other cabins, every plank and stone set just so.

Continuing on, my jaw hangs low as I approach a deep stone-lined, semi-circle in the ground.

An amphitheater, Lii says.

Thoughts of gladiators fighting to the death in ancient Rome race through my mind. Very few of these survived the AI War, but digital reconstructions fascinated me a few years ago. I sure as hell hope they don't expect us to duel. Sitting on the top step, I listen to the echoes as I call out and clap. Gradually, the amplified whistle of the breeze starts to creep me out, so I move on.

A while later, I reach the cafeteria at Southgate. The label on the cottage next to it says "Fontein." So, they stationed a counselor at each exit, probably making sure campers don't sneak out.

Or maybe they're worried about something else getting in...

I shake my head. "Great! Now I'm thinking about vampires."

Continuing around the wall, a steep crag of granite rises up to my right. After walking below the cliffside for several minutes, I come upon a forty-foot-tall waterfall that dribbles down the rock face. Grey and purple formations mark the rivulets where water contacts stone. At its base, a milky pond overflows into a stream running toward the center of camp. A mystical haunt hovers around this pond, a vibe they skipped over in the brochure.

I skirt the walls around Eastgate and pass another counselor cottage labeled "Ms. Merryweather." Hypothesis confirmed: counselors at each exit. The northeast part of camp is littered with cabins like the northwest. "Wagon Wheels" and "Celtics" stick out as interesting names.

I recognize Northgate when I see it, huge and unsettling. I hope this place won't be as freaky when the other campers arrive. I'd hate to get lost–

A nasally voice breaks through my thoughts. "Who the hell are you? And what do you think you're doing?" I jump, not having seen a single person along my walk. Turning, I face a pale, flat-nosed man in an immaculate black overcoat, black slacks, and shiny dress shoes. As if this place wasn't spine-chilling before, this ghost of a man tipped it into a whole new realm. Can nanos reanimate corpses? His too-perfect attire belongs in a gleaming skyscraper, not surrounded by evergreen trees and wild shrubs.

"I–I'm Mazz Becker." He definitely looks like the sort of upper who expects blockers to show respect, so I add, "sir."

"What are you doing next to my cabin?" he asks, his pale blue eyes burrowing into me.

He's Counselor von Steiner, Lii informs me.

Having learned long ago not to trust Lii, I ask him, how do you know without signal to the outside world?

Local network, he says as relaxed as I've felt him in over a year.

"I'm just walking around camp," I say, rocking back on my feet as he steps menacingly close.

"Likely story." The sneer on his face tells me all I need to know; he concluded that I'm a trouble-making blocker. Not to be trusted with a paperclip.

Lii says, *Rule sixteen: once a blocker, always a blocker.*

"I'm just going to my cabin now."

He eyes me, squinting, and growls, "Go. And no more shenanigans."

Who says shenanigans? Is this guy for real? I almost tell him that I wasn't doing anything, but rules twelve and seven combine: arguing won't persuade an ass flap like him.

Instead, I try to not roll my eyes and say, "Sorry." I walk the remaining twenty yards to my cabin, sure that his pale blues are on me the whole time. I swear he's sniffing me out. Can nanos do that?

CHAPTER NINE

Assembly

I t feels better to be inside Steadfast Corner and away from von Steiner. Miles smiles, his attitude a complete opposite of the tweaker outside. "Mazz, come meet Naren. He just arrived from India."

"Pleased to meet you," says the slender, tan-skinned camper with an accent. He looks similar in age to me but taller and healthier. I snap a quick glance at his neck and verify what I already knew; he's another upper. Like Miles, he wears fancy synthetic camping gear.

"This is your first year, right?" he asks.

"Uh, yes." And I'm immediately identified as a noob. "You?"

"No, I've been coming for years." He smiles broadly with a grin that is uniquely his, slightly crooked and wrinkling his nose above his nostrils. He and Miles seem too nice to be uppers, which means they're probably playing at something. Naren says, "I'm happy to tell you anything you want to know about camp."

A ton of questions flood my mind but I don't know where to begin. Anything dumb that I say can and probably will be used against me. "Uh, okay."

"Do you want to grab a snack?" he asks, an eyebrow raised. "Ms. Abigail makes the best chocolate chip cookies."

"I can't afford that," I say.

Lii buzzes me with annoyance. *Don't highlight how different we are. Just say "no" next time.*

"Not to worry, my friend," he gently claps me on the shoulder. I almost cringe away, uncomfortable with the intrusion on my personal space. Coming into contact with scavengers, Resistance, or enforcers brings nothing but trouble for blockers. Unaware of my discomfort, he says, "They're free. The counselors want us to eat as many as we can. All the snacks have booster nanites, don't they?"

Is he pulling my chain? Rule twenty-two: nothing is ever free. I haven't had a cookie since Reunification Day, so I go along with it and say, "Sure. Let's go."

Walking back toward Southgate, Naren asks, "Why did you come early?"

"I'm not really sure, but I sort of had an accident last week. I think they were afraid someone might follow me if I traveled by bus and train."

"Yeah," Naren says. "You have to watch out for the shockknights."

"Shockknights?"

"Ah, you must be a norm-born," he says.

It takes me a moment to figure out what he means. Knowing the answer, I ask, "Are most campers norm-born?"

"Nah," he says.

Once an outsider, always an outsider, Lii says. *An adaptation of rule sixteen.*

"Most of us have parents that are nanos. Only a few nano-borns come each year." We walk in silence for a moment. He shakes his head and says, "They should have told you about the shockknights though. They're a secret group who kidnaps and kills nanos."

Too many questions gurgle up. It was pretty obvious from Bender's behavior and the fortress walls around camp that they're scared of something, but hearing it outright is another story. The first thought that pops to the surface is, "Why are they after us?"

"That's the question, isn't it? Nobody really knows, or at least not for certain. While they could be anti-AI zealots, I think they're a government agency that wants to lock us up. They may think they can steal or replicate our skills?" The prickly sensation on the back of my neck hints that being a nano may not be all unicorns and rainbows. All-you-can-eat cookies are awesome and all, but if I'm dead...

"Mother says their leader goes by the name Tollere, but supposedly nobody has ever seen him and lived to tell the tale, so I don't know how she'd know." Naren's smile clashes with the serious nature of our conversation. Is he messing with me? "But, don't worry. They hid Camp Astrid and put up all sorts of barriers. Nobody can find us."

"That's what I heard." Yet, if I learned one thing in Ms. Dillinger's history class, it was that nothing is foolproof.

"Yeah. They fortified camp with all sorts of defenses like refracting light to camouflage camp, jamming signals, and tweaking magnetics. Stuff like that."

We walk in silence for a bit, but the quiet bothers me, so I ask, "What kind of nano are you?"

"I am a nano-terran and nano-ventus. Mother gave me rock skills and Father gave me wind skills."

Naren leads the way into the cafeteria. He seems so casual, walking in as easily as I'd enter Latisha's container. Wooden picnic tables with attached benches fill a huge open space, big enough for two hundred campers. On a table to my right, platters of cookies, cinnamon rolls, donuts, candy, and nano-bars make my eyes bulge. I've never seen so many sweets in one place before. Such extravagance feels flagrant given how many blockers starve every day.

"I know, right?" Naren says, with an ear-to-ear grin spread across his face. He grabs three chocolate chip cookies, each the size of his palm, and takes a large bite. "They have loads of nanites baked into them, so they're good for you."

I grab a cookie and take a small bite, expecting to taste the nanites as medicine or metal. Or one of Lii's blundered sims of tofu. But, no, sweetness with a hint of bitter explodes in my mouth, far better than any blocker cookie. When nobody storms out and demands payment, I take another bite, not as large as Naren's, but large for me. I can't believe my luck, a nano-bar and a cookie in one day.

"So, you're from the blocks, right?" I nearly roll my eyes. Here comes the judgment. My ears grow hot. "Yeah, don't worry. There are a few other blockers here too. I've heard that it can take a while to get used to all the food. You'll burn through your nanites fast once you get into your specialty tracks, so the sooner you stretch your stomach, the better."

Huh? I take another bite while I wait for the punchline. Naren takes a bite out of his second cookie and says, "And grab a Nano-Milk. It's the best way to stock up on nanites."

I reach into the fridge and grab one, looking around in anticipation of someone popping out and slapping me in cuffs.

Apparently unaware of my nervousness, Narren says, "So, what kind of nano are you?"

I don't know quite how to answer him. "They told me that I'm a kinetic. I think that means I can move and teleport things and phase, whatever that last one is." I cringe at how much of a noob I'm coming across as.

He holds out a fist for a bump and says, "Wicked. I always wanted to be a kinetic." He looks impressed. "I never met a teleporter or phaser before–other than Dr. Fontein, and she doesn't count because she has nearly every skill."

So, now I'm an outsider three times over: norm-born, blocker, and unusual nano-skills.

Throughout the day, more and more campers arrive, gradually filling the bunk beds in Steadfast Corner. Justin, a short olive-skinned guy with a bright smile, stands out as being a nano-electric. He zaps everyone when he fist bumps them.

Ding, dong, ding-a-long, a bell rings somewhere off in the distance. I don't think I've ever heard a physical bell resonate like that before. Unlike simmed chimes, this one hits an inner tuning fork.

"Assembly," Miles bellows above the din of my cabinmates cheering for bots that look like ancient warriors. Naren explained that the battle bots operate intelligently with weak AIs, and repair themselves after each sword or ax fight. Nano-gadgeteers build them with skills that aren't otherwise possible—or legal. Noted. Nanos skirt the laws.

"Wrap it up," Miles calls out like a drill sergeant, not mean, but commanding. "Three-minute warning." My cabinmates grab their nano-mechanical figurines and stow them away. As soon as we're assembled at the front door, standing two by two, Miles orders, "Fall in." As a whole, we set into a steady half-walking, half-marching pace. We pass other groups along the way, all of whom are clumped chaotically. They range from about six years old to maybe eighteen.

After a few minutes, a gentle murmur grows louder until we stand at the top of the amphitheater. Campers are everywhere, bumping into each other in attempts to walk in every direction. "How many campers are there?" I ask.

"Over two hundred," Justin answers as we descend the stone stairs. If most of them are nano-born, there must be tons of nanos out there. Parents. Singles. Couples.

A number of adults stand at the bottom, on the semi-circle stage. I recognize Dr. Fontein and Mr. von Steiner. Where is Bender?

Bam! The air gushes out of my lungs with a quick, painful jab to my stomach, barely below my sternum. Fear spikes within me as the ability to breathe temporarily escapes me. I fall forward into a face-first dive but Miles pulls me back from an epic tumble with cheetah-like reflexes.

"Watch where you're going, blocker!" someone growls from behind me. A six-foot Adonis of a guy turns his sandy-topped head just enough to make eye contact. I know that look. They tell the same story we replayed over and over at Desmond High; I don't belong. Once my incidents start everyone will look at me like that.

With my guts twisting in on themselves, I feel like I did

when I teleported with Bender. Then, the guy melds into the crowd and my innards decide I can breathe again. "Don't mind him," Miles says. "Pyro hates anyone who isn't a pinnacle." Having never met a pinnacle before today, I find myself stunned at having encountered my second. Uppers are one thing, but pinnacles? I mean–

"Ah-hem," Dr. Fontein's voice resonates through the animated conversations as we find our seats. The chitchat dies down as the last stragglers meander into the amphitheater and take their seats. "I'm pleased to see new faces, and equally delighted to see so many returning ones."

"We have many exciting activities planned for you, from swimming and rock climbing to capture-the-flag and war games." I don't recall any mention of war games in the pamphlet. "We'll have the obstacle course here in the amphitheater."

"You will each have personal challenges. At Camp Astrid, and life in general, your friends will be your greatest resource. Rely on them to overcome your unique task."

"Let's introduce your camp counselors so I can let you go. Mr. Roberto's talents are nano-pathy and nano-aquas." A man with slicked-back hair and a thin mustache steps forward. A wisp of cloud coalesces in front of him in the form of a Pegasus. It launches into the air with flapping wings and flies into the skies. Thunder echoes through the amphitheater as campers stomp their feet and clap.

"Next," Dr. Fontein says. "Ms. Quin will help those of you who want to take nano-botany, veterinary, or agriculture tracks." A slender, muscular woman with blond hair steps forward to even more boisterous cheers. Campers call out for "Flowers." Every-colored roses blossom at our feet. All around me, flowers and petals fly, some like snowballs and others like fireworks.

"Next, Mr. von Steiner leads the nano-hacking, electric, and gadgetry tracks." Nobody claps and he doesn't do any tricks.

"He's totally miserly," Justin whispers. Dr. Fontein introduces a giant counselor, but Justin keeps talking so I can't hear. "I take nano-electrics with von Steiner and it sucks. Not even the other counselors can stand him."

The campers cheer for another counselor who sends flames flying into the air in the shape of a dragon, which turns toward us and dives down to ignite us on fire. Cries of joy and terror meld together. Just as I think it will swallow me in an inferno, the flames vanish. Feet stomp in unison, resound throughout the arena. Stomp, stomp, clap.

After a moment, Dr. Fontein continues. "Ms. Merryweather leads the nano-kinetics and magnetics tracks." Kinetics. That's me. She looks fierce in a black hoodie that shades her face. She doesn't move a muscle and doesn't perform any impossible nano-abilities.

"She's the toughest counselor in the bunch," Justin says. "But, don't worry. You might be okay." I nod, not at all reassured.

"Mr. Braunwyn leads nano-history, meditation, and ethics." The amphitheater goes silent.

"Bor-ing!" Justin says loud enough that it echoes and laughter breaks out through the stands.

"That's enough, Justin," Dr. Fontein says, tilting her head and crooking an eyebrow, then continues introducing counselors, but I struggle to keep track of them with my belly gurgling from all the sweets.

"Finally, we have a new counselor, Mr. Bender, but he couldn't join us today. Bender will lead our new nano-phasing and teleportation tracks." A hundred heads swivel my way. Whispers ripple throughout the stands. I lower my head, wanting nothing more than to teleport away. If only.

Justin says, "Nano-phasing and teleportation are really rare and can be dangerous." I don't want to be rare. And "dangerous" doesn't make it any better.

Dr. Fontein claps her hands, bringing all eyes back to her. "And that is it. Come down and sign up for your tracks. In an hour the gong will ring for dinner." Conversations break out everywhere as campers descend to the stone stage. I try to ignore the eyes that follow me the whole way down.

"Do you know where you're heading first?" Naren asks.

"Ms. Merryweather's kinetics track."

"Good," he says and disappears into the crowd.

As I reach the stage at the bottom, the crowd thickens and I feel claustrophobic. How can they stand so many people crowding in like this? Pyro's eyes flash red as he pushes toward me. With a wicked crook to his lips, he mouths the word, "blocker." The frayed cuff of my right pant leg bursts into flames. My heart beats loudly. Am I screaming like a frightened toddler?

Drop and roll, Lii says.

There isn't room to roll without being trampled. The heat sears my calf and shin. Campers scatter away. My world squeezes tight around me. Pop!

When the world flexes back to normal, I'm sitting in the stands where Steadfast Corner sat only a minute before. Fortunately, the fire snuffed out and my pants aren't too badly singed. My ankle is bright red but I've suffered worse burns apprenticing with Mom and Dad, so I walk it off.

Lii says, *With all the nanites around here, I'll fix you up in no time.* He sounds giddier than an enforcer in a gun shop. *Hehe. Camp Astrid is a snow globe of joy!*

Down at the center, a group of guys around Pyro point and laugh in my direction as if lighting me on fire was the funniest joke in the history of humor. Ignoring the new chafing of my charred pants, I walk down the steps as if I couldn't care less. Though I steer clear of Pyro and his friends.

"Mazz!" Miles calls out. "Where'd you go?"

"Nowhere," I say, looking around. A misfire is embarrassing enough without the fact that I ran away from a bully, inadvertently or not. Recalling rule twenty-four–the best lies have a nugget of truth–I add, "I don't like crowds."

"I signed you up for kinetics, so let's drop our names for teleportation and phasing."

"You're taking those too?" I ask. "I didn't know that you could..."

"I'm a nano-adapter," he says with an easy wink. "I can learn to do any nano-skill."

"Nice." I can't imagine learning my three skills, not to mention everyone else's. How does he manage?

A large group of campers encircle Dr. Fontein next to the phasing and teleporting sign-up sheets. A girl who can't be older than ten asks, "Will I have time to take the aquas, pyrus, and culinary tracks?"

"Most campers only take two tracks," Dr. Fontein says. "Otherwise it digs into fun time."

Under my breath, I say, "Great. There goes fun and games."

After Miles pens his name on Bender's two tracks, I lean down to do the same. Pyro's name holds the top spot on both lists, written in perfect penmanship. "Piece of crap."

"Gotta go," Miles says. "There's someone I gotta see." He winks, and ducks into the chaos.

And like that, I'm alone despite being surrounded. Not awkward at all. I wind my way out of the dwindling madness and follow two teens as they walk up the amphitheater steps hand in hand.

"Hey," a female voice calls out from behind me accompanied by the sound of jogging footsteps. A dark-haired, green-eyed gal a bit shorter than me leaps up the last few steps. "I saw you teleport. That was amazeballs."

"Uh, thanks, I guess."

"I'm Scarlett," she says, pushing a braid out from in front of her eyes. "My mom thought I was going to be a red-head, you know, Scarlett."

"Hi, I'm Mazz. At school, they call me Spazz." What the? Why did I lead with that? Idiot.

Maybe the mountain air is getting to you, Lii says.

A sputter of laughter escapes her lips. If her mouth was filled with a drink, she would have spit it all over me. "Sure," she says. "Everyone is talking about you. You're really unique." The way she says this makes me feel awkward yet proud. "You signed up for teleportation, phasing, and kinetics, right?"

"Uh, yeah. And you?"

"Botany and aquas. They go well together, you know, plants and water." A delicate flower with long peachy-orange petals sprouts from the braid she was just fiddling with.

"No way! How'd you do that?"

"It comes naturally to me, like eating or drinking. I'm also taking hacking this summer. I want to see if I can speed up my brain." We stand in silence.

Lii says, *We really need to learn how to small talk.*

It's not like I had a lot of people to chat with this year.

"What are you up to now?" she asks.

"I don't know. Maybe I'll go to the pond and see if I can skip rocks." I've never done it before and always wanted to try.

"Mind if I join you?"

"Sure," I say brightly, happy to have someone to hang out with. Plus, her smile is beau-ti-ful. We walk to Southgate, then along the crag to the pond. With Scarlett at my side, it doesn't feel so ghostly. But, the longer we go without talking, the harder it is for me to think of something to say.

Finally, she asks, "Which bus did you come on?"

"I didn't take a bus. Bender teleported me in."

"Why? Do you live on some distant volcano or something?"

"No, I um, I think that I drew some attention with an accident."

"So they're afraid that the shockknights are onto you," she says as we come to a cloudy pool. That confirms Naren's explanation and description. Twice in one day.

I plunk a stone into the pond. No skips. After a while of considering questions about the shockknights, during which thoughts fall short of reaching my mouth, I decide it's best not to show fear in front of a pretty girl. I change the subject. "Why is von Steiner such an ass-a-saurus?"

"I heard a nano-aquas put a permanent water spring in von Steiner's bladder so he constantly has to pee," Scarlett laughs with a snort. I really like her smile. And the way she tries to cover her snort with her hand as if that will block the sound makes it all the better.

Filled with a sense of ease opened up by her snort, I say, "I bet his nano-electric skills backfire, constantly zapping his nose hairs." Joking like this, we barely make it back to Southgate before the bell sounds for dinner.

Entering the cafeteria, she says, "See ya." I wave, but she already turned and bounded off. I look around for the Steadfast guys and spot most of them at a table left of middle.

"I got you a plate," Naren says. Instead of a third of an algae tofu block, the plate is filled with real turkey, genuine mashed potatoes, and fresh corn. He piled twice as much on his own plate. Barely loud enough for me to hear above the conversations around me, he says, "You'll want to go slow. I hear blockers have a hard time adapting to the portions." This mountain of food doesn't strike me as going slow.

Upon stomaching the whole delicious plate and a Nano-Milk, I sit quietly and listen to my bunkmates' banter. I try to focus on their boisterous conversations about battle bots, but my gurgling innards make it hard to pay attention.

Justin kisses his fingers and says, "Do you remember those chocolate croissants that Wyatt brought back to the cabin last summer? They were tre' magnifique."

I hadn't realized that Miles had slipped away, but when he returns, he has a platter of dessert in one hand and a stack of folded papers in the other. My cabinmates dive into chocolate-covered strawberries like a pack of hyenas. As tempting as they are, I'd puke if I forced one down.

"Schedules everyone," Miles says as soon as the frenzy dies down. I inspect mine: kinetics after breakfast every weekday followed by phasing in the afternoon. Someone marked "To Be Determined" next to teleportation. I guess I'll find out when Bender gets back from doing whatever he does.

The rest of the evening passes in a blur. I follow the others back to our cabin, where I climb into my bunk and flop down. While they gather around another battle bot competition, I close my eyes. I guess I won't mind being hunted by shockknights as long as I get to eat like this.

CHAPTER TEN

Kinetics

"**U**p and at 'em," someone bellows entirely too early for a sane individual to face reality. "Time to wake up and greet the day." I blink my eyes open and struggle to focus on the underside of Steadfast Corner's canvas roof, unsure if it's real until I feel the dampness of the fabric.

"Breakfast jog in three minutes," Miles barks like an army officer. I roll out of bed, mostly ready, having fallen asleep in my new Camp Astrid shirt. True to his word, Miles claps his hands three minutes later and we slow jog in a two-by-two formation, feet stomping down in unison. My mind quickly clears up with the sweet, crisp morning air and the light exercise.

As we enter the cafeteria, Justin asks, "Can you smell that? Ultimate olfactory bliss." No argument there. The scent of spicy cinnamon, sweet maple syrup, savory scrambled eggs, and salty bacon hit my nose like the best bouquet of aromas ever known to humankind.

Thwack! I don't remember when the floor came up to meet my ass. My gut, tailbone, and skull yell in protest at the sudden fall. A guy I don't recognize towers over me, looking down as one might upon a worker ant. His nearly black eyes creep me out. "Watch where you're going, boy." The way he seethes, *boy*, really means lowly blocker scum.

Miles pulls me to my feet and pats me down as if dusting off a dirty towel. "Why don't you take a seat?" he says quietly.

"Not until he apologizes," the guy says as if I smell like the waste treatment plant I helped Dad with last summer. He stands tall and proud, six feet with powerful shoulders. With a smirk, he says, "This *boy* should watch where he's going."

"It was an accident," I say, not even knowing what I'm apologizing for.

"Mazz was clearly worse for the wear, Henri," Miles states with a look that could intimidate a tiger. The black holes of Henri's eyes are now mirrored in Miles's.

"What's going on here?" Mr. von Steiner inquires, slithering up from behind Miles, face manically happy as if he found a clue on a scavenger hunt. He eyes me like Justin eyed the bacon only seconds ago, ready to savor his favorite treat.

"Nothing, sir," Henri and Miles say together, neither taking their eyes off each other in a staring contest. Henri knocks Miles's shoulder as he struts to the Eagle's Nest table, where Pyro fist bumps him. If only I had control of my skills, I'd teleport him into that sewage plant. Von Steiner follows me to my seat and stands over me for a moment before moving on.

Seconds later, all thoughts of the conflict are gone as I savor my first taste of a real breakfast. The soft French toast and real maple syrup balance perfectly with the crispy bacon. I can't help but moan. Naren seems to get a kick out of watching me eat.

After breakfast, as I bus my dirty plate with the rest of the Steadfasters, Naren says, "Don't forget to grab a nano-bar or two. You'll want them during each track to freshen up." I can't imagine a world in which I'd want to eat before lunch but take one like everyone else.

The camp's gong resonates within my bones, a perfect rightness of place. In the courtyard, black and electric violet banners hang from tall wood poles, each with a track labeled on it. Avoiding tight bunches of campers, I edge my way to the "Kinetics" flag. Miles claps me gruffly on the shoulder and says, "Kinetics should be fun. Are you ready?"

I take a couple of quick steps to keep from falling with the nudge. Did he mean to knock me over? Nah, he seems genuinely nice, to a fault. But then again, he was fierce when he stood up to that guy Henri. Lii, what's my rule about falling?

Don't do it, Lii says.

Taking Miles at face value with his do-goody facade, I say, "I have no idea what to expect. Justin said Ms. Merryweather is the toughest counselor of the bunch."

"Don't worry, they always go easy on us on the first day of each track, even Ms. M."

"Hey, Bethany," Miles says as we saunter up to the kinetics. He fist-bumps a very tall, Hispanic gal a couple of years older than me. She has a plain but beautiful face and a powerful demeanor that could only belong to an upper. Her camo tank top and dark-gray tech pants give her a badass female warrior vibe. I can easily imagine a gun in her hand. But she's all smiles for Miles.

"Penny." Miles fist-bumps a red-head gal. Her light blue eyes twinkle with the glow of intelligence and sharp calculation.

"Bethany and Penny, meet Mazz. He's in Steadfast with me." To me, he says, "They're cabin leaders too; Wagon Wheels and the Celtics. I remember those cabins near Eastgate from my self-guided tour.

I hold out my hand to shake while Bethany attempts a fist bump, resulting in an awkward case of paper beats rock. Smooth Mazz. Very smooth. Now would be a perfect time to dissolve into another dimension, but no, I'm stuck here. With Penny, I manage a simple fist bump without embarrassing myself.

"You're the new nano-kinetic everyone is talking about," Bethany says in a nonchalant tone, but her eyes hint at a level of respect, a sentiment I'm not used to.

"He can also phase," Miles says.

"I know," Bethany says, tapping her temple with a wink. I look back and forth between them for a moment. "So you've only known about being a nano for a few weeks."

"Uh." How could she know? I haven't told anyone.

Catch up, Lii says. *She's a nano-path.*

This must be freaking you out, she says with her lips upturned in a closed-lip smile. I must look ridiculous because all three of them are laughing. I shut my caveman mouth. It isn't even eight am, but I've had more than my fill of being laughed at.

"Sorry, man," Miles says as soon as he can breathe again. "The look on your face was like a shocked fish. Mouth wide open and eyes bulging."

When Bethany stops laughing, the supple smoothness of her puffy lips catches my attention. The gentle curve of her cheeks accentuates her upper-born looks. She might be the most beautiful woman I've ever seen. A warm stirring echoes with the sounds of a lion's roar. The glow of a perfect golden summer sunrise highlights her perfect cheekbones and lends a sparkling depth to her brown eyes.

Shaking me hard, Miles says, "Don't get sucked in. She'll have you washing her laundry and doing her dishes if you're not careful." I shake my head to clear the feeling of pure joy. "You better learn to close off your mind or every nano-path will know your deepest darkest secrets."

Pyro and Henri join our group, chatting to each other and ignoring us. Damn. Both of these fart nuggets are here, and nobody else.

"Yeah," Bethany says. "Your mind resembles a leaky water balloon, randomly spewing chaotic thoughts in all directions and entirely too easy to mold. You should try–"

"Heh hem," Ms. Merryweather interrupts. Under her black hoodie, the stark counselor wears dark metallic piercings in her nostrils and down both earlobes. Her dark bushy brows and shaved head lend intensity to piercing brown eyes. She radiates a stern appraising and precise countenance. I get a chill when her shaded eyes meet mine. Stern as hell.

"Walk," Ms. Merryweather says, her voice scratchy. Turning, she leads us through Southgate and east along the camp's wall, in and out of ruins. I follow, keeping one of the cabin leaders between me and the Eagle's Nesters at all times.

Plants, vines, and shrubs grow thicker near the walls than in the rest of the forest. In some places, they're so dense that I can't see the fifteen-foot-tall walls at all. Is this natural barrier another form of defense against the shockknights? This place really is a fortress.

In my head, Bethany says, *As long as you don't wander outside camp alone, you'll be fine.*

WTF? Are you reading all my thoughts?

Not intentionally. You broadcast at a million megawatts. I can't block you out.

"This will do," Ms. Merryweather says when we reach a large knee-high foundation that doubles as a grass clearing. "Gather in a circle." This spot tickles my skin like a staticky sock.

Nanites galore, Lii purrs

Once we're all seated on the damp grass, Merryweather says, "We all know why we are here. You want to learn how to move objects with your mind. But I want to know 'why?' To impress a special friend? To learn neat tricks? Or hurl the perfect curveball?"

"McFadden," she says, looking at Bethany, "Why are you really here?"

"I want to protect myself," Bethany says. Does that mean she's afraid of the shockknights? With nano-pathy, couldn't she just take over an enemy's mind?

Everyone should be frightened of the knights, she says in my mind again. *But not here. Not near Ms. M. Can you imagine anyone going up against her?*

No, I can't.

"Good," Ms. Merryweather says, then turns to Miles. "Mr. Williams?"

"I want to be a nano-marshal, ma'am," he says. "I want to protect our way of life." Nano-marshals? Do they have our own police?

Yes, Bethany interjects. *But I think you mean 'we,' not 'they.' You're one of us now.*

"Mr. Ellister, tell me."

Pyro says, "I like rock climbing." A wry smile tells everyone that he wants us to know he's lying.

"I see. How about you, Mr. Siler?" She looks none too pleased.

Henri says, "As a pinnacle, I'll be safer with nano-kinetics."

Henri always "lets it slip" that his daddy is a pinnacle.

"Ms. Killian?" she says to Penny.

"I think it will help me with nano-gadgetry. I could kinetically assemble nano-bots rather than pinching tweezers under a microscope.

"And you, Mr. Becker?"

Panic freezes my brain. I should have thought about an answer instead of listening to the others. Are the grinding gears in my head audible? I clear my throat to stall for time. After what feels like millennia, I find myself saying, "I want to stop weird stuff from happening around me."

"Satisfactory," Ms. Merryweather says, though I get the sense that our responses underwhelmed her, particularly Pyro's and mine. "You should know that less than a quarter of the very few campers I allow into kinetics show any promise at kinetics. Let's see if you can beat my low expectations." An uncomfortable silence settles over us. No, not silence. The woods make their own noises, but the background sounds don't cut through the awkwardness. She evaluated each of us and found us lacking, perhaps with the exception of Bethany.

Ms. Merryweather's intense gaze falls upon me. My insides gurgle, whether from too much breakfast or from her harsh glare, I can't tell. Is she like von Steiner? Already made up her mind that I suck because I grew up in the blocks? My ears dial up the heat. "I hear that Mr. Becker may have the strongest inherent nano-influence we've seen for decades. However, he has less experience than anyone I've ever let into my tracks."

Henri and Pyro snigger at the latter part of her assessment.

Screw those two, Bethany says, rippling of anger. *They look down on anyone who isn't a pinnacle. As a blocker, you're particularly worth keeping around as asswipe repellant.*

I choke on a laugh, drawing Ms. Merryweather's considerable

focus to me. "Mazz's responsibility is to help the rest of you learn kinetics, and you will help him harness his innate influence. Understood?" Pyro and Henri scowl at Ms. Merryweather's edict.

"You should also know that more than one kinetic has died from self-inflicted misfires." I gulp involuntarily. "Telekinesis can kill." Bethany illuminates a picture in my mind where a man's head sticks through a cement wall, blood trickling down to puddle on the ground. He lost in a head-on collision with a skyscraper.

A familiar constriction twists inside my chest as scenarios of fatal accidents flash through my mind. Whether Bethany's or mine, I'm not sure. Kinetically pulling a pencil from a desk to my hand only to have it stick through my eye into my brain. Hanging a towel on a hook only to have it wrap around my neck and strangle me. A woman turns her head so forcefully that it snaps her neck.

My heart pounds heavily; Ba-bump, Ba-pump, Ba–Between beats, I bounce away. Pop!

"Umph," The back of my head bursts like a cracked watermelon. I tenderly rub the new bump on my noggin, gradually realizing that I smacked my head on the wood edge of my bunk in Steadfast Corner. Looking around, I'm relieved that my bunkmates aren't here, meaning I won't have to explain my misfire.

I roll out of bed and run down the path toward Southgate. At first, I stumble on the uneven forest floor but quickly figure out how to place my feet for trail running. As I dash under Southgate, a highly recognizable voice, both stern and nasally, brings me to a halt. Von Steiner says, "Where do you think you are going, young man?" I twirl on the spot and sure enough, there he is, wearing his smug grin and immaculately pressed attire.

"I–"

"Cutting out on your first track, I see." Von Steiner steps closer, each inch making me feel greasier. "Do you think you're above the rules? No going outside camp walls without a cabin leader or counselor."

"I didn't mean to," I say. Those words always seem to pop out of my mouth.

"Sure," he says with a smile that doesn't match the disdain in his squinting eyes. I barely know the man and I hate him as much as the scavengers.

Hoping that I might appeal to him by confessing the truth, I say, "My heart rate got too high and I teleported away on accident."

"Likely story," von Steiner says, sarcasm dripping from his thin red lips. He looks like a hungry vampire. Are there nano-vampires? Blood would have tons of nanites in it, right?

Von Steiner reaches out, grabs my arm, and twists it behind my back like an enforcer. Panic implodes inside me for the second time in minutes, tugging at my center like water through a fire hose. This time it comes on so fast that it feels like one of those painful hiccups that happen while you're gulping down water.

Pop!

"Ow!" My noggin hits my bunk again. Groaning, I touch the spot and find a sizable lump. Blood flows from my nose. Unsure what to do, I slink out of the cabin in case von Steiner comes to look for me here. He's freaky. Dangerous. Not right in the head. How could they let him be a counselor?

On instinct, I run down the path leading toward Southgate then up a route toward another cabin. I spot a bramble surrounded by a tight ring of redwood trees. The thicket reminds me of places Laticia and I hide back home, or as close as I expect I'll find in the woods. I wish I could skate the paths here. Giant wheels would be legendary. I dive into the thicket and catch my breath.

Damn! My nose bleed got all over my new shirt. What now? I can't go to Southgate with von Assnugget looking for me. Maybe I should hide out here until lunch.

While waffling back and forth between my options, I hear heavy breathing and soft steps on redwood needles. Wait, that sounds more like a dog sniffing for the scent of its prey. The soft steps on the forest floor draw closer. "Little Mazzy," von Steiner's unmistakable voice says in an off-pitch sing-songy voice. "You can't hide from me. I can smell you. Your blocker clothes and blocker blood stand out like too much garlic."

I peak out through the bushes. Von Steiner pushes through the undergrowth only feet away. Surely he can hear my heart pounding. I hold my breath.

Pop.

My gut drops out from under me and my lungs want to explode. My tailbone hits something hard and I'm somewhere in the forest looking up at treetops.

"Ahh!" someone yells in addition to me. The kinetics group towers over me, watching me in varying states of surprise. Henri jumped to his feet and now looks down at me like I'm a tarantula. My heart pumps wildly, and my ears fill with the rush of blood, bu-bump, bu-bump. Don't jump. Don't jump.

"Welcome back," Ms. Merryweather says, voice steady and raspy, void of emotion.

Calm yourself, Bethany says. The sensation of standing at the shore of an emerald green waterhole with little waves washing over my feet fills my being. Granite walls rise up high to the left and right. A small waterfall pours over rock at the far end. My pounding heart eases up as the ripples lap at my feet.

"Let's continue," Ms. Merryweather says and retrieves books from her satchel. The hardback books float to each of us. So cool!

I want to learn that, Lii says, emanating as much wonderment as me.

"Read chapter one." I marvel at the hand-made and hand-printed book. After ten minutes of reading about the challenges of nano-kinetics, Ms. Merryweather asks, "What is the major point of the chapter?"

Penny says, "Nano-kinetics requires three core features; a location to focus on, a strong will, and inherent ability."

"Correct, Ms. Killian."

The rest of the morning we discuss the basic points of

kinetics. I find it boring and difficult to pay attention. My thoughts keep returning to von Steiner's predatory sniffing. Each time Bethany pushes back on these thoughts and chastises me for not focusing. *Try eating a nano-bar,* she suggests. *You're probably low on nanites after your 'adventure'.*

Surprisingly, I do feel better after demolishing the bar. My bloody nose also clears up.

You got the nosebleed because you overused your influence, Bethany says. *And, you'll need to learn to calm your own mind sooner rather than later. I'm not going to keep calming you down.*

On the walk back to camp, I want nothing but to become invisible. Sadly, invisibility isn't one of my nano-skills. Miles claps me on the shoulder and asks, "What happened back there?" The others gather close, even Pyro and Henri.

"I teleported."

"That's awesome," Miles says, clapping me on the shoulder again. He's definitely going to knock me off my feet one of these times.

"Not so awesome." I really don't want to get into this conversation, especially with the Eagle's Nesters here.

Word will make the rounds as soon as you enter the cafeteria, Bethany says. *Every nano-path will unwrap your thoughts like Cocao Cubes.*

"What do you mean?" Miles asks.

Reluctantly, I tell them about my accidental jumps away from von Steiner. Miles shakes his head. "I hate it when Von Steiner does that. He sniffed me out a few years back after I... well, he sniffed me out and it creeped me out." He shudders.

"On the plus side," Bethany says. "You probably pissed him off something fierce. I bet he's apoplectic. That's always a mark in the bonus column."

CHAPTER ELEVEN

Phasing

A fter lunch, I stand by Dr. Fontein beneath the black and purple "Phasing" flag. In the cafeteria, news of my ordeal with von Steiner made the rounds. I couldn't count the number of times strangers of all ages glanced back and forth between me and Steiner. Von Stuffiness stank-eyed me the whole time with those pale blues. Creepy dude.

Glad to leave the gossiping cafeteria behind, Bethany and Miles flank me as if protecting me from Pyro, who also stands beneath the phasing track. "It's just the four of you," Dr. Fontein says. I wish more campers could buffer me from Pyro.

Don't let him get to you, Bethany says. *He hates anyone with skills he can't obtain, which is everyone because he can't tap into any nanites except those that control fire, and barely at that. Every year, he tries new tracks, and every year he fails.*

I almost laugh. It brings me too much pleasure that Pyro sucks as a nano.

"Follow me," the head counselor says, leading us through Eastgate and on a meandering set of animal trails. After about ten minutes of winding here and there in random directions, we enter a large field with light blue and yellow flowers peppering lush grasses, and a brook that runs southward through the middle. At the center of the field, three redwoods support a wood platform at least twenty feet off the ground.

"Here we are," Dr. Fontein says. "I'll meet you up top. She disappears and reappears on the platform. For a split second, two versions of the head counselor exist, the departing and arriving versions. "Come on up." Ascending last, I find Bethany, Miles, and Pyro already gathered around the head counselor, listening intently. From their quick glances my way, I get the feeling that they're talking about me.

"So," Fontein says when my butt plants between Miles and Bethany. "What do you think exists at the core of phasing?"

"The person doing the phasing?" Bethany says.

"Yes, Bethany. Sometimes for natural nano-phasers like Mazz, but not necessarily for those who learn the skill. Today, you will focus on these stones." She passes out four rounded black stones that would be great for skipping at the pond.

"Phasing ensues when you stay right where you are, but you transfer an object between dimensions or planes of existence. It is the opposite of teleporting, where you instantly reappear in another place, but in our dimension." I try to commit this to memory; Phasing means different dimensions but the same place. Teleporting means different places but in our dimension.

"Now, think about a strong emotion, positive or negative. Something that motivates you. If it isn't strong, phasing won't work. Now, focus on your rock. Get to know the stone in your hand. Turn it around and memorize each grain." I twiddle the smooth black stone over and over, trying to figure out how it differs from any other smooth black rock. They all look the same to me.

"Recall a memory that might induce a strong reaction." I consider using von Steiner's attempt to stalk me down but decide on the memory of the truck-bus crash. I imagine the truck's jagged crack in the window, the peeling paint on the bumper, and the giant beam it carried. I focus on the rattling of the loose nuts that held the seat in front of me. My imminent death. Pop!

I hit something unforgiving and ricochet back to the

platform. Agony wracks my whole body, splintering every nerve, even ones I never knew I had. I groan in pain. What was that? Nobody told me that being a nano is painful as hell.

You hit one of the defenses around Camp Astrid, Dr. Fontein says in my mind. She feels like a volcano, solid and dangerous, filled with pent-up energy. Yet, she also emanates a reassuring calm, an immutable, unflappable anchor. *Don't worry. I blocked Bethany from your mind. We can talk like this and they won't overhear us.*

As the invisible spider mandibles stop piercing my nerves from scalp to toenail, I vow to never repeat that again. New rule: Don't screw around with the wards around camp. My nose is bleeding again. Dr. Fontein taps my knee and my nose clears up.

Keep focusing on your stone. You are supposed to be working on phasing, not teleportation. So, perhaps you could choose a memory that isn't quite so intense.

Yes, ma'am. I return my attention to the stone, searching my mind for an appropriate memory.

You're worse than a toddler, Bethany groans, sending forth peevish spikes in my direction. *Brain rambling this way and that.*

Perhaps annoyance will work, like being sent to the principal's office. Nothing happens. Maybe something funny. Willing the rock to phase, I close my eyes and visualize when Rhenate's tater tots flew across the lunchroom. Everyone's faces were hysterical. Nothing happens.

I don't really care if I can't phase, because I'm at a legit camp, not stuck apprenticing for Mom and Dad. A rightness of being wraps me in a glowing warmth. I belong here at Camp Astrid, surrounded by nano-enabled weirdos like me.

Realizing that I stopped focusing on the rock, I redouble my focus. For the third time today, a falling sensation surprises me. My already bruised tailbone smacks down on something hard. I squint, sure that this time I broke my butt. I flop to my side, trying to take the pressure off my backside. Rule number fifty-two: being a nano hurts.

Opening my eyes, the first thing I see is the brilliant blue sky, which tells me I'm not in my bunk. Next, I see Dr. Fontein, Bethany, Pyro, and Miles staring at me, trying but failing to stifle their laughter. Everyone but Pyro that is. He laughs outright and points at me like I'm a monkey in roller skates.

"What happened?" I ask, standing up and rubbing my tailbone.

"You levitated," Miles says. "You were like a mystic Tibetan monk, levitating peacefully a foot off the ground. Then it looked like you realized it was impossible to hover in mid-air and fell like a cartoon." Bethany plunges the image into my head. Her crisp memory of my guru-like flub is hysterical. I join in the laughter, conjuring an image of Master Mazz dressed in an orange Kāṣāya robe and sporting a bald head. I am the master of peace and harmony.

"Well," Dr. Fontein says. "That will conclude today's lesson. Do you think you can find your way back to camp?"

"Yup," Miles says confidently. "Bethers and I used to come here for our nano-path track." How many skills does Miles have?

Nearly all of them, Bethany says. *That's one of the reasons for the rift between Steadfast and Eagle's Nest. Pyro absolutely hates Miles.*

"Well then, I have business to attend to." She dematerializes, leaving me wondering what "business" she and Bender are up to.

I spend the rest of the afternoon getting to know my cabinmates. Brooks Rollins has the coolest skill: nano-vibrus. He can shake the air any way he wants, which means he's a one-man rock concert. He lays down some of the most incredible beats I've ever heard.

Later, as I enter the cafeteria for dinner, dozens of faces pivot my way, many laughing while others whisper. I'm torn between checking to see if my zipper hangs open and not wanting to be seen fiddling with my flytrap. I decide to own it because I'm pretty sure my blunders today are part of the collective camp knowledge.

You need to close off your mind, Bethany says from across the room. *Your thoughts are like a Reunification Day fireworks display:*

visible from miles away.

Scarlett, the gal I skipped rocks with, approaches my table and asks, "Is it true?"

"What?"

"Did you teleport and levitate today? I heard you teleported away from von Steiner a couple of times."

"Yeah," I say, unsure whether to be proud or embarrassed. Humiliation wins out and my ears and cheeks burn hot.

"That's amazing." She winks and raises a fist and I bump it lightly. "All of us would teleport away from him if we could."

"Ah," Justin says loudly, a large bite of pizza still in his mouth. "You're only here for a day, and you already have a girlfriend? I've been coming for years, and I haven't landed a tall and handsome even once. How's that fair?"

I'm afraid my ears might go supernova. Without wasting a second, Scarlett says, "I am *not* his girlfriend." I'm unsure if I should be insulted by her knee-jerk adamance or impressed by her strength. She holds her empty hand over Justin's head and tips it over. A stream of water pours out of her thumb, splashing over his buzz-cut head.

He jumps out of his seat, yelling, "Ahhh!" and shakes water off him like a soaked poodle. The entire cafeteria erupts into fits of laughter and gleeful points at Justin. Having the attention siphoned away from me feels good.

"Nice move," Bethany says, walking up from behind Scarlett. "Now, if we could do that to the rest of the boys…" Her eyes linger over Miles with a wicked smile. "But we should get a move on; von Stinker is on his way."

The mean-spirited counselor winds through the picnic tables in our direction. "What happened here?" He fixes Justin and me with squinting eyes–especially me.

"I–I just spilled some water," Justin lies.

"Liar." Crap. Can he read minds too?

Nope, Bethany says. *He'd make everyone even more miserable if he could.*

"It's what happened," Miles says, stone-faced serious. Nearly everyone at the table holds their breath. I'm afraid some of us might run out of air before von Steiner walks away. I want to disappear again as he looks me over like I'm a dung beetle. He probably wants to shock me for hours with his electric skills.

"Alright," von Steiner says, doling out one last round of squint-eyed anger. "I'll be watching you, Steadfast." As he walks off, probably looking for some other campers to terrorize, we collectively let out sighs and stifled laughter.

From her seat a few tables away, Scarlett crosses her eyes and sticks out her tongue. I laugh and contort my face in what I hope is a goofy look. "See," Justin says, looking back and forth between us. "They're totally going out." Steadfast breaks into more laughter, and I join them.

After dinner, we head to the campfire set up in the amphitheater. Counselors tell jokes. Mr. Roberto plays a beautiful acoustic guitar decorated with a red and black rose flare. We sing along, sometimes completely off-key. Everyone laughs and enjoys marshmallows and s'mores. Even Pyro seems to be having a good time, though his eyes reflect the fire more than anyone else. S'mores are tied with bacon for first place on my favorite foods list, even better than cookies.

By the time I climb into my bunk and drift into the cloudy blackness of sleep, my belly and brain ache, equally overstuffed.

CHAPTER TWELVE

Emerald Lake

I reflect on my first few days as we walk back from phasing at the platform. I'm starting to get into the rhythm of the days including how much we're expected to eat. My skills continue to stubbornly misbehave, but with fewer painful accidents. I suspect this has more to do with my quick reflexes and constant expectation of misfires than any improvement in my skills.

I try to focus on the funny incidents rather than the painful ones, like when Bethany's long black hair stood straight up making her look like a cartoon gnome, or when Miles's shirt disappeared. We still don't know where it went.

Miles pulls me into a gentle noogie and asks, "So, you aren't going out with her, huh?"

"No," I protest for the ten-thousandth time. "We're just friends." Scar and I have been hanging out each afternoon. We've been skipping stones and carving, both of which I find oddly gratifying even though I suck at both. Dad's knife was designed for maximum damage to an assailant, not detailed woodworking. Scar doesn't seem to mind when I borrow her pocket knife. Naren joined us yesterday, but the rumors continue.

Keep to your story, Bethany says. *But every nano-path worth a damn knows you haven't ruled it out.*

"For now," Miles jokes, letting me go.

"Tonight?" Bethany asks Miles with a flutter of her eyebrows.

"Yup," Miles says with a sly grin.

Pyro also nods. "Tonight."

"What's tonight?"

"Don't worry about it," Miles says. "Cabin leader stuff. Let's head to Emerald Lake."

"Perfect," Bethany says. "You coming, Mazz?"

"Sure," I say, nervous about having never swum before.

"I just let Penny know," Bethany says.

Fifteen minutes later, I'm dressed in the only shorts I own, and we step through Westgate with the cabin leaders. Miles invited Naren and Justin, Bethany brought Scarlett along. Penny invited a statuesque dark-skinned gal named Ing. Part of me wonders if Bethany brought Scarlett just so they could poke fun at me, but nobody seems inclined to test Scarlett's wrath.

They banter and joke far better than me, but I'm content to listen in and laugh along. Justin is the funniest by far, both intentionally and unintentionally. He has a knack for shoving his foot in his mouth, flip-flops and all.

When we reach Emerald Lake, I recognize it from the clear, green-tinged water hole that Bethany uses to calm and focus my mind. It's just as beautiful in person, with a gentle waterfall at one end and a granite cliffside looking down into the clear waters.

Down below, campers splash noisily and swim about. Others lounge on the flat rocks on the other side. Miles drops his towel, flings off his sandals, and yells, "Last one in is a hairy bagel." He leaps over the cliffside, which must be a hundred feet high–

More like fourteen, Lii corrects me.

–and splashes into the water like a bomb. The others jump in after him, squealing and yelling on their way down. Then, I'm the only one standing on the cliffside. What's scarier? The height of the cliff or the fact that I don't know how to swim?

Perhaps you should have thought of that before you agreed to come along, Lii says.

"Mazz, come on down," Miles yells up to me with hands cupped around his mouth. His body floats impossibly far out of the water.

Nano-aquas, Lii says.

Miles's voice echoes off the stone wall and everyone stops what they're doing to watch. They chant, "Ju-ump. Ju-ump."

Ughh. I have to do it now.

No, Bethany says firmly. *It's not a good idea. Go in at the shallow end.*

I push off my sneakers and peel off my socks to the chanting of "Ju-ump. Ju-ump," which has drawn even more campers to watch. Now would be a great time to teleport away, or even better, levitate down. But despite my anxious nerves, neither happens. All for the better. I'd probably end up teleporting my shorts to wherever Miles's shirt ended up.

I step to the cliff's edge, my heart pounding, sweat beading on my forehead. I want to step back but feel compelled to jump. There is no choice other than stepping forward, one large leap for me, and an even larger one for my fear.

Then I fall, too fast, leaving my guts behind. I flail my arms and legs wildly as I pitch forward. My heart trips over itself, beating a completely new mega-spaz rhythm. I'm about to hit face and belly first.

The cheering stops and a collective, "Uuuuh," takes its place. Pop!

I'm several feet above and out from where I jumped, falling faster this time, but now I rotated head down. This is gonna hurt. Far-off screams fill the air only to be replaced with another pop. I fall even faster, looking up at the sky, wind racing through my hair. Why the hell did I jump? I can't see the water!

Smack! My back explodes with the stings of a thousand scorpions as I come to a startling halt. My head snaps back, then whips forward. If I were a toy doll, my head would have snapped off. Where my arms and legs are, I have no idea. My chest burns for air but floods with burning water instead. I should do something, but my body and mind flounder in opposition to my new reality.

The overhead, a layer of water thickens as I sink, feet leading the way. Pop!

My legs collapse under my own weight and my shoulder thwacks down on something hard, followed by my left cheek, like getting cold-cocked by a nano-terran. A new explosion of pain burst from my neck. Oh no! Did I break it?

I convulse as my chest constricts, expelling water onto the black-speckled white rock. More water spews from my mouth with shredding coughs, my neck pushing forward, back arching up then down involuntarily. Air rasps in and out of my throat, launching me into a spasm of coughs. Someone kneels beside me, patting my back, propelling more water out of my mouth. He's saying something, but I can't make sense of it. Eventually, my lungs return to their normal job of keeping me alive, though invisible bands bind my chest and each breath aches like I swallowed sandpaper.

"You're okay," Miles says. "Nothing looks broken. You'll be fine. Focus on your breathing, steady and as full and slow as you can manage."

"Thanks," I say. I sit up, which causes another bout of hoarse coughs. The group I came with stands above me, worry marring their upper faces. Genuine concern for me even with my blocker status.

We're all nanos here, Bethany says. She seems pissed.

"You had us scared," Miles says.

You were stupid, Bethany says, her anger washing over me. As if I'm not angry enough at myself. Don't you think I know? I feel sick. Each time I teleported, I gained more and more speed. If I teleported back to the rock surface instead of hitting the water, I would have splattered on the granite like a bug on a windshield. The best-case scenario would have been broken bones, with death a very plausible outcome. Curse rule fifty-two: being a nano hurts.

Ing, the gal from Penny's cabin, kneels at my side and places her hand on my chest. Warmth fills me and water seeps out of my mouth painlessly. My lungs stop aching and my throat no longer burns. My cheek stops throbbing.

She's a nano-medic, Lii says.

Scarlett holds out her hand and water spills out of my clothes, leaving me as dry as when I came.

Lii says, *It's good that we have friends who will take care of us, even though they egged you on in the first place.* After numerous attempts to convince them that I'm fine, they don't stop nagging me when I agree to head back to camp and see Ms. Abigail, the nano-medic counselor.

Naren offers to guide me back through the wards, and we head off. We walk slowly at first because when I push faster, I end up stopping to lean over in more rasping fits. The nanites in my body should have taken care of everything by now, but they seem resistant to doing their job.

You depleted our nanites when you teleported, Lii says. *That's why we're so tired.*

Half an hour later, we should have reached Westgate, even with my slow trudge. I mention this to Naren, and he admits that we are "pleasantly off course." After another ten minutes, I recognize a moss-covered rock formation that I've seen before.

"We're running in circles," I tell Naren.

"I know. Where did I make the wrong turn though? I have walked this route many times." Rule fifty-one: don't mess with the wards.

"Maybe we should go back to Emerald Lake," I say.

"Yeah," Naren agrees, seeming as happy as ever. His perpetually happy personality keeps me from wandering down a tunnel of anxiety. It's hard to get lost in the blocks but here...

We reach the swimming area in under ten minutes. "Why'd you come back?" Miles hollers up to us after dunking Bethany. Standing on the cliff, I'm too embarrassed to answer Miles, but Naren apparently has no such compunction because he says, "The wards turned us away."

"No problem," Miles calls up. "This place is so last hour anyway. Bethany, we should get back to plan for tonight anyway. You know, the cabin leader stuff."

Liar much? They're probably going to hook up. I've seen how their eyes keep connecting. Ten minutes later we head back along the path, Bethany and Miles bumping into each other more often than would happen naturally.

I don't see the junction where we turned off last time, but in fifteen minutes, we reach Westgate. I'll need to learn the paths in and out of camp so I don't get lost again. It was embarrassing enough the first time. A second time would be disastrous, especially if I don't have the cabin leaders to rely on. That, and rule two: always have an escape route.

CHAPTER THIRTEEN

An Outing

I'm stuck in a bad dream, but I can't wake up. Pyro stands opposite me on the amphitheater stage covered from head to toe in steel armor, wielding a flaming two-handed sword. My hand grips around a dainty butter knife. He attacks and I panic. Pop. Onlookers laugh as I land in Bethany's lap, a baby bottle in hand. In horror, I realize that I'm dressed in nothing but boxers. She looks pissed and pushes me away. Everyone chants, "Mazz! Mazz!" like a loud whisper rolling through the crowd.

The amphitheater turns to misty gray, then blackness. "Mazz." The whisper continues as someone nudges my shoulder. Blinking in the darkness, I grapple with the long tendrils of unconsciousness. Miles continues shaking me.

"What is it?" I ask, the anxiety of my dream spilling into reality.

"Shhhh," Miles whispers. "Get up."

"What's going on?"

"Just get your clothes on," Miles says. I really need to do my laundry. They're starting to get smelly. "Quickly and quietly." He leads me out the cabin's back door, his footsteps silent. Outside a few inky silhouettes stand in front of us shrouded in a moonless night.

"Follow me," my cabin leader says, striding away confidently.

I try to stay close enough to see his onyx outline but not so close that I flat tire him. "Quiet now." He steers me under something that blots out the starry night sky.

Northgate, Lii says. After a dozen disorienting paces, I emerge from the other side and the stars return. The sounds of footsteps mark the way forward follow behind, hidden by darkness. We walk in silence. I stumble on roots and rocks, nearly falling every thirty seconds. This has to be whatever Miles and Bethany were planning. My excitement outweighs my fatigue from the day's ordeals at Emerald Lake. That fiasco still shakes me. I could have died.

Ten minutes later, we reach a field. To our left, something glows in the middle of a large crater. Descending the crater walls, the golden light dancing from its center illuminates rectangular stones standing taller than two of me and wider than three uppers. The megaliths form a ring backlit by flickering light that casts long shadows into the crater. Above, a ring of horizontal stones lays atop the vertical stones like a crown.

Stonehenge, Lii says.

Unlike the real thing, this one shows no signs of crumbling, weathering, or missing pieces. Miles leads me between two upright stones where more campers wait on long wooden benches. They surround a raging campfire, chatting and laughing amongst themselves. An electric excitement fills the air.

The concentration of nanites in here is off the charts, Lii says, almost purring.

Looking around, I recognize Scarlett and Bethany among a group at the front. Scar sticks her tongue out at me as we approach them. Miles sits next to Bethany with me on his opposite side. Penny and Ing sit next to Justin, who gesticulates like a wild man as he tells them about a battle bot fight. Both look bored.

How does everyone have so much energy? I'm drained like a faucetless sink. I ask Miles, "What's going on?"

"This is The Gathering," Miles says as if that explains

everything and turns back to Bethany, whispering something in her ear.

"The Gathering?" I ask, after nudging him.

"Oh, yeah. I keep forgetting that you're a norm-born. We gather together campers with unique skills and those who achieve impressive feats for a ritual. That now includes you. Surprise."

Penny stands and walks to the fire. She turns to the assembly of campers, holds up her hands, and bellows, "Let it begin!" Her voice carries loud and clear, cutting short the various conversations.

The crowd responds as one, "Let it begin!"

"For those who haven't been here before, don't worry. You only need to bring your offering up and toss it into the fire."

Miles places three grimy gears in my hand. "I brought an offering for you," he explains with a nod of encouragement. The random scraps of metal match the set in his other palm.

One by one, the campers stand and walk to the front. They toss their offerings reverently into the fire in a ritualistic manner more appropriate for an anti-AI cult. Some of the offerings let off sparks or burn with green or blue flames. Others shoot towering flames into the sky or create shimmering mirages in purples and greens like an aurora.

I nearly trip when it comes time for me to toss mine in. When will I get used to walking on natural ground? I toss the offering into the fire, and the entire upper ring of Stonehenge bursts into towering flames. Yells of fright erupt through the assembled crowd, followed by laughter and clapping. Scar gives me a double thumbs up. Pyro and Henri snigger with a look I'm growing used to seeing on their faces.

Miles claps me on the shoulder and tosses in his own offering. The flames erupt from the upper ring of stones exactly like mine. Everyone cheers again, whooping and hollering excitedly.

Nano-adapter, Lii says.

Planting my butt back onto the bench, I ask, "Why isn't

Naren here?"

"Because we can only invite so many people," Miles says with a shrug and a "what-can-I-do?" sort of tweak to his face. "The Gathering is invite-only."

"Thanks," I say, feeling a comradery among this group of nanos, even with Pyro and Henri here.

"No problemo," Miles says with a fist-nudge to my shoulder. We watch the last of the group toss their offerings into the dancing flames. "Now watch this," Miles says as the last campers sit back down.

"Let it continue," Penny yells over the roar of the flames, which are now rising higher and higher. Images shine blue and white within the orange and yellow inferno, ranging from people to vines and plants. At one point, I see a black silhouette of a guy in a run-down container. I look around to see if I can spot another blocker but can't make out anyone who stands out.

Once the fire burns down to a reasonable size, Penny sticks giant metal tongs into the fire and pulls out what looks like a metal rod contraption with all sorts of gears, switches, and dohickeys. Some of the components glow white-hot. She sets it down on a flat-topped rock next to her.

Panny says, "For those who are new to The Gathering, we come here once a year to create a device called a wonkit. We fill the fire with nanites of all varieties. This place combines your mechanical offerings and infuses the device with one of our skills. We never know what the fire will create until it's over."

"Some devices only work once, and some work for decades. The Gathering has created everything from the machine that built this Stonehenge to a healing box. Let's find out what type of machine we created tonight." Penny licks her finger and touches the wonkit tentatively. She pulls away and laughs. "We'll give that another minute."

A Hispanic gal close to Penny extends her finger at the wonkit and an ice-cold wind blasts it, curling a chill around our Stonehenge. All these nanos have so much control over their innate skills. Will I gain control of mine by the end of summer?

Or will it take years?

How about being a little patient, Lii says with a hint of grumpy old man. *You're less than a week into camp.*

In the already cool night air, I shiver, wishing my clothes were thicker. When the nano-ventus finishes her arctic blast, Penny sticks a finger to the device and says, "Well, why didn't you say so in the first place?" She grabs the cooled wonkit from the tongs and turns the rod around in her slender hands, rolling it this way and that. All those strange gears and switches. It's like one of those needlessly complicated devices that make no sense.

A Rube Goldberg machine, Lii says.

Yeah.

"Hmmm," Penny mutters. "Should I rotate this gear?" A few onlookers yell "Aye" and "wahoo." Justin blows a loud raspberry and points both thumbs down, drawing a round of laughter.

"What about this toggle?" More campers holler and clap. Penny shakes her head and moves her hand up and down a shaft, searching for something. She places her pointer finger at an old metal switch as if it was drawn in magnetically. "How about this one?" Everyone whoops and hollers wildly, some like a basset hound, others like madmen standing on their benches. The look on Scarlett's radiant face could light every bulb in the blocks.

"This switch it is," she bellows over the rowdy crowd. Penny flicks the switch. Reality glows with blue and violet like everyone and everything is made up of millions of glowing particles. But as soon as it began, the hallucination dwindles and I sit alone. Did I jump forward in time or something?

No, the stars haven't shifted, Lii says like a history teacher.

How will I get back to camp? Is this some elaborate joke at my expense? Would Miles really do that to me? There's no way Bethany would let him get away with it.

Before my thoughts spiral too far down the vortex of fear, everyone rematerializes, some laid out on the ground and others standing in confusion. Some laugh loudly while others wince and rub bruised tailbones or elbows.

"Where'd you all go?" I ask.

"Where'd *you* go?" Miles counters. "One minute you were there and then you and the wood benches disappeared. Everything tweaked into glowing purple and blue with a dusk-like sky. When Penny flipped the switch again, you, the benches, and normal color came back."

"We phased," Penny shouts over the boisterous conversations that sprouted up everywhere. "Everyone calm down. It was a simple matter of a rare nano-skill. While uncommon, this year's wonkit picked up on one of Mazz's skills: phasing." She points at me. "He can phase in and out of our plane of existence. That's what we did."

"How do you know?" someone calls out from the back row.

"I don't *know*, but it's a highly-educated guess."

Several campers try to speak up, but Bethany yells over the crowd, "Shut it!" accompanied with a mental push demanding silence.

Penny continues as silence steamrolls through the crowd. "Mazz didn't jump with us. He wasn't pulled in, which tells us that whatever affected us belongs to one of his skills, right? From one of Mr. Braunwyn's books, I read that the other plane looks blue and purple."

The crowd stays quiet for several heartbeats, then bursts into conversation all at once. A dozen nearby teens clamber close to me, several pawing at my shoulders, asking, "Can you really phase?" "When did you start?" "Did we really phase?" "Does it feel strange like that every time?" "It was hard to breathe in there."

Pyro's gaze reflects angry orange and yellow. Is he gonna set me on fire again? He smiles wickedly as my shirt sparks. An uncomfortable shrinking in my gut pulls me in, out of control. This place supercharges my teleportation, sending me out so fast that I don't have time to look to Miles for help. Pop!

CHAPTER FOURTEEN

A Round Trip

Searing pain smacks my body, from my brain to the soles of my feet as I slam into something entirely immovable. I collapse, recognizing the feeling. I bounced off Camp Astrid's wards, breaking rule fifty-one, again.

My hands scrape on gravelly dirt, my backside bruised. Are other nano-skills this painful? As my eyes adjust from the bright firelight of Stonehenge, the stars emerge in the sky. The tip of the barely-risen crescent moon casts long shadows from the tall redwoods and Douglas fir trees that surround me. The faint line of a road flanked by crumbling buildings comes into view.

Where am I?

Lost, Lii says.

Not helpful. What now? I need to get back. I could pick a direction and walk. No. The wards would run me in a wild goose chase. Could Dr. Fontein or Bender find me out here? Wherever here is.

That's your best bet, Lii says. *Wait for the calvary.*

I could try to teleport and hopefully bounce back to Stonehenge but bouncing off the wards again isn't an appealing notion. That, and I haven't been able to teleport on purpose yet. I'd be more likely to teleport by trying kinetics or phasing. Any other options?

Stick with option A, Lii says. *Sit and wait for morning or for a counselor.*

Teleportation it is then. I sit cross-legged on the dirt road, exactly like we do in phasing and kinetics, and select a piece of gravel from the road. I can't make out much detail in the darkness. I roll the rock over, feeling its edges, weighing it in my palm, and squeezing it in my hands. I try to recall the feel of the truck accident and tap into that fear, the rattle of loose bolts, the shocked expressions of the passengers. I lean into the thought that I'm about to die.

That familiar constriction yanks me inward, tugging me to my bunk bed in Steadfast Corner, pop, but then I hit the unwavering wall of Camp Astrid, like running full out into a cement wall. For the second time in under a half-hour, splinters shoot through every ounce of me. I'm left with a whole-body maelstrom of pain. I pat myself down to make sure all my parts are still in the right place. I didn't break any bones, but with this amount of pain, I wouldn't be surprised if I had.

Even though I'm plunged into complete darkness, I instantly recognize where I am. I woke up to these coarse sheets and this comfortably small bed for as long as I can remember. My bunk in the blocks, with its summer smell wafting in through the container cracks. It is so familiar that I could live a thousand years and never forget it. Not waiting for the aching to fully dissipate, I peer down to where my parentals sleep. Of course, they aren't home during their night shift. I lean back in my bunk and wait for the feeling of being shredded in a woodchipper to subside.

What now? Clutching the rock in my hand, I want to blame it for my current situation. I should have stayed where I was. Stupid, Mazz. I expect Lii to weigh in, but he glitched out.

Then I think of something. While I'm here, I might as well go see Laticia. It would be an awesome surprise. I gingerly climb down from my bunk, too stiff to bound down the way I usually do. I flip on the single lightbulb and write a message for my folks. If I'm still here in the morning, I'll come back and see them.

A few minutes later, I'm at Laticia's container knocking at the door with my signature rap, tap, rappity tap so she knows it's me. I have to knock the pattern twice before I hear her mom yell, "wake up and get the door." I know her folks nearly as well as my own, and they are as familiar with my knock as she is.

She flings the door open and slams into me with a hug, something we have rarely shared in the past. My whole body pulses with pain. "How?" she whispers in my ear as she clings to me. She pecks at my cheek, lips feeling warm and gentle, but stirringly unfamiliar. I want to return the gesture, but wonder if the kiss was an accident in which case I'd mess things up.

"I teleported," I tell her. "Let's go to our hiding spot. I'll tell you all about camp." We walk silently, taking advantage of the dark sky and deep shadows to stay hidden. A block over and six containers up, I crawl into a collapsed section between two off-kilter containers. My shoulders barely fit between a hidden hole in the wreckage. Did the hole shrink?

We put on weight, Lii says, not bothering to hide how stupid he thinks I am.

"Tell me everything," she says, squeezing my hand in the impenetrable darkness. We can't see each other, but I know exactly where she is. We're close enough that I feel her minty breath on my cheeks. "How is camp?"

As tired as I am, I'm eager to tell her all about what I've seen, heard, and done. I downplay my new friendships with Bethany, Penny, Ing, and especially Scarlett, focusing on the guys. I get the feeling that she wouldn't want to hear about them. It shouldn't matter, but it does. What rule is that?

Lii says, *rule nineteen: don't poke a slumbering bear.*

Laticia's apprenticeship with Mom and Dad is going well. She's getting my summer rations for her efforts. Plus, a high-paying skill like welding is a ticket to a better life, ensuring that she won't wither away. We could be a team like Mom and Dad. Well, maybe not like them, but friends working together.

After an hour, we've caught up. Telling her everything makes my experiences feel more real, as if they were a dream before and now they have taken form as an undeniable anchor in my mind. The last few days don't fit into the rest of my life, delineating a before and after my nano identity.

"I need to get back," I say, realizing that people at camp might still be looking for me.

"Go," she says, her breath closer than before. "But take this with you." Her lips touch mine, first tenderly, then passionately. The stirring of emotions we shared before I left for camp intensify. I follow her lead, our touch natural, built on years of trust and friendship, yet filled with nervousness at changing everything between us. She feels like Bethany did when she toyed with my mind. But these kisses are built on years of memories and friendship. She pushes me back and lies on top of me, her slender body a mere paper-weight.

How long we stay like this, I don't know. Then she pushes herself up, mouth inches from mine, and says, "I wanted to give you something to come home to. Don't forget us as you take on your new status as an upper."

Her words sting. "I'm not going to change," I say, though I know my words are false. I don't need to see her to sense that she knows it too.

"You're already bigger than a week ago," she says. "Taller and more muscular."

"Really?"

"Yes," she and Lii say as one. We sit in silence for a moment, her breath warm and appealing. "Can I watch you teleport?"

"Yes. Let's go back to my container." We walk back home, sticking to the shadows as we've done so many times before. My mind races and clogs from the last hour.

Back in my container, I sit on the floor, cross-legged, staring at the piece of gravel I brought with me from the road. I struggle to think of anything scary enough to counteract my confuddled mind. Laticia watches me from the posh chair Bender summoned, her gaze filling me with comfort. I don't want to leave her. Will we be able to pick up where we left off when the summer ends? Pop.

She is gone. Home is gone. The clangs of the blocks are gone. The sweet scent of the empty forest and the brackish scent of the dirt road announce my return to the woods. I'm not at Stonehenge, but I'm content that I didn't bounce against the wards. In the light of the risen moon, I see my footprints from before. "I guess I'm walking."

We could always stay put and wait for someone to find us, Lii says as if I'm an idiot.

Nope. I'm walking. I choose to head southward and begin my walk, careful not to trip on potholes that crop up every few strides. If The Gathering was north of Camp Astrid, then most likely I bounced back in that direction, so south makes the most sense. Maybe I'll see the flames of Stonehenge, which are outside the wards. Soon, I come to a fork in the road, and stand still, unsure of what to do. I ponder for a while, the moon shedding a bit of light on the situation. If I felt tired before, now I'm nearly depleted to the point of falling down. My feet drag, scraping my well-worn heels on the gravel.

You've been using too many nanites with all this teleportation, Lii says. *You're almost out, and there aren't as many nanites around here. More than back home, but way less than camp.*

Shortly, I come to a junction in the road. What now? I recall a stupid phrase I heard once, "When you find a fork in the road, take it." I take the southerly branch. In another few minutes, the road curves east, and I find another fork, one southward and the other eastward. I choose the southbound route again, hoping that it will take me closer to camp. In the next half hour, I take four more southward forks, one left, two right, and one straight ahead.

Then, when I reach the fifth intersection, I notice elongated footprints matching my own dragging gate, one track leading left and another set right. I yell out to the sky and shake my head in frustration. Defeated, I plop down by the side of the road cursing the wards. What now?

I don't know when I fell asleep, but when I open my eyes, a pair of blinding headlights are rumbling up the road. I grunt to my feet and dust off my clothes, though in the darkness I doubt it will make much difference.

The SUV has an angular black frame, decked out with fat knobby tires, reinforced bull bars, and all kinds of gear mounted to the roof. As it rolls up, the dusty passenger-side window slides down, and a man from inside asks, "Lost?"

In a word, yes. Even though this isn't a dark alley, I'm pretty sure rule thirty-one still applies: avoid strangers. In the dim, bluish light of the car's dashboard, the man's face is chiseled and rigid, but his eyes are kind, framed by the short black hair of someone very serious about obedience and order. I must look completely out of place, a blocker lost in the woods.

"My name's Mariotto," he says jovially with a French accent. "I take care of the roads around here. You're from Camp Astrid, no?"

When I fail to respond, Mariotto asks, "Which nano-skill landed you all the way out here?" His face splits into an inviting smile. Still not responding, he says, "It's okay. I wouldn't trust a random guy in a truck either."

He fiddles with something by his knees, then looks off to the distance, the clear sign of entering a sim. Aloud he says, "Hey, uh, Camp Astrid, this is Mariotto. I found one of your boys out here alone." I have no idea what the person on the other side of the link says. "No, he wisely didn't tell me his name. Smart kid. A blocker, maybe fourteen or fifteen." I don't bother to correct him. Uppers always misjudge my age.

"Will do. Out," he says, eyes returning to the focus of the physical world. "We're supposed to stay here until a counselor comes and gets us. I couldn't drive through the borders if I tried." Leaning over, he pushes the passenger-side door open. "Hop on in. It's more comfortable and a lot warmer in here."

My exhausted mind beckons me to get in and relax for a bit, but then I notice that Mariotto wears shiny gray armor, like some sort of modern knight. A black semi-automatic rifle rises in my direction. Details of the gun grow vivid. The long barrel with a silencer, a sight, and a black stock, his finger on the trigger.

Pop.

Unable to keep my legs under me, I fall. My lungs heave in and out rapidly, my heart beating hard to keep oxygen cycling to my head. I'm surrounded by the unmistakable ring of Stonehenge. I let my head fall to the trodden grass next to the warm, dwindling fire, and I close my eyes. Several sets of feet pad over to me, the unmistakable sound of running.

"Thank the nanites," Bethany says from six feet above me. In my head, she says, *It's good to have you back.*

"I knew you'd bounce back," Miles says, almost laughing. Warmth flows out my nose yet again.

"About time," von Steiner says with his disdainful and distinctively nasal voice.

"It looks like you've had an adventure," Dr. Fontein whispers, resonating with calm and security inside my mind. Miles picks me up in a rib-crunching hug as easily as a child squishing a stuffed animal. "Put the poor boy down," Dr. Fontein says, her voice somewhere between a laugh and a patient teacher. "He's been through quite enough already, don't you think?"

"Yes, Dr. F," Miles says and sets me on my unstable feet. I lean so far to the side that I nearly fall, but Miles's firm grip shores me up.

Dr. Fontein hands me a chocolate nano-milk and says, "Why don't we sit down for a spell while you tell us your tale." I shakily pull the cap off the milk and drink up. After gulping down half the bottle, I feel a skosh better. Without anyone poking or prodding the fire, it unnaturally flares up on its own, warming my cold muscles.

Gaining strength from the milk and warmth from the flames, I recount the events of tonight, occasionally pausing to swallow more of the nanite-rich goodness. I tell them that I needed to rest at home instead of the truth that I spent time with Laticia while they were out searching for me. Why? I'm not sure because Dr. Fontein and Bethany surely read the truth.

I won't tell anyone, Bethany says with a wink, *but I can't guarantee about other nano-paths tomorrow.*

Contrary to the fatigue I feel, I am more focused than usual, able to organize my thoughts and recount details I normally would have skipped over. I'm pretty sure that it's Dr. Fontein's immeasurable, yet soft influence. When I'm done recounting the night's activities, Dr. Fontein says, "It is good that you bounced back to The Gathering."

"Yes, ma'am."

"Who was that Mariotto guy?" Bethany asks.

Dr. F tilts her neck with an audible crack, eyes glinting with the thoughts of someone wiser than time. "This is not for sharing, understood?" A powerful wave of energy emanates from the head counselor, a clear threat of what will happen if any of us let her secret spill. Her boundless reserve of power unnerves me. "I only tell you this because Mazz has a right to know what sort of danger he was in and so he knows the consequences of leaving camp again. The rest of you need to know because I want you to look out for him."

Each of us nods in turn as she looks over us appraisingly.

"An Imperium battalion called shockknights, of whom I assume you have heard countless contradictory rumors, look for Camp Astrid every summer. They know roughly where we are, but they cannot find us. Our defenses steer them away, just as they did with Mazz today–"

"Ah!" I scream as a leopard bounds out of the darkness, open-mouthed and teeth bared. I jump to my feet to run. I begin to port away but only manage to fall over my bench as Dr. Fontein yanks my essence back. Scrambling to my feet, sure that one of us will die, I realize they are laughing.

"This is Tiny," Penny says between giggles, hugging the large cat as it nuzzles into her lap. She scratches it behind the ears as one might a house cat. "She's super nice. I sent her out looking for you."

With waves of calm rolling over me, Bethany's distinctive presence in my mind, my heart returns to a more normal rhythm and the clenching of my chest subsides. I don't like how easily Dr. Fontein and Bethany can influence me. Do I have free will, or am I going to be hostage to their whims from here on out?

Dr. Fontein says, *We will only influence you when your actions endanger yourself or other campers.*

Agreed, Bethany says.

"Pet her," Penny says of the leopard. Now that I look closer, the giant cat was built from gears and knobs and levers, much like the wonkit we made earlier. "It's okay. She's my familiar. She won't bite." Scarlett and Naren told me about familiars, nano-enhanced mechanical creatures whose AIs are bound to their masters. Scarlett has a gecko and Naren has a monkey, which they were encouraged to leave at home. Why would Penny be allowed to bring hers?

I shakily extend my hand, hoping the mechanical feline won't rip my arm off at the shoulder. I touch her, gears rough but not jagged against my fingers. Soothingly so. Tiny perfectly suits her form, mechanical and exotic. I scratch her behind the ears as I've often done with simulated cats over the years and she purrs deeply, craning her neck into my hand.

"She likes you," Penny says with a twinkle in her eyes. After a moment of quietness, while I get used to the feline miracle, Penny says, "I've heard all sorts of stories about the shockknights, but who are they really? And, *why* are they after for us?" She emphasizes the word, "Why."

"They work for a cabal of the Imperium's highest-level supremes, all of whom are nanos. The shockknights maintain power for the select few, either keeping others from gaining power. They keep nanos in constant fear in hopes to separate us, ensuring that we don't rise up against them."

How can she possibly know this?

"They capture us and remove our skills," Fontein says sadly, confirming what Scar and Naren told me. While I haven't known about nano-influence for long and I don't have control over mine yet, the idea of having them stripped away sickens me. Like losing an arm.

"How do they remove nano-skills?" Miles asks.

"The shockknights' leader, a man named Tollere, is responsible," Dr. Fontein says with a bitterness to her tongue and a matching aura I wouldn't have thought possible before learning about nano-influence. "The deceased and very few survivors had the mark of a right hand imprinted on their chests. Their AIs were rendered permanently inert."

Lii lets out the mental equivalent of a cat's hiss. To him, an AI death is as bad as a human death. Once, I heard that losing one's AI causes the worst pain one can ever endure.

"Tollere has a unique nano-skill similar to Miles's but instead of additive, he extracts skills permanently without regard for his victims." Dr. Fontein lets the thought percolate for a moment before saying, "To make matters worse, the shockknights have added nanos to their ranks. Some may be conscripted and others volunteers, but most are made. We think Tollere imprints loyal norms with the nano-influence he siphons from his victims."

"But, why?" I ask, the words spilling out before the thought registers.

"Some people need power the way the rest of us need water or air. Mazz, as you know better than the rest of us, life isn't always nano-refracting rainbows and mechanical unicorns. Desperate and angry people will do almost anything, even, and sometimes especially, at the cost of others. Much like the scavengers in the blocks."

"So Camp Astrid is like a candy store for Tollere." Miles's brown eyes blaze. His inner peace-keeper must bristle at the notion.

Dr. Fontein says, "Precisely. But you have nothing to fear as long as you remain inside Camp Astrid's defenses or with a counselor." Her eyes defocus, not the look of someone simmed out, but of a wise woman pondering great thoughts. She snaps out of it and says, "Well, enough ghost stories for one night." The head counselor stands and the fire dies to black soot.

"Mazz, you are with me. The rest of you know your way back." My body shrinks and sucks into a pinprick of a whirlwind, stops for the briefest of flashes, then rages back into a tempest. This happens three more times in rapid succession, after which we stand outside Steadfast corner. I cough and gag like when Bender teleported me.

When I right myself, she says, "I will let you in on a secret. When you gain control of your skills, you can teleport multiple times through the wards, like skipping a rock on water."

"Uh, thanks." I'm not sure when or even if I'll master my skills, but someday it could be useful information. It fits into rule two: always have an escape plan.

"I did something I loath to do, but it was necessary," Dr. F says. "We can't have tonight's adventures spreading through the camp like nanites on the wind. So, I cordoned off tonight's memories as you told us about them. They won't crop up unless you intentionally focus on them."

"Now, off to bed. You've had enough excitement for one night. You'll need your sleep for tomorrow. I stashed a few nano-bars under your pillow in case you wake up with a hankering."

I nod, then creep into my cabin, quietly crawling onto my bunk. Despite being exhausted, I can't help but replay today's insanity over and over in my mind. Emerald lake. The Gathering. Getting lost in the woods. Laticia. The gray-armored knight, Mariotto. How close was I to being captured? If he'd shot me, would I have a handprint on my chest right now?

CHAPTER FIFTEEN

Sunrise Meditation

T he camp gong sounds.

"Argh," I groan, sounding like a bullfrog. Morning came too quickly. All night I dreamt of shiny-armored men trying to hunt me down. Six times I woke up in strange places. At one point I jolted awake in the cafeteria lying under Steadfast Corner's table. Another time, I roused to the uncomfortable cement of the girl's bathroom floor on my face. Each time I had to sneak back, sure that von Steiner would catch me. The latest accidental teleportation landed me on the doorstep of Wagon Wheels, Bethany and Scarlett's cabin. I only reached Steadfast Corner a few minutes before Miles shouted us awake.

At least I didn't wake up dangling by branches in a tree or cold and wet in the milky pond. From what I've gathered, most nanos stop using skills in their sleep when they stop wetting their beds. Nobody found out last night, but they will as soon as nano-paths listen into my thoughts at breakfast.

"Three minutes until morning march," Miles hollers. I peel myself off my pillow and consider skipping breakfast. I zombie-march to the mess hall, legs responding like day-old tofu.

As I enter the cafeteria, my mood improves. The smell of freshly baked cinnamon rolls, syrup-covered pancakes, salty

bacon, hot chocolate, and scrambled eggs can raise anyone's spirits. Last night, I munched through the nano-bars Dr. Fontein placed under my pillow, but my stomach growls for more.

Not until I fill my plate and sit down do I notice that all eyes have turned to me. Their eyes are metal needles pointing to me like I'm magnetic north. The cafeteria buzzes with energy as they whisper and stare. A girl no more than nine years old walks past and whispers the word "teleported" to her shorter friend.

Am I sweating? Why am I always at the center of attention? I didn't ask to go to The Gathering. I didn't ask for the wonkit to choose my skill, a skill I don't have control over. And I definitely didn't want to accidentally jump away. I keep my head bent down to avoid eye contact with anyone and walk out into the brisk morning air, wanting to be alone. I find a chair out on the front porch and plunk down in it, closing my eyes as if that will stop everyone from gossiping.

"What happened?" Naren asks, sitting in the chair next to me. "Why is everyone staring and whispering about you?" Reluctantly, I retell the story of last night. I avoid mentioning the part that Dr. Fontein warned me not to repeat though it feels weird not telling him.

The bell gongs in the courtyard for the morning track, but I barely touched my plate. I lost my appetite. As I re-enter the mess hall to return my plate, my feet fly out from under me and I splat on the floor with less grace than a rhinoceros ballerina. My pancake smushes into my chest. To my left, a group of campers breaks into boisterous laughter.

"Look," Henri says to Pyro with malice in his nearly black eyes. "The lost blocker fell on his ass. Mazz, us about your *trip*."

"Ignore Henri," Naren says, pulling me to my feet. "He's an idiot."

"Ah, man!" My unfinished pancake sticks to my last clean shirt, the syrup seeping through to the skin.

Naren says, "He is jealous that you are admired and he is…"

"An ass," Ing whispers as she passes.

"He can have the attention," I say, wiping the leftovers off my shirt. "I've had more than a lifetime of gawking."

"I brought metal fines today," Ms. Merryweather says once we sit in our usual kinetics spot. She pours a few flakes of metal from a vial and they float in mid-air. "Sometimes campers find it easier to focus on a single large object." The flakes spin in a circle so fast they look like a solid grey bracelet. "Other times, it's easier for the mind to focus on smaller specs or even just one tiny grain."

"It isn't the object's size that matters, though beginners never believe me," she says. Her grains twist so quickly in a complicated interweaving mosaic that it looks like a metal bust of a Persian man on an ancient coin. "Today, each of you will focus on three metal shavings."

After Ms. Merryweather pours three tiny flakes into my hand, I find a spot to lean against a half-crumbled wall. I'm too tired to sit upright or think straight. I wish I drank some nano-milk at breakfast. I close my eyes, trying to focus, but my attention won't narrow in on the task at hand. I keep taking a detour into the events of last night.

Focus, Bethany says peevishly in my head. *You can't let those thoughts slip while in the presence of other campers.*

My lips purse, my nose crinkles, and my eyes dart angrily to Bethany. A puff of air aggressively flings her hair wildly and forces her to blink. You're the one listening to my thoughts, I mentally shout back.

You're louder than a buffalo stampede, Bethany growls. *I can't concentrate with your thoughts screaming in my head.*

Fine. I'll try harder, I say, though I have no idea how I'm supposed to do that. I repeat the word, focus, over and over in his head. Even still, mental souvenirs from last night push into my head. The Gathering, the excursion to see Laticia, the encounter with the shockknight.

"Argh!" Bethany throws up her arms, stands, and stomps away. "How am I supposed to concentrate around you all?" I redouble my efforts to pay attention to the fines in my palm. But before long, I realize I am not paying attention to anything but my anger over my habit of drawing attention.

Look, Lii says. The metal flakes float lazily inches above my palm but instantly fall into my open hand. I groan, annoyed that none of my skills work how I want them to.

"Hey," Miles calls out. "It's working! It's working!" Miles's flakes wobble as mine had moments before. Only Miles is actually trying to make them float. I almost chuck my flakes out of frustration. Instead, they burn into my clenched fist.

"How'd you do that?" Bethany asks, coming back over.

"I don't know," Miles says. "It just worked. One second they were laying there and the next they floated."

"Did it work for anyone else?" Ms. Merryweather asks, looking around at each of us. I think about keeping my "success" a secret but realize that Bethany already knows the truth.

She casts a disapproving look my way, saying, *Speak up, or I'll do it for you.*

"I kinda got mine to work."

"That's good," Ms. Merryweather says, not approvingly, but not as sharply as usual. Looking back and forth between Miles and Bethany, she asks, "Would you two be willing to run an experiment for me?"

"Sure," they say in unison, Bethany looking far more confident than Miles.

"Bethany, I want you to dive into Miles's mind as he tries to levitate his metal filings again. Alright?"

"Sure, I suppose," Miles says, sounding like he'd rather not.

Bethany smiles. "I've always wondered if there was anything going on inside that hot-air balloon of yours." The smile on her face and raised eyebrow tell of a connection between them that is more than friends.

"When he levitates the flakes, I want you to share the sensation with the rest of us."

"Okay," Bethany says, a fierce glow to her eyes.

Miles breathes in and out slowly, turning his attention to the metal grains. Within a minute, they lift off from Miles's hand, shakily balancing an inch above his palm. Almost imperceptibly, Ms. Merryweather's lips slide up at the edges. "Good."

A few seconds later, a powerful tug yanks my mind out of my head, a thick milkshake sucked through a straw. It takes a moment to get my bearings, but when I do, I see and feel the world from Miles's perspective. Intangible tendrils of energy, like the wispy tentacles of a jellyfish, reach out to the flakes.

Then I'm thwomped out of Miles's consciousness, a helpless mothball pulled through a vacuum cleaner. I crash back into my body, a part of me left with an ache I can't identify, a part I never knew existed. The intensity of having my essence unceremoniously pulled away, then roughly pushed back, leaves me dizzy and confused.

Blinking myself back to normal, I look around at the others. Bethany wipes blood from her nose with the cuff of her synthetic sleeve. Sweat rolls from Miles's brow and he breathes hard as if from a strenuous workout. Penny has a radiant smile. Does she want to do it again? Pyro leans over, breathing heavily, face pale and maybe a hint green. Is he about to blow chunks?

"You did well," Ms. Merryweather says to Miles and Bethany. "That was impressive. You two have come a long way. You remind me of..." For a second, her stern features soften, her eyes distant. I'm curious. What was the trailing end of that sentence?

"Thank you," Bethany says to our instructor.

"That was so nano," Penny laughs. To Bethany, who is still staunching her bloody nose, she asks, "Is that what it's like for you all the time?"

"No," Bethany says, an angry torrent of emotion buffeting me. Through pursed lips and clenched teeth, she says, "It's usually more like a constant onslaught of competing podcasts turned up to full blast. I have to close myself off to it all or I'd go nuts. And, some people are louder than others." She twirls her eyes in my direction.

Ms. Merryweather claps her hands together and says, "Miles and Bethany, you take a break. The rest of you, try and repeat the sensation you felt in Miles's head."

Within seconds, Penny levitates her own flakes, to which the group cheers. As soon as Bethany returns her considerable will to the task at hand, her flakes float. Miles picks her up on his back and prances around the small clearing like a horse, her laughing the whole time.

At the end of the levitation track, Penny weaves her flakes in a Celtic pattern. Henri, Pyro, and I continue struggling. I'm happy for my friends, but...

A bit jealous too, Lii says. *It's not a good look on you.*

Walking back a few minutes later, I ask Bethany, "Why don't we always learn that way, but by sharing the counselors' experiences?"

"Do you think they want campers, even cabin leaders, in their heads? Plus, they're so used to their skills that it would be hard to tease out what they're doing. I couldn't teach you telepathy because I've been able to do it for as long as I can remember. Could you teach someone how to breathe or blink?"

Miles puts his hand to the side of his mouth as if revealing a secret. "The real reason is that no other nano-paths are as good as Bethany. She's something of a prodigal child." She nudges him on the shoulder as if to say, "shut up." But she's smiling anyway.

"Two brownie points for Miles," Penny says with an exaggerated double wink.

At lunch, I tell Naren about my lack of progress. In response, he says, "Perhaps you should try meditation."

"Why?"

"It may help you focus. I meditate all the time."

"I didn't sign up for that track," I say, casting about to find an excuse to avoid one of the most boring tracks at Camp Astrid.

"I am sure there is room," Naren says. "Nobody ever signs up for Mr. Braunwyn's tracks."

"Stop. You're making it sound so fun." I cram an oversized bite of turkey sandwich in my mouth wishing Naren to drop it.

It works, Bethany pipes into my head. *I take meditation to tune out everyone's thoughts. It could help you stop broadcasting to everyone.*

Thanks for the unsolicited advice.

Until you learn to stop yelling in my head, I'll give you any advice I see fit. So the sooner you master meditation, the sooner you'll get rid of me.

They're right, Lii says.

"Alright," I grumble to all three of them.

After Saturday breakfast, Naren and I stop by Mr. Braunwyn's cabin. I nearly backed out several times, but the idea of closing my thoughts to nano-paths wins out. If it works, maybe I won't be the central cog in Camp Astrid's rumor mill. I knock at his open doorway. "Mr. Braunwyn."

"Yes, come in," says the most monotone voice I've ever heard.

Naren nods at me to enter first as if I might abandon him. My jaw drops as I step inside. The walls are covered in shelves, and those shelves are stacked with paper books. And nearly a third of them are graphic novels. Staring in wonder at his treasure trove, I recognize a bunch of the titles. Enamored by his collection, I barely notice him.

"You like them?" he says, his voice so boring that his three-word question nearly puts me to sleep. He is the living embodiment of a tranquilizer dart. Is that his primary nano-skill? But his collection of original graphic novels has my eyes dancing like a spastic kangaroo.

"This is incredible," I say, reaching out to touch one before catching myself.

"Go ahead," he says. "Their purpose is to be appreciated and enjoyed. It is a pleasure to meet someone who appreciates them." I carefully pull one off the shelf. On the front cover, a buffed man with three blades coming from his fists stands in a fighting stance in a yellow, blue, and black uniform. The title says, "Wolverine," in matching blue scrawl. It looks and feels ancient.

As I thumb through the pages, Mr. Braunwyn asks, "What can I do for you young gentlemen?" His slow, sedating voice is like an advertisement for the Professional Association of Boredom.

"I'm Naren Rai and this is Mazz Becker."

"Yes." Mr. Braunwyn's glossy eyes slowly roll to focus on me. "You are the kinetic who teleported out of The Gathering."

"Uh, yeah," I say. After an uncomfortable pause where Naren and I look back and forth between Mr. Bruanwyn and each other, I say, "Naren said that I need to learn to focus and, well..."

"Meditation could help you." The fact that his mellow brain could think fast enough to finish my sentence doesn't seem possible. What animal am I thinking of?

A sloth, Lii says.

"Yup, that's it," I say to Lii and Mr. Braunwyn." The nearly catatonic man's eyes defocus even more, and he says, "The only track that fits your schedule is sunrise meditation."

"What time does that start?" I ask, sure I don't want the answer.

"Fifteen minutes before sunrise," Mr. Braunwyn says impassionately. "Tomorrow, that's 5:17 am."

My eyes bulge of their own accord. "5:17 am? Really?" No wonder this guy is comatose; he's so exhausted that he's stuck in slow motion. How can someone so blah give such horrible news. I already sleep too little. Soon I'll be like him, dragging through life at a koala's pace.

"Thank you, sir," Naren says merrily. "We will be there." He pulls at my arm. I reluctantly set down the graphic novel and follow Naren.

"Feel free to browse my collection any time," Mr. Braunwyn says.

"Ur. Thanks," I say over my shoulder. I doubt the price of admission, an onslaught of tranquilizer voice, is worth the reward of a special viewing.

◆ ◆ ◆

Lii wakes me at five o'clock for my first sunrise meditation with the gentle tones of a wind-chime, much nicer than I'm used to. Camp seems to agree with him.

Naren and I slip out the back door of Steadfast Corner into the darkness, the cold splashing me awake. "Come on," Naren whispers, waving at me to walk faster. He sets a half-walk half-jogging pace south until we follow the signs pointing to Eastgate. I stumble a few times, still gaining familiarity with the unevenness of the forest floor.

"Welcome," Mr. Braunwyn says as we approach the towers of Eastgate, his slim figure a black silhouette against the first signs of light. He ushers us inside Eastgate's tower as emotionless as a robot.

Welcome to the group, Bethany says as I reach the top. *This will help.*

"I hope so," I grumble, eyelids heavy, shoulders drooping. "At this hour, it better."

Through chattering teeth, Naren says, "It can't hurt." I'm not so sure. Next time I'll have to wear warmer clothes. Looking eastward, beautiful pink clouds with orange whisps shine in the sky. The sun paints the far-off mountain peaks in golden light.

Do as we do, Bethany says. I retrieve a floor mat and lay it flat before sitting on it. *Don't worry. It's pretty simple.*

"Let's start with a thanks to the day," Mr. Braunwyn drones. Bethany flashes a cartoon image of a Miles-shaped man standing and holding arms stretched wide to either side, one leg stretched wide, as he leans toward his other foot. I do my best to match the others but I'm pretty sure that wobbling isn't supposed to be part of the pose. The skies remind me of an impressionist painting I once saw in art class.

Monet, Bethany offers. *Take in the moment and feel what you feel. Notice the sunrise, your mind, and your body. Let go of everything else.*

My mind isn't enjoying this and my body is freezing.

"Release your thoughts of yesterday," Mr. Braunwyn says. If he keeps using that dreary voice, I'll meditate myself to sleep. "And switch sides. Release your worries for the coming day."

Easy for you to say.

Those are the thoughts you need to let go of, Bethany says. *They don't help.*

But–

But nothing, Bethany interrupts with an emotional force like a bulldozer. *You need to focus on being here and now. Enjoy the sunrise.*

Okay. The next half hour of sunrise continues to aggravate me. At the end of the session, I spot three butterflies, one purple, another orange, and the last yellow. I marvel as they hover around Mr. Braunwyn.

Those are Mr. Braunwyn's familiars, Bethany says. They flutter through the air exactly like the animals they represent. As much as I disliked waking up early to freeze myself, I have to admit that the sunrise was the most beautiful of my life.

CHAPTER SIXTEEN

Teleportation

"Cheer up," Naren says as we enter the mess hall for breakfast. After a week of morning meditation, I'm no closer to finding my inner self. "You will get a hang of it. I know–"

"Bender," I practically yell, thrilled to see him.

Naren startles and looks around as if someone might attack. "What?!"

I jog over to the counselor's table. Bender stands and fist bumps me. He smiles broadly, but the expression only makes him look haunted. A fresh quadruple scar on his temple looks as if Tiny tried to rip his head off. It must be fresh because medical nanites should have healed something like that within a couple of days.

"Don't worry about this," he says, having noticed me staring. "Head back to your table. We'll see each other in phasing. Today you'll have your first teleportation track too, so eat up."

After another frustrating kinetics track, I introduce Miles, Bethany, and Pyro to Bender. They seem nervous in his presence. Probably the scars. Without wasting time, Bender says, "I hear you've been playing with rocks out at the platform. I'll meet you there." He disappears with a faint pop.

When we arrive at the platform, Bender hands out four

bowls of every-colored Fruity Bombs. As we take our spots around him, he hands us notebooks and pencils.

"Your goal today is to phase a single Fruity Bomb from the bowl while tasting the rest and writing down how they taste. You must use a unique word to describe each bomb. And don't worry, I had a special batch mixed up with extra nanites. They're healthy."

"Nano," Miles says with a goofy grin, a bit less tense about Bender. I suppose it's hard to be intimidated by a counselor who offers you candy.

"If you run out of Fruity Bombs, let me know, and I'll refill your bowl. Now get to work. I shall return shortly." Bender vanishes. I smile at Miles and Bethany, but ignore Pyro, then dive into our challenge. I set aside one orange bomb and scoop up several more colors. Green: sour. Yellow: sweet. Another yellow: tart. The list goes on. At some point, I forget about phasing the bombs. When I remember, the orange one is gone.

I look up, and Bender has returned. He looks at me with a knowing look. "Your Fruit Bomb phased about a minute ago." The other campers stop writing and listen in. "Why do you think it worked?"

"Because I wasn't paying attention?" My usual blunder.

"Precisely. Phasing differs from other skills. You don't push an object around or force someone to hear your thoughts. Instead, you slide an object between planes of existence. We don't understand the other dimension even though scientists can detect that it exists and nanites draw upon that plain for energy."

"Usually, people only notice the other dimension when they aren't paying attention. People call it a sixth sense. It feels similar to those inspired thoughts that pop into your head when you shower."

"Let's try it again," Bender says as he subtly shifts his fingers, filling our bowls with more candy. "Bethany, listen in to Mazz like you did in Merr–Ms. Merryweather's track."

"Will do," Bethany says. I feel a gentle presence, mildly

pulling a part of my essence into her mind. With so much practice at linking us all together, she feels less invasive every day.

I focus on the activity at hand. Pink: sugary. Red: fresh. Yellowish-with brown polka dots: funky.

"Wait, where did it go?" I ask.

Bender claps his hands together and nods. "Bethany? Did you get it?"

"Yup," she says.

"Would you mind sharing the sensation with us?"

"On it," she says as if she thought he'd never ask. She draws my whole essence into an in-betweenness, a limbo. She replays the sequence of the last few seconds with shocking attention to detail, far better than Lii and I can do. A tingle like washes over me. I recognize it from some of the accidents and once when I lost my best pair of socks. Then the sensation fades and my mind returns to normal.

Within seconds, Miles's Fruity Bomb disappears. Soon after, Bethany phases hers too. By the end of class, the three of us can make our sweets disappear at will. Each time we get it, Pyro's glower deepens. I'm pretty sure that Pyro's hair is only a twitch away from igniting.

As the lesson comes to an end, Miles says, "That was wicked! Hands down, the best lesson I've ever had."

"That is precisely what I am here for," Bender says. "My goal is to be wicked to the campers, just like von Stinker–I mean von Steiner." He winks at me with a twinkle in his eyes.

"Mazz, shall we start on teleportation?" he asks as the three cabin leaders stand to leave. "Or has phasing drained you?"

"Let's do it," I say, full of excitement. I'm sure the smile on my face could power a whole container block. I can't wait to learn how to teleport.

After the others have left, Bender says, "This group works well together. Well, minus Pyro. You will do well to stick with them." I nod, my eyes accidentally looking at the four red stripes on the side of his head. Who or what could have done that? "Do you know how teleportation works?"

"No idea."

"Well, neither do I, and neither does anyone else. It has to do with micro-wormholes and quantum entanglement, but that lies beyond my expertise." My excitement falls like a bag of bolts.

"But fortunately, you and I do not need to understand it to use it. The best minds in the world have tried to invent teleportation devices but have thus far failed. If they knew about the two of us, they would want to dissect our brains to figure out how it all works." Bender tries to laugh off this last bit, but I can tell that his "joke" has more than a nugget of truth.

After an uncomfortable minute, Bender asks, "Do you know teleportation comes instinctively when something frightens you?"

"Because physics breaks down when my world approaches an end?" I guess, sticking my tongue out and screwing up my face.

"Humorous, but no," Bender says, his lips curling up at corners. "Teleportation feels like folding in on oneself. When you are afraid, your stomach lurches and your body wants to shrink down."

"I hate that feeling."

"The more you practice, the less it will screw you up," he says. "The basics of teleportation involve folding in on oneself and thinking of the destination. The more familiar you are with the terminus, the easier it is. It is even easier to jump to a spot you can see. Today, you will teleport one foot at a time.

"Okay," I say, excited to begin.

"For the first few tries, crumple your body inward and twist, like so." Bender demonstrates with a quick bending motion where he twirls, pulls his arms in, and hunches his body into a crouch. He disappears and reappears a foot forward. Or, rather he starts taking form before fully dissolving, so for a second, there are two of him, incredible and mind-bending.

A roll of blue tape snaps into his hands. He marks five blue lines to the platform, each a foot from the last. "Start here and aim for this line here. Each time you do it, you get Sour Tape, okay?" A package of the sweets crinkles in his previously empty hand.

I step to the first line, take in a deep breath, and then try to crumple myself as quickly as I can. I end up on my butt, but not due to any nano-skill unless you count clumsiness a skill. I'm glad none of my friends are here.

"Not a bad start," Bender says, stifling a laugh. "Perhaps this time, do not hold your breath. You look as though you might burst into pieces. Instead, try scrunching yourself up as you exhale quickly."

It can't hurt. Well, no. Most of my experiences with nano-influence have been painful in one way or another. Nevertheless, I straighten up as tall as I stretch and take a deep breath. As I blow air out, I curl down into a ball. Meanwhile, I close my eyes, fully expecting to fall over again.

Nothing happens, except almost falling over. I open my eyes and stand up, prepared for more advice. I can't figure out the look on his face. "It was about as graceful as a tadpole out of water, but you did it, my boy." Looking down, I stand at the second piece of tape.

You missed the popping sound, Lii says. *It was pretty quiet this time.*

"As you get better at it, you will not need to scrunch your body," Bender says. "But for now, keep it in the mix."

"Why didn't it make much of a popping sound?" I ask.

"The better you are at teleporting, the quieter it is. With sidelongs or teleporting other things, there is always more noise."

At Bender's encouragement, I step back and try again, this time keeping my eyes open. For an instant, I am both the "me" behind the jump and the "me" in front. Next, I port two feet forward. Then five. Next, I bounce to the ground and back up to the platform. After my thirty-fourth jump, my stomach protests with uncomfortable burps, and my body is spent from the overuse of my skills.

"Well," says Bender with a clap as I sip at a nano-milk Bender summoned. Where does he keep getting these things? Not from Camp Astrid because the wards would block him. Breaking my distracted thoughts, he says, "I think that is quite enough for today. I'll see you tom–."

"Bender, can I ask you a question?" I say. A question has been nagging at me.

"Sure. What's up?"

"Why aren't there more blockers here?"

"Several reasons," Bender says, sighing as if he knew I'd ask at some point. "Most nanos can use their influence to elevate their status in some way. Very few blockers elevate to upper status. People with even the slightest nano skills account for a good percentage of those that do. Some of the weaker nanos may not even realize what they can do. The second reason is that few blockers encounter a high enough dose of nanites to manifest their natural abilities. You, going to an upper school, were exposed, which kicked your influence into overdrive. Their soap. Their paints. The Cocoa Cubes from that enforcer. It all added up."

"So, there might be more blocker nanos out there?"

"Yes, and lots of them," Bender nods. "Blockers probably outnumber upper nanos by three to one, but we can't identify them. Unlike you, most only possess weak influence, and their rare accidents wouldn't draw attention."

"Okay," I say, not feeling as alone despite being the only blocker in a hundred miles.

"Anything else?" He scratches at the white scars on his temple.

"Yeah," I say. "How can we influence nanites when they designed our AIs and the nanites so they couldn't work together?"

"Simple," he says. "Nanites evolve the way viruses do. Nobody really understands what these changes do. You know of AISystems, right?"

"Everyone does. The manufacturer of almost all nanites

everywhere."

"Yeah," Bender nods. "They try to combat these anomalous variants, and the variants continue to evolve to fight back. It's like the viruses of old, constantly adapting to vaccines. AISystems, the Imperium's manufacturing arm, would hate to admit it but Dr. Fontein says that more than ninety percent of nanites are rogue. They mostly behave the way they were designed, so AISystems and the supremes don't make it publicly known. You should also remember that the highest-level supremes of the Imperium are all nanos. They ruthlessly maintain power with nano influence, so the rogue nanites work to their advantage."

"Got it," I say. "But why are some people nanos and others not?"

"Again, we only have theories," Bender says with a shrug of his shoulders. "Dr. F thinks that someone sabotaged the AI manufacturers with a hidden software or hardware virus. Like nanites, AIs are too complicated to fully understand. It also has a genetic component, since most nanos are nano-born, not norm-born."

"Thanks," I say, mind contemplating these knowledge bombs.

"Sure, sonny," he says, nods, winks, and disappears, leaving me alone on the platform with my thoughts. Maybe if we knew why some people are nanos and others are not, we'd know how Tollere removes our skills.

CHAPTER SEVENTEEN

Capture the Flag

Six groups of cabinmates cluster together in a small ruin-strewn clearing surrounded by dense forest to the north of camp. Mr. Winston, the strength and speed counselor, stands in the middle of the groups. His flat-top haircut, army-style clothes, and chiseled features make him seem like a lieutenant colonel in a delta force squadron.

"You know the rules of regular capture the flag," Mr. Winston says while his entire demeanor says, "Don't even think about messing with me."

Pyro's Eagle's Nesters stand to our right, looking cocky all decked out in matching camo and commando boots. Penny's Celtics don't look daunting in their athletic wear, but Miles told us that they are cunning and not to be underestimated. Miles arranged a truce with the Celtics before the game. We won't go after each other's flags until one of our groups gets two flags.

"Whoever retrieves the opponent's flag and brings it back to their territory will win that flag's territory. We have six teams, each with their own pie slice of land in which to stash their flag. Lii offers me a file from Mr. Winston and displays a map with the boundaries of each team shaded in all the colors of the rainbow.

It's amazing how much better-behaved Lii is out here.

All these nanites do an AI good, Lii says.

Realizing I just zoned out, I refocus on Mr. Winston. "–You must return your enemy's flag to your pie slice. If you capture another group's flag, you get any flags they captured. The first camp to retrieve four flags wins."

"You may only use your skills three times, so conserve them. You may not–I repeat, not–use your skills to hurt anyone. You may not use any weapons, makeshift or otherwise. Any foul play will result in an immediate forfeit. Understood?"

"Yes," most of us say, with a round of nods.

"If you are tagged in another group's territory, you must sit down. If you are tagged again by your teammates, you may return to the game."

Mr. Winston hands a red flag to Penny, a yellow flag to Miles, an orange one to Pyro, and so on. "On the whistle, run and place your flags in a spot that can be seen by your opponents. On the second whistle, the game begins." Without waiting or asking for questions, he blows a piercing note, and I run after Miles, with the other teams scattering to their territories.

Forest running during the day turns out to be similar to fleeing from scavengers in the blocks. Instead of dashing between vendor carts or leaping over wraiths, you have to dodge trees and bound over ferns. I find myself at the head of the group with Miles, holding back on my speed so I don't get ahead. I suppose that's one advantage of being so wiry.

Miles finds a ruined building with four tall walls and a caved-in doorway to stash the flag. "Gather round and listen up." He divides us into offensive and defensive groups. I'm in the forward group with Miles, Justin, Brooks, Joseph (a nano-celitas–speed), and Tanner (a nano-ventus–wind). Naren and the others are in the rear guard.

"We go in pairs," he says. "Understood? We–" The whistle blows shrill, echoing through the woods. "I'm with Mazz. Pair up and Go."

Miles dashes off towards Pyro's Eagle's Nest territory, and I follow easily keeping up. "This is a game of stamina," Miles says as we run. "Conserve your energy and your skills as long as you can."

"Got it." Within a minute, we cross into the orange Eagle's Nest territory.

"Quiet now," he says. "Your footsteps are too loud." I hadn't realized how much noise I'm making and how quiet Miles is. I force my steps to land between branches and twigs, working to tread delicately, and am rewarded with fewer crunches and snaps.

I wish my clothes were made of fancy synthetic materials like my cabinmates instead of these blocker rags that swish with every stride. Note to self: next time, wear my Camp Astrid shirt.

Shortly after crossing the border into Eagle's Nest territory, we spot our first set of defenders. We must have missed Pyro's forward ranks on our way.

"There!" one of them shouts, pointing at us. Their camo acts as a chameleon skin, adapting to the background, making them nearly impossible to make out. How much do clothes like those cost? Probably enough to feed a blocker for a year.

Miles pivots to the left, and I follow on his heels. The two of them are slower than us, but they don't have to keep up. They only need to stay between us and the flag, making us run two paces for every one of theirs. But their defense strategy gives away the rough location of their flag.

Miles whispers, "Split to the right. I'll draw them off to the left." I skid to a halt and duck behind a dilapidated building, count to five, then dash in the opposite direction. As Miles predicted, both of the defenders follow him. I head toward where I think their flag is, trying to keep my worn-down tennis shoes from treading too heavily.

"Incoming," a hoarse voice yells. A thick, muscular Eagle runs at me, by all appearances intending to run into me rather than tag me. I stand still as if frozen by fright until I can practically taste him, then sprint at an angle around him, barely dodging his outstretched hand. This feels like a low-stakes version of running from scavengers. With the Eagle's considerable weight, I hope he will run right by, but I don't look over my shoulder to find out. I wish I had my skateboard, not that it would do much good in the forest.

I dodge in and out of more ruins, then slow and quiet my steps as I weave between a group of broad redwood trunks and dash around a bush with tiny purple berries. The trees make it hard to keep my bearings, but I'm pretty sure I'm going in the right direction based on the square foundations.

Henri stands menacingly between me and the doorway to a ruined building with head-height walls and a dense cluster of saplings growing from within. His chameleon uniform makes his slow, stalking movements hard to discern. Unlike him, I stand out against the green backdrop.

I bolt around a structure to the left, hoping he will follow me. He doesn't. I nearly run around Henri's building, with him shifting easily to stay between me and the doorway. The broad-shouldered Eagle steams toward me, prepared to slam into me again. This time, I slide to the left, my face narrowly avoiding his swinging fist. So much for not hurting each other.

Okay, a different strategy. I have to be more aggressive. I hope Miles is fairing well. In the distance, indistinct yells punctuate my concerns.

Keeping my momentum from the slide, I rebound to my feet and beeline for a wall of their defended building. Who needs doors? I run up the side of the wall, feeling lighter than normal, and land belly down on top. I flop over the other side as that hulking Eagle's Nester slams into the wall, shaking rocks loose. So much for playing nice…

Inside a jumbled mess of rock, tree, fern, and shrubs impede any movement. Branches crunch underfoot and my shirt catches on underbrush. I cast my head around in search of their flag. A few steps further, I spot the flag half-buried beneath a mound of branches. I press through a thicket and stumble over rock. Then I have it, but I trip, and Henri bolts at me. Sure that I won't be able to escape, I do the only thing I can think of. I throw the flag over the near wall in hopes that one of my cabinmates will have an easier time snatching it.

On my knees, I flinch as Henri nears. I can't avoid the blow he is about to "accidentally" land on me. My senses heighten, and the pit in my stomach begins to tug me in. But then his palm slams into my chest, and the teleportation stops. I can't move.

He kneels down and presses his palm to my chest, pinning my paralyzed body in place. "You should scurry back to where you belong," he says with a sneer. Pain consumes me, shooting from my chest like snake venom. An explosion from within detonates every nerve in my body. I convulse as he keeps pressing his hand into my chest. My heart drums an uncertain funeral dirge. The taste of blood coats my mouth, but I don't care. All I want is for the pain to stop.

The strength ebbs from my spasming muscles and I lay still. Henri's hand follows me down. I don't know when it happened, but I lost the will to live. I'll do anything to make it stop. Blackness creeps in at the edge of my vision, telling me that I'll soon be unconscious.

"Oh, no you don't," Henri says. He pulls his hand away, stands, towering over me again. The pain stops, but I am hollow. A husk of myself. I lack something precious, something core to who I am, an essence stripped from me.

"Poor little blocker has nothing to say?" he asks under his breath. "You don't belong here. Go slither back to your flea-ridden container."

He leans down and presses his hand to my chest again. The pain is less severe this time, but scarier. My eyes blink closed and I cannot open them. The hollers nearby lack character and intensity. Is he Tollere? The world fades away into a black abyss of tortured emptiness.

"Wake up," Miles's disembodied voice says. He shakes my shoulder and I blink my sticky eyes open. He kneels over me, patting me down. "What happened?"

"Henri," I rasp, unable to say more. Miles helps me sit up. Every fiber of my body aches. As memories flood back into me, I panic and turn my head from side to side, looking for Henri. For his hand. I regret the motion immediately. I want to vomit.

"Here, eat this," Miles says, offering me a nano-bar. Halfway to Barfsville, I don't feel like eating anything. I push it away. He unwraps the package and places it in my hand. I'm too weak to argue and barely strong enough to chew on the bar.

With a smile, he says, "We beat them. Got their flag." A fraction of a smile raises my cheeks. I don't feel like the victor in this head-to-head but imagining Henri's face when he realized he'd lost warms my tired heart. "The group of them was so focused on you in here that Brooks snuck up and snatched it without getting noticed."

"Serves him right," I croak, feeling a smidge stronger after forcing down a few nauseating bites. "He took my–" I don't know what he took. Some key part of me.

"Your nanites. He's done this before. I'll tell Mr. Winston and Dr. Fontein," Miles says. "But Henri receives special considerations, so I doubt anything will come of it. Because he's...you know." I don't know at all, but I nod anyway because the caramel glued my tongue to the top of my mouth.

"Rest up and eat up," Miles says, handing me two of Ms. Abigail's raisin-oatmeal cookies. I should have brought snacks. New rule: always have nano-bars on hand. Standing, Miles says, "We need you back in the game. We're pushing into Argonaut's territory."

Lii's presence returns. *I feel a bit better,* Lii says. *Keep eating. Amend rule fifty-two to include nano-milk.*

"Catch up when you recover," Miles says, then nods and runs off to the next section of the wheel: red. He disappears, weaving silently between the trees like a ninja.

Alone, the memory of Henri's black eyes and excruciating hand occupy the entirety of my thought. So much for not using your abilities to hurt each other. I'll throttle him, make him hurt as much as I did. Make him feel as empty as I do. How did he do that?

A thought returns to my mind; is he Tollere? I hadn't noticed before, but my shirt tore at some point. My ticker pumps faster and my desire for revenge doubles at the sight of a red, puffy handprint on my chest. Tollere leaves the mark of a hand upon his victims. My breath hitches, choking me. Did he remove my skills? Will I be left, a norm, destined to return to the blocks?

Lii? Nothing. He has been so good since we arrived at Camp Astrid. Did Henri's attack disable him? Will Lii ever come back?

My appetite returns as the first nanites do their job. I devour the oatmeal cookies, craving more. Only weeks ago, I couldn't down more than one. I've already adapted. I rest for about half a minute more, then slowly rise to my feet, joints grinding and muscles straining. I take a few steps, and some of the kinks work themselves out. After a few more staggering paces, I feel a skosh better. Not good, but better.

I set off at a slow walk, not capable of anything faster, but resolved to stay in the game if for no other reason than to irk Henri. By the time I reach the red zone, my body hurts less, but my strength has waned again. If only I had nano-milk.

Not seeing Miles or the others, I walk as stealthily as my infirm muscles will allow, avoiding sticks and trying to stay on game trails. An Argonaut approaches and I duck behind a giant mossy log. I prepare to run as he clomps forward on heavy feet. My chest hurts with every heartbeat and he continues on his way.

I lean against the wet fallen tree for a minute, letting my body rest before slinking farther into red territory. I take it slow and easy, trying to reserve my strength in case I need to run for it. Where are my cabinmates? Then I spot Joseph, sitting on the ground, a sour look firmly planted on his face. An Argonaut stands nearby, protecting his prisoner of war. I may not be useful in my current state, but if I can tag him, he will be back in the game. It is a good trade.

Summoning as much strength as I can, I run full out to Joseph, only to trip over a set of vines a few feet away. I tumble into an uncontrolled roll and slide on the thick layer of forest floor smack-dab into Joseph. He immediately stands and creates a twister between us and his guard. He isn't hurting anyone, but someone would be nuts to walk into that, with branches and dirt sucked up into the vortex.

He pulls me to my feet and runs off, but I'm all out of juice. Empty. Useless.

I slump to my backside, panting from exertion and pain. The tornado dissipates as Joseph speeds between the trees. The Argonaut with shaggy brown hair and a bland face tags me easily. I don't put up a fight against gravity as it pulls me into a lying position. I find myself looking straight up at the towering trees and clear blue skies above, not caring a nanite's backside about my state, only concerned that Henri will find me again.

If I can ever control my abilities again, I'll teleport him into the Mojave desert. Shortly, a whistle blows twice and the red around me turns to yellow. My team got another flag.

"Here," the Argonaut says. His features are utterly forgettable. He could blend into any mix of uppers and never be noticed. "Take this." He hands me three granola bars. I don't have enough strength left to eat.

Holding his hand out, he asks, "May I?" Before I can answer, he places his hand on my shoulder. I prepare for another bout of torment, sure that this round will end me. I try to roll out of the way, but I'm too slow. Instead of torture, vitality flows into me, filling me with calm and peace.

He is a nano-medic, Lii says, his existence returning to me for the first time since Henri's palm touched my chest.

"Mazz, technically I'm not supposed to do this, but I figure you won't tell." He smiles genuinely, a sense of understanding and compassion molding his features.

"Thanks, uh…" I wish I knew his name.

"Devin," he and Lii fill in the blank simultaneously. "I hope you win. We blockers need to stick together." What? I glance at his neck, something I haven't bothered with since I arrived, and sure enough, his neck sports the two marks of a blocker. He doesn't look like a blocker, full cheeks, meat on his bones, and clear-eyed. He isn't dressed like one either. He looks the part of a combat medic, a white cross on a red band around his bicep. "Go, show them what we're made of."

I'm surprised at how strong I feel as he pulls me to my feet. Not complete, but well enough to get back in the game. "Thanks, Devin."

He nods as if to say, "Get going."

"Thanks." I nod back, hoping that he understands how much I appreciate him. The comradery fills me with as much vitality as his healing touch. I'm not alone. I wave and run toward purple territory, Starry Skies's domain, a girl's cabin if I'm correct. Entering purple's borders, I try to balance speed with silence. I want to bound forward as fast as I can but need to look for signs of the defenders and the flag.

Someone shouts out to my right. I run in that direction, hoping that the noise will guide me to the flag or maybe a tagged teammate that I can release from purgatory. Off in the distance, another double whistle cries its shrill note, meaning that another territory has fallen. I come to the edge of the clearing, skipping from tree to tree for cover. Thirteen cement pillars stick out of the ground and the purple flag hangs from a piece of rusted rebar atop the center one. Four Starry Skyers surround Miles and Brooks who sit at the pillar's base.

A slender gal of Asian descent with her blue hair up in a ponytail zips around so fast I can barely see her.

Nano-celitas–speed, Lii says.

I can't do this the old-fashioned way. She'd catch me so fast I wouldn't know what hit me. What can I do? If only I could summon the flag kinetically, I'd be able to stay hidden. If I could phase, unphase, grab it, then phase again it would be perfect. Nobody could touch me. But if don't want to see what would happen if I messed up the phase.

So teleportation it is. I exhale and scrunch up, hoping I can pull this off quickly. I rematerialize next to the pillar and tag my cabinmates. Brooks holds out his hands and releases an atomic-bomb level shriek at the pitch of squeaky brakes on a blocker bus. The sound forms some kind of shield around us. I barely manage to think past the wailing onslaught to my ears. Relying on my plan and instincts, I jump up and snatch the purple flag.

Without turning around, I port back to my hiding place, abandoning my teammates. I run as fast as I can without sounding like a tank. I hotfoot it between trees, leap over a puddle, duck under branches. I'm home free. Yellow territory is close enough to taste.

Then it hits me. Not a physical blow, but a mental one. Similar to Bethany, but different in the way voices are easily distinguishable. I come to a full stop in front of Ing. She is the most beautiful woman I've ever seen, glowing in golden light like a goddess. Spectacular. Her ebony skin has a perfect sheen, eyes large and lined flawlessly with long lashes, dressed in the most perfectly fitted sequined gown. Love. I will do anything for her.

"Here. Take my flag," I say, my voice distant and my hand holding the red token of my love. "You are my one and only purpose for living."

My yellow territory lies only ten yards away. That color repulses me. I want to gag. She smiles at me sweetly and wordlessly beckons me to carry the flag to her section. I comply, happy to serve.

Then a blur passes me by. It's Joseph I realize too late. He stole my love's treasure. I need to get it back at all costs. I reach out with my mind and summon him, my enemy, kinetically lifting him from the ground as easily as a feather and floating him back to me.

"Let me go!" he screams. "You're not yourself."

I mentally yank the flag from his hands and leave Joseph to dangle three feet off the ground. She lends me unearthly power, sparing godly focus and purpose. Anything for my only reason for existing, Ing, the one whom I would walk to the end of the Earth.

Mazz! Miles yells in my head. *Let! Go!*

Now, two undeniable gods tug at my essence, paralyzing me. On the one hand, Ing, my goddess draws me in with love and promise. On the other, the god of friendship commands loyalty. Any action I take will shatter me like a thin layer of ice over a warm pond. No matter which one wins, I lose. Only in the grasp of both do I have meaning, to serve.

Then my lady's flag is gone. A second later, a whistle blows three times, and my precious deities vanish, replaced by mortals. My sense of belonging to higher powers fades into depression. I am lost without their direction and attention.

"We won!" Miles bounds up to me, screaming in excitement. "We did it!" At my quizzical look, he says, "You dropped Joseph and he ran it home." I didn't win. I lost purpose. I lost love. I lost true friendship. I lost everything. For the second time today, I consider death a release. Once physically injured. Now mentally devastated.

"Sorry, Mazz," the mortal Ing says. While still pretty, she's now dressed in a forest green tank top and comfortably black yoga pants. Her glow is gone. The corners of her eyes downturn in a look of concern. "I didn't realize how susceptible you were."

I slump down, put my head between my knees, wishing I'd never been born. Tears sting my eyes. While I still love her for what she was, I know she doesn't share my feelings. No physical wound could be crueler than what they left me with.

A foreign sense of warm comfort wedges its way into my being, and I yell, "Stop!" I dare for a second to look up at my fallen angel. "Stop fiddling with my insides," I plead. Miles squeezes my shoulder and I brush his hand away. "Leave me alone."

"Okay," Miles says. "Whatever you need."

"I'm so sorry," she says, sounding truly remorseful. I hate to hear the sorrow from her even after what she did to me. I only want her to be happy.

I wipe tears from my eyes, but more spring forth, unbidden and unwanted.

CHAPTER EIGHTEEN

Obstacle Course

Naren, Scarlett, and I sit in the amphitheater stands as others line up to practice on the obstacle course that the counselors assembled overnight. We cheer on the contenders and occasionally laugh when they epically fail. A cluster of campers a few seats down busily wagers on which campers will make it how far. It's almost enough to forget about Ing and Mile's battle over my mind. Almost.

An Argonaut camper, Herald, announces each attempt as a parity of a world championship sporting event. "And Miles Williams steps up to the first obstacle, only to realize that his nose itches," Herald says seriously. "Everyone wants to know; will he resist the urge to scratch mid-course. His influence over itches might mean the difference between success and failure. And here he goes..."

The first time I step up to try my hand at the course, I try teleporting through the first obstacle, only to find myself dangling upside down above a foam pit. "You can't cheat, blocker, " Henri yells above the laughter.

"Rookie mistake," Herald says. "It never gets old."

After lunch, I try another go at the obstacle course and make it to the fourth out of ten obstacles with nothing but balance and reflexes honed by skating. But when I reach the fifth obstacle, I'm completely at a loss. Everyone except those with nano-aquas fails at this obstacle, a water-filled chasm between two landings. Others have tried everything from boldly leaping across to hopping in random directions in hopes that an invisible platform might be out there somewhere.

"This is going nowhere fast," Scarlett says. "We aren't getting enough time on the course to make headway."

"Do you have something in mind?" Naren asks.

Conspiratorially, Scar leans in and asks, "Do you want to sneak back here tonight?"

"Sure," I find myself whispering. I really should stick to rule ten: think before you speak.

"I'm in," Naren says a little louder than I'm comfortable with.

"Midnight," Scarlett says with a wry smile and a twinkle to her luminous green eyes.

Shortly before midnight, Lii blares an annoying tone inside my head. With Naren, I slink outside into the cold night's air. Along the path, we see someone's black silhouette in front of us, moonlight illuminating a slight female figure the size of Scarlett walking toward the amphitheater. She walks slowly, keeping a quiet foot.

We sneak up silently until I can recognize her. "Hey, Scar," I whisper, concerned that my voice will carry to a counselor's cabin dispersed around camp.

Even in the dark, she visibly jumps, spinning on the spot. She holds her hands out in front of her, looking like a predator prepared to pounce. "You scared the crap out of me," she curses quietly. As I near, she gently punches me on the shoulder, as much a push as a thump. "I nearly had a heart attack."

"Sorry," I say, pleased and apologetic at the same time. Laughter wins out, resulting in another push-shove. This proves that my stealthy strides are getting better.

"Let's go," she says pulling my hand forward. Her fingers are warm and soft, stirring a sensation similar to how I felt about Ing. How do I feel about Laticia? Then her palm slips from mine and I can't tell if it was ever there.

When we arrive at the amphitheater, I'm thrilled that the lights are on, shining down on the obstacle course. This won't be as easy as during the full light of day, but beggars can't be picky. You get what you get and you don't give a sh..."

The obstacle course isn't easy, and if I were any shorter, I'd have a much harder time at the hurdles. If Laticia was right, I've gained an extra inch or two, placing me in the optimal size for competition: tall enough to reach each challenge and skinny enough to launch myself nimbly.

For no apparent reason, Scar pushes me forward to be first. The first four challenges are easy. The fifth challenge is too long of a span for me to leap over in a single go. A few feet below, a dark shoulder-depth pool reflects the starlight with every ripple, portending the punishment of my inevitable failure. It will chill my thin blocker body to the bones in no time and doubly so when I get out.

"Try levitating a disk of water and skip off it like a stone," Scarlett suggests a little louder than I feel comfortable with given that we're not supposed to be out of our cabins. Her whisper carries through the amphitheater, magnified by the perfect acoustic design of the ancients. "And don't worry," she says, "I'll dry you off if you take a plunge."

Right. Nano-aquas. And, what's this "if" stuff? It's "when."

Way to be positive, Lii says.

"Thanks," I say, imagining my epic fail. Drawing on my nano-kinetics, I tug some water as if it is a stone. I know I can lift larger objects because of the welding accident and when I was possessed by Ing, but never intentionally.

On my first attempt, water spills over the sides of the "disk", uselessly flowing back into the pool. On my fourth try, I manage to levitate a funky-shaped globule of water to the height of the platform. I might have to spend all night working to get this right, and don't want to keep Naren and Scar waiting any longer than necessary. They need practice too.

I back up as far as I can on the platform, which is much too short to get up a good steam, still concentrating on my liquid disk. I sprint two quick steps forward and spring to the hovering water blob. Split between the effort of levitating the blob and leaping, I slip at the platform's edge and the giant droplet falls. I meet the shin-sized teardrop, but with my face rather than my foot, immediately followed by a belly flop into the pool.

I sputter my way out of the pool, the frigid water motivating me to move as fast as I can. True to her word, seconds later my skin and clothes are dry again. "Thanks," I say.

"It's just as much for me as you," she says. "You stink less this way." She screws her face and I can't help but laugh along with her and Naren.

I smell my armpit and pretend to wince. "I guess I'll have to fall in a few more times."

Scar steps up to the course. She proves to be stronger, but less agile than me, easily overcoming the first four challenges. Unlike me, she forms a set of flat-topped liquid toad-stools and effortlessly walks across. If only I had that type of control. The sixth challenge launches pressure-sensitive beanbags in a complicated pattern, forcing the contestant to dodge, duck, shimmy, and weave. A single hit means you're out. She fails right out of the gate, running headlong into a pair of beanbags.

After a few curt curses from Scarlett, Naren takes up the first position. He is much slower and far less coordinated than Scar, taking his time with each obstacle. At this rate, we'll be here all night. When Naren gets to the pool challenge, a billowing wind rises up under him. He holds out his jacket by the pockets and it fills with air like a hang-glider on an updraft. He leaps and soars across the expanse faster than a falcon, but smacks into the other side like a crash test dummy. Definitely worse for the wear, he bows out of the sixth challenge in favor of watching us run the course several more times.

By my fourth attempt, I can manage a decent disk, but can't get enough spring from the water to reach the far side. I'm shivering, too much to have another go even with Scarlett's best efforts. While I'm pretty sure Scarlett could run the course many more times, I'm caput. "Let's call it a night."

We walk back in silence, attempting to stay under the radar in case any counselors are out and about. It takes me too long to hear a male voice from ahead. No. Two voices. One the unmistakably Mr. von Steiner's and the other familiar enough that I should know who it is, but made harsh with quiet anger so I can't place it.

Holding my hand out to stop Scar and Naren, I crouch down and motion for them to do the same. As one, we dodge off the path, Naren the quietest and Scarlett the noisiest. "What are they saying?" Scarlett asks barely louder than a breath.

"I have no clue," Naren says.

I don't know why, but I inch closer, careful not to step on sticks or trip on ferns, scurrying from the shadows of one tree to the next. Von Steiner's nasally voice carries through the forest loud enough to be heard, but not understood. His pour victim isn't more than a whisper. After slipping two trees closer, then behind the waist-high remains of a brick wall, I can make out von Steiner's words. "Go ahead." He speaks with his usual blend of condescension and contempt.

The other voice hisses something too quiet to make out.

"I'll have no choice," von Steiner snaps. He sounds like he might devour his prey. I raise my head above the wall to get a glimpse. Why is this so important to me?

Lii's annoyance with me presses against my mind. *We should follow rule nine: Don't chase trouble.* I ignore him. A brick falls from the wall. Both shaded figures turn in my direction as I duck back into the embrace of darkness.

"What was that?" von Steiner asks. A large owl takes flight with a "hoo" as if to help me out, but more probably because I startled it. I breathe slowly in and out to calm my nerves the way Mr. Braunwyn always says.

After an excruciating pause, von Steiner says, "I warn you." Apparently, the conversation is over because the sound of heavy footsteps fades into the distance. Is it possible to identify someone by the rhythm of their footsteps?

Not likely, Lii says.

Listening to those footsteps, I almost miss the much quieter feet walking toward me. At the last second, I hear von Steiner wolf-like sniffing. My heart rate goes through the roof and I, bounce away faster than a rocket full of monkeys. Bam! I wince as my head hits my bunk. I need to leave a pillow at the top of my bed.

"Huh?" Justin stirs in the bunk next to mine.

"Sorry," I whisper. "I, uh, have to go to the bathroom."

"Uh-huh," Justin groans and rolls over.

Naren! Scarlett! I left them behind. Did von Steiner sniff them out? I can't get back to them without getting caught. I'll have to wait for Naren to know whether he got away or not. I step into the cold and squat in the shadows. After a few minutes of shivering, von Steiner walks past alone. Naren and Scar didn't get caught. My anxiety doesn't fully abate until Naren walks up to Steadfast Corner so silently that he's only feet away before I make him out.

"Thank the nanites," I whisper and hold out my fist for a bump.

"I thought you were a goner," he says, softly bumping my fist and shaking my shoulder.

"Sorry I couldn't jump back to you."

"No worries, my friend. It was dicey there for a moment. Von Steiner was almost upon us, but something distracted him and we got away. In the end, it was a pleasant evening for a stroll." I tilt my head, perplexed by his perpetually happy mood. I can imagine the funny crinkle of his nose as he smiles.

"How about Scar?"

"Once we lost von Steiner, we split up," Naren says. "She will be just fine." Relieved, I tell him about the one side of the conversation that I overheard.

"So what?" Naren says. "Who doesn't von Steiner threaten."

"I don't know. There's something…"

Naren shakes his head and says, "Your gut instincts aren't enough to keep me from sleep. We have morning meditation in four hours."

"Ughhh," I groan. Morning meditation. With a shared nod, we sneak into Steadfast Corner, slip into our bunks, and attempt to fall asleep, me failing for some time, the engines in my brain overcoming the exhaustion of my body.

CHAPTER NINETEEN

The Challenge

After my third week of intense back-to-back tracks, I'm thrilled to have another weekend break, especially two days off of morning meditation. Now, lazily crunching on extra-crispy bacon, after sleeping in for a few hours, I'm taking great pleasure in doing absolutely nothing.

I fight back a stabbing memory of losing my deities, Ing and Miles. The empty place within me seems at once unidentifiable and entirely tangible. I try not to hold it against them, but feelings don't always match logic. Bethany explained that, while unconscionable, they never could have predicted what a deep-rooted trauma it would cause.

I close my eyes and focus on my bacon. Mr. Braunwyn should use bacon to help with meditation. It would be a lot easier to focus on inner happiness. "What's yours?" Justin asks, breaking into my moment of food-induced trance. He holds a three-by-five note in one hand and a half-eaten sausage in the other.

"My what?" I ask before seeing a similar note in front of me.

"Earth to Mazz. What's your challenge? On your note..." He shakes his note as if I've been smacked between the eyes by the dumb fairy.

Turning over the note, I read a single line.

Teleport Steadfast Corner.

"Ha!" I laugh. "That'll be the day."

"Don't worry," Miles says, peeking over my shoulder. "They don't give you challenges unless they think you can handle them." Despite the reassurance, I couldn't imagine a reality in which I could teleport a whole cabin, complex and interconnected, heavy and voluminous, especially on purpose. I'd be more likely to phase the ground below us and collapse the cabin in on itself with everyone still inside.

"What did you get?" I ask Justin, not wanting to focus on the impossible this fine day. Don't let it get you down, I told myself.

Justin stuffs his mouth full of cinnamon bun and says, "They want me to summon a lightning bolt out of the sky. As if that's safe." He imitates someone getting electrocuted until he coughs on his food and the contents of his mouth fly out of his mouth and land on the table. Everyone nearby laughs at his expense, but he doesn't seem to mind.

"It suits you perfectly though," Miles says and makes a "zz-zz" sound. "Weather and electricity."

Swallowing before he speaks this time, Justin says, "It's also a perfect way to die." Then, he asks Naren about his challenge.

"I have to create a golem," Naren says happily. He tilts his head, looking at his card again in the strangest combination of joy and concern. "They can't expect me to make a stone creature sentient, can they?"

Miles shakes his head, dispelling any fears with his confidence. "Nah. I'm sure they mean a human-like bundle of rocks that you control. You don't have the gadgetry skills to infuse one with an AI of its own."

"That's awesome!" I say, holding out a fist to bump. My cheeks rise as I imagine a giant rock man smashing Henri and Pyro like caterpillars under a kids foot. Naren shrugs his shoulders and smiles back, calm and content as ever, unaware of the dark nature under which I found pleasure.

My cabinmates continue talking about their challenges and ways to overcome them while I drift back into a bacon-induced stupor. Contemplating my challenge can wait for another day.

Today, we'll visit Emerald Lake. This time, I'll go in the easy way.

◆ ◆ ◆

"Naren," I say as we lounge on the sunbaked rocks above Emerald Lake. "Why don't elite campers or alumni or parents give away Camp Astrid's location?"

"I believe that some try but cannot. I think it has something to do with Mr. Roberto, the nano-pathy counselor. I think he does something to our minds that makes it impossible to remember if we try to tell someone who means harm to campers."

"Really? I can't believe it. If parents knew, they would never let the counselors mess with our minds."

Naren shakes his head, still looking up at a cottony pillow in the sky. "You have it wrong, my friend. They wouldn't let us come if Mr. Roberto didn't mess with our memories. It wouldn't be safe. Besides, you wouldn't know if you could or could not until you tried, in which case, screw whoever tries. It's a minor price to pay for safety."

"So they messed with everyone's minds?" I guess I isn't only me that they mess with. It's all of us. I don't enjoy the idea any more because I'm among company. The more I know about them messing with my gray matter, the more it bothers me. It makes me question how many more times they've tinkered with our perception without us knowing.

I can't figure that out either, Lii says. *I suspect it is more than anyone knows.*

This train of thought flushes out a thought. Is this a cult? Are we the bad guys, trained by evil "counselors," a generation of nanos taught to fear the good guys? Nah. I can't believe that. Though I'll watch for any evidence that suggests that I've been recruited to the wrong side.

"That is what Mother said but I doubt she really knows. Besides, I doubt Dr. Fontein would invite anyone who would give us up like that."

CHAPTER TWENTY

Traitor

A few midnights later, I don't feel much like tackling the sixth obstacle. Since I figured out how to levitate a thin disk of water and three-sixty mid-jump like a skipping stone, I can now skim across obstacle five, but not without a wet sneaker.

"Have you made any progress on your teleportation challenge?" Scar asks.

"Not nearly enough," I say, exhausted from the day's intensive schedule. "There's no way I'll ever manage my challenge. A cabin is too big and too complex. How about you?"

She shrugs. "Mine's easy but boring. The nano-terrans dig the moats at the gates faster than I can fill them with water. I stopped going to the nano-aquas track so I have enough time."

"You got this!" Scar whisper-yells as Naren jumps across the pool, lifted by air. He lands unsteadily on the far platform. "Did you see that? I can fly!" It didn't look much like flying. Flailing describes his wind maneuver better, but what he doesn't know won't kill him. On the sixth obstacle, he doesn't make a full step before getting pelted.

The three of us climb the amphitheater stairs and walk silently back to our cabins, sure to be careful after that encounter with von Sketchy. Overhead, the constellations are hard to spot through the innumerable sea of glittering stars in the Milky Way. The tales of Greek gods, fables, and magical items littering the stars were fascinating to me when I was younger. Gods. Ing and Miles flash into my head. Once again, I descend into a downward spiral. When will this feeling go away? Or will it haunt me for the rest of my life?

"What's that?" Scarlett whispers, stopping me short both mentally and physically.

"Wha?" I ask.

"Shhhh," she admonishes me. "Listen. That." Scarlett points behind us, but I don't hear anything. She waves me and Naren off the path into the darkness, away from the moonlight.

Whoever it is, appears to be talking to himself. It's the same voice I heard the other night, though with less anger. "–It's worth it. It's a transaction, that's all. Nothing more." Then he is past us and I can't make out his words.

"Let's follow," I whisper, not sure why I feel compelled to pursue. If that's a counselor, we should avoid him, not spy on him.

Rule nine, Lii says peevishly. *Don't chase trouble.*

"I don't know about this," Naren says. For the first time, his ceaseless smile fades, worry lines accentuated by the moonlight.

"Stay here if you want," I hear myself say and turn to the path, continuing on as quietly as I can. The sound of Naren and Scar following barely reaches my ears. The man keeps muttering. I wish I could get closer. Pop.

Without meaning to, I teleport. Where am I? Good. Outside my cabin. I dash into the dark shadows of a tree near the path, waiting for the man to pass again.

A moment later, the man's heavy footsteps approach along with his muffled voice. "–angry. They don't appreciate what they have. For Della and Duncan. The choice is obvious. And their ungrateful attitudes make it so much easier." Daring to peek, I see a man in a bulky black jacket with a hooded drawn up. Damn it. Without that hood, I'd see who it is. He passes by again and my opportunity to hear more has come and gone.

A moment later, Scarlett and Naren catch up. Lii helps me recite his words to them. "Let's keep following."

"Why?" Naren asks, shadows pulling at his downturned eyes.

I agree with Naren, Lii says. *Stop chasing trouble.*

"I'm getting sketchy vibes."

Scar nods. "Me too. And we'd lose him before we could warn a counselor."

Naren shrugs and says, "Okay, but if we get in trouble, it's your fault."

We walk to Northgate following the muttering man through a propped-open door. With a shared look of trepidation, we nod at each other and soft-toe it through the darkness under the tall gate.

We follow the noisy clomping and muttering voice of the dark figure as he walks north along a well-worn path, the one we walked to capture the flag. It meanders through ruins and tall Douglas firs, then fields of tall grass. Each time we reach a clearing, the three of us fall back to hide in the forest and then press forward to catch up once he's in the woods again.

While we can't understand him, his constant muttering makes it easy to follow and masks our quiet feet. After a quarter-hour of walking, the grumbling man stops in the middle of a field. For a moment, I think he spotted us, but he paces back and forth, then kicks at the dirt, frequently turning this way and that. We duck behind a rusted automobile carcass.

"Is that Stonehenge?" Naren asks, pointing into the distance.

"Yes," Scarlett says. I can barely make out the column and capstones above the crater's edge. After shivering in the cold for a moment, she asks, "What's he waiting for?"

"No idea," I say. "But he seems nervous, which means we were right to come."

Seven minutes later, headlights beam through the forest accompanied by the heavy cracking of branches and the high-pitched whine of a powerful electric engine. A large black SUV drives into the field shining floodlights on the hooded figure. Backlit as he is, we can't see anything but a silhouette.

Two figures in shiny armor hop out of the SUV, look around, point rifles around, then approach the hooded figure.

At barely a whisper, I say, "Holy crap. They're shockknights." My words hit home in the way that my thoughts hadn't as if the vibration of my hushed voice transformed the notion into physical reality. My mouth dries. My throat constricts. Fear and anger mix together, a billowy tempest.

Against the backlighting from the SUV lights, it is impossible to identify either of their faces, but their armor glints different colors. Their profiles suggest a slightly female figure in green and a reddishness to a male.

"How do you know?" Scarlett asks, not so much questioning my certainty as curious about how I know.

I think of holding my lips. I could say it's just a hunch. A covert meeting in the middle of the night. As promised to Dr. Fontein, I kept the secret of my encounter with Mariotto this long. Why break my word now? Because those *are* shockknights, and my friends have a right to know.

It's like with Laticia before camp, Lii says. *They deserve to know.*

Listening to Lii, I cave and tell them an abbreviated version of my short brush with death followed by what Dr. Fontein said. "That's the same shiny armor and the same SUV."

"We should go back," Naren says, his whisper carrying a tone of uncharacteristic worry.

He's right, Lii says. I recognize how dangerous this is, and almost agree with Naren but this is too important to walk away from. Someone from camp is meeting with shockknights. We need to uncover as much info as possible before heading back.

If only I had control over my skills. I'd be able to do something. Kinetically crush them or something. What Bender or Ms. Merryweather would do to them...

Can we make a new rule? Lii asks. *Don't bring your malfunctioning nano-influence to a gunfight.*

"I wish I could hear them," Scarlett whispers, mirroring my own thoughts. The urge to teleport closer nearly pulls my stomach inward, but I manage to push it back. At least I have that much control now.

"I wish we could go," Naren says. I'm annoyed. He's all smiles, but when it comes to something truly important, he crumbles under fear. Scarlett, on the other hand, grinds her teeth and scowls like she might rip them apart.

The hooded man gives something long and skinny to the woman knight, who gives him something small in return. "That was this year's wonkit," Scarlett whispers sharply. The peculiar phasing device switched from being an oddity to a secret weapon. Within a minute, the exchange is over, and the knights return to their SUV. It rumbles out of the meadow, red taillights disappearing into the forest.

"Traitor," Scarlett says, anger seething through her hushed voice. "How could he?" My thoughts exactly. Moments later, the double-crosser passes by. If I knew what kind of skills he has, I'd take him down right now. Every counselor must have abilities well beyond the three of us. I can't put Scar or Naren at risk.

If he had one wonkit, Lii says, sounding like a scholar, *he may have more, and who knows how dangerous some might be. A lightning hammer? A glove of fire? An amulet of nanite-disruption?*

Lii, you know how much I hate it when you're right. So, we follow him back to camp, wordless. How I want to strategize a foolproof plan to capture him. He no longer mutters to himself, so we stay farther back in order to stay hidden from view and hearing. I couldn't have found our way back in the daylight, not to mention in the dark, so we need the traitor to lead us back to camp.

A thick fog sweeps in, obscuring our view and canceling our ability to trail him. The combination of mist and moonlight creeps me out. The ruins don't make the situation any less spooky. Sinister questions burn holes in my mind. Why would anyone work with the shockknights? For what possible reason could a nano turn on their own kind? What if he doubles back and ambushes us? What did the knight give him? A map?

It could have been anything, Lii says. *Possibly, instructions on their next rendezvous. A weapon? Names of campers they want?*

We hang farther back as the Northgate's towers of loom tall into the sky and count out a minute from when the traitor steps through the gate. Naren pulls at the door, but it doesn't give. He tries pushing instead. Nothing. He jiggles the foot-long handle until it starts making noise. "Shhhh," I hiss. "Von Steiner will hear us." I don't need to say how much pleasure he'd take in lugging us to Dr. Fontein.

"We're locked out," Naren says. For someone whose face constantly shines with joy, he sure turned a corner into Worriedville. I suppose his distress warrants merit. His worry lines mirror my state of mind.

"Not to worry," Scarlett says before I have time to do just that. "Mazz, teleport to the other side and let us in."

"I don't know if I can." Bender and I haven't covered teleporting to somewhere I can't see. Yet, I have teleported to my bunk a dozen times.

You never did it on purpose, Lii points out.

"Okay," I say, not feeling at all okay. It's our only and best bet. "I can do this," I say. I repeat it several times in an attempt to build false confidence. Rule twenty-nine: fake it until you make it.

With the billion angry and worried thoughts rampaging through my mind, I'm already in the right state of mind for the jump. Pop. I want to vomit as I push my way through a tiny hole, then almost shout out in triumph when my head knocks into my bunk. Damn! I thought I left my pillow over that board. I Hop out of bed and give my usual refrain of going to the bathroom, then sprint back to Northgate. After a minute of fumbling in the pitch black under the towers, I unlock the door and let them in.

We slink to Steadfast corner and away from von Steiner before we halt to whisper. Scarlett says, "We lost him." I hate to agree, but she's right. He could be anywhere inside the walls by now, thigh I suspect he returned to Eagle's Nest.

Don't let your grudges lead you astray, Lii says, sounding like a disappointed teacher.

"My gut says it's Pyro or Henri."

Your gut is biased.

"It could be anyone," Scar says. "Even a little girl with nano-lumus skills or a wonkit. It would be the perfect cover."

My gut was right about following him tonight. I let the matter drop, sensing that Scarlett and Lii's logic won't budge with a feeling in my digestive system.

"Want me to walk you back to your cabin?" I ask, not liking the idea of her wandering camp alone with a traitor in our midst.

"Because I'm a girl?" she snaps, still quiet, but no less venomous. "Not a chance." Her hand goes to her hip in a "don't mess with me" pose.

Naren says, "We'll talk about this tomorrow, okay? There's nothing we can do tonight."

A half-hour later, after replaying the night's events in my head in a continuous loop, the last thought in my mind is that tomorrow morning's meditation is gonna hurt.

"Mazz," Bethany says after a particularly lackluster morning meditation dulled by the cold bite of the heavy fog. Over the last couple of days, Mr. Braunwyn has been half short of a one-eighty nose kick, though it's probably because he never shined with any luster to begin with. "May I have a word?" she says with a smile, but her tone and mental push tell me that I'm in trouble.

"Uh, yeah?" My chin lowers, my neck pulls back, and my face contorts in a "What the?" look.

Follow me, she says. *And think about your comics until I say otherwise.* Her frothing emotions splash through me like flesh-eating acid. I can't imagine what I did to her, but I wouldn't be the first guy to miss the subtleties of a female mind. Rule thirteen: don't try to understand the complexities of the fairer gender. Naren follows us, and I half expect her to cuss him out, but she doesn't. Only twenty yards from the gates, she opens the door to her cabin, Wagon Wheels, and ushers us in.

Scarlett's cabin too, Lii reminds me. For some reason, Lii's comment makes me nervous. It feels different from Steadfast Corner but is surprisingly similar. Perhaps a bit more colorful and the walls are straiter but basically the same.

Instead of her cabinmates, I find Penny, Miles, and Scarlett. Rounding upon me, she yells, "You're an idiot, Mazz! You followed a stranger out of camp?"

"Uh," I stammer.

"Don't you dare deny it. I spent the last half hour trying not to blow my lid. Your thoughts are as transparent as, as, as some transparent thing. You see how mad I am?"

"But I–"

"And what if the shockknights caught you?" Her arms are talking, matching her words' and telepathic fury. By they, she means Scar and Naren.

"They didn't–"

"But they could have!" she yells at me.

"But they–"

"You are in so! Much! Trouble! I don't even…" She shakes her head like Mom does when anger boils over the edges of her emotional pot.

She can read your thoughts, Miles says. *I wouldn't make any more comparisons to your mom if I were you.* I constantly forget that Miles has pathic skills, especially around Bethany.

"We have to tell Dr. F about this, you know?" Her hand goes to her hip like my–very awesome friend who will give me a pass this time. She smiles despite herself.

"It was stupid, you know," Miles says seriously. "It's one thing to come upon one shockknight by accident, but to walk into a covert meeting is something else entirely. You need to be more careful."

"Do we really need to go to Fontein with this?" I ask. The idea of her piercing eyes and immense well of power directed at me makes me squirm.

"Yes," Miles, Penny, and Bethany say in unison. Bethany adds her telepathic double-speak for emphasis.

"Look," Miles says. "Nothing gets past Dr. Fontein. She's like Bethany. She'll sense your thoughts. And so will half the other nano-paths in camp."

"So, what do I do then?"

"Go to her right now, and confess everything," Bethany says. "She'll deal with it. I'll take you myself and block your mind from eavesdropping as we go."

A knock raps at the door. "May I come in?" says Dr. F, her resonant Afrikaans voice unmistakable even through the door. Without waiting for an answer, the door props open. "I hope I'm not interrupting your pre-breakfast tea party."

"Uh," several of us say at once.

"I overheard some rather enthusiastic conversation and decided to investigate. I assume you understand."

"So, you know," Penny says. Of course, she knows. She nods. "Good. It's done."

"So it is," she says sadly. Turning to me, she says, "I cannot allow your memories to spread like wildfire through my camp."

She's gonna do the encryption thing again. Everyone messes with my mind without consent. I'm not a reprogrammed robot. I still suffer daily from what Miles and Ing did to me.

Unfortunately, I have to, Dr. Fontein says. *Until you learn to block your thoughts from others or learn to stay out of trouble, we may need to do this from time to time. I hate to do it, but...*

Her warm but calculating presence probes my brain and the memories of last night flash through my mind at agro-speed. Then they drop from the forefront of my attention. "All done." I think back to last night, and the thoughts appear, categorized and clearer than I could normally conjure them. But as soon as I think about how embarrassing it is to have Dr. Fontein privy to my thoughts, the memories cut away.

"What about the traitor?" Penny asks, red eyebrows

furrowing her freckled forehead.

"Not for any of you to worry about. I have it well under control."

How true can that be with a traitor in our midst?

Not for you to fret over, Fontein says with the addition of her seemingly bottomless well of power carrying her message to the core of me. She fixes me with a stare that practically hurts.

Yes, ma'am, I mentally say, though I'm not sure I can stop fretting about something like this.

And don't think that Henri's hand incident went unnoticed or unpunished. If you didn't notice, everyone knows what he did thanks to your leaky mind. Almost everyone stays clear of him now. The news even spread to the adult upper and pinnacle nanos. This bit of news is nearly enough to make me smile.

"Well," Dr. Fontein says, a smile creasing her cheeks. A stack of Ms. Abigail's cinnamon rolls appears in her hands. She hands them out, keeping one for herself. Mmmmm, they're still warm and gooey. "I'll be off. Do try to stay out of trouble, won't you?"

Once the door closes behind her, an uncomfortable silence sets in. Penny breaks the silence. "The traitor is a double agent. That's the only explanation for Fontein's reaction." I want to argue, but I'm thinking of creating a rule about never arguing with a nano-hacker. They're too bright.

Good call, Lii says, groaning in pleasure at the nanites in the roll. We sit in silence again. I need time to digest her statement. The cinnamon bun in my mouth gives me time to do just that.

"So," Miles says, breaking through the awkwardness that settled over us. "Now that you know that we know about your midnight outings, we're gonna join you at the obstacle course tonight. I want to see your progress."

Standing in the amphitheater next to the obstacle course, Miles says, "Let's see your skills." The glimmer in his eyes shows a deep-seated eagerness to celebrate our successes not degrade us for our shortcomings. Part of me struggles to hold a grudge against him for what he did to me, but his persistently kind behavior makes it difficult.

Without discussion, it is clear that I'm up first. I don't know why, but we all know it to be true. Bethany's influence? I breeze past the first few obstacles. The cabin leaders cheer me on, unconcerned about making too much noise. I use my water-disk maneuver to get across the pool.

"Great use of kinetics," Miles hollers. Bethany gives me a whoop, whoop.

Now comes the hard stuff. I haven't traversed more than two-thirds the way across the beanbag shooters yet. I can't outmaneuver the bags no matter which combination of stopping, ducking, or running I choose. The projectiles account for my shifting strategies and home in on me. Scar and Naren remain equally frustrated by the unbeatable barrage.

It was one thing failing in front of Naren and Scarlett. It will be much more embarrassing failing in front of the cabin leaders. Scar, Naren, and I are peers, even if they wield their skills with far more control. I decide on a strategy: an all-out run with a high jump in the middle and a slide at the end, sure the bags will shoot me down, but my speed might win out. Here goes nothing. One. Two. Three.

I sprint, holding my arm out to protect my face from being hit. I don't mind the body shots, but the face hurts. By mid-obstacle, I'm surprised that I haven't been hit. I leap over two projectiles. Without losing my momentum, I keep running, my arm still shielding my face. Then my foot catches. I hit the floor hard and keep sliding.

"Way to go Mazz!" Miles yells. To my surprise, I slide all the way through the onslaught. I didn't get hit once.

"Cheater!" Penny yells.

Cheater? What?

The bags disappeared before they hit you, Bethany says.

Really? They did?

Yeah, she says in that tone reserved for complete morons. *You phased them.*

Sweet. I mean. Of course, I did. Hehehe. Okay. Now what? I never thought through the next obstacle, a series of swinging foam swords guarding a meandering line of sturdy lily pads above a foam pit. At least it's not the freezing water. Impossible. It reminds me of an overly complicated tunnel needed for a hero to reach a self-destruction button on a starship. Completely unnecessary and unbeatable in real life.

Way to stay positive, Lii says. *Great motivational speech.*

How now brown cow? Time to wing it.

Your instincts outmatch your brain any day, Bethany says. Was that a compliment or a dig? Possibly both. I suppose she would know after rummaging through my thoughts so many times.

Instincts, I tell myself. Don't overthink it.

I time the first leap to avoid the horizontal head-height basher and maintain my forward momentum to bound off to the near edge of the second pad, where a blue noodle slaps down in the middle of the pad, only inches in front of me. The trailing wind buffets my eyes with damp air. I teeter and bend my knees to keep balance on the lily pad's edge and the foam basher almost hits my flailing hands. I gain a steady footing and step forward between downward swings, the blue club swooshing by too close for comfort.

The next sword swings by at shin height moving fast enough that it looks like a green circle. This is the pad where best daytime contestants fail. It must be possible, but I don't see how. Rely on instinct. I jump off my pad, trying to gain enough height and distance that I can fly over this pad to the next one, I instantly know I've messed up, like an ollie McTwist where I land too far forward on the board.

I land belly down on the pad, something painfully nudging up beneath my sternum. Surprisingly, the basher isn't whooshing overhead, or more importantly, smacking me over and over on the cranium. Laughter and clapping echo in the amphitheater and my cheeks redden.

"Go Mazz!" Miles hollers. I'm belly down on top of the noodle, pinning it in place.

Graceful, Bethany says, wreaking of humorous sarcasm.

Hey, it worked. That's all I care about. I'm still on the pad. I pin it in place with my knee, then my foot. It relies on one of those weak motors that take time to build up speed and force, so it stays put under my sopping shoe.

The next pad has two yellow noodles: one that slaps down and another that swings across at belt height. Only Miles managed to land the yellow pad, with a short stop and an impressive limbo. I suspect he uses a combination of nano-skills to achieve inhuman reflexes. Go with my instincts. I try to bust a Miles, but don't have a tenth of his enhanced reflexes. The next thing I know, I'm in the foam pit. Instincts only carry me so far.

Until you master your skills, they're the best you have. Which isn't bad.

Each of my friends takes a stab at the obstacle course. Naren and Scar get pelted at the bean bag obstacle. Miles makes it past my personal record by two pads, bouncing off the yellow pad and doing a flip to the orange pad before over-rotating and ending up face down in the pit. Bethany falls one pad short of me by what seems like pure determination. Penny's movements are economical as if she planned out the precise measure of muscles needed for each obstacle.

As Naren attracts another round of beanbags on his second run, Miles says, "You guys have some serious skills."

"Did you have any doubt?" Scarlett says with one of those "be careful what you say next" poses. He raises his hands in the universal, "I don't want a fight" stance. Scarlett's face breaks into a smile and she snorts. "Ha! Bethany is so right about you. You're too gullible."

As the echoes of laughter at Miles's expense fade, a seed of thought grows into a strangle-vine, forcing words from my mouth. "Do you think the obstacle course and capture-the-flag were designed to prepare us for a possible shockknights attack?" My words throw dry ice on our collective mood.

"I do," Penny says. She responds so fast and confidently that I have no doubt that she speaks with authoritative truth. "The challenges too. My nano-enabled 'egg launchers'. Bethany's communication hub. Scarlett's moat. Naren's golem. Mazz's teleportation of campers. Each of us plays a key role in a synergistic plan."

My jaws tighten and my neck hairs prickle. Fontein disguised preparation for war as a series of games and personal challenges. Her insistence that we need not worry rings false.

With a conspiratorial look, Bethany says, "Despite what Dr. F says, we should watch Northgate for the traitor." Miles agrees with Bethany instantly. Penny argues that Dr. F has it covered. I want to believe that Penny but fear that Bethany is right. In the end, Bethany's force of will wins over Penny's smarts and we resolve to guard Northgate every night, trading shifts regularly.

If Camp Astrid isn't safe, with its powerful counselors and fortified walls, is there anywhere safe from the shockknights?

In short, Bethany says. *No.*

CHAPTER TWENTY-ONE

War Games

Several nights later, I stand, prepared to walk the fourteen steps back to my cabin after my shift on watch and muse how summer at home isn't that different from this, other than the stench. Apprenticing with Dad comes with nighttime duties. I can't wait to wake Naren and crawl back under my blankets.

There's someone up ahead, Lii says in an uneasy tone that snatches my attention. I teleport behind the stone half-wall on my right and duck. I peek my head over the wall and spy a man so large it can only be Mr. Winston. He pounds on my cabin door and bellows, "Wake up Steadfast! Three-minute drill! Paintball wars." While Fontein trains us for a possible attack with games like paintball wars, Miles trains us for a rapid response with his daily marches. Every night, Camp Astrid appears more like a military school than the night before.

A group of campers tromps up the path toward me. Faex! I gotta get back to my cabinmates before anyone notices I'm gone–especially Mr. Winston, who scares the crap out of me. When Mr. Winston turns back to the path and stops the other group, I teleport to my bunk as easily as tying my shoelaces. I pocket the nano-bars that I stash under my pillow just in case. I should probably carry some with me everywhere I go in case I run into Henri or the traitor, though they may be one and the same.

Within three minutes, we march two-by-two with Miles at the head. Who's going to watch Northgate if Miles, Naren, and I are out playing paintball wars?

Before I mentally say a single word in Bethany's direction, she says, "Don't. Just don't. Miles already filled me in. I don't need you yelling incoherently in my ear too." I funnel my thoughts to the tranquil waters of Emerald Lake. I should have known that Miles had it under control.

The other group walks haphazardly, some alongside us and others stretched out ahead or behind us. I recognize Devin among their group. The Argonauts seem like reasonable guys from what I can tell. If Devin fits in with them, they can't be all bad. Though it would've been fun to put a smackdown on Pyro and especially Henri.

About five minutes later, we arrive at the same spot where we played capture the flag. Or rather, we built a cohesive combat team through a low-stakes nano-enhanced contest. At least this time, they didn't bother to mask it. Mr. Winston didn't call it "paintball match" or "game." This time we fight in a simulated "war."

"The goal today is to "kill" every opponent on the other team," Mr. Winston says, his sonorous voice stern and demanding of order. Simulated killing, not tagging. "The paintballs glow in the dark when fired."

"Steadfast is yellow and will start in the west. Argonauts are red and will start in the east. Here are your guns. You will not fire until the second whistle." Mr. Winston goes over their operation and repeats that we are to keep our fingers off the trigger until we aim to shoot.

"Treat these as true weapons, loaded with real rounds," he continues. There it is. He hands the semi-automatic paintball rifles out. It feels heavy in my hands, like a real gun. In the dim light, it resembles the very real gun that Mariotto pointed at me, complete with a silencer.

This is an exact replica of the one Mariotto pointed at us, Lii says.

I notice a pile of masks resting by Mr. Winston's feet, unused and unmentioned. Shouldn't we have received our masks before handling these? Particularly if he wants us to treat the guns as the real deal.

"To balance out the teams," Mr. Winston says while I review the rifle's operation, "Mazz, is not allowed to teleport."

I crack to attention and almost say, "I didn't do it." My tongue nearly moves of its own will, but I squelch my instinct. This is Camp Astrid. I can follow rules twelve, seven, and twenty-five. I say, "Yes, sir." Mr. Winston is too scary to cross. It still feels unfair, even if the Argonauts are younger and teleportation is a dead useful skill in a game like this.

"No rough stuff," Mr. Winston says menacingly. I'll play fair if they do. I mentally kick myself. This is Devin's team, not Eagle's Nest. "At the second whistle, two minutes from now, the battle will begin." He blows the first shrill note to mark our dismissal.

"Steadfast," Miles calls out. "Fall in." As one, my cabinmates stomp jog, snapping our fingers to make it easier to stay in formation. Exactly one minute later, Miles stops us and calls out names. He divides us into a forward offense and calvary. I'm on the front line again.

Miles hands out tags and sends a program to our AIs. Lii illuminates a yellow dot marking each of us in the dark. Good. No friendly fire.

Miles says, "Now, scatter."

I run off to the south and east, making way too much noise. I practically scalp myself on a low-lying branch and curse before I realize that I gave away my position. Damn! I'm bleeding. Too quickly, the whistle blows, carrying through the woods. The trill reminds me of thrillers where monsters and demons pop out from the shadows.

I run south and eastward. Warmth flows down my forehead

and gunks up my right eye, the eye I use for aiming. I pause behind a tree to wipe it away and blink it away. I pull off my abused Camp Astrid shirt and cinch it to my forehead to keep blood out of my eye. A body shot will hurt more this way, but if I can't shoot with blood in my eye, I'll be a sitting duck. All the more reason to avoid getting hit. The night's air chills my torso and raises goosebumps. My senses sharpen.

I slowly walk east toward the enemy with a concerted effort to step quietly. With any luck, the other team will stomp into me. I take up a strategic position behind a pile of cement rubble and wait in the dark, the smell of sap mixed with the acrid scent of blood filling my nostrils. I never realized how noisy the woods are, creaking in the gentle breeze, ominous, unsettling.

The crack of a stick sounds to my left. Is that normal? Or is someone or something coming? I try to push the image of a demon with horns and a tail stalking me. As quietly as I can, I ready my rifle and point it in the direction of the noise. No yellow dot, meaning one of them. I can't see the Argonaut directly but make out pieces of his silhouette as he moves against the background of filtered moonlight.

I pull the trigger twice fast: double tap. The first paintball flies where I meant it to go, but the second flies wild. The gun kicks like a real one, or as real as the ones I used in sims. While the rifle issues almost no noise, the balls impact with an unexpectedly loud thwack, like a real round. Two yellow splotches glow in the dark, one illuminating the chest of an Argonaut, and the other lighting the tree behind him.

"Umph," the Argonaut collapses on the ground, curled up and hissing. Nobody told me they'd hurt like that. He takes a few breaths, then cups his mouth and yells, "Out!" I hope I don't have to shoot Devin after what he did for me. The still grunting Argonaut sits up and turns to face me.

Why so loud?

It's a clue that we're nearby, Lii says as if I'm an idiot, which I feel like now that he explained it. *And the direction he's turned tells his teammates where we are.*

Clever. With my position blown, I walk, heal first, feeling for branches. The warn-thin soles of my shoes and the new hole at my big toe make it easier to find branches as I prowl slowly, far quieter than the creaking trees and rustle of the breeze through bushes. I maneuver around to the "dead" Argonaut, whose feet still point to where I was rather than where I am.

Good. I take up a position behind another tree with a good vantage of my prior hiding spot. Sure enough, a barely visible enemy walks through the dark woods. I strain to see his silhouette and double tap where I think he is. This time I prepared for the all-too-real rifle's kick. Both shots fly exactly where I aimed, but only serve to illuminate a tall Argonaut when they hit a nearby tree. Damn!

A snap to my side warns of another enemy who snuck up from the other side. Without a thought, I drop the gun to its sling and press out my hands. Four red paintballs explode in bright splatter marks two feet in front of me, glowing on a shimmering glass-like surface. A kinetic shield. How did I do that?

This is not the time to plant our feet and find out, Lii says. I run away in a zigzag pattern, fleeing the glowing red balls that streak past me. A bright light sparks to life overhead and follows me.

Nano-lumus, Lii says as if I care right now.

Red splatters hit trees on either side of me.

The two Argonauts in pursuit make twice the noise I am. From sims before Lii started glitching, I remember that as long as they're running, their shots should fly wild. A pair of eyes glint in front of me with a reflection from the light overhead. I stomp to a stop, hoping to bounce to the side when the paintballs fly. Time grinds to a standstill. A double tap of red flies at my chest. I mentally prepare for the impact. This is gonna suck. Why does being a nano always hurt? Damn rule fifty-three! I can't avoid them. Momentum is not on my side.

But the impact doesn't come. The balls pass right through my chest, which is disturbingly transparent. Time speeds back up. The teen's eyes widen as I nearly barrel into him. I pull my trigger at belly level as I pass by, a point-blank shot to the gut. He grunts. I feel a little bad for the kid. Normally, I would stop to make sure he's okay, but with two Argonauts on the chase, I don't dare stick around.

"Sorry," I say and duck behind him. He lets out three more grunts. Friendly fire. Poor guy. Two red balls bolt by my head from ahead. I grin as one of my pursuers grunts. Friendly fire. The light remains in place, and I dash into the darkness with red balls flying wildly after me, and one through me.

"Ahhh!" I scream. Someone reaches around me, wrapping me up in many arms and slamming my back into them so hard that my brain rattles in my skull. My opponent's arms are so rough and strong that they scrape my arms like I'd taken a spill on a skateboard.

Not arms, Lii says. *Branches. Nano-botany.*

A short Argonaut approaches, gun raised, preparing to take an easy shot to the head. I strain to raise my gun but am totally immobilized, even my head, which twisted sideways.

Snap, snap. Two yellow splotches glow brightly, one on the Argonaut's shoulder and the other on his gun. "Damn it!" He grabs his injured shoulder and sits down and points his feet at me. The branches don't let go, and his glowing "wounds" bathe me in yellow light. I'm a sitting duck.

The yellow dot of one of my teammates bobs toward me until I can make out Miles's smiling face. He places one hand on the downed Argonaut's head and extends the other one toward me. The tree's branches unfurl, slowly releasing me from their prison.

"The advantage of being a nano-adapter," Miles whispers. He furrows his brow, angles his head as if disgusted, and asks, "Did you know that your chest is missing?"

I look down, and sure enough, part of me is gone. It doesn't hurt, but my guts and muscles glint in the yellow glow of the Argonaut's paint-balled shoulder. Sick! In my panicked run, I didn't know how the rounds passed right through me, but now that I do, I feel sick. Uckfe! Am I dying? Where is my heart?

From what I can tell, Lii says. *You're just fine. All your nanites are operating as normal.*

"You phased your body?" Miles asks, pulling me away from the yellow glow. "Clever."

Trying not to panic about accidentally losing a chunk of my body, I decide to let him believe it was on purpose. What he doesn't know won't hurt him: rule thirty-four. Hopefully, Bender or Dr. Fontein can fix this.

"No time to waste," Miles says. "You run that way. Speed is your friend."

I follow his instructions, not able to move quietly as I weave between trees. A dim halo illuminates my body, or rather the two halves of my body. Miles trails me by thirty feet but as quiet as a great cat. What the? I'm the bait. He's the trap. Nearly tripping on a large fern, I decide that I might as well play up my role. I clomp up and down with every step and stomp on as many twigs and branches as I can. I slap my hands through the brush as I run by.

Only seconds after becoming the worm on the hook, I slam into a howling wind that stops me mid-stride. Twigs and dirt blast me, stripping the outer layer of skin from my body. My right knee overextends and buckles under me. Glowing red pellets fly from multiple directions. Among the hailstorm of streaks, six paintballs make contact from head to foot. The one to my groin hurts the worst, even more than the one to my bare-skinned spine. Tears well up in my eyes. I barely have enough mental faculty to yell, "Out," so another volley doesn't bring on more punishment.

Through my yell, three sets of rapid double taps snap, followed by two curses and a grunt. The whistle blows.

"We won!" Miles yells and pads quietly up to me. He may have won, but I definitely didn't. This seems to be a developing pattern for these contests. It's gonna take a hot minute until my privates stop smarting. And I won't be able to get part of my body back until we reach camp.

"Walk it off," Miles says, pulling me to my feet. "You do make great fish food."

"Next time you get to draw the attention," I say, trying to sound as if the pain doesn't bother me.

"Nah," he says, clapping me on the shoulder. "I'm too good looking to get mutilated like that."

"Miles," I say. "This was a training exercise to prepare us for a shockknight attack, right?"

"Yeah."

CHAPTER TWENTY-TWO

Tiny

A t the end of our phasing track, Bender says, "You did great today. You're really getting the hang of phasing things out. Faster and larger every day. Tomorrow we're going to work on phasing things back into our plane of existence." After the paintball accident, I've been itching to learn to unphase.

Miles and Bethany improved massively over the last few weeks, phasing rocks, snacks, and various types of office supplies like rubber bands into the other dimension, each time faster and larger. My phasing skill skyrocketed this week, launching me past Miles and Bethany's ability to phase a coffee mug or tape measure, to phasing rocks that weigh more than me. Meanwhile Pyro floundered, not even able to phase a grain of sand, so he gave up yesterday. I don't mind his absence. If he weren't such an assnoid, I might feel bad for the guy.

"Sweet," Miles says with an excited look in his eye, then walks to the rope ladder with Bethany. I'm jealous that they're going to meet up with the others at Emerald Lake. Last time—entering the cold water from the shallow side—was tons of fun and felt spectacular on a hot day like today.

Interrupting my thoughts, Bender says, "Today, you learn to teleport objects other than yourself. Decades ago, a healthy sense of humor motivated teleportation for me. We shall see if the same is true for you."

"A creative mind can make almost anything funny," he says. "For example, a stapler seems pretty boring, but if you imagine stapling a kick-me sign to von Steiner's butt..." A stapler appears in his hand. "See?" Where did he summon that from? He must have a warehouse of random things to draw from. "Don't tell von Serious that I used that example. He was always an arse when I was a camper."

"You were a camper here?"

"Yeah," he says. "It was a couple of decades ago, Mer and I came up together." A far-off gaze glazes his eyes, his expression mournful instead of happy like I'd imagine. Snapping back to the present, Bender says, "This piece of popcorn isn't inherently funny." He places one on the platform between us. "But if you imagine shoving it up Henri's nose, it's hilariousness to the nth degree, right?"

I want to ask him what he knows about Henri but settle for a smile. "I want you to imagine how your school principal would look with this buttered snack stuffed up her schnauzer and force it to appear in your other hand."

I concentrate on the piece of popcorn while picturing Principal Jean with the popped kernel lodged firmly up her snout. The popcorn sputters out of existence but doesn't rematerialize in my other hand.

"Hold on a sec," Bender says, raising a finger. He vanishes, then reappears a second later with the kernel floating above his hand. "Poor Ms. Jean. She had no idea why she suddenly sneezed this out of her nose."

"No!" I start laughing uncontrollably. "I didn't just..."

"Yes, you did." I can't help but imagine her jumping up from her desk and screaming my name, somehow knowing that I'm involved. Or, I suppose she might be enjoying summer vacation on a beach somewhere, then all of a sudden her nose stretches out and everything smells of salty butter. I would feel bad if she hadn't sent me home without proof so many times.

"This time, make sure you focus on your other hand as the destination." He places a new puffed kernel between us. "And for good measure, why don't you imagine someone else's nose. I'd hate for her to experience that twice in one afternoon. She might get a phobia of popcorn."

I imagine the kernel choking Henri, with Pyro giving him the Heimlich until it flies out of his mouth and into one of their chums' mouths. I'm pretty sure that the camp's wards will protect Henri and Pyro, but the image plants a smile on my face all the same. The kernel dematerializes and lands in my hand.

"Ha! You did it!" Bender says pointing at my hand. "Who is the best instructor ever? Oh, yeah, this guy." He points his thumbs at his puffed-out chest and his teeth present themselves in the most genuine smile I've seen since we met. The sadness and stress behind his eyes vanish, leaving a proud and happy man, if only for this moment. The scar at his temple practically vanishes before his million-watt cheer.

In rapid succession, we try a peanut with the thought of plugging von Steiner's ear, a gummy worm in Scarlett's pretty hair, a real worm in Miles's mouth. Each shows up in my other hand. How did Bender retrieve a worm on demand? His stash of random stuff must be enormous.

"You picked that up fast," he says, eyes still twinkling with delight. "Want to try something more challenging?"

"Sure," I say, wondering what I should teleport next.

"Try to imagine something you have at home–back in the blocks, not Steadfast Corner–and summon it to your hand. It has to be something you know well. Like a well-used shoe or a favorite pair of socks. Imagine every piece of it in as much detail as you can. Wait, don't choose a toilet or anything that will damage your folk's container."

"Got it," I say with a laugh. For a second, I fear that their toilet will appear in my lap involuntarily. I picture my pillow. The one here at camp is too puffy, not that I ever have trouble slipping into sleep given the full schedule and nighttime activities. But retrieving my pillow will be...

Like home, Lii says. *You don't want to admit it, but you miss being surrounded by blockers.*

I imagine my pillow's constantly escaping fluff tickling Justin's ear, making him swat at himself. The pillow snaps into existence between Bender and me.

"Excellent, sonny."

"I did it!" I pick up my pillow, jump to my feet and swing it over my head. I lean my head back and puff out my chest, then yell into the wilderness, "I am a god!"

Bender laughs. "And you are so very humble, aren't you?" The pillow swings back around with a will of its own and smacks me in the face. "Even gods aren't above a good pillow fight." Several more pillows appear and batter me.

All I can do is curl up with my hands over my head and yell, "I give. You win!" The barrage ends, and the pillows vanish, leaving us alone with stupid grins. Only if all counselors could be like Bender, especially von Suckitude.

As we approach the amphitheater for our regular midnight training, I hear a slight snap of a twig behind us and startle. Everything sets me off these days. Between my sleep deficit, the constant menacing looks from Henri and Pyro, and the threat of shockknights, they should change my name to "Jumpy." Naren and Bethany say that meditation should help with my jitters, but it just adds to my fatigue and gives me more time to imagine horrible scenarios.

I spin my head, but before I can whip around, something crashes into my back, slamming me down and knocking the wind from my lungs as it pins me to the ground. With my nose pressed into the dirt and my knees protesting angrily at hitting the dirt so hard, I teleport twenty feet to my side.

I resurface beside a mossy tree to the sight of a giant mechanical leopard who pivots and pounces at me with its powerful haunches launching smoothly and front paws outstretched to tackle me. At odds with my fear, laughter from down the trail sounds like my friends, not the jeering of Henri or Pyro. I teleport to them.

With a smile, Penny says, "You remember Tiny, don't you?"

"Tiny?" Naren says skeptically.

"She's quite sweet," Penny says in the way one might talk about a baby. "She likes you, Mazz. You smell like strawberries." After bounding up she licks my neck and nuzzles into me with a rumbling purr.

"Tiny? Really?" Naren seems incapable of getting his head around the cat's name.

"I know, right?" Penny smiles. "I named her when she was a little gearbox that fit in my hand." Tiny nudges Penny's hand for a scratch on its neck, then lays down at my side, belly up.

"You mean familiars grow?" I ask, tentatively reaching out to rub her belly, hoping that she won't spontaneously turn into Danger Kitty like so many sim-cats do.

"Yeah, by adding nanites and gears and stuff they put on mass," Penny says. "They really are the finest examples of nano-gadgetry, aren't they?"

"Yeah." The large cat's gears, knobs, switches, and dials create a smooth but malleable surface that ripples under my touch a bit like natural hair. She rewards the gentle scratching at her belly with a low, resonating purr that can be felt as much as heard.

"Come on," Penny says with a wave. "We're wasting precious obstacle course time. You can pet her when we get there."

While the others practice, I spend my time playing with Tiny. She's remarkably gentle, even while wrestling. At one point, she stands up with me on her back and I ride her up the Amphitheater stairs holding on for dear life.

Before I know it, the hour is up, so Tiny and I have to separate. As I move to walk north, where our paths diverge, she pins me on my back. She noses at my chest then looks down at me with her teeth bared. Uh oh. Her head pulses forward and back several times as her maw opens above me. A shrill grinding and rattling emanate from her core, not at all like her purr or playful growls.

Is her head moving the way a house cat might when hacking up a hairball?

Something goopy and heavy slides from her mouth. "Gross! She puked on me." Tiny steps off me and nuzzles her face into mine, getting greasy sputum on my face before pouncing off to Penny's side.

"It's a familiar," Penny says between giggles. "Tiny really likes you. She wouldn't do that for just anyone."

"Uh, thanks." In the moonlight, I must look ridiculous because a laughing affliction spreads through my friends. I pick up the egg-shaped mass composed of a series of levers, gears, and innumerable other minuscule mechanical devices. I'm sure Tiny thinks she did me a favor but being puked on is an experience I never put on my to-do list.

Note to self: bring your blanket on your next stint at guarding Northgate. Shivering sucks. And remaining silent and still doesn't lend itself to keeping warm.

I whittled a couple of sticks with Dad's shark K-bar. It wasn't until tonight that I noticed the slight glint of the Alpha Force emblem. I wonder how Dad got this. These types of nearly indestructible knives, with their atomic-sharpened edges, are rare. But my shivering made it too dangerous to mess around with something so deadly.

I try to ignore the cold, but I'm failing. Actually...Why not. I summon my blanket from my bunk and imagine wrapping Henri in it and rolling him down a hill to knock over bowling pins at the bottom. "Aw, that's better."

As I wait for nothing to happen, I practice phasing rocks out of existence. I'm getting faster at it every day, and it saps my energy less and less.

"I wonder what Dr. Fontein is up to," I whisper to myself, picking up another batch of pebbles to phase. Surely, she has plans for us, but she isn't telling anyone, or at least not the campers. The fact that she is worried, with her seemingly infinite supply of power, terrifies me. She and the counselors seem impossibly skilled. The shockknights must be equally dangerous if she is concerned. I teleport a pebble from my left hand to my right and back again.

To make matters worse, if Tollere is stealing nano-skills, then wouldn't rare skills make me a greater target. "You're a kinetic, a phaser, and you can teleport," I tell myself. The only other nano like me is Bender, and with his abilities, I can't imagine anyone ever harming him.

Looking down at my pebbles, I realize I've been phasing and unphasing the same pebble over and over without thinking about it. As soon as I pay attention, the pebble phases out and doesn't return. "Steaming pile of recycled tofu!" Phasing sucks.

Studying a piece of quartz-rich stone that glimmers in a stray ray of moonlight, I phase it out. It doesn't phase back. "With my inexperience and backfiring skills, I'd be an easy target."

"And who would make you a target?" von Steiner's distinctive voice asks. I look up to see his undeniably clean shoes first, the wrinkleless pants, the fine white shirt, then his pale-faced. He looks far more menacing in the spotted moonlight filtering through the trees. So much for watching Northgate.

"Nobody," I say lamely. Even I know I don't sound convincing.

Von Steiner sneers at me, face so pasty that it practically glows. "Don't lie to me, boy. Why are you out of bed?"

"I was just making up a story. It helps me practice my skills." Rule twenty-four: the best lies have a hint of truth.

"And you want me to believe that?"

"My skills work better when I'm distracted," I say.

"That, I believe. Someone as undisciplined as you would have to resort to such tactics. But you'll have to tell Dr. Fontein why you're out of bed at this hour." A glimmering-eyed smile makes him look even uglier. "Come with me."

As much as I dislike von Sneers-a-lot, I follow him. I won't be able to use the excuse of accidentally teleporting away this time. Everyone is sick of me popping around all the time. I've been jumping off nearly everything, twisting, teleporting, and landing somewhere else. It's better than skating.

We walk wordlessly to Dr. Fontein's cabin near Southgate. A million and five choice words want to escape my mouth. I grind my teeth so I don't let a few slip. As we walk by the cafeteria, he says, "Now is your last chance to come clean. Either you tell me, or we wake up Dr. Fontein, and you tell her."

"No need," Fontein says, as she walks out of the cafeteria with a cupcake in each hand. "It would appear that my midnight sweet tooth served me well tonight. You know that Ms. Abigail makes the most amazing key lime cupcakes. My favorite."

Closing the distance, the head counselor asks, "So what seems to be the problem?"

"Well, sir, I caught Mazz out of bed at Northgate making up lies in the middle of the night."

"Is that so?" Dr. Fontein asks, not looking at all surprised or concerned.

"No, ma'am," I lie.

You might consider that I can read your thoughts, Fontein says, with the mental equivalent of a chuckle. Even as good nature as she seems, the well of power within her is uber-intimidating. Noted. Never lie to her again.

"Hush, child," von Steiner nearly shouts, his hand shaking as if he wants to backhand me.

"Why don't we hear from the boy?" Dr. Fontein suggests.

Stick to the truth, I remind myself. "I've been working on my phasing skills." True. "I don't have enough time to make progress during the day." True. "I wake up at night and practice." True.

"But you were talking to yourself," von Steiner says, shaking his head with a look of contempt.

"My skills come easier when I'm not focused on them," I say. "Talking to myself allows me to do things I normally can't." My truthometer still pointed to the green.

"It is so for many beginners," Dr. Fontein says, going along with my charade. "And isn't your cabin right next to Northgate?"

I nod hopefully. "Yes, ma'am."

"So that's that," Dr. Fontein says.

"But–" von Steiner stammers.

"But you found a camper trying extra hard to master his skills. Do you really think that's a punishable offense?" the head counselor asks, winking at me.

"I–"

"I thought not," she continues. "I'll walk young Mazz back to his cabin. Why don't you head in and grab yourself one of these key lime cupcakes?"

"Yes, ma'am. Alright…"

After von Stammers disappears into the cafeteria, Dr. Fontein hands me a cupcake and says, "Why don't you tell me what this is really about?"

"Uh, ma'am?"

"I already know, but I want to hear it from you anyway." I take a bite of the cupcake, vying for time to formulate my thoughts. She says, "I'll help you get started. You and your friends decided to ignore me and opted to keep watch for the traitor. And…"

"And we want to capture him or at least uncover who it is."

"Of course," she says, taking another bite of her cupcake. "Mmmm."

"Why aren't you concerned about it?"

"Oh, but I am," she says. "But these are not concerns for you. Your challenge should be your focus. Leave this business to the counselors."

"But, ma'am. I–"

"Tell the others to stop their nighttime stakeouts," Dr.

Fontein says, a hint of her will pushing me to comply.

"But–"

"But nothing," she says. A bit more strength nudges me. I don't want to be the focus of her seemingly bottomless reserve of energy. I nod.

"Good. And look, we have arrived at your cabin. In you go."

I wave and tiptoe inside, careful not to wake anyone. I summon my blanket back from my cold hiding spot. While I wait for my bed to warm up, thoughts clunk around my mind like mismatched cogs. How can Fontein be so calm about all of this? Who is the traitor? Is he a double agent like Penny said? Should we keep the night watch going despite what I promised? Are we actually safe in Camp Astrid? Will my family be safe at home? I drift off to sleep, imagining von Steiner working with shockknights to capture the younger campers and slaying the counselors.

CHAPTER TWENTY-THREE

Purple and Blue

The platform outside Eastgate feels more suited for lounging today than lessons. With the gentle breeze, it is that perfect temperature that brushes ever so gently across my skin. The skies are a rare shade of clear blue. I'm struggling to focus on Bender's words. I know he's talking about how to unphase things, which is something I desperately want to learn, but I stopped listening a few minutes ago.

It's not my fault. A rather large purple butterfly flew by and distracted me, with its gentle bob and weave. It hovered above Bender's head for a flutter or two before moving on. I wonder where it went. Is that all it ever does? Meander here and flutter there? Not a care in the world? It doesn't have to worry about shockknights. No concerns about all the nanos reading my mind.

"Mazz," Bender says, snapping his finger in front of my face.

"I didn't do it," I say before realizing no incidents had spontaneously sprung to life.

"If you're going to be distracted, go be distracted somewhere else. I won't mind. Really. I'll take the day off too. I can really use some time off."

"Sorry, I'll stay."

"So, I was saying: to phase something back, you need to know where it is. There are two ways that I know of. One, you phase the outer layer of skin on your fingers. For some reason, it stays with you and you can feel things in the other dimension. I think it has to do with the continuous bonds between nanites within you. The second method is that you can phase an eyeball."

The former sounds like a much less disgusting approach.

"When you can directly observe the object, you simply phase it again, and it will come back into our plane of existence. Then you can phase your fingers or eyeball back. Got it?"

"Yeah," we all say, Miles and Bethany more enthusiastically than me. I'm not sure I like the idea of shifting a part of my body into another dimension, even if it is the outer skin of my hand. That, and I want a break from constant practice. Tomorrow, on exploration day we'll try something new and everyone goes camping.

Unaware of my inner dialogue, Bender says, "Since it seems to be working for this group, we're going to work with more candy. This time, sugar-covered Sour Bugs appear in front of us in every color of the rainbow.

I set about the task, nervous that I might flay myself. To my surprise, it works exactly as advertised on the first try. The Sour Bug and the skin around it vanish. While it feels normal, I can now see the muscle underneath, making bile rise in my throat. Observing the texture and temperature of the sugary bug, I phase it again and it reappears.

"It worked!" I say in surprise. Skills are coming easier and easier. I stand up and do a goofy victory dance with arms raised over my head, accompanied by, "Who's the best? Oh yeah, me."

Miles and Bethany match my success in moments and join me in a congratulatory group dance. Miles sends me a digital file for a song to spaz out to. Even Bender joins in, casting a few fireworks into the sky. Where is his stash of endless things? Does he have a warehouse somewhere?

Later in the session, Bender tells us to phase one of our eyes so that we can see the alternate plane of existence. This proves to be more difficult until Bender conjures three small mirror shards so we can see the eye we're phasing.

He reassures us that "You don't need to worry. If something goes awry, I am here to help." No amount of encouragement will calm my nerves. The idea of phasing a thin layer of skin skeeves me out but sending my eye into another dimension grapples with every ounce of common sense I possess.

I know, right? Lii says. It should be a universal rule, one for which we need not state in our list. As it is, it violates rules nine, twenty-eight, and especially rule twenty: don't sever any body parts.

Nothing happens. More zilch-a-maximus continues to fill the time until I give up. Then the sound of sand sifting through an hourglass accompanies the strangest scene I've seen outside the digital world. With one eye in this new reality and the other in a purple and blue fun-house mirror sort of world, my mind can't make heads or tails of reality.

My eye pulses, blurring a smidge with the beat of my heart, which tells me that blood vessels connect through the transition between domains, though uncomfortably so. I blink, but my vision doesn't darken as a lifetime of blinks informs me that it should. So strange. Each twitch of my eyelid grinds on my disembodied eye as if dust, or an eyelash, or sand found purchase there.

I close both eyes to focus on this new landscape. The deck is translucent, spawning a sense of vertigo. The grasses below ceased to exist, leaving bare purplish earth, void of everything except strangely strewn rocks and a scattered pile of candies. Rather than looking continuous, billions of tiny glowing dots swarms of bioluminescent krill.

The tree trunks holding our platform stay where they are, but fuzz at their peaks and edges. Their branches and needles grow more and more blurry and transparent the farther they extend from their trunks. The sky swirls with glowing bluish patterns like a mashup of clouds and flocks of tiny synchronous birds. Mesmerizing.

Bender, Bethany, and Miles glow blue and purple, blazing far brighter than anything around, but are otherwise transparent, pure energy. Bender and I glow brighter than Miles and Bethany. Bethany shines with hints of green, while Miles radiates more white. We are magnificent, ethereal, beautiful. Bender's scars stand out as the only dark spot in this dimension.

Back in normal reality, Bender says, "Well done, Mazz," A tangible, normal eyeball appears in Bender's glowing head, though reflecting the violet and lapis in an unnatural tinge. My voice shrieks a bit more like a frightened toddler than I would have hoped for in front of Miles and Bethany. The eye swivels and the attached red muscles stretch and contract sickeningly. A wrongness at seeing his inner workings revolts against a billion years of evolution. Creepy like a muscular jellyfish, optical nerves splaying backward from his ophthulm.

"This is so cool," Miles says as his eyeball appears, equally disturbing. A memory of a mystical creature flashes to mind, a beholder beast, capable of pushing humans' fears, apathy, and rage. At odds with me, Miles says, "Just like The Gathering. Amazing."

Seconds later, Bethany's eye materializes too, with a verbal "Wicked!" Eyeballs shift left, right, up, and down, taking in this strange place.

Bender's whole body takes form in this bizarre landscape, as plain and solid as it would be under the mauve and azure stage lights. His mouth moves, but I can't hear him. Noted: sound does not transfer between planes. So strange. He motions for us to return with a set of complicated gestures. It takes me a moment to phase my eyeball back. The gentle swishing sound in my head accompanies my orb's transfer back into the only domain I've known up until now.

"That was amazeballs!" Bethany says. "Disorienting, but incredible. And beautiful with all those lilacs and sapphire specks." Perhaps beautiful the way grass-covered graveyards under the giant oak trees are serene, haunting.

"Do you know why it looks blurry and strange like that?" Bender asks. When we don't hazard a guess, he says, "The longer something stays stationary here in our domain, the more solid it is in the other dimension. Bases of tree trunks are stable over long periods, therefore as solid as the ground. Branches less so, and leaves even less so. Grasses sway even in a gentle breeze and regrow every year, so they don't show up at all other than a slight haze that covers the ground. They built this platform three years so, thus its translucence."

"So, why do we luminesce so brightly?" Bethany asks.

"Ah, yes," Bender says and smiles. "Now, this is Dr. Fontein's theory and only a theory. How many nanites do we consume on a daily basis?" Without pause, he answers his own question: "Billions if not trillions. Every microscopic nanite draws upon the energy at the barrier between the dimensions, so each glows."

"And we glow in different colors," Bethany says, "because we each inherently draw different kinds of nanites into us."

"Excellent observation," Bender says. His smile reveals his teeth, happy enough that I almost don't notice the scar on his temple.

"Now, comes the fun part. We'll phase our whole bodies," Bender says with a rapid flutter of his eyebrows, alternating curiously. "Down a nano-milk to supercharge yourselves," he says as three milks take form in front of us.

I drink mine up, the warmth diffusing through me, easing the tension that built during our eyeball experiment. I close my eyes and imagine my body, all of its six hundred forty muscles, two hundred six bones, nine hundred ligaments, and three pounds of brain that combine to form all that I am. For the second time today, it works on my first try.

This time, a desert sandstorm of dry heat spanks my whole body, penetrating my clothes like they weren't there. Trillions of specks swim toward me, drawn by an invisible force, collecting on my skin then absorbing into me.

Lii growls like a happy wolf scratching his back on the

ground.

As my heart pounds harder, I realize I haven't drawn breath in half a minute. I don't want to inhale here.

"It's fine to breathe," Bender says, fully in this domain, accentuating his point with a deep intake and outflow of blue-purple air. His voice is high-pitched, like underwater. "It will feel peculiar, but it's okay. Sorry, I forgot to tell you about the breathing thing. It is so natural for me." I take in a breath and immediately cough. Something between air and water fills my lungs, the taste sour and brackish. "Just breathe," he says. "You'll get used to it."

I take in another gulp of air, not sure if I'll ever get used to this, barely managing to keep from coughing. The air smells acrid, like a crisped rat at a vendor's cart. Now I understand why we didn't teleport fully into this domain before the eyeball experiment. I would have flipped out.

This universe overlays ours yet overwhelms me with alien discomfort. So strangely bizarre. Bender says, "It has always been here even though you never knew it." I knew we were sending rocks and candies into this place, but it felt like a card trick or a digital hack in a sim. Seeing may be believing but immersing myself here elevates my acceptance of this reality to a new degree.

"Look up at the stars," Bender says. "The light of the sun blends day and night into perpetual dusk or dawn."

"Wicked!" I'm not sure if Lii is influencing me or if my feelings are entirely my own, but this place feels welcoming now, inviting despite the staggering heat and heavy air.

Watching the billions of sparkling lights close in on me, I ask, "Why are the nanites drawn to us?"

He pauses for a moment, then says, "Dr. F and I think that because the original nanites were designed to heal people, they are all attracted to people. What we can't explain is why they are attracted to us more when we're in this dimension or why nanos draw different types faster than others."

"I think this is enough for today," Bender says. "Let's phase back. This domain draws nanites and energy to us like a black hole. If you stay here too long, you'll have to unleash it, and that may hurt one of us in the process." I kinda want to explore, but recognize what Bender means. It explains why I feel better, caffeinated, manic, elated. With supercharged ease, I cascade into normal reality, the joy of body flowing with me.

"You did it," Miles says, clapping me on the shoulder in congratulations even though he wasn't able to follow us into crazy land. Yet, his hand never touches me, bouncing off an invisible barrier only a hair's width from me. An accidental kinetic shield, from which Miles yanks his hand away and hisses.

"Sorry," I say. "I didn't mean to." Miles really is a genuinely nice guy, always doling out compliments and encouragement. From me, congratulations sound false, even when I mean them. Does rule fifty-three, the one about pain, extend to people around me? I hope not. Miles's ultimate kindness deserves better.

He is the best, Bethany says, an admiring look in her eyes.

Bender says, "Mazz, I officially cancel teleportation today. You had your fill of strange today and I have business to attend to." The way he says "business" and scratches the white remnants of the scar, raises the hairs on the back of my neck. The clenching of his jaw makes me think he means something dangerous. He vanishes before I can ask about it.

CHAPTER TWENTY-THERE

Exploring

After shoveling a second helping of pancakes into my expanding stomach, I join Scarlett and Naren under the purple and black rock-climbing banner in the south courtyard. I try to not pick at the really annoying cuticle on my pinky, something made harder by the idea of dangling from a rope on the side of a giant rock cliff. I could still opt to do something a bit saner like archery or tomahawk throwing, but then I'd be alone among gossipers.

In typical Mazz fashion, you insist on proving how dumb you are by following your friends into something you know you shouldn't, Lii says as if channeling Sigmond Freud. *Remember the Emerald Lake debacle?*

I gained a healthy respect for heights precisely because of Emerald Lake.

While waiting beside Ms. Merryweather and Mr. Braunwyn, the excursion leaders for today, the three of us dive into a heated discussion about the best foods on the planet. While Scarlett loves avocado, which I had for the first time on Mexican night, and Naren swears by sushi, something I never want to try, I waffle back and forth between bacon, s'mores, and mint-chip ice cream.

Once a large enough group of us have gathered, Ms. Merryweather guides a group of us along the inside wall of camp to the southeast. As I recall from my first day, the path in this section of camp winds over and through rock outcrops and hard-to-navigate swaths between densely packed trees. I let Scarlett and Naren lead the way as I dig into my cuticle.

Up ahead of us, a kid who can't be more than eight years old enthusiastically bounces over rocks and swings from branches. If he can do this, then so can I.

A girl with a tidy black bob cut and a drab-gray uni-garb like a janitor's uniform walks up to my side and says, "You are Mazz Becker." It was a statement, not a question. Her stilted, emotionless words sound almost accented.

"Uh, yes," I say, pretty sure I'm displaying a what-the-hell expression.

"Mr. von Steiner does not like you," she says as if reading a fact sheet.

"Duh!" I look at Scarlett and Naren, and they both laugh at me. I mouth the words, "Save me."

"You teleported away from Mr. von Steiner," she continues, apparently missing my discomfort.

"Yeah, what of it?" I'm starting to get pissed off at this intrusion into what was already looking to be a stressful day.

"I do not like Mr. Gregorovichivov von Steiner either," she says in a peculiarly monotone way. That explains why he goes by von Steiner. With a name like that, I would too.

"Oh," I say, completely confused by her. Is she messing with me or something?

"I wanted to say, hello."

"Okay. Hi." Awkward much? She didn't even tell me her name.

"Mazz, meet Lily," Scarlett says, a smile hidden behind her hand. "She's an incredible nano-hacker, but she also has some nano-aquas skills. That's how I know her."

"Yes," Lily confirms. "Scarlett Tansy, seventeen, born in

Springfield–"

"That's enough," Scarlett says, cutting her short.

"What are you doing here?" Lily asks Scarlett. Now it's Scarlett's turn to feel awkward. "Naren and Mazz's bunk in Steadfast Corner. Why are you walking with them?"

"We're friends," Scarlett says, clearly miffed. It's my turn to chuckle in her direction.

"Yes," Lily says as if number crunching on an unanswerable problem. "I do not have friends." I nearly choke on a laugh. I think I understand why she doesn't have any BFFs. Yet, not having friends at Camp Astrid is absolutely tragic. Camp Astrid is the only place I've found kinship in the last year–except for Latisha that is. Laticia.

"Would you like to walk with us?" I offer before I know the words spilled from my mouth.

"Really?" Scarlett asks, looking thoroughly put out.

"We would love your company," Naren says with an easy smile, always the positive one.

Lily tilts her head oddly and says, "That would be satisfactory. Does this make us friends?" Silence. My brain stops working. Ignoring our uncomfortable break in the conversation, she looks at me and asks, "Did you know that you are only the second camper with natural teleportation skills to attend Camp Astrid?"

"Really?"

"Yes," she says. "I know things." I don't think she is bragging but stating the truth about her reality.

"How?" Naren asks.

"Things are known," she answers cryptically. She provides no additional details.

"Who was the other camper?" Scarlett asks.

"Aldrich Robertson, aka Mr. Bender," Lily says as if a purely logical AI replaced her gray matter. It makes sense that Bender was once a camper. "Forty-one, born in Southampton, England. He–"

"We get the picture," Scarlett says. She must be tired of Lily's eccentricities from prolonged exposures but I could use to know more about Bender.

Lily continues. "Did you know that Mr. Bender–"

"Look at Mazz's new girlfriend," Henri exclaims from behind us. His cabinmate, Reuben, laughs in that way that burrows under your skin, a splinter under the fingernail, an agoraphobic sneeze. "What? You couldn't find a human, so you settled for a robot?"

"Shut it, Henri," I find myself saying, ramping up for a fight.

"Ooooh," Henri feigns fear with his hand over his mouth. His sidealong thug steps closer, as if ready for a brawl. "I'm sooo scared. The special little blocker is gonna use his special skills on me. You wouldn't dare. You'd be booted from camp faster than you could spell nano. Do you know who my dad is?"

"Pinnacle Alberist," Lily says. "Age, seventy-three. Born–"

"That's enough," Scarlett says, pulling her farther away from Henri.

The urge to kinetically fling rocks at Henri and his friend pulses through my veins, thick with potential. My hands stiffen in an open position as if carrying large stones in them. My eyes flitter to the side of the trail where plenty of stones lie, ready to inflict their damage.

"He's right," Scarlett whispers in my ear, placing her hand on my shoulder. I set my jaw and allow her to quickly guide me forward. "He's not worth it."

"So, how long have you two been dating?" Henri calls after me. "Is it new and exciting? Or have you been hiding it for a while now? Are you embarrassed by Lily-bot?" I pick up the pace with long angry steps. What an ass with a capital A! I flex my fingers as if I'm strangling his throat and the thirty-foot-tall tree in front of me splits down the middle with a loud crack and a bunch of creeks.

Oops!

Why don't you check your anger until you have better control of your influence? Lii asks.

I keep rage walking, making Scarlett, Naren, and Lily double-step to keep up. The crunch of the tree was extremely satisfying and seems to have had the unintended bonus of shutting Henri up.

"I don't like him," Lily says emotionlessly from behind me, shuffling to catch up. "He often says untrue things." In a strange way, I like her more now. If Henri doesn't like her, then she must have something redeeming about her.

A few minutes later, as we reach the cliffs Ms. Merryweather says, "Gather 'round." She claps her hands together to get our attention. She looks at me pointedly, giving me a you-know-better expression, even if it wasn't intentional.

"While Mr. Braunwyn and I set everything up, you can wander. But I want you all back here in fifteen minutes for a safety briefing."

Not wanting to be anywhere near Henri, I suggest that we explore. "I'm in," Naren says with his usual upbeat attitude. Scarlett nods as well. Lily seems lost in her own thoughts, staring at the cliffs. I think about interrupting what must be boring calculations but decide better of it.

The three of us run, bound, and scamper over rocks and between trees at the bottom of the cliff, investigating nooks and overhangs. Then we reach a spot where the stream tumbles out from the cliffside into a pool.

"Is that a cave above the waterfall?" Naren asks, his neck craned back and hand shadowing his eyes. Most people wouldn't have noticed, rarely looking above them as Miles said a few weeks ago.

Scarlett does the same. "It's what? fifty feet up? With it wet like that we won't be able to climb–"

My body, already tense with too much residual anger and skin-deep energy, I pop up to the cave's mouth. "Whoa." While the cave mouth is small, with barely enough room to stand next to the underground stream, the inside widens and extends dozens of feet into pitch-black depths.

Stepping clear of the edge, I call down, "It's huge in here." My voice echoes. Vertigo spikes when I look down at them, ba-bump, ba-bump.

Back away from the ledge, Lii suggests.

Noted: don't look down again.

Cupping her hands around her mouth, Scarlett hollers, "Cool, but we gotta head back. We can explore more later."

After returning to the group for the brief but thorough safety lesson, we group up in fours or fives per climbing rope. Lily and a pencil-thin, maybe seven-year-old boy in a too-large camp shirt and orange shorts join our group.

"My name is Edo," he says. "This is gonna be awesome." We introduce ourselves, though he clearly knows who I am, an expression of what?

Admiration, Lii says. *Awe.*

Lily starts to provide details about us as we say our names, and Scar interrupts her each time. Edo lives on a small island at the north end of what used to be Japan. One of the few islands that recovered from the AI War.

With no interest in dangling off a cliff by a sketchy rope, I have other plans. Without sharing a word between us, I know that Scarlett and Naren have similar thoughts. The cave. Scarlett explains to Lily and Edo that we want to explore the cave, and invites them to join us. Lily seems...not excited, but maybe interested. Edo requires a bit more persuasion, but in the end, agrees. Yay for peer pressure.

When we reach the waterfall, I teleport to the mouth of the cave. Now comes the tricky part: teleporting them up without turning them inside out. It should be the same as teleporting nearly anything, right? No problem. Following everything I've learned from Bender, I think of Scarlett and everything I know about her: Her athletic figure, chin-length bangs, green eyes, smooth lips–

Pop! She coughs by my side, leaning over as if she might spew. I almost say, "I didn't mean to."

Again, acting before thinking.

I pat Scarlett on the back. "Are you okay?"

"Yeah," she croaks between coughs. She stands tall,

swallows, and nods. "A little warning next time. That was awful."

"Sure," I say, not about to tell her that I teleported her by accident. That would go over like a plane without wings.

I count down for Naren, relying on the cave to amplify my voice and lean my head over the edge on one, and he materializes at my side, looking like he might teeter into the subterranean stream. Scarlett grabs him and pulls him farther into the cave. After Naren recovers, I repeat this with Lily, then Edo. Lily seems curious, but otherwise unaffected by my rough elevator service.

"Can we do that again?" little Edo asks, hopping up and down as if he's discovered the greatest roller coaster in history.

"This is amazing!" Scarlett says as she walks farther into the cave.

"Cah-ray-zee," Naren agrees, following close behind her. I'm not sure because it's dark in here, but he might still be a tinge green.

"This cave was excavated by three nano-terrans," Lily says as if lecturing about a boring old archeology site. Is she related to Mr. Braunwyn? Or has she taken a course on how to make anything monotonous?

"How do you know?" I ask.

"I know things," she says. Who says that? I want to like her, but she's so...different.

"Notice the perfectly squared path at the back," Naren says.

Edo scoops up a few pebbles into his pint-sized hands and they flicker on like flashlights. "Here. Take one."

"Wicked," I say, snatching one and turning it over in my fingers. I'm twice as old as this munchkin and he has way more control over his influence than I do. Edo smiles, exposing two missing canines.

"Look here," Scarlett says. A spectacular stone statue of a life-sized great wolf stands naturally within the cave. Someone crafted a perfect masterpiece, with details so fine it almost looks like someone transformed a live wolf into stone. Is that possible?

"This resembles Mother's work," Naren says. "She uses nano-terran skills to mold rock into perfect statues for the rich and famous. Of course, her patrons don't know how she does it."

After a minute of gawking and touching the statue, Scarlett says, "Let's keep exploring." The nano-carved path follows the stream along a natural tunnel running deep into the earth. Doorway after doorway feeds off the central cave, each leading to an empty square room about the size of Steadfast Corner. This place could hold hundreds of people.

With our rock-lights flickering in every direction, bending distorted shadows across every surface, we explore farther back. Nobody seems particularly interested in straying far from the group. Idiots die this way in every horror sim ever made. Hundreds of feet in, we reach a flat wall blocking the path. The stream comes from farther back, but without any room around it. "This is not right," Lily says, making me jump. I hadn't realized that she stood only inches behind me. Noted: no sense of personal space.

"What's not right?" I ask after a few intense heartbeats.

"The tunnel does not stop here," she says in her calm, factual manner.

"How? Why?"

"I know things," she says.

That is *not* an answer. I want to yell, "How do you know things?" but decide to follow rule nine. Or is it nineteen?

Neither and both, Lii says. *You don't have a rule that applies perfectly.*

"She's right," Naren says, looking this way and that. I get the impression that he expects vampires to attack at any second. I don't blame him. Holding his hand to the back wall, he says, "I sense there is an emptiness behind this wall."

"How do we get through?" Scarlett asks, feeling around for a lever or a switch or something.

"I don't know," Naren says. "I could "dig" away at it, but it might take a while, and we better get back to the others before someone notices we're missing."

"I hate to admit it," Scarlett says, "but he's right."

"Fine," I say, one part happy to move back toward daylight and another part reluctant to stop exploring. "This place is mega though."

We return to the mouth of the cave and I teleport them down one at a time, making sure to count down each time. We'll have to come back and explore more. With one more look back at the cave and the magnificent wolf, I teleport down to the base of the cliff.

We walk back toward Ms. Merryweather, laughing and chatting the whole way. "I rather enjoyed that," Lily says in her emotionless way. "Do friends break rules and sneak off often?" The rest of us look at each other awkwardly. How do you answer a question like that? I mean, I'm an outcast, but she's...

"Not often," Scarlett said sympathetically. I'm not sure she's right. We sneak out of our cabin nearly every night. On one of our first nights at Camp Astrid, Scar and I were pulled out of our beds to join in The Gathering. The three of us followed the traitor to a meeting with shockknights. Against direct orders from Dr. Fontein, we keep a stakeout for him. Just now, we snuck off to explore a cave. Perhaps breaking rules and sneaking around is what friends do together.

Or it could be a "me thing." Laticia and I slink about at night a bunch, holing up in one hiding spot or another. I mean, I–

"Mazz, Earth to Mazz." Scarlett waves her hand in front of my face.

"Whah?"

"Who do you think created that cave?" she asks.

"Don't know." In the presence of Edo and Lily, I don't want to say the first thought that springs to mind. Whoever built it wants a place to hide the campers in case the shockknights come for us. With a look from Scarlett, her eyes express more concern than I want to see. Her thoughts fall along a similar grain as mine. In contrast, Naren smiles in his signature perma-grin.

We return the unused rock-climbing gear to Ms. Merryweather, then wait for her to pack everything up.

A few minutes later, we walk out through Eastgate and hike

on a trail I'm not familiar with. We keep bantering about the cave quietly but mostly happily so the others won't overhear us. During the hour-long trek, Scarlett and I exchange a few more anxious looks that convey the deeper, darker concerns we feel.

When we reach our overnight campsite, a huge mostly flat clearing with a marsh at the center, there isn't much to do, so Scarlett and I decide to whittle sticks for marshmallow roasting. While we adventure out to look for the perfect sticks, Scar and I share our aligned thoughts about the cave's purpose: an evacuation point should the shockknights come. I don't like to see unease shade her eyes.

Eventually, we decide to bring this up with Miles and the others later. We should "live in the moment" as Mr. Braunwin always says. It's a beautiful afternoon for a stroll.

After carving a sharp point on a straight shaft, like an arrow, I join up with my bunkmates who have gathered into a circle, telling stories. I keep stamping down my concerns about the shockknights and the cave so all the nano-paths won't overhear my thoughts. Relax. The counselors have everything covered. Just relax.

Yes, Bethany says, puh-lease relax. *I've heard your worries and passed them along to Miles and the others. I can't enjoy this outing while constantly sheltering your thoughts from all the nano-paths.*

Where are you?

Unfortunately, not far enough away. So you're as loud as ever.

Not my fault!

Let's try something, she suggests, a sense of dangerous adventure wafting from her.

I'm pretty sure I've had enough adventure for today, so I preemptively cringe at asking, Like what? I don't like the eagerness her thoughts resonate with.

When you phased your whole body yesterday with Bender, I couldn't hear you. *Everything was blissfully quiet for the first time all summer.*

So? I say. Do you really think I'm going to phase away all the time?

No, she says, indignation wafting off her thoughts. *I want you to phase your brain.*

Ha! Like that's any better. I can do without scrambling my brain, thank you very much.

Losing your brain might be an improvement, she snorts. *Don't worry, you'll be fine.*

So says someone every time someone wins the Darwin Award. I'll have that put on my gravestone, "you'll be fine."

It can't be worse than phasing your eyeball.

Then, why don't you do it first? I say.

Because I'm not the one blaring my thoughts all over camp, Bethany said. *Did you know I can even hear you when you're dreaming? And Ing isn't hot enough to fill your unconscious hours. Do you really want me and others to know things like that?*

Fine! I try to relax, but the extra time doesn't seem to be having the right effect. I can feel Bethany's mind metaphorically tapping her foot. I imagine the insides of my head and my brain's shape. I shake my head roughly from side to side then up and down, feeling the edges of my inner skull. Then, with a deep breath, I phase my melon.

Bethany, did it work? Nothing. Bethany? "Wahoo!" I yell to the surprise of my cabinmates. Belatedly, I realize I have a sharp stick in one hand that I just waved around wildly in front of Brooks's face. New rule: phase my brain around nano-paths.

The counselors send us into the large field to find spots to park our sleeping bags and tents. Naren and I decided to tent up together from the beginning. We would have included Scarlett, but she said she was going to bunk with Ing. The thought of them in a tent together doesn't compute. I know they hang out, often invited by Penny and Bethany on outings, but I don't know how to put them into the same box.

We squish our way across a thin marsh in the middle of the field to a secluded camping spot on the far side from the fire pit, for which other campers are gathering wood. Being my first time camping out in the wilds, and not atop our container block with Dad and Laticia, I want a bit of quiet to get the full experience.

It takes a surprisingly long time to figure out the tent. Poles everywhere. The ultra-light fabric is too tight in some places and too slack in others. Naren, who has done this before, basically pops it up without me. It seems unnecessarily complicated. Finally, he gets it to work and I bow and say, "Well done, Sir. Naren."

"Excellent work, Master Mazz," he says even though I was more of a hindrance than a help.

We walk back across the marsh to the giant unlit fire ring. My left foot catches on a bushel of grass. I reflexively reach out with my kinetics to catch myself, something I recently realized has been helping me with surviving skating fails for years, but all connections to my kinetic influence are gone.

Instead, the soggy ground flies up and smacks me in the chest and chin. I'm soaked in mud. Cackling laughter erupts behind me. No surprise. I turn to find Henri and Reuben pointing and smirking as if my trip to Splatsville was the funniest thing they'd ever seen.

In all fairness it probably was, Lii says. *How many times have we watched compilations of epic fails like this?*

"Grow up," Naren says as I try to scrape off the layer of mud clinging to my clothes. New rule: bring extra clothes on overnights.

"Oh, grow up, says the little Pakistani." He poorly imitates Naren's accent. "I am a weak and pathetic blocker-lover, but I tell pinnacles to grow up." Most pinnacles are born into leadership, rarely having to leave their skyscrapers to mingle with uppers, other than the uppers who act as their servants. Someone like me would never have met one in person. I guess even uppers are looked down upon. Supremes probably look down on pinnacles with the same scorn. Who looks down on them?

"I am not Pakistani," Naren says, irate, which might upset the natural laws of the universe. "I am Indian."

"Big difference," Henri says as he walks past and bumps Naren's shoulder with a rough body check. He nods for Reuben to follow. I really, really want to kinetically tug on Henri's fancy hiking boots, which shed mud like huskies waggle off snow. I want him to fall flat on his face. Give him a whiff of his own crap. Again, the reflexive urge to connect with my influence encounters a blank. This area must be nanite-poor. Probably why we're out here.

"He's a jerk," Edo says, as Naren pulls me to my feet. "You wouldn't believe what he did to Devin. He's a blocker like you. He only gets away with it because of his dad." I'm pretty sure I know what he did to Devin.

"Are all of the Eagle's Nesters pinnacles?" I ask.

"Most of them," Naren says. "Many pinnacles are nanos. Especially nano-paths and medics, who can influence how people feel."

That night, we have an amazing time and I forget all about Henri, Reuben, and Pyro, who seem to hang out together the way Scar, Naren, and I do. The campfire rampages wider than I am tall and twice as high. It dances to its own hypnotic rhythm, swaying, undulating from side to side, and springing into the air. Oranges and yellows ripple with threads of blues and greens, red embers simmering below.

We sing funny songs that I have never heard before. Lii feeds me the lyrics so I can sing along as best as my unpracticed, off-key voice can. The blocks are too congested to sing unless you're a natural. I bounce around the fire to the beat of the drums. To add to the fun, Brooks uses his nano-vibrus skills to create amazing percussions that seem impossible, and probably are for anyone else.

As I bounce, laugh, and howl with the other campers, Bethany bounces with me for a moment, and mouths the words, "I can't hear you." She smiles from ear to ear. Then, she's gone into the throng.

Later, the counselors tell stories. Ms. Merryweather tells a tale of a counselor that went mad when the campers pushed her over the edge. She snapped one day and started taking locks of hair from the campers. If they misbehaved, a lock was gone. The next time, the whole head. If the campers continued to be bad, there went their eyebrows. If the campers continued with their naughty ways, there went their eyelashes. One day, another counselor asked, "What do you use to shave their heads?"

"Oh no, my dear," the deranged counselor said, "I don't shave their heads. I pluck them out one by one."

Argh, I wince despite myself.

Dr. Fontein tells a story about a camper who died and haunts these woods. After seeing the alternate plane yesterday, I can't help but wonder if ghosts do actually traverse the earth in that purgatory. Every few seconds she strikes the fire ring with a shove, making a grating clanking sound three times.

"A young camper goes missing." Clank, clank, clank.

"A cabin leader's body is found drained of all his blood." Clank, clank, clank.

"A wolf gutted, left for the ravens." Clank, clank, clank.

"A counselor venture out to–"

A ghoulish face runs into the ring howling in a shrill cry and waving hands to the sound of clank, clank, clank. Screams ring out, including mine, as campers run in every direction, tripping over log seats and other campers. I don't teleport away to my relief. No slamming into the camp's wards or finding myself lost in the woods. The constant practice and meditation really are working.

Afterward, we roast marshmallows above the low coals, the smoldering leftover of the fire. I couldn't care less when someone steals my roasting stick after my fourth s'mores.

I decide to sleep outside the tent, having weighed the risk of mosquito bites against the opportunity to gaze up at the brilliant stars, which are much brighter than I've ever seen before. As I lay here and think about how perfect today was, minus both encounters with Henri, I fidget with the familiar Tiny gave me. The nano-mechanical device put on some serious weight over the last few days. How is this thing growing? Whatever. Life can't get better than this.

If only the shockknights didn't exist, life would be perfect. Faex! Now I'm thinking about shockknights again. Can't I have a single night without worrying about them and whoever the traitor is? And if there is a better time to attack than now, I don't know when it could possibly be. We're outside Camp Astrid's protective wards. We're disorganized. We just made a giant campfire so big it could be seen from orbit. How could the shockknights miss this? And how am I supposed to sleep now?

So many questions. Who is the traitor? von Steiner? Henri? Pyro? Can I even trust my friends? How well do I really know them? Von Steiner seems too weaselly to so openly reveal himself. But Henri and Pyro might be smug enough to walk about without a care. They don't seem like they'd miss any sleep over betraying uppers and especially blockers like me and Devin.

I trust Bender, Merryweather, and Fontein. They are too powerful to succumb to threats, blackmail, or stoop to backstab the nano community. Mr. Braunyn is too "at one with himself" to motivate himself into betrayal. I don't know the other counselors much or at all, so it could be one of them. Can I even rule out the younger campers? A nano-lumus, like Edo, could shine any outward image by tweaking and bending light. And it would have been even easier in the dark.

I definitely can't sleep now. I might as well pop over to lean against a tree for a while. I mentally scrunch into a teleportation. Nothing happens. Whah? To add a kick, I think about the vertigo-inducing ledge at the cave earlier today. Nothing.

I teleport my familiar from my left hand to right. Nothing. I levitate my familiar with nano-kinetics. Nothing! This isn't the too-common feeling of a misfire. Instead, I can't tap into my influence at all. It isn't there.

Oh, faex! Did Tollere already steal my abilities? I feel my chest for the scar of a hand. Few. It feels normal. Regardless, I stand and scan the dark clearing for any signs of knights. Nothing moves. No shiny armor reflects the light of a billion stars in the Milky Way. But if they're dangerous enough to make Dr. Fontein nervous, they're scary enough to sneak into this clearing and make off with campers.

What's going on? An empty pit fills the space where my nano-influence used to be. Trying to calm myself, I inhale and exhale deep breaths. Calm yourself, Mazz. You're over-reacting.

You haven't tried phasing, Lii says. *Maybe we can still do that.*

I phase my familiar and the outer skin of my hands. It vanishes. The telltale sifting sensation of sand falling through an hourglass tingles my callouses. Thank the nanites! I unphase my familiar and that works too. I phase my whole body. The phased night glows as dull and eerie as it was during the day, hundreds of bodies alight with purple and blue nexuses of nanites. With this altered vision, I see everything, from trees to the snuffed fire pit.

While some of the campers shift in their sleeping bags, a tent full of kids play with battle-bots, and a couple engages in more than sleep, the clearing remains still. Four figures stand still at the edges of the clearing, not watching over the slumbering lumps, but guarding like gargoyles fending off demons, threats from outside. Each glimmers with unique shades and colors of blue and purple, one an addition of green like Bethany.

Good. We're safe. A figure at the center glows brighter, a brilliant white pulsating figure. Nobody's gonna screw with her. At the far side of the clearing, I recognize Bender's particular blend of glow, so similar in nature to mine, but deeper rooted in his bones.

Returning to the problem at hand, I consider my situation. I can phase. Can I unphase myself? I should have thought about that before jumping in full-bore. I shift back and the darkness in the meadow returns. Yes!

No! Bethany booms in my head so loud it hurts. Her anger knocks me like Pyro's punch to the gut. Pah-lease shut up. I just got to sleep.

Sorry, I mentally whisper. I phase my brain again so she won't scramble my noggin.

"Got it," I say aloud, then look around to make sure I didn't wake up anyone else. I unphase my brain, focusing on the clear waters of Emerald Lake, and teleport my familiar from hand to hand. It works. I rephase my brain before Bethany goes ballistic on me.

Rule fifty-eight: I can't phase brain and teleport or use kinetics at the same time.

CHAPTER TWENTY-FOUR

Misbehaving

A few nights later at the obstacle course, Penny asks, "Did you hear?"

"Hear what?" I ask offhandedly as I scratch Tiny behind the ears. We already played a round of "teleport me, teleport you," in which she tries to tackle me while I send one of us twenty feet away.

She makes that horrible grinding sound and regurgitates a small lump of greasy gears and a strand of chain links onto my familiar. The rapidly growing mass twists levers and gears to incorporate the new addition. My inattentive, "Hear what?" was just a polite way to fill the void between Penny's words so I can watch my familiar's transformation.

"Two more nano families went missing," she says.

"Huh?" Splick! Now she has my full attention. "Whole families?"

"Is that the third one this summer?" Bethany asks.

"The third one that we know about," Penny says. "There could be more."

"Do you think the shockknights got them?" Naren asks. "Or did they go into hiding?" I hope it's the latter. Crapola. Are my parentals in danger?

"I have no idea," Penny says, an edgy crack creeping into her distinctively clear and logical voice.

"This is why Camp A is so important," Bethany says. "We need to re-double our training to protect ourselves." I knew that the challenges, obstacle course, and war games were Dr. Fontein's way to train us in case the shockknights attack but I hadn't thought past summer. When school starts back up, my constant practice will protect my family, even if I can't use my skills without misfires. Camp is about survival.

Bethany grasps hold of my being, trapping me in place and blocking my desire to phase my brain. My paintball gun hangs loose in my hand. Tap, tap, tap. My chest glows green as two paintballs hit dead center and another nails me in the belly button. I drop, gritting my teeth through the sting of the impacts as Bethany releases me. She didn't imprison me harshly. I had most of my free will, but couldn't shoot one of her cabinmates or flee for safety. I hate how easily she did it, but don't hold it against her. It's her strength.

I sit and wait for the war game, brain phased.

"Hey Mazz, wake up," Miles says quietly. He sounds one part concerned, another part happy, and a third part confused.

"What?" I grumble and flump over, tired from having nightmares about zombie nanos biting norms, converting them into zombie nanos, and so on.

"Why is Steadfast Corner outside Northgate?" Miles whispers.

I sit up, instantly awake and attentive. "What?"

'You heard me," he whispers, shushing me with a finger to

his lips.

"You mean..."

He half-smiles and cocks his head. "Yeah. You teleported it."

"Crap," I say, wide-eyed. I palm my forehead. "I was having nightmares."

"I know. You were talking in your sleep."

I double-checked that my brain was phased before falling asleep last night. I must have unphased my brain then teleported the cabin. "Please don't tell the others."

"Sure," Miles says in a hushed tone. "I'll say you did it as a joke demonstration of your challenge."

Miles returns to his bunk, and a few minutes later Naren and I leave for morning meditation. Outside, Naren turns his head from side to side and upturns his palms in the universal WTF pose. I swear him to silence and explain what happened.

"It's fine," he says. "Everyone will believe it was a joke and a fantastic one at that. Only if you could teleport Eagle's Nest into Emerald Lake..."

Sunrise meditation sucks several levels more this morning, with images of zombies still rattling around in my head. Once the infinitely futile attempt to calm my brain reaches its end, I can't wait to get out of here. As a crap lier, there isn't really any place for me to go. If I go to the cafeteria, people will know, even with my brain phased.

"Mazz, hold up," Mr. Braunwyn says. Faex. Kill me now. One more word from him might leave me as angry and braindead as the zombies I keep pushing out of my mind. I hope my involuntary eyeroll and suck-an-egg expression will dissuade him from striking up a conversation.

"Why don't you come and delve into my graphic novel collection. I think you could use a good distraction and some time away from the other campers." He's not wrong. I have thought about his collection plenty of times, and a respite from the rumor mill would be a nice change of pace.

"Sure," I say with a nod.

We walk across camp in silence, which suits me just fine.

I don't have anything I want to say to him and couldn't care less about discovering my inner peace. His three butterflies flit around him as we walk.

He welcomes me into his cabin and says, "Take your pick of the caboodle." I'm pretty sure that's not a real phrase, but the less we talk, the better. I grab the thin one with the clawed wolverine-man I saw before. He motions me to a pillow on the floor without a word, which is fine by me.

I carefully flip the pages, making sure not to crease or overly bend them. I'm drawn in by the retro style and pre-AI storyline. Wolverine is flawed and filled with rage but fights on the side of good. After the first, I move onto another, then another, disregarding the growls of my stomach. I would summon a few candy bars from the cafeteria, but don't want to gum up the frail pages.

I stand and retrieve my fourth issue in the series when Mr. Braunwyn breaks the silence. "We have more in common than you might think." Damn. I could have stayed here, content all day without him saying a word. This conversation already bores me. How can I escape the ensuing tedium?

"How so?" I ask, wishing I knew a way to cut the chit-chat short.

"I'll tell you a secret if you promise to keep it to yourself."

"Uh, sure." He can't have any secrets that I'd be interested in. Does he have a pet rock? Or a large stash of rubber bands?

"I'm a norm," he says. Now that, I was not expecting. But he's a counselor at a camp for nanos. It doesn't make sense. A friendly smile with more emotion than I've seen all summer crosses his face. "You heard me. A norm."

"But..."

"I used to be a neurosurgeon. I specialized in patients with odd brain-AI connections. Mostly after severe accidents." Why is he telling me this? Can my brain be expected to keep this kind of news safe? If I unphase for a second, the news will slip.

"One day I met a girl who kept getting shocked by inexplicable jolts of electricity, often frying electronic equipment around her, even if it wasn't touching her. A group of soldiers showed up, handcuffed me and the girl, and hauled us off. Dr. Fontein rescued me and relocated me, my wife, and my son, like witness protection."

"You have a wife?" I say, unconvinced that anyone would marry this sleep-inducing, emotionless bore-fest of a man. Faex! I didn't mean to sound so incredulous. Aiming to sound interested rather than surprised, I add, "And a kid?"

He smiles. "Is it so hard to imagine?"

I want to say, "Yes," but manage to get out an unconvincing, "No." Someone intentionally married this guy? Really?

"I owe Fontein for saving us," he says. "That's why I come here every summer."

"Why are you telling me this?" I ask. "I can't unknow it."

"So, you know that no matter how much you stand out here, as a blocker, as a norm-born, as a rare nano, you aren't nearly the outsider that I am." Huh. What do I say to that? How many others know?

The gong to mark the end of breakfast and the start of the first track sounds in the distance. Saved by the bell. "Uh…"

"Go on," he says. "Keep my secret, okay? They'll give me unending hell if the others find out I'm a norm."

"Got it. Ur. Thanks." I do feel better. I may stand out like a toe among thumbs, but he's…some other analogy I can't think of. Maybe I judged him too harshly. He isn't trying to kill me one droning word at a time. He's just trying to survive the summer.

I quick-step it back to meet up with the kinetics crew, dodging in to grab a crumble-top blueberry muffin and a couple of candy bars. I know where Ms. Abigail usually puts the muffins, so I probably could have summoned them, but that's a good way to end up with a handful of oatmeal. I don't need to break rule fifty-seven again. I avoid two congratulations for my "prank" with the excuse that "I'm late. Gotta go."

After our short walk to the usual kinetics spot, I'm having a hard time concentrating. My mind keeps bouncing back and forth between my accidental teleportation of Steadfast and Mr.

Braunwyn's secret. I can't unphase my brain or I'll divulge his secret. Why did he have to tell me? While it makes me feel like less of an outcast, I'm now stressed that I'll let the bomb drop.

"Let me guess," Bethany says after levitating a fist-sized rock above her palm. "Mr. Braunwyn told you his secret."

"What? You know?"

"Everyone knows," she says. "I'm surprised you didn't. It's really obvious. Every year he tells some unsuspecting kid, who inevitably lets it slip. How could you not spill the gears with nano-paths running around this place? The rumor always gets out and blows up for a few days. Most campers go along with the ruse. Anyone who believes him gets ridiculed as a gullible fool."

"So he played me?" I say, anger flashing red hot. "Fraker!"

"Sorry, Mazz."

"I'm taking a walk," I say through clenched teeth, unphasing my brain.

"Sure," Ms. Merryweather says calmly, probably concluding that I'm a halfwit for believing that boring shart. Over her shoulder, she adds, "Don't go too far. Stay within hearing distance."

"Don't worry about that," I say with a devious smile. I follow an animal trail for a minute until I reach another small grass clearing encircled by a crumbling hip-height foundation. This is perfect.

I kick at the foundation, knocking a pillow-sized chunk of concrete loose. Focusing, I kinetically lift the block so it rests in my hand. Ms. Merryweather keeps telling me that it shouldn't make a difference if the stone levitates in mid-air or balances weightless in my hand, but it feels natural this way.

I "throw" the cement as far and fast as my kinetics will allow. It bolts across the field and slams into the trunk of a hundred-foot-tall Douglas fir, not the tree I was aiming for, but the affect is perfect. The collision releases a low thump that stirs something primal inside me. I jump up and down and shout like a mad man as branches fly.

I know I shouldn't be encouraging this, Lii says, *but it's too fun to stop.*

I knock loose another block of cement and catapult it even faster, barely hitting the same tree. The cement deflects and flies off at an angle, carrying bark and tinder with it. The rumble of the strike resonates in my lungs, and the tree sways from side to side. I found the perfect solution to every frustration I've ever felt.

Destructive much? Bethany asks.

It feels good. Too good to stop.

I know, she says. I'm sharing your experience with the group. I hope you don't mind. It's incredible! For once, I don't care. All I care about is throwing the stones and the destruction they're causing, far more therapeutic than skipping rocks on a pond. I pound the tree–and sometimes other trees by accident–until it cracks and leans over toward me.

"Oh, frak!" I yell, running as the huge Douglas fir falls, reminding me of the swooping dragon illusion during the assembly on the first day, ready to swallow me whole. But this tree is very real. I barely manage to dodge behind a wide-based redwood tree before the fir hits down. The rumble fills my lungs and shakes the soles of my feet.

My heart pounds and my lungs heave and ho. Branches fly. I crave water. The air tastes of sawdust and iron. Sweat beads at my temples. I shake, not cold, but full of adrenaline.

That was stupid, Lii says, though I get the sense that he'd do it all over again if given the chance.

Stupidly fun. I walk around my protective redwood to see the corpse of a tree. I did this. I can't believe it. I climb up some branches, my left hand struggling to obey, and stand on my vanquished foe.

We have a bloody nose again, Lii says. *And our left hand isn't reporting back properly. You over-used our nanites again.*

I could care less. This was worth it. Though I do care because I feel weak and a bit dizzy, a combination of my new vertigo from Lake Emerald and the pounding in my head. Plus, my left hand resembles a hook, muscles spasmed tight. I lower myself to straddle the tree, catch my breath, and stretch out my cramped hand.

I–Lii craps out.

I blink twice as a chunk of cement rises into the air all on its own. I check my hands, as if they're practicing kinetics on their own, then look over my shoulder to see my friends standing behind me, concentrating together. The large rock wobbles high in the air under their combined focus. Bethany counts down from three and they smash it onto the remaining base of the fir tree.

A round of cheers erupts from the cabin leaders when a thump echoes through the clearing, not as loud as mine, but still fun. "That was so nano!" Penny says, doing a little dance. Miles and Bethany join in on the silent dance party.

"Who's badass?" Bethany says. "Oh, yeah, we are." Joy flows through her mental link with Miles and Penny. She really is getting good at this telepathic group link.

After everyone calms down, Ms. Merryweather says, "Mazz, I'm disappointed." Crap. Here comes a lecture about how I need to respect nature or some BS like that. "You wasted a ton of energy. You could have done it much more efficiently. Watch this."

With a gentle flick of her fingers, Ms. Merryweather sends three chunks of concrete flying hundreds of feet into the air. As one, they fall, smacking down on a second tree, pulverizing it into nothingness, branches flying and the sound growling through the surrounding valleys like nothing I've ever heard before.

Wood shrapnel bounces off an invisible spherical barrier around us. Without it, we would have experienced death by a million splinters. She stands still, awesome and terrifying, not even breaking a sweat.

"Do it again," Miles says. His expression is that of a little boy asking a magician to pull a coin from behind his ear.

Ms. Merryweather shakes her head. "I think we enjoyed enough destruction for one day." After a bit of pleading, she says,

"Just once more." This next explosion is even more impressive than the last, filling me with overwhelming awe, glee, and dread. Bits bounce off the shield Ms. M formed, sending a shockwave in the opposite direction. With three trees destroyed, she says, "We tortured the trees enough for today. Time to head back."

On our way to Southgate, I feel better despite the awful start of the day. Ms. Merryweather pats me on the shoulder and says, "That was fun. But perhaps find a less destructive way to lift your spirits next time?"

"Sure thing," I say. However, I'm unsure if I can keep that promise. It was just too fun.

"I hear you had a frustrating morning," Bender says after we're done with our phasing track.

"That's one word for it," I say, not wanting to get into details. All the prying eyes and whispers at lunch just served to frustrate me. Scar, Naren, and I took sandwiches for a walk along the creek, up to the pool at the cliff, where Lii pointed out that the waters were incredibly rich in nanites.

"Well, let's tap into your destructive bent," Bender says with a mischievous bob of his eyebrow. "Let's play another game of smash."

"You know about that, huh?"

"I think everyone on this side of the planet heard you. But–" The next moment, we stand on a black stone outcrop in the middle of a giant salt-flat, me feeling queasy. I try to remember that Scarlett and Naren suffered the same fate when we explored the cave, perhaps even worse.

The sun beats down so hot I can practically hear my skin burning. My throat instantly dries out. My eyes squint. Lips begin to crack. In every direction, hexagonal cracks break up the flat, parched surface stretching into the blurred horizon of mirages. How did Bender find this place?

Bender continues, "This time, teleport these boulders into the air and smash them into the ground."

My already parched throat croaks as I laugh. This is going to be so much fun! Does my face look as maniacal as I think it does? I aim to misbehave.

Humans always have the capacity for more ruination, Lii says in disgust.

The first egg-shaped boulder phases rather than teleports. Bender brings it back for me. On my next attempt, I manage to teleport it fifty feet into the air. My rock comes down hard with a thud that tickles my toes. Dirt and smaller rocks fly in all directions but don't reach us. It may not have landed where I meant it to, but I don't care. My lips are so dry that I have to lick them before I can fully smile.

"Well done, sonny," Bender says, and we fist bump.

I send the same rock higher this time. It rewards me with a gratifying explosion, sending more debris flying from a new crater, this one closer to us. I flinch as a spherical shield, like Ms. Merryweather's, keeps the shower of flying dried mud clumps from raining down us.

"Hells yeah!" I shout. With an unstoppable smile on my face, I bring down another rock from twice as high, yielding a much better hailstorm and digging a third hole far larger than the other two. I find myself jumping up and down, laughing like a maniac.

When my wild laughter dies down, Bender says in a very formal voice, "We shall henceforth dub this crater, Mazz's Hole. Mer's–I mean, Ms. Merryweather's kinetics have nothing on teleportation," Bender says. "But don't tell her I said so." We fist bump. "Hey, do you think that crater is a little lonely?"

"We wouldn't want that, now would we?"

"This time, I want you to kinetically pull down on the boulder while it falls." I nod and teleport it up. Struggling to focus on it right, I reach out mentally and tug as best as I can. It comes down at as a streak.

BOOM! Even with Bender's shield, the blast throws me backward like a limp rag. I skid to a halt on my back and knock my head.

I try to open my eyes but thick dust clogs the air, forcing me to close them again. That annoying high-pitch nheeeeee in my ear skewers my brain. An acrid burnt smell mixes with an earthy scent of dried mud. Someone pats me down roughly. After another few seconds, the smell disperses and I open my eyes to find a bubble of clean air surrounding me. Bender is bent over me with a look of terror on his face.

"Are. You. O. K?" he mouths slowly with exaggerated emphasis on each syllable and points at me followed by the universal okay signal with a circle and three fingers up.

"Yes," I yell, though I can't hear my own voice above the all-consuming spike through my ears. Wait. Am I okay? Bender's face bleeds from multiple scratches, a particularly bad gash streams gore from under his left–or is it right–eye.

As sensation returns to my body, my back and chest hurt but my right elbow screeches with a new echelon of torment. Looking down, my blocker shirt has new holes, some of which waft with black smoke. My thick pants, the ones I wear to apprentice with Mom and Dad, fared better. Not unscathed, but better. My head lulls back as the world warps in all directions at once.

He sprays water over my head, first biting at my cuts, then transitioning to a pleasant tingle as the water seeps in. I sputter as the salty-sweet concoction spills into my mouth and up my nose. When I blink away the fluid, my eyes function almost normally.

The pain in my arm magnifies as I try to bend it. No! Elbows can't bend that way. This isn't right. Bender kneels on my chest and clutches my forearm. I contort, not in control of my clenching muscles. He twists my hand to my belly, rotates my wrist outward, then pushes my hand toward my shoulder. A quick jolt accompanies a reaper's touch to the inside of my elbow, and the pain snaps to an almost tolerable level.

Bender summons another bottle of that saline and splashes me down, soaking my shirt and pants.

"What. Year. Is. It?" Bender yells, his mouth exaggerating

each word, blood streaking his face. At some point, the piercing shriek in my ears shriveled to a howling squeal.

"One hundred two years AAI," I answer, mimicking his overemphasized, one word at a time style.

"Where are you?" he asks.

"No clue," I shout, looking around and shrugging. My throat scratches, raw, dry. "You never told me."

"Right," he says, palming his forehead. "You'll be fine."

I manage to sit up, right arm cradled to my belly, and survey my wounds. Soaked crimson runs from dozens of cuts, reminding me of the shattered window at school. Rule fifty-three: being a nano hurts, but less with every heartbeat.

Lii must be seriously busy. Two nano-milks appear in Bender's hand. He passes me one. I gulp the chocolate milk down in one series of large gulps. Meanwhile, Bender paces back and forth, drinking his own. Between the saline spray and the nano-milk, Lii's efforts already reduced the major pain.

My ears pop and I hear Bender say, "–stupid! Bender, you really buggered that up." He turns and paces the other direction, gesticulating angrily, favoring his left leg. "You're supposed to look out for the boy, not get him killed. The first–"

"I'm fine," I tell Bender. "Or, at least I will be." His face is ashen, fear and self-loathing plain to see. He returns to crouch at my side, silently looking me over again, checking Lii's progress with my various scrapes. His cuts have re-knitted, well underway to recover, all but the white claw mark at his temple, which remains unchanged.

"Let's make more craters," I say with the best smile I can marshal.

"Absolutely not," Bender says, having missed my sarcasm. "General Fon–Dr. Fontein would kill me. We're done here. Dr. F will make confetti out of me as it is."

"Rule thirty-four," I say. "What they don't know..."

"Rule thirty-four?" he asks. I explain how I started making rules when the "incidents" started happening and list a few of them for him. "Not a bad approach to life. Perhaps I should make a rule about not accidentally killing you."

"So, we don't tell anyone," I say, then know how stupid that concept is with my leaky skull.

He nods. "Are you up for a jump?"

"Sure," I say, not looking forward to the nausea, but not wanting to stay out in the beating sun any longer.

Pop.

After a minute of losing a battle with my stomach, I look around at a dim warehouse, the air cold and dry. Floor-to-ceiling shelves hold supplies of every kind, boxes of Band-Aids and permabond, crates of jackets, a pallet of chicken noodle soup, endless mac 'n cheese, and on and on.

A crisply folded set of green army fatigues appear in his hands. A pair of new black combat boots settle at my feet and he places the clothes on them. "You needed some new clothes anyway. These should fit."

He leads me to a chlorine bathroom with benches and lockers, and a giant, many showered basin that smells of chlorine. I expect the cold water of home and Camp Astrid, but finding hot water with a strong head. Blood streaks the shower floor pink and red, dirt threading strings down the drain. The soap smells of vanilla and honey, leaving my skin soothed and clean, no doubt leaving a residue of nanites. I linger in the euphoric spray longer than I would at home, comfortable, not shivering.

I dress in the clothes Bender provided, a synthetic camo top, durable tactical pants in forest green with a black tactical belt, a luxurious pair of black socks, and a sturdy set of shiny black boots. I look in the mirror and a stranger stares back, still small but passable as an upper, shoulders broadened, face filled out, dressed like a warrior, like Bethany and Bender. When I return to the blocks, I will stick out like an emu.

I step out of the bathroom. Bender eyes me with a smile somewhere between proud and haunted. "You look good, sonny. You remind me of…" Who do I remind him of? Someone with a militaristic background like Bender. What happened to that guy?

With ghosts in his eyes, Bender says, "Time to head back. I think that's enough excitement for one day." He snaps his fingers and we stand on the trail outside the wards of Eastgate. Bender holds a large black backpack that wasn't there a second ago. He hands it to me and says, "This is for you. Consider it a gift. Or a bribe for keeping the accident between us."

"Uh, thanks," I say, unsure what else to say. He already gave me a set of upper clothes. What else could this be? The bag wears scratches and frayed fabric telling of previous use, including a tan name badge reading "Major B." I set it down and unclasp the strap and look inside.

"I have somewhere to be," Bender says, eyes shifting, jaw set, then jumps away.

Inside the bag, I find a complete change of clothes, all black, an enforcer-style bullet-proof vest, a quarter canteen, a multi-tool, a well-worn first aid kit, seven nano-bars, a nano-milk, and two syringes full of grayish-purple stuff. In a pocket, I spy a red bandana with a white cross on it. Is this his way of preparing me for war?

CHAPTER
TWENTY-FIVE

Traitor

I groan as Lii blares an alarm in my head to wake me for sunrise meditation. It grows harder every morning as summer slides closer to autumn and the days grow shorter. The cold of the often-foggy mornings lingers longer every day. Worse still, these changes mean summer will end soon and with it camp, which makes finding "inner harmony" more difficult. The concept of returning to life as a norm for another nine months is depressing. Add to that my dislike of Mr. Braunwyn both in general and for his attempt to set me up for ridicule, and I nearly back out. If not for Naren, and fear of Bethany's persistent insistence, I would back out completely.

As I pull on my shoes, I think about my unfinished challenge, unless I count the accidental teleportation, which I don't. While I keep teleporting larger and more intricate objects with each passing day, I can't move anything as substantial and complex as a cabin full of all sorts of things.

"Let's go, Mazz," Naren whispers, nudging me to move faster in his ever-happy way.

Outside, a morning mist cools my face like a million tiny pins of frost. In the darkness, a haze gives camp a sinister feel. All around us, water drips from trees like a very slow rain, tapping eerily on the forest floor with each droplet.

I pull my hoodie tight, grumbling. I'm tempted to do what any sane person should, get up and return to the warmth of my bunk. Most mornings I want to teleport directly to Eastgate, but Naren gets really queasy when I teleport him. I nearly leave him to walk on his own but decide that I don't have enough friends to start leaving them behind.

As we step onto the path, the hairs on the back of his neck give me an unsettled feeling. It's probably the weird mist or the cold breeze. I shake it off, put my hands in my hoodie pockets, lean my head down, and start walking quickly to get my heart pumping.

Only seconds later, Naren pulls me off the path, putting his finger to his lips, not that we were saying anything in the dismal cold. As soon as we find a hiding spot, the silhouette of the traitor walks along the path, head down, making a noisy swish-swish sound with every step.

Do something, I tell myself. Damn. Through the mist, I can't see him well enough or tell his distance, so I'm limited on what I can do. He passes and I've done nothing.

It's for the best, Lii says. Who knows what kind of skills he has. He could be really dangerous. With him farther ahead, we sneak out from behind the trees to follow the swishing of his pants, barely audible above the dripping condensation off the soaked branches.

After a few seconds, he stops to look around. I could swear he's sniffing the air like von Steiner. I'm entirely too aware that my clothes are not the picture of cleanliness, so I probably smell awful to someone who can transform their nose like that. After our narrowly missed encounter, we follow from farther back and moments later lose him in the dim light.

"Frak!" I whisper. "Where'd he go?"

"No clue," Naren says. We look around for several minutes, knowing he could have turned down any number of paths, stepped off the path, or outpaced us. Without even a mild frustration in his voice, Naren says, "We might as well go to sunrise meditation." He shrugs as if to say, "Oh well. That was fun."

"Sure," I say, kicking my heel into the dirt. Only if we had gotten a better look at him. I should have knocked him over the head with a stick when I had a chance. Why didn't I just knock him out? Stupid.

We continue toward Eastgate, and I fiddle with my familiar, which started twitching last night like a sleeping dog. My familiar measures as long as my leg now, putting on more weight daily. I wear it like a backpack now, an arm-like appendage thrown over each shoulder. It weighs a ton, but for some reason, I can't leave it behind, so I unload some of the burden with a kinetic lift.

"Twitching is a good sign," Naren says. "It won't be long until it reveals its form."

"That's what Justin said." I'm not sure how, but the gears, levers, and knobs are shifting and forming in ways that look like muscles.

"What do you think it will be?" Naren asks for the millionth time, in a tactic he uses to take my mind off the traitor.

"I hope it's something savage like Tiny. A cheetah or a dinosaur."

"That would be so nano! Can you imagine taking your dinosaur out for a walk when you get home?" The scavengers would stay clear of me, not that we have room for any even a small familiar in our container. I keep these thoughts to myself. Naren was raised wealthy, and I don't think he'd understand. He has a monkey familiar back home, and it plays all over the house.

When we arrive at meditation, they've already begun. I dragged my feet on the last leg of the walk because I don't feel like meditating. As much as Naren was able to redirect our conversation, my concern over the mist-shrouded man keeps rearing its head. I wish I had just...

During meditation, I can't sit still. Every droplet of water that forms on my nose reminds me that I didn't act. I let him go. I should have done something. I will be responsible when he betrays us all.

Unphasing my brain, I mentally say, Bethany?

What? she asks, annoyance spilling out of her like cold riptides preparing to drown me. I'm getting swallowed whole by her anger as images of the traitor flash before me unbidden. Then it stops and Bethany's anger lifts.

Where? When? All hints of Bethany's irritation are gone, replaced by urgency and worry. I need not tell her anything because she already knows as much as I do. I hope she didn't see the part where I changed my underwear.

And this wasn't a dream you had before waking? she says though I know her question is wishful thinking.

Ask Naren, I tell her.

A nano-second later, I feel a new happy presence in Bethany's mind, Naren.

Hey, Naren says peacefully.

Why did he return this morning? Bethany asks. *You get up at the same time every morning, right?*

Is Venus in retrograde? I ask since she knows everything we do.

C'mon. Be serious, Bethany growls.

"Mr. Becker, relax those shoulders," Mr. Braunwyn says in his perpetually boring voice, completely ignorant of our mental conversation. "You seem tense today."

"Sorry," I lie. I'm not sorry at all. I want to smack him in the face with one of the butterflies hunkered on his shoulder. Underneath that serene exterior, he's an ass. Sticking to lies, I say, "I didn't sleep well."

"All the more reason to reset," he says in his monotonous voice. Even in this horrible weather, his non-emotional tone isn't perturbed one bit. "Double your efforts to calm yourself." That makes absolutely no sense. If I work hard at it, how can I be calm?

Don't worry about him, Bethany says. Only the traitor matters. *Why was he walking faster this morning?*

Probably to make it back before the light of day, Naren says, no sense of concern washing through our connection. *It's easier to sneak around in the dark.*

True, Bethany says.

Maybe he had to go to the bathroom really bad, I offer, seeking to diffuse my tension.

Forget you, Bethany says with a blast of anger. I'm bringing the others in. Damp wind gusts through my hoodie like a screen door. The droplets stick to my stinging cheeks, spilling down to my chest as I enter cobra pose. My clothes are starting to soak through. While the others are dressed in synthetic clothes that wick away moisture, my gashed and torn blocker clothes cling to my body like a second skin.

Five more beings enter our circle of minds through Bethany. Each time she practices this multi-link the others get clearer and clearer. She rifles through my memories from this morning as easily as Lii could.

Dr. F isn't worried, Scarlett says, *so we shouldn't be either.*

Dr. F didn't see what Mazz and Naren just saw, Miles says.

Neither did we, Scarlett says. *Not really. We don't know what they saw, only a misty outline of a person. That could be anyone in camp doing anything.*

We should go to Dr. Fontein, Penny says, logic backed by an instant influx of a five-point argument.

And be shut down again? I mentally scoff. Dr. Fontein didn't listen to me last time. This time the evidence is even weaker. No thanks.

Then we should keep watch for the man in the hooded jacket, Bethany says. *Even if Dr. F doesn't want us to, now that Mazz can phase his mind, we should be able to keep it secret.*

We'll take shifts, Bethany says firmly, with confidence and adamance radiating from her as strong as a Q4 tank.

I'm in, Miles says enthusiastically. The rest of us agree but without Miles's eagerness.

Good, Bethany says. *We're decided. We'll watch the path at Northgate again in shifts.* Penny instantly sends us a watch schedule. As raindrops start to pelt down on us, everyone drops out of Bethany's head, leaving me uncomfortable and alone with her as if trapped by a tiger. *Mazz, do I need to tell you to phase your brain to keep all this secret?*

No, I say, though you did sorta just tell me.

Smartass.

A few nights later at half an hour before sunrise meditation, I sit, freezing near Northgate, my cold fingers mindlessly fiddling with switches on my familiar, which has grown to Tiny's size. It is too heavy to carry around, so I teleported him here and hunker down under my blanket. I've already decided that I will skip meditation this morning in favor of getting out of the breeze in the relative warmth of Steadfast Corner.

"Plus, I'm gonna need some rest before our capture-the-flag semi-finals." I need all my energy if I'm gonna be of any use.

Tiny is here, keeping me company, quietly purring beside my familiar, perfectly content with the cold. Tiny keeps upchucking nanite goo and gears onto my familiar, spurring its growth nightly. Where she finds the nanites and metal scraps, I have no idea.

With only eight days left at Camp Astrid, these nights spent watching for the hooded man strike a bitter chord within me. I want to enjoy every ounce left of camp before returning to norm life. I don't want to spend them on the lookout for some creepy guy in a hood.

Dr. Fontein has it covered, I tell myself. Why am I wasting time like this? Surely she, who seems to have every skill imaginable, would know everything going on around here. If it was truly dangerous, she would've told us last time. But, the others take their shifts without complaint, so I resolve to do the same.

Tiny sits up quickly and nudges me on the hand with her

snout, growling a low rumble. Looking up, I see him, hood and all, striding toward Northgate with a quick, purposeful stride. My heart pounds loudly in my temples and rage rises inside me.

"Go," I whisper to the leopard, her cue to sprint off and wake Bethany, who will telepathically rouse everyone else. As much as I don't want to, I leave my familiar behind and shadow the traitor. I'm tempted to disregard the promise I made about not engaging him on my own.

The bright moon makes it easy to see the path and trail the turncoat. The biting wind covers the sound of my footsteps. Alone in the cold, all my senses are drawn tight, ready to spring loose at any sign of threat.

About fifteen nerve-racking minutes later, the back-stabbing nano stops short in the same field as last time. Stonehenge stands in the distance, preternaturally shining in the predawn light. I duck behind the shelter of a crumbling cement wall and wait. At least the shockknights' black SUV isn't here yet. I watch the man pace back and forth, trampling the same grass over and over.

Unlike last time, I'm not defenseless. In fact, I feel powerful, my nanites thrumming, prepared to batter him. I want to act, but Penny said we can't simply capture the traitor. We need to catch him in the act and neutralize the shockknights. But I–

Don't do anything stupid, Lii says as stern as I've ever felt. Wait for our friends. I hate that he's right. I could easily teleport the man a hundred feet into the air and let him fall. I could do the same with the SUV when it arrives. Why not?

Because you're not a murderer, Lii says.

I could make an exception. I'd be justified.

It's a bridge that once you've crossed it, you can't go back.

Again, he's right, but it doesn't make this any easier.

Headlights twinkle through the gaps in the woods, sending rays into the meadow. The SUV pulls up in front of the traitor, bathing him in light, perfectly silhouetting him so I can't see anything of his features. Like last time, two knights in shiny armor, one man glinting red and the other a woman gleaming green, hop out of the SUV and approach the hooded traitor.

"Hey," Miles whispers in my right ear, nearly causing me to cry out, heart pounding in my chest, bah bump. A couple of months ago, I would have accidentally teleported away in fright. But not tonight–early morning–whatever. This time, I aim to introduce them to the definition of smackdown.

"What did we miss?" Penny asks as my heart pounds at a less distracting volume.

"Nothing," I whisper. "They just drove up and hopped out."

I can't tap into the traitor's thoughts, Bethany says. *He knows how to block off his mind.* She invades the armored man's brain and quickly subdues his ability to sense her presence, sharing what the knight hears and sees. A black face mask hides the hooded man's face. No wonder we could never make out who it was. His eyes dance red in the lights of the truck. Pyro.

It could be any nano-pyrus, Penny rebukes. *Or a nano-lumus. Not a nano-path, though. He would have sensed you last time.*

"The deal is still on," the hooded man says, his voice familiar but muffled under the mask.

The armored woman nods. "Tollere will honor the deal." A mental smile that doesn't reach the knight's face tells of the lie. Tollere plans to kill the traitor.

"He better."

"And you'll get us into Camp Astrid?" she asks.

"Tonight is the night," the traitor says. "I'll guide you in." Again, the knight's inner happiness tells of deceit. They already know how to get in. They simply wanted the traitor to draw the counselors away from camp.

Faex!

"Good," the man says. "This is the motherload." A mental image of Mr. von Steiner kneeling, pressing his hand to the chest of a convulsing black-haired man on the wood floor of a handsomely-decorated kitchen. A restrained woman screams, "No!" Her wide, watery eyes never leaving the man as her scream turns to a hiccup and her shoulders shake with sobs. The memory drops as he blinks back to the present.

I can't believe it.

Von Steiner is Tollere! His distinctive pale skin and white-washed blue eyes. Yet his lashes downturn at the corners and tears drip from his cheek, an expression I'd never expect from von Steiner.

He's a doppelgänger, Penny says. *Look at his bald head. That black scar across his neck. Probably an avatar. If physical, then a nano-lumus or a nano-morph.*

I wouldn't put it past von Steiner though.

No, Penny says, not to my thought, but something far more dire. *My AI can't connect to my comms nanites. Somehow, they jammed every way I know how to reach the outside world, and I know them all.*

I can't penetrate camp's defenses from here, Bethany says, a dangerous blade at the corners of her mental voice.

Shh, Miles hushes us. *The traitor gave the knight something.*

It's the wonkit from last year, Penny says, anger boiling through Bethany-Net. *A healing box.*

"For Nulla," the red-armored knight says into a large radio attached to his chest. Dozens of headlights blink on, shining rays through the forest, crunching over the uneven ground.

"I can't sense any of the drivers," Bethany says in near panic. "It's not possible."

"Mazz," Penny says aloud as confusion clogs up Bethany's mental link, "Bring down the trees. Block the SUVs in the forest."

How? I don't have any boulders. A thought occurs to me. Not worrying if it is too big, I teleport a crown stone from Stonehenge to a spot high above the forest on the far side of the field. I can't aim it, but the teleportation worked. An incredibly satisfying thunder echoes in the distance.

The two shockknights in the field spin on their feet, don their helmets, then aim their semi-auto rifles at the hooded jacket man. Three black-armored knights jump out of the SUV, swinging their guns outward in search of a victim.

"I can't read their minds anymore," Bethany says, dismay bumping up against me.

"Their helmets and armor block our influence," Penny says definitively. Without giving me a chance to comprehend, she hisses, "Strike their SUV, then keep demolishing trees."

I pluck another crown stone into the air a hundred feet into the air above the black car. It smacks down hard, but off-target, sends dirt flying in all directions, and knocks the knights along with the debris. The giant stone leans over and crunches the top of the SUV, pinning it in place.

Drop more stones in the far forest, Penny says. Faster. At the edge of my being, I sense her orchestrating Miles, Scarlett, and Naren into a coordinated strike. I pound two more crown stones down on the far forest, unable to aim them. Am I hitting the trucks? Faex! Did I kill anyone?

Now isn't the time for an existential crisis, Lii says. *They've come to invade Camp Astrid. To capture us.*

The shockknights rise to their feet only to fall over again. It probably has something to do with Miles's kinetics skills, Scarlett's plant skills, and Naren's wind. The traitor limp-runs back toward the path to Northgate, only to be tackled by one of the black knights.

Black-armored figures emerge from the forest on the far side, pointing guns in every direction. They fan out, helmets turning in every direction. I reach out mentally and try to kinetically fling them into the sky, but they don't budge.

Their armor won't let you affect them directly, Penny says.

The shockknights turn toward us as one and start firing, bullets pelting the trees overhead.

They have a nano-path, Bethany says, a smoldering calm squaring my mind.

Weeds sprout at our feet, clinging to my ankles. As quickly as they sprouted, they flatten in a wide circle surrounding Scarlett. "Mazz, grab their guns and get us out of here."

Wincing as I reach out my hand, I summon the closer knights' rifles kinetically. The slings around their bodies snap, and the guns fly but fly over our heads into the forest. More gunfire. I peek my head up for a second when the rounds stop, then repeat the trick, only to feel my fear smash me into an infinitesimal hole.

Pop.

CHAPTER
TWENTY-SIX

Return

I squint my right eye, wincing at the feeling of a hot poker sticking into my brain. I find myself yelling as I fall to my knees and press my hand to my head. I teleported too many of us. Warmth flows from my nose again as it always does when I abuse my influence.

We–Lii glitches. Something didn't go right. This isn't the spot outside Northgate where we played capture the flag. It takes a moment to figure out where we are. The ruined walls of a concrete foundation surround us, only feet from the path near Eastgate, outside the wards.

The others lean over or on their knees, retching and coughing. I can't imagine what it would feel like to ride along as we squeezed through my first seven-person teleportation.

"Teleport. Ahead," Penny says between coughs, wiping filth from her mouth. "Warn Dr. F. We'll catch up."

"Go!" Penny yells, not angry, but insistent.

Pop. Pop. Pop. I materialize at each landing point in a blur, following the path I take on a daily basis. On the last port, I knock my head on something hard. I meant to go to Dr. F's cabin near Southgate but–misfire. I know exactly where I am: Steadfast corner. I can only see the faint light of daybreak through the canvas roof with my left eye, my right eye reporting only blackness.

"Wake up!" I yell. "Shockknights are coming!" I want to regroup with my cabinmates but stick to Penny's plan. I need to get to Dr. Fontein.

Pop.

I stand inside the cafeteria instead of Dr. F's cabin, the pain in my right eye spiking again. At least I'm close to Fontein's cabin this time. I dash outside and run the twenty strides to the head counselor's door.

"Dr. Fontein!" I smack my knuckles on her wooden shack hard enough to hurt. No response. The window remains decidedly dark. The sound of creaky floorboards never comes. I pound on the door again and call out several more times. Nothing. My mind grinds to slow motion. What would Penny or Scarlett do? Think.

I phase my body intending to walk in, but the sifting sensation of phasing itches my eye as only it slides into the other dimension. Brilliant white-blue light doesn't radiate through the translucent doorway, a clear sign that she isn't home. My good eye grates like paper in a shredder.

What now? I need another counselor. Bender. No. I don't know where he stays, and I'm pretty sure it isn't within a hundred miles of camp. After seeing that knight's memory, I never want to see von Steiner again. Even if Penny is right about Tollere being a doppelgänger, he'd sooner electrocute me than listen to me.

Ms. Merryweather. Next to Eastgate. As soon as I imagine her cabin, I port.

Pop.

My left eye returned to this domain but a screw twists at the back of my right eye and now my left clenches painfully. Someone screams next to me. I stand, teetering on the edge of Eastgate's tower, too high to survive a fall. I rotate my arms wildly as if they are wings that could help my body from teetering over. The memory of Emerald Lake's bluff fills my head and my world flexes this way and that. The taste of blood intensifies.

Pop.

I bounce off something painful, the camp's fortifications, which end I have no idea and land on my face at the bottom of the tower where several campers mill about in wait for sunrise meditation. The air knocked out of my lungs fights against my fear of the shockknights. Seconds later, I push to my feet and pound on Ms. Merryweather's front door. "It's an emergency!" I croak. I clear my throat and yell this time, my vocal cords straining in protest. A light flickers on and shines through the cabin window.

Ms. Merryweather emerges, shining me in the good eye with a headlamp, a sour look on her face. "Mazz, what can be so important that–" She cuts short, probably noticing my bloody nose and wincing eye.

"Shockknights are coming from Stonehenge."

"What's this nonsense?" she asks, her face the portrait of intensity.

"Miles and the others are on their way back as we speak."

"Back from where?"

"We followed a sketchy guy from camp to Stonehenge. He met with warriors in shockknight armor." We don't have time for this. Every second counts. I stretch my cramped left hand with my right.

"Why didn't you go to Dr. Fontein?" she asks, head cocked and scratching her brow.

"She isn't here," I say, frustration mounting to the point of anger. I recall the knight's thought about "drawing the counselors away." In an attempt to not panic, I huff then say, "We don't have time."

She reaches out and touches my temples with a cold hand. Memories of my last few minutes–has it really only been minutes?–flip through my brain.

She pulls her hand away and says, "Jump to Northgate. Fulfill your challenge. Teleport cabins to the pond at the base of the climbing wall. There is a cave to hide in the cliffside." When I don't move, she yells, "Go! Now!"

She extends her hands down and flies over the treetops to the southwest. She can fly?

"What's happening?" one of the sunrise meditation campers yells from the base of Eastgate.

I have no idea what to say, but words pour out of my mouth anyway. "Shockknights are coming! Run to the pond by the rock-climbing cliff." I port away before she can ask questions.

Pop.

CHAPTER TWENTY-SEVEN

Northgate

I materialize on my bunk, my left hand cranked even tighter. My right eye stops hurting, but that worries me even more. Nobody seems to have moved since I was here only minutes ago. I roll off my bunk and yell, "Wake up!" I try to sound like Miles but my voice fails me miserably. "Shockknights are coming!" Nobody moves.

Justin says, "Shut your pranking mouth," then rolls over. I wish we hadn't said my accidental teleportation of Steadfast Corner was a prank. The nano that cried wolf...

"Shockknights are coming!" I yell again, my voice hoarse, grinding in my throat. Anxiety builds inside me like a growing thistle. I wish I had Bethany's ability to mentally push people into motion.

"Where is Miles?" Brooks asks.

"He's probably out with Bethany," someone says, which gets a few snickers.

This is taking too long. Even in my adrenaline-fueled state, I'll never be able to teleport Steadfast Corner. I failed at my challenge, a challenge perfectly suited to my current predicament. I may not be able to port the cabin, but maybe...

I port my cabinmates to the cave, but the supporting wood from several bunks vanish, dumping their occupants to the floor.

"Help!" I yell above the cacophony that is Steadfast Corner. "We need to get everyone to the pond by the cliffside. There's a cave there." A loud explosion echoes through camp from the north, lending strength to my words. All voices go quiet.

"Divide up and get the whole camp to the cave." Nobody moves.

"Go!" Justin yells, a harshness and command that goes against everything I know about him. My cabinmates jump to, pulling on shoes. I wish I could motivate people that way. Justin says, "Split into pairs. Start at the northern cabins and work your way south, half on the girl's side and half on the boys. No three-minute drill this time. Act now."

"I'm with you," Justin says. As he squeegees his feet into his boots, I pull out the kevlar vest Bender gave me and fasten it tight. I retrieve a nano-milk from the go-bag, then hike the black combat backpack over my shoulder. Once ready, Justin asks, "What do we need to do?"

"They're coming from the north," I say. I wish Penny or Bethany were here. They'd know exactly what to do. What would Scarlett do? She'd meet any threat head-on. "We need to protect Northgate."

We step out the back of Steadfast as another explosion rumbles through camp, this one accompanied by flames from Northgate. I look to Justin. He nods. In the early-dawn light, I can't fully make out his expression, but if I'm not mistaken, his jaw is set, stoic, not at all like my ever-goofy cabinmate.

They're here, Bethany blares into my head as if the explosions hadn't announced their arrival. *Penny is about to launch her "egg" catapults. It should buy us a few minutes.* I don't bother to respond as I force my feet toward Northgate, keeping to the trees. Gulping down the nano-milk, I am all too aware that I'm breaking rule nine: don't chase trouble, and more important rule one: try not to die.

Another firey explosion thunders ahead of us. As I reach the clearing around Northgate, I hide behind a large redwood, tilting my head out to see. Von Steiner stands in the courtyard, blasting lightning from his fingertips through a hole that used to be a heavy metal gate. The interwoven wood of the towers burns and smokes. Each electric strand cracks the air like a bullwhip.

Von Steiner's pale hands and face glow purple-blue in the light of the electric arcs, his face every bit as angry as Tollere's was sorrowful.

Penny's catapults didn't take into account their weird armor, Bethany says. Penny's cold fury bleeds through Bethany-Net, lending a little courage to combat my fear. The connection to my friend's emotions gives me more purpose and focus than I could manage on my own. I'm not doing this for me. I'm pushing on for all of our sakes.

Muffled snaps of gunfire fill the silence between lightning strikes. Von Steiner falls to the ground, limp. Lifeless?

Three black knights step through the blown-apart gate, pointing their rifles here and there.

"No!" Justin yells, stepping forward and shooting lightning bolts of his own at the knights. His electrical discharge doesn't flash as brightly as von Steiner's but makes quick work of the three black knights. His face flickers with an angry snarl with each bolt.

I watch in horror as Justin falls to his knee. Two more knights step into the courtyard, one pointing his rifle at Justin, the other scanning back and forth. Justin topples, every inch closer to the ground intensifying my anger, fear, disbelief, and need for revenge. Is he dead? No. A dart sticks out of his neck. They came to capture us and deracinate us, not kill us.

Two shockknights turn my way and fire. I hold out my arms defensively, hands protecting my head and neck. Rather than feeling holes riddle my body, darts bounce off an invisible barrier. Another accidental shield.

"No!" I scream and my kinetic shield streaks forward, flattening the shockknights into the camp's sturdy walls.

They hit with a sickening crunch and remain pinned for a moment before slumping to the ground like nothing more than undercooked pasta. Did I just kill them? The thought shadows a hidden place within me. I didn't mean to. It was reflexive.

It's okay, Bethany says, backing her word with purpose and resolve. *You are protecting us all.* I feel my inner turmoil dull but not fully leave under her mental pressure. More black knights step through Northgate, pointing their guns in every direction.

I duck for cover behind the tree, not trusting that I can summon another shield. A few soft thumps and much more intimidating louder thwacks hit the trunk in front of me. No amount of war games could compare to this. They're coming for us. They're coming for me.

Do something, Bethany commands like a senior officer.

More knights stream in to replace the last, firing as they go. A stone giant lumbers into the courtyard from the south, barreling toward the knights. The knights shoot at the creature but the bundle of stones isn't perturbed by the puny bullets or darts. With surprising agility, the golem knocks into the two knights, sending them flying out through the gate. The golem approximates a fighting stance, blocking the gate.

Thirty feet to my right, Naren gives me a thumbs up and smiles. How in all that is nano can he possibly smile at a time like this?

Boom! The stone monster flies apart, flames exploding through the courtyard. As I duck back behind my tree, stone fragments clobber down and smack against trees.

More knights storm through the gate, stepping over flaming stones. They home in on Naren and fire. I focus on the leading three black knights and teleport them a hundred feet into the air, but they remain fixed to the ground.

No. Penny says through Bethany-Net, her breakneck logic lashing against my mistake. *Their armor protects them from direct nano-skills.*

They continue firing at Naren. The rounds don't impact the trees with loud thwacks like they did at the field near

Stonehenge. Instead, they're quiet thumps. More darts.

Naren falls to the ground with an "umph."

Naren! Bethany howls in my head. His essence slips from Beth-Net. *He's knocked out.*

Naren's rocks. I bob my head out from behind the tree trunk as quick as I can, spotting the black knights, and kinetically launch the stones horizontally at the growing group of invaders, like a giant shotgun blast. No aim or fine control. Only brutish rage. Daring to peek my head out again, I watch the stones knock the knights off their feet.

Even with that armor, the hailstorm of stones must bruise and batter them on the insides. Hopefully, I didn't kill anyone. I try to bash them again with the rocks, but accidentally teleport them into the air. They take too long to crash down, but when they do, they're spectacular meteors. Dirt and knights eject from the impact zone. Did I see an arm fly away on its own? I want to vomit.

My left hand curls tighter, clamped into an impossible chaos that reminds me of Gunther's bootless toes back in the blocks.

"Retreat!" one of the knights yells. I let them go, some crawling, others supporting their wounded comrades.

Get Justin, von Steiner, and Naren to the cave, Penny says. Numbed by my own actions as much as by the attempted shockknight blitz, I follow her instructions and port them, one at a time, to the pond's shore outside the cave. Please, please, please let them arrive at the right place. Or did I phase them by accident?

No time for second-guessing, Penny says through Beth-Net.

A knight, dressed in red armor but with bare hands, steps forward with some form of a fuzzy translucent shield in front of him. I kinetically snap branches off the tree above me and send them flying at the red knight. Only one flies true. The on-target branch smacks into the man's amorphous shield.

Oh, No! They have a kinetic. Fraking traitor!

He's a nano-magnetic, Penny corrects me. *That shield is a million metal fines.*

The shield diffuses a bit, and a glinting spear shoots toward me. I duck behind the tree and am rewarded with the sound of metal smacking on wood, not on my chest. The metal inside the tree emits a drilling sound. He's going to bore through the tree and hit me.

I imagine the metal fines as they grind their way through the tree and try to phase them. The sawing sound stops, only to be replaced by a gurgling. The red knight falls along with his metallic shield, a metal drill bit sticking out of his chest. The sound of him hitting the ground reverberates with a clatter that carries more weight than can be heard with ears. I accidentally felled a man with his own weapon. There is no denying it; that was a mortal wound. I didn't mean to.

Nicely done, Bethany says. I'm not convinced she's right. I'm never going to forget that. I want to puke, but Bethany pushes those thoughts from my mind.

Bullets hit the tree in front of me, keeping me pinned down and terrified. In a blink, I port to the other side of the clearing, splintering into a million pieces and reconstructing again. Teleportation has never hurt like that before. I shake my head to clear my thoughts, aided by Bethany's calming influence and Penny's mental scaffolding.

I go to rip more branches off a redwood only to phase a section from the trunk of the tree. The hundred-foot-tall redwood squeals and falls onto four black knights, sending a rapid percussion of breaking branches through the courtyard. I'm breathing too hard, whether because of fear or exertion I couldn't say.

My whole left arm contorts, torqued at the elbow and shoulder to pin my folded wrist beneath my armpit.

You've over-extended on your nanites, Bethany says.

I wish I could check in with Lii. I pull a branch loose from the fallen tree and kinetically club the closest shockknight and yell, "Stay down!"

I fall to my knee, panting, the right side of my face numb.

A silver streak flashes across the ground from the south and dives onto a black knight as he attempts to recover his feet. Tiny. The mechanical cat tosses a man wildly to the side and pounces on another. Bullets ricochet off her. I watch, mesmerized by the display of raw animal ferocity and mechanical power as she downs another black-clad knight.

Then there are two Tinys, each ravaging a knight. No, this latter one resembles a dog. No, a wolf. I recognize its gears and knobs and the two rust-colored streaks that run down his metal ribs. I can see through his eyes and feel the mechanical strength in his jaws as they crunch through the armor. We're bonded. He emanates loyalty. The name, Rusty, clicks into my thoughts.

Stop watching and do something, Bethany says.

Still on my knees, I kinetically yank on a section of Northgate's right tower, only to phase the section instead. The tower teeters, then collapses under its own weight into the breach in Northgate. Two knights, one of whom is peppering Rusty with bullets, crumple under the falling mass. I don't care if I killed the knight who was shooting Rusty.

You do and will care, Bethany says. *But you can't think about it now.*

I sink to my butt, exhausted. I need a moment to rest, recover from my constant expenditure of sugars and nanites. I can't see anyone moving except the two familiars. I need nanites.

An explosion shakes the ground under me. The stones, metal, and wood planks that I collapsed into the breach now fly in every direction. They didn't bother to search for survivors under that pile. Instead, they blew them up like no more than burning wood.

It takes a moment before I realize that my distorted left shoulder has a several-inch chunk of wood buried in it, an inch above my armpit. Blood seeps out on my shirt, joining the stains from my nose. So much blood.

I lean against the tree. I can't keep doing this. I have to get out of here.

Help is coming, Bethany says. *Just a little longer.*

A green knight steps through the newly formed channel,

brown and green whips dancing around her like a medusa, but with snakes poking through each major joint instead of her head. she turns toward me. The tree in front of me groans as branches bend down, seizing me tight. My shoulder screams and my ribs creak and pop. She's crushing me.

I try to teleport away but accidentally phase into the purple-blue dimension. I crawl away like a three-legged dog behind a thick, purple tree a few yards farther into the woods. Rusty bounds to my side, having slipped into this sauna of a dimension with me. Nanites press into me. My crushed chest hurts worse in the thick, hot air. The vines of the green knight glow bright aqua, but her armor is jet black.

My chest. I can't stay here for long even with all these nanites replenishing me. I'll suffocate long before my ribs heal. Without intending to, I re-emerge in normal reality, gasping for air.

Several black knights race through the new hole in the wall accompanied by a blue knight. There are too many of them.

She's almost here, Bethany says.

Who? Thoughts are coming slower with wheezing breath.

Do something!

I find myself teleporting a section of the burning planks, stone, and metal of Northgate's tower high into the air to rain down on them. The green knight smacks the larger projectiles aside. The blue one releases an explosion of lightning overhead, clearing a swath above him. The rest of the debris crashes down, flattening three black shockknights, nothing more than origami under a kid's foot. The rumble of the heavy logs and metal sickens and bolsters me. While I neutralized some of the immediate danger, I just smashed–no, obliterated, probably killed–humans.

Think of it as nullifying, Penny says, a calculating wall of reason nudging against my head.

I need to "nullify" more of them. Cling to that. The thought helps me detach a smidge from the malignancy of it all. "Nullify."

Tiny and Rusty launch at the blue and green knights. From Rusty's perspective, I watch as lightning crackles out of the blue knight's hands, encasing both of them in searing pain. Every servo and muscle within Rusty fires at once, and he collapses to the ground.

Drawing on my anger, I lift my hands, attempting to throw the green and blue knights flying. I can't latch onto them, but the earth beneath them bursts up like twin geysers, sending them tumbling twenty feet in the air. The green knight's vines fan out and she transforms into a green-yellow butterfly, gliding smoothly down. She reaches out with a green vine and hooks the blue knight by the ankle before he crashes down.

Dangling by his feet, the blue knight extends his hand at me. Electricity courses through my body. My muscles convulse, arms and legs thrashing about. My skin burns. The acerbic scent of burnt hair and ozone fills my nostrils. My heart pounds, stops, and pounds again in my ears, washing away every other sound, I fall to the ground, exposed and defenseless.

The sky overhead is lighter now with beautiful pinks and oranges painting a few fluffy clouds. My body goes limp. The peacefully canvased sky calls to me. Am I dead?

No! Bethany yells, a forceful bear of a growl attempting to intimidate me into action. *Get up.*

I can't.

Someone flies over the treetops.

Ms. Merryweather, Bethany says, relief poking through my fear like a shining spear of hope. Earth and trees fly about like giant darting hummingbirds. So much chaos and power unleashed it shakes the ground.

She'll hold them off. Come to me. Bethany sends me a mental image of where she is, hidden in the bushes where von Steiner nearly sniffed me out. I can't even crawl. How can I get to her?

She slams her presence into my mind and seizes control of me more forcefully than Ing ever could. My deadened body folds in on itself, robbing me of the glorious sky. Is this what dying feels like? Squeezing into nothingness.

Pop.

CHAPTER TWENTY-EIGHT

Eastgate

Bethany and Penny stand over me. Why are they so tall? And so worried? I've passed from this realm to the next. I'm dead, right Lii? Nothing. Why is Bethany's nose bleeding? Did she die too? Why can't I see the gold and rose sky? That's where I wanted to die. Not here tucked into a clump of bushes, under a tight ring of trees.

"You're not dead," Bethany says, leaning down to cup my cheek the way Mom does.

I'm not?

As the ubiquitous pain from the lightning recedes, Bethany says, "You have some broken bones and the lightning fried you pretty good."

"Broken bones? Lightning?"

"Minor fractures. You're fine," she says, a weak tug of her lips forming a crooked smile. Fine? Minor fracture? "Your med-pack had a syringe with nanites in it. The nanites from the injection will take effect in a minute."

Someone is making god-awful noises to my left. Spotting my glance, Penny says, "That's Ms. Merryweather. She's incredible."

"Right," I say. "Did you know she can fly?"

"Yeah," Bethany says, though her concentration has turned elsewhere. She wipes her nose and takes a sip of nano-milk.

"We're conducting defenses from here," Penny says. "Rest for a minute. We need you up and healthy." She hauls me to lean against a tree. Rusty belly crawls to stay at my side. His back legs aren't moving. Poor guy.

Penny hands me a nano-milk and says, "Drink up. You have work to do." The devilish twitch of her cheek makes me nervous. Bethany and Penny both hold shockknight rifles slung casually over their shoulders, each with one hand resting on the handle, prepared for battle. They stand, viscous and natural, as comfortable as we were in paintball wars.

"What 'work' do you have for me?" I ask Penny, my voice sounding stronger than I would have expected. With every breath, I feel better. My ribs clack, making me wince. Perhaps not with every breath. Then they feel tender but much better.

I alternate between a gulp for me and a slurp for Rusty. The sensation of an invisible fifth limb allows me to feel him healing too. His legs mend themselves and twitch as the nanites from the milk do their job. "Good boy." I pet him behind his upturned chest.

With restored energy, I summon more nano-milk from the cafeteria, restock my backpack, and twist open another to share with Rusty.

"Can you stand?" Penny asks. I slowly rise to my feet, not trusting myself. My muscles wobble like a toddler's. With a flutter of her eyebrows she asks, "Ready to get out of here?"

I nod, not feeling the least bit ready for whatever she has planned but forcing myself not to shy away. I'm not doing this for me. I'm doing this for my friends, for the other campers, for the very few blockers like Devin.

"Good," Bethany says. "Take us to Eastgate." This sounds like violating rule nine: don't chase trouble. How many rules have I broken today?

Pop.

"Geesh!" Bethany yells. "Give a gal some warning. Count

down or something. That was awful." Waves of nausea slosh over the edges of her mind, almost bringing my nano-milk back up.

I don't bother responding because at that moment Eastgate explodes, throwing me off my feet. Mid-impact, I teleport all of us, including the familiars, behind Ms. Merryweather's cabin. I land on an air cushion, but my ribs jar painfully.

Take it easy. Lii says with venom, momentarily snapping into my conscious thought. *I'm still working hard in here to fix you up.*

Bethany and Penny look sick but their high-end upper clothes blocked the scratches and scrapes more than my rags. Note to self: wear upper clothes when I get into a fight. I peek my head out from behind the cabin to find a green knight emerging through the freshly smoking gap between Eastgate's towers. I prepare to act, not sure what I'm about to do, but Bethany's hand stays me.

Ms. Quin, the nano-botany counselor, leaps from the tree above me into the courtyard. Tendrils reach up from the ground to catch her and gently set her down. The green knight's blade-like tentacles lash out at her, but her tentacles perry the blows.

Three black knights aim their guns at Ms. Quin but can't hit her without the risk of hitting the green knight. Noted: the black knights are expendable. The other colors aren't.

As Ms. Quin and the green knight battle with many sword-like appendages, the black knights begin to fan out, flanking the counselor, preparing to shoot the counselor from the side.

With clear shots at them from our angle, Bethany and Penny let loose a deadly volley from their stolen rifles. They fly and crumple to the ground, likely wounded, not killed because of their armor.

Bethany and Peny turn their aim toward the green invader, but her vines puff out into a yellowish sphere, like popped corn. Ms. Quin's lancing tentacles can't penetrate the makeshift bunker. Bethany leans forward, gun braced on the ground for a precision shot. The bullet ricochets and hits our counselor's leg, toppling her.

Ms. Quin cries out in pain, clutching her shin. A green sheath encases her lower leg. She rolls to her feet and limps away from the gate.

I phase a section of Eastgate to block the knights' breach as I accidentally did at Northgate but the stones, metal, and wood appear on top of the green knight's protective orb. None of my skills will do what I want them to. But the effect on the tower is the same, and if greeny emerges from her cocoon, she'll have a ton of weight to deal with. I don't want to squish her if I don't have to, but this way, I doubt she'll be able to return to the fight.

Black knights climb over the rubble of Eastgate, firing in our direction. I summon a shield in front of us, but it doesn't take form. I need to figure out how I do that. The green knight's protective shell blocks the black knights from shooting Ms. Quin.

I try to phase the tower on the other side of the gate, but send wood, metal, and cement shrapnel exploding in all directions, nailing three of the incoming knights back through the gate. I'm nullifying, not killing or maiming.

More knights rush in, and a black knight who was already inside the camp's walls runs south along the inside of the wall and slips into the woods.

We can't let him find the cave, Penny says through Beth-Net.

Rusty. Hunt him down. Without pause, he and Tiny bound off, limping but faster than any human, especially one weighed down by armor.

Phase greeny's plant shell, Penny says, cool and collected. For once, it works, and the green knight crumples under a heap of scrap. Ms. Quin dodges behind a cabin as Bethany and Penny draw the black knights' fire.

Pain of a flavor I've never felt before lances through me. Every bone in my body breaks at once. My skin boils. My fingernails peel back. I convulse with muscles knotted, even sinewy flesh I didn't know existed. Contorting, I fall. Unfk! Reality twists into a fathomless abyss that pierces through me like a thousand porcupines.

Bethany snatches control of my mind and the torture cools to a low simmer. *It was all in your head,* she says. It didn't feel like it was in my head. From Bethany's dominating perspective, an image presses forward, showing a purple knight without one of those weird helmets that the other knights wear.

His beard reminds me of Bender's, which unleashes a different kind of twinge through me that pokes at Penny's concept of nullifying. They are human under those helmets, with unique faces, eyes, and lives of their own. Lives that I ruined or snuffed out.

Nullified, Penny reaffirms, cold symmetry adding structure to my mind.

The simmering pain dies completely as the full force of Bethany pushes mercilessly into the purple knight. He freezes in a perfect imitation of a statue, Bethany's core so angry and spectacularly frightening. A purple aurora borealis shimmers around her, whether mental or physical I can't tell.

"He's going to wake up with complete amnesia," Bethany growls. Her spirit shines with a smoldering outrage. "How dare he use his influence like that?"

Returning my attention to Eastgate, vines have sprouted between the legs of the remaining black knights, crawled over their backs, buckled their bodies, imprisoned in Ms. Quin's trap. The hole in Eastgate closes with a chaotic web of plants, trees, and ruins of the towers.

Eastgate is secure, Penny reports to someone other than Bethany and me, someone cordoned off in a different section of Bethany's mind. How does she do it?

It's a group effort, Bethany says. *Miles, Ing, and especially Mr. Roberto form our nano-pathy backbone.* The burden of responsibility lightens a skosh at hearing that others fight alongside us, even if I can't see or sense them.

Through my bond with Rusty, I watch and feel the forest floor glide under me, the sensation of his powerful "muscles" propelling him between the trees, Tiny at his side. Ahead, a black knight turns and fires at Rusty. Pangs of pain ricochet off me–

no, Rusty. Then we descend upon him, tearing at his armored shoulder with Tiny mangling his leg, breaking bones until he stops moving.

"No time to relax," Bethany says. "Ms. Quin has Eastgate. Take us to Westgate."

Fatigue grips at me. My thrashing under the purple knight's onslaught re-injured my partially healed shoulder, broken ribs, and burned skin.

Pop.

CHAPTER TWENTY-NINE

Westgate

Westgate is a chaos of crackling flames, flattened bodies, smoldering clothes, and black armor fallen. Mr. Winston's giant form lies among the motionless forms. Is he dead? Six black knights form a human shield around an orange knight with fire sprouting from her bare hands.

Bethany tackles me as they swing their guns toward us. Something explodes in my chest as we fly behind Mr. Braunwyn's fancy cabin, a knock that expels all the air in my lungs. She lands on top of me, amplifying the deadly pain in my abused chest. My left foot bellows angrily with a sickening crunch. Bethany leaps off me, one hand pressed down on my back. Crack. Was that my heart?

No, Lii says, angry, pushing through our glitchy bond. *Your ribs cracked. I just had them mended.*

My lungs ache for oxygen. I can't breathe. I can't breathe.

Stop getting hurt! Lii yells.

The clang of bullets bouncing off metal pings in my ears. No. Bullets hitting familiars. Without meaning to, I teleported Tiny and Rusty with us. They're protecting Penny, who fell short of the cabin. Ping. Ping. Each of the blows stings through my connection with Rusty. White-hot flames wrap around him but don't burn his metallic frame.

I teleport the three of them behind Mr. Braunwyn's cabin, but not before Penny's clothes ignite under a blast of flames. I reach out to grab her feet but can't bend properly. Instead, my mind reaches out with tendrils and teleports her next to me, protected by wood and stone. Upon rematerializing, the fire has squelched, but blackened fringes of synthetic fabric have fused to her skin. The smell of burnt flesh wrinkles my nose. I try to stand, but my ankle won't support my weight.

Fire consumes the edge of the cabin, fanning around the corner toward me.

Her hands, Bethany says and sends me a mental image of the orange knight's bare hands. *Teleport them somewhere.*

On my knees, I sneak a look around the burning cabin. A new fountain of flames flies at me, releasing a rush of heat that fries my left arm. The heavy smoke all around me eats at my lungs. The frayed threads that ring the many holes on my left leg burn like candles on a gasoline and kindling cake. Inch by inch, the burnt nerves report back like sizzling fajitas.

New rule: don't get cooked alive.

New rule, Lii says angrily. *Stop getting hurt.*

"Get up!" Bethany yells down at me as she blindly shoots a few rounds around the side of the cabin. Another wave of heat buffets off Mr. Braunwyn's cabin, searing my already singed flesh.

"Fight back!" Bethany yells with both her voice and a mental command.

I flop to my left side, landing on my side. With the orange knight's hands highlighted by flames, they make easy targets. I mentally push, and she screams, holding her missing hands to his face, lit by the flames all around her. While no blood pours from her severed wrists, I can see bone and flesh on her stubs. My misfire accidentally phased her hands rather than teleported them. Gross, but not as awful as teleporting them. Either way, I'll never unsee it.

All six black knights' rifles turn down toward me. Rusty bounds in front of me, blocking a mixture of darts and bullets. Bethany fires wildly with one hand and pulls me behind the burning building with the other.

A ricocheted dart tugs at my good shoulder. In a panic, I grasp for the dart seeking to draw it out before the knockout juice kicks in. But it isn't embedded in my skin. Instead, it dangles in the folds of my oversized shirt.

Behind the tinderbox of a cottage, I grab at the dart and its needle jabs into the sensitive flesh under my middle finger. It registers slowly, being only a minor pinprick compared to my burns, ribs, and ankle. Too slow, I pull my hand away. My finger numbs as I dislodge the poker. Damn! I'm done for.

Penny's intelligence pokes through my thoughts. *Most of the sedative was lost with its strike to your shirt. You'll be fine.*

Someone shouts, "Help!" from inside Mr. Braunwyn's cabin. I can't believe anyone could still be alive inside that conflagration. Filled with all those books and graphic novels, it is the perfect design for a giant campfire.

You keep the knights busy, Bethany says. *I'll get whoever is in there.* The numbness in my finger spreads up my burnt arm and wounded shoulder, soothing my raw mental edges. So much better.

Stop using our nanites! Lii complains. He's furious with me. *You already depleted us. You will kill us if you keep–.*

I port to the other side of the quickly combusting cottage, wishing the numbness would dull my ankle's shrieking. I kinetically wrench the guns out of the black knights' hands. I wheel the rifles around one hundred and eighty degrees and fire, double tapping each trigger to the chest. To my surprise, it works. The knights fall, crumpled but not bleeding, their armor blocking the bullets.

Stop. Using. Our–

I drag the knights by their harnessed rifles, faster and faster, and launch them through the flames of Westgate.

Smack. Something slams into my chest and again into my

ravaged arm, throwing me onto my back.

We're hit, Lii says. *Double tap.* Panic from Lii and me. Weakness and shadow beckon me. As the numbness of the low-dose sedative warms my body, my mind grows fuzzy. I fight to breathe through the smoke and constricted chest. I flounder to my side, eyes squinting against the sting of dry ash.

Someone appears in the sky. Ms. Merryweather's black beard and dark skin look funny.

Blackness.

CHAPTER THIRTY

Wolf Cave

A yellowish radiance floods between my eyelids. Too much light. A woman's silhouette shades my eyes and an angelic voice says, "Welcome back."

I recognize her, my beautiful Ing, the incomparable woman who visits me in my dreams. I reflexively phase my brain so she can't toy with me again. I don't hear the sifting sound. It failed. She smiles sweetly, but not lovingly. She's a memory in my head, but not as my goddess. She conveys dispassionate concern for my wellbeing and health, nothing more. Her beauty is worn thin in a way that doesn't suit her high cheekbones and deep brown eyes. She tumbled from the stars.

Coldness quivers through me, each shake smacking me with pain. Arms. Ankle. Chest. Head.

Burned, sprained, broken, concussed, and depleted of nanites, Lii says, as grumpy as a hungry scavenger.

Weightless. No, floating.

Bathing in a pool of nanites.

"Can you sit up?" Ing asks, helping me up upright. I'm in the shallows of a milky gray pond inside a well-lit cave. The movement pinches at my chest, the exertion throbbing in my skull. "Good job," she says. "We're safe here."

Rusty, in the water laying against my leg, licks at my charred, swiss-cheese shirt. The burns hurt, but not as bad as I would have expected. I roll my ankle and wince. My shoulder throbs, wrapped by white gauze and immobilized by my belt.

We're fine, Lii says. *No thanks to you. Are you done hurting us yet?*

Yes.

Stay put while I suck more nanites from the pond.

Stalactites litter the ceiling of the huge cavern, each glowing. Bodies line the milky pond, bandages covering arms, legs, and heads of the wounded, Mr. Winston the most obvious among them. His clothes cover only a minor part of his body. Several young campers, no more than ten, lie half in the pool unconscious for who knows what reason, too young for this.

"Take it slow," Ing says. "Your wounds haven't healed yet, especially the bullet hole. Your AI is doing great with the nanite-rich water."

Memories return to my mind like a deathly torrent. "Shockknights!" I yell, though my voice cracks, weak and raspy.

"Shhhh. It's okay," she says soothingly, the faintest of calming influence washing over me. I phase my brain and it works this time. She squeezes my good shoulder as if to comfort me, but it only serves to mash one of my many scrapes. "Dr. Fontein and Bender arrived in time. After what you did, the counselors took care of the rest."

"Good." I can't think of anything else to say, so I mindlessly repeat, "good."

"Mazz!" A female voice squeals in excitement. I turn my head too fast and develop a serious case of the spins. A double vision of Scarlett runs at full sprint to me. She leaps on top of me, splashing water everywhere and knocking me back to the cave floor. "You're awake!"

"Ugghh," is all I can manage as she bounces up and down on me like I'm a trampoline. My partially mended wounds send excruciating shockwaves through my body, launching me into a fit of agonizing coughs.

"Sorry," she says, hopping off me, face full of excitement and embarrassment, her clothes soaked through like mine. Pulling me gently into a sitting position again, she laughs and squeezes me in a hug that hurts, but not nearly as much as the bouncing and not entirely unpleasantly. "You did it!"

She kisses me, her lips warm and tender. What?

I do believe she just kissed you, young man, Lii says. *Do you want me to tell you about the birds and the bees? When a boy and a girl–*

Shut it, Lii.

"I, uh. I did what?" I ask, my temples pounding with each heartbeat. Did she just kiss me? Is this real?

"You kept them from getting in," she says as if I fell out of the dumb tree and hit every branch on the way down, which doesn't sound too far from how I feel.

Devin, the blocker from capture-the-flag, attends to a small girl with a savage gash on her forehead. He looks up and gives me a nod, a gesture of blocker kinship that I didn't know I needed. Rule sixteen: once a blocker, always a blocker.

The scent of freshly baked bread wafts from an oven carved into the far rock wall, fueled by smokeless flames. Wyatt, from my cabin, shifts loaves around in the kiln with a giant spatula. "This place is incredible."

"Yes, it is," Scarlett says. "It's the wolf cave we explored. C'mon. Let's go say 'hi' to the others. You can soak in the waters downstream." She helps me stand, then supports me, her shoulder under mine, as I test my ankle.

It'll hold, Lii says. *But be careful.*

Scarlett dries my clothes and shoes with a wave of her hand, her body anchoring me both mentally and physically. I still shiver, frozen everywhere except where we touch. While Scarlett guides me, limp-stepped, along the stream and into the long tunnel, I ask, "What happened to the shockknights?"

"The rumor is that Dr. Fontein sent them off the coast of Port Saint Johns, the most shark-infested water on the planet. It sounds like something someone would make up, but it would definitely serve them right."

I can't argue with her. Can they swim in that strange black

armor? Would Dr. F actually kill them all? With that scary intensity of hers, I wouldn't put it past her.

Oh frak. How many did I kill? Murder. I stumble under the weight of that question only to be caught by Scar with an firm arm reassuringly wrapped around my waist.

We can debate about self-defense versus murder now or later, Lii says. *You choose. Either way, your actions land us on the right side of justice.*

Scarlett leads me forward, an odd crook to her lips, unaware of the darkness gnarling my mind. Her body heat comforts me far more than Lii's words. I wish I could wrap myself up in her.

Careful there, Lii says. *I like her and I don't want you to screw things up for us.*

In the side rooms off the central tunnel, campers sit on the floor or lean against the walls, a dozen in each. Some are young, not even half my age, and others older like me, but they all look tired.

But largely unharmed, Lii says. *That's the important thing.*

Eyes and whispers follow me as I limp by. More than a few gazes linger on Rusty. Gawkers are the least of my concerns right now. Scarlett guides me to where Miles and Bethany stand. Miles looks strong and in his element. Bethany's clean-shaven scalp, pasty white, boasts several raw burn splotches that haven't fully healed.

"Don't make a single comment," she says. "It burned in the fire." She looks as fierce as Ms. Merryweather now. I don't even open my mouth. "And you should look at yourself."

Remembering the lightning and flames, I touch my own head only to find patches of raw, hairless scalp. I must look downright comical. No wonder everyone was staring at me. Bethany's changes from one of cheer to concern, telling me that I look less silly and more damaged.

Miles says, "It is good to see you upright."

"Rumors of my demise were a little premature," I say, attempting a smile, but feeling stings of resistance in my cheeks. What happened there?

I haven't been able to heal the splinters from the shrapnel at Eastgate, Lii says. Miles gives me a broad smile and claps me on my goodish shoulder, making me wince. Why does everyone need to touch me? I need more nanites.

Sit with your feet in the stream, Lii says. *It will help.*

As Scar helps me sit, Miles says, "Be happy. We won." The cool water does feel good on my bare feet even though I'm freezing. Where are my shoes? Scar leans close and puts her arm around me, adding her considerable warmth to my cold body.

"None of us won today," my disembodied voice says.

"Take the wins when you can," Miles says. I nod and weakly smile in consent, though I don't agree. My cabinmates pile out of the side room, boisterously asking to hear everything.

"Shut it," Justin roars. "Mazz has been through enough. Let him be." He waves them back into Steadfast Corner's temporary room. Relief fills me at seeing that he survived intact, a memory of him crumbled on the ground shading my thoughts. Justin, who lingers a moment, is usually the last person to cut a conversation short.

I sit, now flanked by Naren on one side and Scarlett on the other. While Naren smiles in his standard, nose-wrinkling manner, Scarlett and Justin seem different.

They struggle with the same burdens as you, Lii says.

Rusty leans on my back so I am now propped up on three sides. Rusty runs hot, adding his heat to Scar's. I almost feel comfortable. How does Naren look as happy as ever?

You should ask him, Lii says.

A couple of younger campers run up close, eyes wide, pupils glued to me and Rusty. "That's him. He–"

"Shoo," Scar says, fanning them away like particles of dust. Vines waggle out of the rock at them. The green knights' vines lance through my being. The kids run back down the hall, their shrill squeals reinforcing my memories of our ordeal. I don't know if I'll ever be able to hear a scream or a shriek again without recoiling from those memories.

"How long was I out?" I ask.

"It's noon," Scarlett and Lii say. Noon. We are all still in the cave five hours later.

"The counselors haven't let everyone out yet?" A thought clanks into place. "That means..."

"We won't be safe until we leave Camp Astrid." Scar squeezes me around the waist, unleashing a round of raspy coughs. "Penny says the shockknights won't be able to regroup for a day or more, if ever. So we have a bit of time." While I wouldn't ever argue with Penny's insanely bright mind, I don't feel confident about anything when it comes to shockknights.

My mind resembles a world championship ping pong match, each thought hollow and smashed hard. Where is Dr. Fontein? Ms. M? Bender? Hell, von Steiner? How long can we hold out here if the shockknights come back? Then my mind settles on, "Who was the traitor?"

Scar's body tenses, muscles shifting powerfully next to me. "Pyro's cabin and four other campers went missing. We're pretty sure it was one of them."

"So, Pyro or Henri." It fits. They're the closest to supremes that you can find at Camp Astrid. They looked down on us all, viewing us as no more than oxen, raised to do their bidding. If I could get my nanites on them...The idea of sacrificing your fellow nanos is, is...

"It's unforgivable," Scar says, watching me carefully. I want to tear them apart cell by cell. They're like the various colored knights. How many nanos have turned on our own kind? I'll kill them.

No. Don't think it, the thought oozing, lava spilling from fissures within. Without meaning to, I whisper, "How many did I kill?" I can't remember them all. I feel sick.

"The question is, how many of us did you save?" Scar says, leaning her head on my shoulder. "It was us or them."

I open my mouth to tell her that I don't think it works that way but close it again. I don't have the strength to tell her that I'll always remember what I did. I'll always see the knights crumpled, drilled through, buried by logs, and pummeled by rocks, impaled by metal, shot, tossed dozens of feet. During one blink, I see the red knight falling, the sound of him gurgling, of him hitting the ground. During another, the pain caused by the purple knight adds to my shivers. Will I ever sleep again?

Little eddies flow around my feet, soothing and peaceful, opposite to the images that clobber my head every time I blink. With the constant flux of nanites from the trickling water, Lii keeps patching me up. I should be able to walk better soon.

I summon one of Wyatt's bread rolls to my hand, pretty sure that it's fortified. As soon as the sourdough hits my stomach, I feel less queasy, more grounded.

Keep eating, Lii says. *We need all the nanites we can get.*

When I offer some to Naren and Scar, they take small chunks but leave the lion's share for me. We eat in silence. When Scarlett's breathing changes, I look down to see that she fell asleep on my shoulder. As tired as I am, I can't imagine sleeping with all the disfigured knights painted on the insides of my eyelids.

Wanting to hear the words aloud, I whisper, "It's my fault. I could have stopped them. If I had just taken care of Pyro out near Stonehenge..."

"It's not your fault," Naren says and squeezes my knee, both comforting and painful. My lips purse on their own as if to hold in a release of energy that might collapse the entire cave. I am a rubber band, pulled to the breaking point, both weak and prepared to unleash uncontrolled energy.

When Naren smiles, the strain slackens some. I smile back, grateful for his presence at my side. For both of them. To share in their warmth both physically and metaphorically. An odd voice inside me utters, *To share in Scar's warmth.*

If you toy with her, I'll throttle you, Lii says. *Understood?*

Hey! I'm not doing anything.

"Mazz," Bender says, kneeling down beside me. He looks like hell, his camo uniform charred in places, blood in others. A rifle hangs comfortably ready from a sling around his torso. Despite his haggard militaristic state, his white scars as sharp as ever, a warmth fills me at seeing him. Safe for the first time since this all began.

With a nod of his head and a sideways glance, he says, "We need your help. Miles, Bethany, Justin. Come." Scarlett helps me stand. I feel remarkably better. She props me up, perfectly tucked under my arm. I'm not sure if I'm leaning on her because I'm still hurting, for her warmth, or for emotional support.

Or other reasons, Lii says with more than a little innuendo.

"What's up," Miles says, happier than I can imagine anyone feeling right now. Is he channeling Naren? He must really think we won today.

Let him have his delusions, Lii says. *We all need to cling to something.*

"Mazz, you're on evac duty," Bender says. He looks hard and edgy the way he did after the welding accident in the blocks. A true warrior. "Normal transport isn't safe, and Fontein and I have other tasks." He has had so many 'other' things to do all the time, I can't help but inwardly growl at his lack of trust in me. Surely, I proved that I'm trustworthy. I expect Lii to make some wise profound statement, but he doesn't. Lii? Nothing.

"But I can't. Too many campers and not enough nanites."

"Not a problem," Bender says. He doesn't look like he wants to waste any time explaining his plan.

"Where do I send them?"

"Bethany will feed you images of their homes from Lily Evergreen. She knows exactly where everyone lives."

That's terrifying. If shockknights captured her, nobody would be safe. The entire nano community would be in danger.

He says, "Don't worry. She memorized every sat image ever taken. It will work."

I nod, but I'm even more worried about the shockknights getting their hands on her. If knowledge is power, then they'd be unstoppable with her stuck in a prison cell.

"Good," Bender says, uncaring or unaware of the dark thoughts tumbling through my head.

"Miles and Justin are security."

"Cabin leaders will escort one cabin at a time to our evac point: Stonehenge. Youngest first. Oldest last. Roger that?"

"Yes, sir," I say. I haven't called him sir since we met. But something feels right about sounding like him. He manages to cordon off the terror. If I act like him, maybe I can do the same. Without further explanation or delay, Bender vanishes.

"Rest time is over," Bethany says and pats me on the shoulder. Why does everyone keep doing that? Don't they see that it's still raw? Oblivious to my pain, which seems so at odds with her core nature, she says, "Let's go."

"I'm coming with," Scarlett says, jaw fixed, arm clamping around my waist. Her face leaves no room to argue.

After a set of glances between the two of us, Bethany says, "Fine." She gives me a look that says, "Tread carefully."

Miles and Bethany dash up and down the long path and update the cabin leaders with our plan. I munch on the fortified bread as I let Scar guide me to the mouth of the cave, passing onlookers in each room. I note that Naren joined us too. Better to ask forgiveness than permission: rule thirty-three.

Someone molded wide, seamless stairs into the cliffside–rock skills no doubt–but with my head reeling from vertigo, I teleport to the bottom. I would multi-port directly to Stonehenge if we could afford to waste nanites. I'll need every last one. And I'm safer surrounded by friends.

Rusty, who ported with me, something so natural that I didn't realize I did it, nudges between my legs from behind and scootches me onto his back. Standing tall, my feet lift off the ground and I'm riding him like a small pony. I suppose every bit of energy helps.

Scarlett walks at my side, a protective eye dancing between me and our surroundings, prepared for any potential threat. She reminds me of a supreme's bodyguard, always ready for an attack. But there is more to it than that and I know it.

CHAPTER THIRTY-ONE

Stonehenge

Twenty minutes later, we stand in the middle of the half-missing Stonehenge, which looks more like the original as a result of my bombardment on the SUVs in the field. How can it only be this morning? The dense concentration of nanites inside the ring gives me a boost, like dangling my feet in the underground cave.

The boys from the Greasy Stains cabin line up in front of me, Lily to my left, Scarlett to my right, and Bethany beside the tiny front camper. Rusty licks the top of my right foot, lying beside me. Miles, Naren, and Justin circle the outer ring of Stonehenge, appropriated shockknight rifles in hand, looking for any signs of trouble.

Penny already rode Tiny back to the cave, her gate powerful and graceful. She'll bring the next batch of young ones soon.

I unphase my mind, worried about how my thoughts will affect the others. I need not have worried. Bethany only linked me to Lily. The barrier between me and Lily is so thin that an almost infinite number of realities flow through my mind. I expected there to be no emotion bleeding through all that information, but so many contradictory feelings vie for dominance, caring for everyone everywhere, that none can emerge as dominant. I can't imagine how tiring it would be to live like that.

Bethany streams a sim into my head from Lily, showing the first boy's tall house on a grassy hill. I see and feel everything from the fresh-cut roses on the dining room table to flies on the horses in the paddock behind his house. The orbital images show exactly where he lives. I know this place more intimately than if I were standing there myself. I count down from three and teleport the first boy, who looks maybe six years old. I watch him bounce up and down, then cartwheel as if teleportation is the funnest ride ever.

I'm impressed with how accurate my teleportation was. And frightened at the real-time nature of Lily's limitless surveillance.

When you learn to focus, act with purpose, and think before doing, you'll have this level of control. Until then, rely on your bonds with others.

The next little camper steps forward and a new sim of a shiny, tinted glass building pops into my head accompanied by a long corridor with flower-print blue and red carpet. The boy appears in the sim and runs into what I assume is his mom's arms. It continues like this until all eleven campers and their cabin leader are gone.

"Take off your shoes, and phase the soles of your feet," Bethany says. That'll draw nanites into you. I look away as I phase the skin around my toes, arch, and heel. I don't need to see that. I hope the others don't look. The temperature hits my foot like walking on coals, telling me that the trick is working. The fatigue that was building inside me dissipates.

While waiting for the next cabin to arrive and focusing on the warmth spreading through my body, I didn't realize that Scar had encased my free hand in both of hers. She squeezes it tightly three times as if pumping it full of life.

Be careful with her, Bethany says, a dangerous edge flowing through her link. *She's strong, but she also has a big heart. Don't go breaking it. I'll crush you like a fly.*

I wasn't even–

You heard me.

I don't let go of her hand. Scar is the picture of imperfect beauty. A rumble stirs inside me, reminding me of Ing. Reminding me of Laticia, who I realize I haven't thought about her in days. The discontinuity of circumstances causes me to look away. We're evacuating the only place I've felt a semblance of community in a year. The only place I have felt full in a way I didn't know existed, powered by a dense supply of nanites. I can't fit Scarlett, Ing, or Laticia into the same box with the images that flash in my mind. They don't belong side by side with my deadly actions.

A cabin of little girls files into Stonehenge. "They're so small. Too young."

"Nobody is old enough for any of this," Scarlett says, squeezing my hand. These innocent humans in front of me are too tender for words. Their faces, more than my own sense of loss, convey what the shockknights stole from us today.

"Thanks, Mr. Mazz," the first one says before Lily and Bethany flood my mind with an understanding of a wood cabin overlooking a serene pond. The next girl lands in the kitchen of a Japanese-style home. These kids have such amazing and diverse homes. So different from the monotony of the blocks.

Each following kid politely addresses me as if I'm a counselor or adult, with "sir" and "Mr. Mazz," neither of which sit comfortably. Awe glows on many of their small faces. Awe of me. Not of my friends, all of whom are more impressive than me.

The sandy-haired girl in front of her cabin leader steps forward to the sim of a shipping container home with chipped orange paint and rusty spots. While smaller than her cabinmates, she doesn't remind me of home with her perfectly fit clothes and well-fed body. Yet, her container stirs a flame for the blocks and a need to see Mom, Dad, and Laticia.

Soon, Bethany says. *You'll be back with them within a day.* I send the semi-blocker home, making sure to land her inside her container so nobody notices and takes interest in her upper clothes.

The ashen-faced cabin leader, I think her name is Brie, steps forward and reaches to shake my hand only to be blocked by Rusty's growling maul and Scarlett's outstretched hand. Vines flow out from under her long-sleeved shirt, reminding me of the many-tentacled green knights.

"Down, boy," I say to Rusty, and place my free hand on Scarlett's shoulder, urging both to stand down. The feeling of the vines crawling under her shirt skeeves me out. Reluctantly, Scar steps back to my side and Brie shakes my hand, saying, "Thank you for saving them. We owe you a debt."

"I–" I don't know what to say.

Say you're welcome, you cretin, Bethany says along with the emotional equivalent of an eye roll. *They need someone to thank. The rumor mill decided you were it. Between your battles and your wolf, like the statue in the cave, gossip abounds.*

"You're welcome," I say, squelching the need to deflect her gratitude.

One cabin at a time, young ones walk up, and we ship them home. Short breaks between cabins let me regain strength, soak up nanites from Stonehenge, and sip at nano-milk. My jaws are sore from chewing through the thick outer crust of the sourdough loaf, my belly uncomfortably distended. By the end of each group, my nose bleeds worse and worse. I must look disgusting or terrifying, or maybe both. Scar's worry lines crease deeper with each batch.

During the middle of the eighth group, which looks like a bunch of ten-year-olds, my eyelids droop shut and gravity tilts. I'm vaguely aware that steady hands lay me down on a bench. "You did great," Scarlett whispers in my ear, running her fingers through my hair and kissing my forehead. Her tender touch soothes me and sends disconcerting ripples of joy through me. "Rest up. We'll–"

"What's that?" Justin asks with an edge that cuts through my exhaustion like my nanite-sharp k-bar. Blinking my eyes open, I follow his upturned finger. A dark dot grows in size, rising above the horizon until it shows itself as an old-school, propeller plane. "Have we seen a plane all summer?"

No, Penny says. It's one of the reasons why Dr. F built the camp here. And I don't believe in coincidences.

I watch, caught in a web waiting for a spider to crawl on invisibly thin strings toward us. It looks like one of those large green propeller planes flown by armies long since passed.

"Mazz!" Bethany breaks through the spell as the hum of the propellers reaches my ears. "Take us back to camp."

I dig deep, calling on Stonehenge's nanites, and propel us into the infinitesimal, backed by surging fear. There are too many of us but I press on, something cracking within me.

Pop.

CHAPTER THIRTY-TWO

Round Two

Through Bethany's telepathic link, I feel a split second of everyone's simultaneous urge to hurl before she shuts it down. Everyone except Lily, who seemed more curious about how we squeezed through a pinhole. While they recover from nausea, I fall to my knees, bowed back, struggling to stay conscious. I look over my shoulder to where the plane should be, fighting to push past my blurry vision.

"Parachuters," Bethany rasps, panting as hard as I am, her from nausea and me from drawing the massive load with me.

Through Rusty's eyes, I watch as a falling dot puffs out into a tiny semi-circle, slowing its descent. Then the next. Ahead of us, Penny leads a group of tweens in our direction.

She rides Tiny to our side in seconds and says, "The shockknights have returned." The expression on her face is one of disbelief. "Mazz, take Bethany and warn the counselors. The rest of us will get these groups back to the cave the old-fashioned way."

With a hand on Rusty, drawing from his strength, I teleport three times fast, pop, pop, pop, through the wards and land at the edge of the pool in the large cavern.

Bethany dry heaves again as Ing, Devin, and Mr. Braunwyn scatter like rats from a container fire. Rusty whimpers and we both collapse into the foggy water. I barely whisper, "Sorry, Bethany, but you have to let the counselors know."

When I don't hear a response, I consider pressing my point, but she rasps, "Done," before dry heaving again. She stands, towering over me, glares down at me for a brief moment, then her eyes haze over like people who are simmed out. "I updated the cabin leaders. How did they regroup so fast? We needed more time."

If only I'd teleported everyone faster. Once again, it's my fault.

"The counselors are ready this time," Bethany says.

While reassuring, I wouldn't bet against the shockknights. "Are Bender and Fontein here? They had 'other tasks' to attend to."

"No, but the other counselors are formidable." Bethany's arms are stretched like she might tear open the fabric of the universe with her bare hands. With Mr. Winston laid out, and who knows what state the other counselors are in, I can't help but question her. Mr. Braunwyn, who looks terrified, is completely useless unless the knights sit around and wait for him to talk them into a coma.

Sitting in the pond, I feel nanites percolating through my skin, filling the empty well inside me. This is how I always used to feel before attending upper school, before I started using their enriched soap so I'd smell better, and before I started absorbing their enhanced nanite concentration. I wish I could drink more nano-milk, but my belly curves too far out as it is.

Something about my skin tingles and visibly disappears, revealing the flesh beneath. No pain. Somehow, I phased it. Now I can feel the nanites flooding my body, warming me, filling me more thoroughly than ten nano-milks. After a few minutes of this, I practically glow. Sitting here, uselessly soaking, grates at my innards as if I'd swallowed sandpaper. I wish there were something I could do.

Can you wish your brain into silence? Bethany says sharply. *I mean–*

No! Penny's telepathic yell slashes through Bethany and me like a katana. From her perspective, I watch campers fall with darts poking out of them, black knights spring from the forest well inside the walls, one holding this year's wonkit, the one that phases people. Penny and the other cabin leader shoot back with their semi-auto rifles. Wind from a younger girl howls and knocks a knight off his feet.

An angry beast from within carries me to Penny's side, already casting out a kinetic blast. I need to figure out how I do that. The knights fly backward like empty bags in a summer storm.

Von Steiner walks out of the trees toward us, dressed in beige linen clothes, so different from his usual garb. His penetrating blue eyes lock on me, both infinitely intense and bottomlessly sorrowful in a way that is so unfitting. He shaved his head bald and a scar rings his neck. Tollere.

His loose-fitting clothes don't stir while my kinetic blast flows around him, or is it through him. He strides forward, unrushed but purposeful, as frightening as Fontein. Why is he barefooted?

You're barefoot too? Bethany reminds me.

Focused by my need to protect my friends and these kids, I phase the ground from under him, but he catches himself with an unnatural wind pushing him up like Naren does on the obstacle course. He continues flying toward me. I freeze, feeling his power within me, rifling through my mind like a sim on fast forward, collecting my recent thoughts, my knowledge of my friends, and the locations of the campers I sent home.

Bethany pushes back on him, helping me find myself again.

Bullets veer around him. I phase a section from the base of a redwood tree and tug at its crown to topple it onto this terrifying transformation of von Steiner. Branches heave to and fro and the tree bends, missing Tollere.

Rusty springs forward to tackle the man but only manages

to rebound on an invisible barrier as if he's a toy-sized puppy attacking a tractor tire. Miles kinetically flings stones at von Steiner, one smacking his cheekbone so hard it indents. He spits blood. A golem lumbers forward to bull him over.

The recovering shockknights shoot at us, and the cabin leaders shoot back, the air a drum circle.

Like a heat-seeking missile, Tollere dodges Naren's stone humanoid and runs unnaturally fast at Miles. Justin steps forward and blasts Tollere in the chest with lightning from his fingertips, but the crackling blue energy barely affects Tollere. If anything, the electrical shock invigorated him.

Weeds rise at his feet only to shrivel and die. His cheek has already healed, impossibly fast. Naren's golem falls apart.

Terrified by his seemingly infinite skills and endless well of energy, I teleport to the cave, pulling my friends and fellow campers with me. The drain is far greater than any I have felt before, towing far too many people along.

My stomach lurches and a vortex pulls me back, threatening to shear me in half. Hopelessness wells up inside me. On one end of the teleportation, a demon hauls me back with a tsunami's force, hellbent on my death–or worse. On the other side, a beacon of light from Bethany draws me toward our only escape. We're not going to make it.

I do the only thing I can. I flex with all that I am and fling my passengers forward while allowing myself to fall back.

Alone with a fiendish predator, the counselor that hated me from day one, I fall to the ground, weakened but relieved that my gambit worked. I need to buy time until Bender and Fontein return. I can't let him reach the cave. All will be lost.

Get up! Bethany yells in my head, though she sounds like an echo of herself.

Rusty, who stands at my side, leaps between me and Tollere, all snarls and snaps, prepared to die in order to protect me. Utterly loyal. Tollere kicks Rusty, the blow sending him tumbling twenty feet back, his neck snapped awkwardly to the side.

"No!" I yell, experiencing part of Rusty's pain as my own.

Tollere fixes me with those eyes, severe yet compassionate, and leisurely strolls toward me. I feel him in my head again, rifling through my thoughts, both present and past. Bethany pushes back on him, a game of king of the hill.

"I'm sorry, Mazz," von Steiner/Tollere says, slowly leaning down with his palm extended. Paralyzed by the fight over my mind, he pauses, his hand inches above my chest. A ghostly chill tugs at my heart. Blood flows freely from my nose, tasting bitter on my tongue. "I wish I didn't have to do this." Grief and regret radiate through our telepathic connection, a mental mirror of his tilted head and furrowed eyebrows. "I was once a blocker like you. If things could be diff–"

Rusty pounces in, but Tollere catches him by the snout and slams him down hard enough to shake the ground beneath us, Rusty's jaw a jumble of gears and levers.

I sense Rusty's version of pain as a missing limb. I have to save him. Drawing on the non-existent reserves within, and the generous supply of nanites surrounding us, I phase. Both Bethany and Tollere vanish from my mind. In this purple and blue world, the human features before me are replaced by an impenetrable black silhouette. The billions of glowing dots in the air glide toward him like a black hole swallowing so many stars.

Run, Mazz, I tell myself. I roll to the right. A stabbing cold cuts through my left ribs where Tollere's onyx hand passes through me. My lung burns of ice. I vault to my feet and jackrabbit, spurred on by fear. A few paces later, I trip to the ground again.

Sure that Tollere is upon me, I flop over. But he stands where he was, arms casting about. I sit, catching my breath, my left lung objecting to the thick air in this dimension. Looking down at my body, I am dimmer than I've seen during phasing track, an empty swath only inches from my heart.

Rusty, fully phased with me, limps to my side, head angled and jaw hanging loose. He nudges me with his broken maw as if to say, "get up." I labor to my knees. With every second in this realm, I gain strength.

Tollere stops sweeping his arms around and faces toward me, disturbingly featureless. Slowly, deliberately, he walks in my direction. Not exactly at me. But then he corrects course, honing in. He can't see me, but he can sense me somehow. Time to get out of here no matter how drained I am.

I slog to my feet, my black-scarred lung frantically begging for air. I stumble away on wearied legs, drowning in this dense air. Rusty limps obediently at my side. A few paces away, I lean against a cabin wall and look over my shoulder. Tollere turned toward me again and continues to follow me. I change directions, round to the other side of a cabin, then trudge farther away. Every time I look back, he follows, but farther and farther behind, a shadow wraith come to kill me.

Ahead, a brilliant flow of purple, blue, and white trickles over a tiny waterfall from one pool to another. The stream that runs through camp. Full of nanites from the cave. I kneel at the stream's edge to scoop nanites into my mouth but end up falling in. I flail to the bottom, expecting to splash and sputter for air, but in this dimension, there is no water, only an intense flow of nanites soaking into me, searing my skin and lungs. The glowing specks swirl into my skin, lodging themselves inside, filling me with arctic blue verging on white, and thistle purple light. The luminescent dots fill me with a rush of energy. Rusty jumps in beside me, with only a fraction of the benefit.

Tollere stops. His nebulous body language suggests that he lost my trail. Then he continues toward me, on my scent again.

I splash upstream through the flow of nanites, accumulating more with each step, feeling stronger and stronger. Reaching the stream's edge, he doesn't immediately follow. He walks a few paces downstream as I head farther upstream. Glancing over my shoulder, he reversed direction and now walks toward me.

I'm running now, splashing most of the flow aside while collecting enough nanites to sear my legs. It dawns on me that the cave and this stream are the heart of Camp Astrid, the true reason we're here: the source of the nanites. Tollere trails far behind now, around a bend in the stream, blocked from view. The energy pulses hot through my veins and threatens to burst free. No matter how bright I shine, my injured lung, which stings of a thousand wasps, remains boundlessly black.

I'm no longer wading through the stream, but on top of it, a runnel of nanites rippling through the bottom of my shoeless feet.

The two plains of existence start to flicker back and forth, faster and faster until they blur into one, a wispy purple and blue overlay on reality. Still standing on the water, I turn to see Tollere rounding the bend in the stream at such superhuman speed that he runs on top of the water as well.

I barely have enough time to launch a kinetic blast at him, coming as naturally as breathing. Unlike last time, this shock wave sends him, water, and river rocks flying dozens of feet, so strong that it knocks over a clump of sapling redwoods. He tumbles through the water but rolls to a stop on a knee.

Locked on me like a predator circling his prey. I feel him trying to push into my mind, but my half-phased brain holds fast as an impenetrable bunker. No. Not halfway between, but fully in both dimensions. Rusty snarls viciously, his jaw clunking back into place.

I need to slow Tollere down. I have no illusions that I can hold him for long, but if I can give the others time to escape... Emboldened by the power running through me and a purpose worth fighting for, I send another kinetic blast, then another and another. Each time, he swings his arm and knocks them aside with some force of his own.

He slowly steps closer. I hold my ground while Rusty steps forward, devoted and resolved. Tollere flicks his finger and water twists up and over me, knocking me about like a plaything. I gulp for air as the flood washes me downstream. My heel hits a rock with a revolting crunch.

The water lifts me high, holding my arms wide and pinning my legs together. "This stream is incredible," Tollere says above the rush of water. "If it were up to me, I'd stay here with you forever."

The water lowers me until I am eye to eye with Tollere. He is haunting–or haunted? He jerkily raises his hand as if being forced to do something he doesn't want to. Rusty dives toward him only to get caught up in another water vortex.

"If you join us, I don't have to do this," he says. "I don't wish this on anyone. You would be a valuable addition to the shockknights." I sense him winnowing into my mind, forcing memories out of me. Chin trembling, he says, "You and Lily."

The notion sickens me. I would never turn on my own. Especially not for those who would attack kids. I couldn't. I won't.

"All you have to do is agree to go with me to Nulla." He subtly shakes his head as if to tell me not to. As if resisting an untold burden that I think has nothing to do with holding me in place, he says, "I'll let the rest of you go."

I stop resisting for a moment. If we could trade my life and Lily's for everyone else's, wouldn't that be worth it? Save the many. But no. If they get Lily, they get them all.

'No," I say forcefully. I dig into the still-growing well of energy within me and let it loose. The kinetic explosion that bursts forth sends rock, water, and trees flying for fifty feet in every direction. Tollere soars, ass over teakettle, a balloon caught in a cyclone. A crater formed under me, yet I stand hovering feet above the ground. Levitating.

Then I realize what I've done. "Rusty!" I appear at his side, not having meant to teleport. His legs are snapped at odd angles. Nanites flow from his body while others blink from purple and blue to black, sacrificing the few to maintain the whole. "What have I done?" I kneel at his side, wishing I knew how to fix him. I pet him gently. His presence weakens in my mind. "No!"

"Mazz!" yells a strained voice from above me.

Tollere stands over me, palm out, hand thrust toward me, but blocked by something other than myself. Bender glows bright purple and blue over Tollere's shoulder, flying with his hand stretched outward. Tollere reverses focus and pounces over fifteen feet into the air, slamming body to body with Bender.

Together, they fall. I can't blast Tollere without hitting Bender too. I won't do to him what I did to Rusty. Bender teleports twenty feet up but Tollere anchors himself to my mentor. As Bender teleports three more times, gaining speed each time, Tollere rides him like a rodeo champion, palm inching toward Bender's chest. Then his despicable hand meets Bender's chest and they fall to the ground with a thud and crack, Bender breaking Tollere's fall.

Spikes fly at Tollere from the side. Ms. Merryweather flies at Tollere, her glowing face fearsome and dangerous. Hand still resting on Bender, the spikes hit home, but clatter to the ground uselessly. Rocks hail down from above, but Tollere dodges to the side, dragging Bender with him.

I summon Bender to my side, only to have Tollere pry his way alongside. With palm pressed to Bender, who looks more withered than any blocker, Tollere reaches up to me with lightning reflexes, planting his palm on my chest as well. We both look confused when nothing happens.

He pulls his hand away to reveal a thin layer of shiny metal on my chest. The sheet of metal deforms into a spike and shoots at Tollere's face, stopping only an inch from his forehead. Rocks pummel down at Tollere, forcing him to leap away. With a twitch of my finger, I teleport Bender and Rusty to the subterranean pond in the cave. Or at least I hope that is where I sent them.

Ms. Merryweather's rocks scream down and blow me backward into the stream. I sputter and flail, injured but not out of the fight. Regaining my feet, I take a fighting stance. My rage over Rusty and Bender flares hot, the plutonium that fuels my internal reactor. As I let a torrent of energy burst forth, a brilliant white human steps between Tollere and myself. The blast of energy flows around the two of them, but Ms. M isn't so lucky, walloped to the ground.

Go, Dr. Fontein yells in my head. *Save the campers. They are all that matters.* Spontaneously and against my will, I find myself teleporting to Wolf Cave.

Pop.

CHAPTER THIRTY-THREE

Southgate

I stand in the middle of the pool in the cavern, enraged by Dr. Fontein's presumption, at being sent away. I teleport back to Fontein's side, but the other end of the teleportation doesn't connect, knocking me back, not as hard as the camp's wards, but enough to make me think twice.

Ms. M places her hand on my shoulder and says, "He blocked everyone out. Don't try."

I rush to Rusty and kneel at his side. He's alive, healing in the pool, but he can't rise to nuzzle into me. "Lay back," I say. I gently pet his back and pull out the branch stuck between his ribs. "You'll be fine," I tell him, though I have no clue if my words are close to truth, possessing little knowledge about familiars.

Looking up, Ms. M holds Bender in her arms, no, hugs him. His lower body floats slack in the mirky pond. Over her shoulder, she commands me to "Port us to Southgate now." She is the incarnation of wrath, love, fear, and sorrow. "Now!" Ms. Merryweather shouts, tears in her eyes.

Infuriated by Tollere, by Dr. Fontein, I teleport everyone in the cavern to Southgate, one single teleportation the likes of which I have never done before. I don't care how sick I make any of them. Everyone but Bender that is. He looked so fragile in her arms.

Too late to tell what happened, I realize that Miles was among the wounded, with Bethany at his side, blood staining the milky water pink. "No!" I scream, releasing a small fraction of my bottled-up fury. A massive stalactite falls to the cavern floor, disintegrating into thousands of fragments.

Drawing on the pool, I glide over the water, taking a natural skateboarding stance over the ledge into the stream. As I pass each room, I teleport the huddled groups to Southgate. Scar tries to get my attention as I pass my friends, but I have no desire to talk. No ability to face anyone. Bender and Miles. I send them along like every other camper.

As I fly out the mouth of the cave, my eyes are drawn to a gleaming gold and white dome covering the center of camp, breathtaking, insane.

I teleport to Southgate.

Pop.

I fly out the other side not reacting fast enough. I fall to a halt with a belly grind. Wheeling over, confident that Lii will patch me up with my surplus of nanites, I find Scarlett standing over me, haloed in an other-dimensional violet and cerulean. "Quite the entrance," she says with a shake of her head.

Casting about, I spy Miles, whose nanites flicker and fade. Bethany propped him up in her lap, arms around him, rocking back and forth. I start to run to him, but Scar pulls me back by the shoulder. Scar draws me into a hug. "There's nothing we can do."

Over her shoulder, a light shines brighter than a thousand acetylene torches. A second later, a thunderous shockwave bulls us over, Scar landing on top of me. My ears ring, my eyes blind, up or down unknown. I blink my eyes trying to get rid of the giant blast-shaped shadow imprinted on my retina. I can barely make out that Scarlett's mouth is moving, but I can't hear anything but ringing.

My mind reels and I struggle to get my bearings. Campers

stumble around, some fine, but many wounded. When Scar and I reach our feet, she turns and I feel the blood drain from my face. The blast embedded a foot-long piece of metal in her back between the spine and shoulder blade.

"No!" I say but can't hear my own voice. She stands, completely unaware.

Ms. Abigail, the nano-medic counselor, stands across the courtyard with Ing and Devin, already triaging campers. I port with Scar to their side, not daring to waste a moment or risk moving her. Confused, she looks pale in the dimming light of dusk.

Ing pushes me back, mouthing the word, "Go."

"Go where?" I ask, but she doesn't pay me a nat's whisker of attention or can't hear me. Probably both. I can't leave Scar. She wouldn't leave me.

With the aid of the other counselors, Mr. Winston corrals the campers that aren't hurt through the gate. All except for Mr. Braunwyn, who uselessly walks around, tears dripping down his face. Where is all of his "find your inner peace" now?

Across the courtyard, Ms. M focuses solely on Bender, who is devoid of any glow. I can't think about him. If I let those thoughts–

Two limping teens fall to the ground at my left, darts sticking from their backs. Two black knights and a teal run around the corner of the cafeteria, firing more darts. I form a kinetic shield around the knights.

More knights circle around us. Orange, red, and green among a dozen black. Vines grow up beneath the densest grouping of campers, fixing them in place. Flames, bullets, and darts bounce off two more shields that I didn't mean to form. Return fire, including Justin's lightning, bounce off the inside of my shields.

I find myself screaming. "How!" My shields fly outward flattening every single one of the knights. "Dare!" I teleport the cafeteria's roof into the air. "You!" I tug it down in dozens of pieces, teleport them up a hundred feet, and tug down running on too much energy. On impact, dirt flies into the air along with wood shrapnel, shock waves bouncing off a new shield I form at the last second.

Nobody could survive that blast. My eyes sting with tears and dust. "Why do you keep making me hurt you?"

Mr. Winston's giant meat hook grabs hold of my arm. He leans down and yells in my ear. I can barely make out "Teleport ffshhh away." He points his finger around at everyone, then throws his thumb over his shoulder. What's he–"Telekssh us way," he yells in my ear again.

"How?" I yell. He repeats the hand gesture, staring me down as if he can intimidate me into comprehending how to accomplish such a huge task.

I nod. Where? And how? Outside the gate first. Then I'll figure out where. I harness the nanites still coursing through me and teleport everyone in a single go to the edge of the defenses.

Bang!

Teleportation sickness even twists my insides. Campers and counselors keel over and heave. Fewer nanites surrounding us here, farther from camp's core, the stream that fed my strength. I flex every muscle and bend the world around us.

Boom!

Everyone falls to the ground, useless. Scar is mercifully unconscious. I can only hope that I'm not making her injury worse. Or Miles. Or Bender. One more time. There are so few nanites here in comparison. This is the real world, not the bubble of existence I've benefited from these last two months.

I pant, sweat soaking me, my lung rasping with every breath. Do I have it in me to teleport again? My duality of dimensions vanished with that last teleportation.

Where to? I bought us some time, but I have no idea how much. At every stage, we underestimated how quickly the shockknights can attack. How soon will they home in on us this time?

"Screw it!" I curse. Pulling upon every nanite inside me, I exhale and physically scrunch myself up, pulling everyone into

the vortex with me.
    Crack!

CHAPTER THIRTY-FOUR

Home, Sort Of

This is all wrong. It is dark, but not like the warehouse Bender took me to after the mudflats. This is the dark street in front of my container home, with sounds of life, a life so different from Camp Astrid, so different from today. Around me cries from campers and blockers call out in surprise at our sudden appearance. Blockers trip over themselves to get out of the way from whatever spontaneous apparition landed in their back yard. Campers huddle closer together to find safety in numbers.

Why did I bring them here? Uppers in the blocks? At nighttime? What was I thinking?

A thick layer of fatigue settles upon me. A rhino might as well have pierced my skull it hurts so bad. My nose bleeds freely. The lack of nanites here terrifies me. Coming from the near infinite well of Camp Astrid to the virtual desert of the blocks, fear pulls at my core.

Blockers form a ring around us, some swearing at us, others gawping.

Mr. Winston walks our perimeter, deterring any potential threats.

I want to check on Scar, to find out about Miles, to apologize to Bender, but the situation just got worse. Gunther steps forward, shoving a pair of onlookers to the side. Velta and the other scavengers flank him, making space for themselves. Gunther waggles his revolver at his side, not pointed at anyone, but menacing all the same.

I push my way toward them, but Justin steps in front of Gunther, his hands zapping bright blue with electricity. While the blockers nearby run, Gunther raises his pistol.

Three things happen at once. I teleport, throw Dad's knife, and my chest crumples in pain as I topple over backward to land on the ground. My head smacks down hard. He shot me? He shot me! Oh, no, he shot me.

Above me, lightning crackles.

"Mazz!" someone yells. I know that voice. I can't raise my head to see her. Then she kneels next to me. Laticia looks healthier than I remember, yet pulled tight somehow. No, worried. She wears a red strap around her arm. I'm hallucinating or Lii glitched with a twist of an overlay. Those are the only explanations. She cups my face. Her cold fingers feel real enough.

Mom's head rises above Laticia's shoulder. A red band adorns her arm as well. She says, "It hit him in the flak jacket. He'll be fine. The enforcers are coming. We need to get them out of here."

Laticia pulls me to my feet and yells, "Come with us." Dad, who I hadn't noticed, leads the way as Laticia drags me along. His bicep is wrapped in red and his hand holds the gun I saw after the welding accident. Since when were they Resistance? Blockers part before us like air before our train of Resistance fighters and nanos. The counselors mingle with the growing group of Resistance, herding the freaked-out campers as they go.

"What's, going, on?" I ask Dad as soon as I can breathe. Between my heavy feet and my painful lungs, the world doesn't make sense.

"We're getting you to safety," he says over his shoulder.

As we walk, winding through blocks, men and women with

the red mark of The Resistance flank us, pushing blockers out of the way. Some carry guns. Not aimed at us, but at blockers around us.

Mr. Winston and Dad talk in hushed tones.

We walk down a set of stairs into the dark subterranean, something we don't do much in the blocks. I have only descended into the gurgling guts of the blocks with Dad on welding jobs for the Guild. The putrid smell coats my nose, my stomach threatening to roll over. My skin sticks to my clothes in the humid air. The pipes and vents hum and rattle.

We wind down stairways, then corridors, then more stairs, surrounded by aged metal and cement. We tromp along in the single-file line, Laticia in front of me and Justin behind. Where is Scar? Moving can't be good for Miles, or Bender. I should help them. No, my feet barely obey my befeebled mind as it is.

A few minutes later, we reach a large, dim warehouse full of goods and supplies. Bulbless light issues forth from hundreds of pinpoints. Nano-lumus. At first, I think this is the same depot Bender ported me to after the mudflats, but that isn't right. The smell is wrong. The waste treatment plant must be near.

Mom and Dad assemble the counselors, minus Ms. Merryweather, who hasn't left Bender, Ms. Abigail, who guides the wounded through a set of double doors, and Mr. Braunwyn who paces, muttering to himself. I want to listen in on what the counselors talk about, but don't have the energy.

I watch Tiny take Rusty, who is balanced on her back, off into a corner of the warehouse. I sense that he is in good hands, and there is nothing I can do. I feel useless again. Too empty to help anyone.

I follow the wounded into a room set up as an infirmary, with cots arranged in rows, most full, but only a few with severe wounds. I only need to check in on three of them. I wind my way through the cots to Scar's side.

"She'll be okay," Devin says, "It will take a while to heal, but she is strong." He pushes me aside, a bottle of permabond and nanite cream in his hands.

Ms. M kneels over Bender, holding his hand, kissing it tenderly. She shouldn't be so vulnerable. She should be all edges and rasp. She ought to know better.

Bender is all wrong too, skin of translucent rice paper and lips chapped. Sunken in with a shallow breath. The mark of Tollere's hand burned a hole in his shirt, exposing a blistering white scar to match the marks at his temple.

I peel off my bulletproof vest, hurting in so many places I can't count. I pull up my shirt to reveal a white scar running beneath my left peck. Holy...

"He lives," Ms. M says as I kneel across from her, touching the tender new scar. She kisses his hand again. "He is strong." She isn't speaking to me but trying to convince herself.

"This is my fault," I say, placing my hand on Bender's shoulder. He has to wake up so I can apologize. So that I can yell at him for risking his life. "I would have been fine. I would have..." I don't know what I would have done, but I would have. We should have fought Tollere together.

"Move," Ms. Abigail says, practically toppling me over. She has a syringe in her hand. "Give me space." I stand and look around. Devin still hovers over Scar, stapling the sides of her cut together.

Bethany huddles over another cot. Miles. I shuffle to their side. The hole between his eyebrows tells me everything I need to know, but it can't be. I won't let it be. "No. No. No-no. No-no." I look to Bethany. She shakes her head, tears streaming down her cheeks. "Miles can't be..."

Bethany pulls me into a hug, sobbing into my shoulder. I wrap my arms around her, her body shuddering, her shaved head scratching my neck. Penny lays a sheet over Miles, then guides Bethany away, leaving me alone with what used to be my cabin leader.

My cabinmates come to kneel and stand around Miles, heads bowed, none of the usual banter and jokes I've come to expect of them. After some time, they lift his cot and carry him away. I would help, but I barely have the strength to stand. I watch the doors close following Miles and his pallbearers.

I return to Scar's side when Devin moves on to other, less severely injured patients. I push a strand of hair from her blanched face, tucking it behind her ear. She will live, and I will be here when she wakes.

My eyes keep returning to the spot where Miles's cot should be. Unlike Scar, he will never awake. Too hard to fathom. He is too kind to die. Too selfless.

I am helpless here. With all my abilities, I can't fix anything that matters. I can't bring them Miles's smile back or return Bender to health.

And what about Dr. Fontein? Nobody could survive that blast. Our insurmountable leader. If she were alive, she would be here now. The only justice is that Tollere will have died in the blast too. Tollere/von Steiner incurred the wrath of justice.

Now all that remains is justice for Pyro and Henri. I will hunt them down and...

CHAPTER THIRTY-FIVE

Reunions

"Mazz," a familiar voice whispers in my ear, someone shaking me gently. "Wake up, Mazz." I raise my cheek from the cot, Scarlett the first thing I see, sound asleep on her belly, some color returned to her face. Someone wrapped me in a blanket.

Looking up, Dr. Fontein stands over me, severely burned and hairless, a patch over her left eye, but intact and alive.

"But how?" I ask.

"By luck and happenstance," she says, fatigue and suffering plain to see. Despite her sharp gaze, she seems so frail, lacking the infinite well of energy she once possessed. Not destroyed but diminished. "You have visitors."

She looks to the side, and I follow her gaze. Mom, Dad, and Laticia stand at the end of the infirmary. I stand. The ten steps to walk to them feel like a hike. Their faces screw up at the sight of Rusty. I stop for a moment and pet him, then mentally nudge him to stay before taking the last few steps.

They draw me into a group hug, a hug I desperately needed.

"Son," Dad says, conveying much of what needs to be said in a single word.

When they let me go, Mom says, "The generals told us what happened."

"Generals?" I ask.

"Counselors," Mom says, guiding me out of the mini-hospital. "They work with us."

The red bands around their arms tug at my attention. "How? Why?"

"Dad and I returned to The Resistance when your skills started to manifest. We left when you were born." My mind clugs with this news. They were Resistance? Are?

We enter a conference room and sit.

"We owe you a lot of truths," Mom says, pressing for eye contact. "You can ask us anything, and we will tell you the truth, unfiltered, unadulterated."

I don't know what to ask first. My shoulders hunch forward like a caveman, towing my brain with them, numb and dumb. "And you didn't tell me?"

"We wanted–want you to make up your own mind," Mom says. "About the Resistance. About your place in the nano world."

"And the counselors are generals in the Resistance?"

"Yes," Mom says, placing a hand on my knee. "Well, the equivalent. They operate independently but can command our troops at that level." So much about Bender makes sense, constantly off on "business" and dressed in different military garb.

"But why would you throw in with the Resistance?" I ask.

"Dr. Fontein informed us that you know about the cabal of the highest-ranking supremes being nano. They are the true oligarchy that controls our caste system, keeping the masses in squaller while they enjoy the rewards. Dr. Fontein and her generals fight alongside us to overthrow the corrupt government." I've never heard Mom talk about our government with such visceral anger. Was it always there? Hidden under the surface for all these years? Or did it fade then re-ignite when she re-joined?

Skepticism narrows my eyes. "So, why did you send me to Desmond High? So I would manifest?"

"Sort of," Mom says. She isn't even denying it. "You started manifesting your abilities last summer. They were subtle at first, only noticeable to someone looking for the signs. We were worried about what would happen if you went from nearly zero nanites to the overload at Camp Astrid. You could have been hurt. Dr. Fontein, Bender, Dad, and I thought the gradual exposure in an upper school would be safer. So, a nano-path got you in and kept you there."

It all makes sense. So many second chances. But so manipulative when they could have told me. "How could you keep this from me. And why would you be looking for signs?"

"Can you trust us that we had our reasons?" Dad asks and leans closer to enfold my hand in his.

I pull away. My mouth whispers, "Nothing." The word comes out as barely a rasp. Nothing is as I thought it was. My parentals are Resistance. They knew about my abilities and kept it from me. I don't know if I'll ever be able to trust them again. They sent me to Camp Astrid completely unprepared. A tightness knots up in my head, threatening to mentally strangle me. "So, Bender? Ms. M? Fontein? You knew them. They're why you knew to look out for my abilities?"

"Yes," she says.

"What about Laticia?" I ask.

"She joined before you left for camp. We let her in on your influence, and our involvement in the Resistance," Mom says. I notice that Mom has more stars on her collar than Dad, her a general and him a grunt. She outranks him, apparently even when it comes to parenting. Is she recruiting me? Is that what this is? "And Laticia joined just like that?" I snap my fingers.

"And you expect me to join the Resistance too?" I say as much as ask. I look to both of my parentals.

"We hope, but that decision is up to you," she answers for them, my father silent, but concerned, her face hard to read. They both gained weight and look healthier since I left, both fleshed out in body and cheeks, somewhere between a blocker and an upper. Come to think of it, so did Laticia. Good food is a carrot, an incentive to work and stay with the Resistance.

"With her father wounded from the textile factory, she knows what it's like not having enough food to eat. She was angry and needed a way to unload. The resistance is what she needed." I look over my shoulder to the open door where Laticia stands. Mom whispers, "And, I think she considered it a way to protect you. She is quite fond of you, you know?" My thoughts bounce between Scar and Laticia, then to Ing, and around again.

Do I want to join? The answer comes so easily, so naturally, so clearly. "I'm in." I want revenge for Bender. Revenge for Miles and his parentals' loss. For Scarlett's unhealing wound. In the names of all the campers who they hurt, mentally and physically. For the worried faces of the little ones. I even want revenge for Henri and Pyro. Anyone who would hunt down little ones like that to capture or kill. To peal out their powers.

I will take Bender's place, a nano-enabled warrior, a point of their spear.

My parentals sigh in unison, Mom in relief and something else, Dad with unease. All business, Mom says, "You'll start as an ensign. As you gain control over your influence and mature, train with us and the generals, you'll move up through their nano ranks." She fills the space with a commanding silence, and intense push to force me into understanding what they expect of me.

"Until you master your influence, you must go into hiding, as do most of the campers that came into contact with the enemy." The idea of going into hiding doesn't affect me, but the word 'enemy' clicks into place perfectly like so many of Rusty's gears while he was growing.

Thinking of him, I realize that I enlisted him into the Resistance too. His sentiment matches my own, but more animalistic anger for his own wounds. Thankfully, most of his injuries have healed under Tiny's administration, both of them hidden away in an empty crate, curled up together like a pack of two.

Mom–General Becker?–reaches into her pocket and hands me a red cuff. I take it and slide it up my arm. She says, "Laticia has new clothes for you, fatigues befitting your new rank. Welcome to the–"

"Mazz," interrupts a woman from behind me. I jump to my feet, prepared to attack. Laticia, hand placed on her sidearm, blocks a woman who looks strikingly like Scarlett, but a shade darker, face freckled, and frizzy dark-red hair.

"Uh," I say. My head floats and I stand stock still, mentally paralyzed.

"Let her in," Mom says. Laticia steps aside like a perfect soldier.

"Thank you." She pulls me into a hug remarkably similar to Mom's.

"Uh," I say again, body rigid, patting her on the back, cheeks growing hot as she extends the embrace.

"You saved my Scar," she says and holds me out at arm's length, giving me a once over. I must look disgusting with blood dried on my clothes, but I wouldn't know it from her expression. I have no idea what to say. "I didn't want to wake you earlier. I hope you don't mind, but I thought you looked cold, so I got you a blanket."

Without waiting for me to even open my mouth, she turns to my parentals and says, "You must be very proud of your son. From the sound of it, he held them all at bay and got everyone to safety. Without him..." She shrugs and lets the statement hang. It suddenly grew very hot in here.

I didn't do enough. Not everyone made it out. My constricting guilt threatens to end me.

It's not your fault, Lii says. *You did everything you could.*

Not able to handle any more praise, I dart out of the room. Should I have asked to be dismissed by the general? How is this going to work? I don't care. I need to be somewhere else. On my way out, Laticia hands me my change of clothes, giving me something to do.

The hot shower feels great against my skin, the water and steam washing a horrendous day of filth from me. If only it could rinse away my memories. Alone, guilt steams up inside me, spurring anger and sadness. I wonder if Bethany could erase the day from my gray matter. Or perhaps the structure of joining an army will help me compartmentalize my feelings. Lii distracts me each time my mood descends to drowning level or to the brink of hitting the tiled wall either with my fist or a misfire.

Once I dress, looking the part of an ensign, with the armband to prove it, I enter the warehouse. I walk to Naren and two adults who must be his parents, the woman dressed in a red saree and the man in a silver, knee-length sherwani. His monkey familiar rests on his shoulder, tail coiled around his arm.

"Mazz," Mrs. Rai says, pulling me into a hug like Scarlett's mom. "Naren told us everything. Thank the nanites you were there." I roll my neck and my Adam's apple bobs up and down with a gulp. I try not to visibly crawl out of my body like a demon at an exorcism.

"Let the boy be, my love," Mr. Rai says.

"If you don't mind, I have to go see about something," I lie, and step away.

You are the worst liar, Lii says.

What I really need is for people to stop thanking me, to stop talking to me completely. I didn't do anything thank-worthy, or at least not enough. Miles and Bender are proof of that. Bender?

I walk down a dark aisle, needing to be alone and not alone. I find the crate with Rusty and Tiny curled up together and sit with my back against it. I rest my hands on my knees and my forehead on the cross of my arms.

If I had been stronger, I–

No, Dr. Fontein says in my head. Her inner strength doesn't push into me but rests outside, a strange, comfortable warmth.

Can't I just be alone? I phase my brain.

Dr. Fontein's presence retreats but does not vanish. *Think of all those you saved, not those who put their lives on the line, those that behaved as you did. The shockknights are to blame. Tollere is to blame. Braunwyn is to blame. I am to blame for trusting him.*

Braunwyn?

I thought you knew, she says. *He triple-crossed us. They have his wife and son. We had a plan, but...*

But Pyro. And Henri.

No, Fontein says, firm, but gentle. *Braunwyn.*

I sink to my butt, leaning against a crate of kid's clothing. I sit, hollowed out like a pumpkin. Crap! I should have looked for them.

There was nothing you could have done, she says. Lii wordlessly agrees.

My brain jams up. Her presence looms at the edge of my mind, not fiddling with me but bolstering me even in her frailty. A nugget of a concept coalesces into an idea, and that idea drips to the forefront as words: Is Tollere dead?

Yes, I believe so, Fontein says.

Good. Even though I know my optimistic question is false, I ask, We are safe, aren't–

"Hey Mazz," Laticia interrupts and slides down at my side.

"Hey." I squint my eyes and massage my temples. Nobody will leave me alone.

"Your girlfriend woke up." Her voice cracks and she purses her lips. A lifetime of friendship bends uncomfortably like a plastic ruler. "She asked for you."

"I don't have a girlfriend," I tell her. I don't know whom I'm trying to delude, Laticia or myself. I don't fully understand what Scar and I are nor what Laticia and I were.

"Yeah, right," Laticia says with a choked laugh. "Keep telling yourself that." Without looking at her, I know her expression. Resentful. Hurt. I should say something, but, what? She fills the painful silence. "I get it. You aren't a blocker anymore. You ascended. You're the unicorn. You look like them. You fought for them. You should be with one of them."

"Am not," I say. Rule sixteen: once a blocker, always a blocker. Yet, I know she isn't entirely wrong. "I'm neither." That isn't right either. "I'm nano, a Frankenstein's monster: a casteless nano." There it is, simple and true.

"I don't blame you," she says, I get the sense that she does.

"She's nice. And pretty. Probably powerful like you. Like I'll never be." She gently hammers her fist on my knee three times, then kisses my cheek, lips wet with tears for what might have been. "You should go."

"But–"

"Go already, Frankenstein's unicorn." She wipes a tear from her eye and half laughs and half cries. "We're good. Back to normal." She sniffles. Strong and courageous. She pushes me.

I stand, confused, lacking the fundamental understanding of words necessary to describe how I feel. Slicing the last strands of what could have been, I nod and shuffle away. Rusty climbs out of the crate and faithfully pads along at my side. Another relationship irreversibly changed. Like Bender. Like Miles.

"Mazz," Scar says, a rasp to her whisper as I kneel at her side so she can see me while laying on her stomach. She holds out her hand, flinching at the effort. This isn't the powerful, confident Scarlett I know but a weak replicant, her hand cool to the touch.

Mrs. Tanzy stands. "I'll give the two of you a moment."

"Hey," I whisper as if my voice might hurt her. If only better words would come.

She tries to sit up but winces before making it an inch. She whispers, "Ms. Abigail told me that the wound won't fully heal. Dr. F thinks Tollere's brand of nano-influence combined with the explosion."

I squeeze her hand. "At least your name makes sense now, Scar."

She starts to laugh, but that sends her into another bout of coughing. She closes her eyes. In less than a minute, her face slackens, and the steady rhythm of her breathing tells me she fell back to sleep.

Ms. Tansy returns to her side, and I take my leave.

CHAPTER THIRTY-SIX

Onward

The night passes in a blur. Parents arrive and families go, transported to and from the warehouse by the now frail-looking Dr. Fontein. Tollere scarred her. Not like Miles or Bender, but I doubt she will return to her full glory, the unstoppable force. So much senseless loss.

While I have confidence in Fontein's assertion that Tollere did not survive their battle, I can't shake the feeling that he survived. At every stage of the invasion, they outpaced us. Without a heavy dose of luck, we would all be dead or captured. Even if Tollere died, some shockknights must have survived, meaning that the supremes remain in power. Any camper spotted and identified is at risk, and that could be any of us, all of us, a whole generation of nanos displaced.

Some families stay. Others move on. Under Penny's and Mr. Winston's guidance, I hand out supplies for families. I never stay in one place long enough for anyone to talk to me. It provides my hands something to do while letting my brain have a break. One by one, Dr. F sends campers and their parents away.

Rusty stays at my side the whole time. My parentals don't penetrate an invisible bubble around me but take turns watching over me, as do the Rais and Mrs. Tanzy. Do they think I'm a delicate flower or something? Surely, I have proven otherwise. Anger flows through me like wind gusts through wheat fields, strong, then calm, and back to strong again.

Whispers–I hate the whispers–follow me along with eyes, and not only ones monitoring me like I might go insane at any moment.

I can't watch as Miles's parents arrive, sobbing. I double my efforts to keep mindlessly busy. Then his father blocks my path. "We heard what you did." Oh, faex! They're going to blame me for his loss. I would if I were them. I do.

You did everything you could, Lii says. *We couldn't have done more.*

"You were incredibly brave, how you thrust them into the cave and allowed Tollere to pull you back. He was lucky to call you his friend. You tried to protect him with your own life." They pull me into a hug, one that I want to throw aside. I am not worthy.

"It wasn't like that. I'm no–There wasn't anything else I could do."

"There is always a choice," he says. I accidentally teleport to the darkest corner of the warehouse. I'm a coward.

It's okay, Lii says. *They'll understand. If not now, then eventually.*

The least I could do was apologize. Some time passes before Laticia finds me and lures me out with a chocolate chip cookie and her infectious smile.

With fewer families coming and going, I busy myself by assembling a "go bag" in case I need to make a quick escape at some point. The first stop is a new bullet-proof vest. Next, I retrieve nano-bars, bottles of nano-milk, and a med-kit. The racks hold everything I could possibly need. Rusty limps at my side, protective and reassuring. For a while, Naren joins me, wordlessly filling a pack of his own, his monkey riding Rusty.

With any luck, Fontein will send us somewhere that I won't have to think about shockknights ever again. But I don't know if any of us will ever truly escape them, or their supreme masters.

Scar and Ms. Tansy vanish with Bender, other patients, and

the medics. I wish I had seen her conscious again before they left. Dr. Fontein teleports Naren and his folks shortly after.

Then Dr. F summons me. My parentals wait for me. If I knew our destination, I would have ported there myself. I regained plenty of nanites down here, but they have been very close-chested about the locations of their long-term safehouses. Apparently, I'm supposed to trust them even though they don't trust me. Did I lie to them? Did I keep secrets? Did I do anything to warrant distrust? No.

They did what they thought was best, Lii says, attempting to sound the voice of reason, though I sense bitterness from him.

Fontein counts down from three.

Pop.

We stand in a similar warehouse, poorly lit, cement walled, racks of every kind of supplies. How many warehouses does The Resistance have? With a closer examination, this appears to be the one Bender brought me to. Every thought of Bender trips up my insides.

Naren finds me a few minutes later and shows me to a room that we'll share. At least one friendly face is here. Offshoot corridors lead to dozens of quarters, each plenty large for blockers.

"Scar is here too," Naren says. "Bunking a few doors down with Lily once she gets out of the infirmary."

We sit on the bunk petting our familiars in silence. After a while, I unburden my mental load on Naren, splintering the logjam holding back my confused thoughts. He commiserates, revealing similar challenges in the aftermath of Camp Astrid. He does most of the listening, patient and nodding his head, asking questions from time to time. By the time I finish, my limbs hang loose at my side, my body slack, overtaxed.

"Come see this," Naren says, pulling me from the bunk. He guides me down several corridors, the third of which is wide enough for a semi-truck to drive down. At the end, he punches a button and floor-to-ceiling metal doors slide open with a squeal and grind similar to those we hear–heard in the blocks.

Humid air sloshes over my face, a sweet scent on the breeze, the likes of which I only experienced in sims. Beyond the doors, sounds of birds and wind-rustled trees match the sway of the canopy overhead and jungle life below. We overlook a green valley, a waterfall spilling down the far side, an overgrown farm below, and a rainforest covering the mountains all around us. I had no idea that such places survived the AI Wars.

"Where are we?" I ask.

"Central America," he and Lii say in unison.

This is perfect, concealed from the world, away from scavengers, enforcers, and shockknights. Here, I need not be a blocker or upper. Here, I am nano.

THE END

Made in the USA
Las Vegas, NV
31 July 2022